O9-CFU-067

DIANA MICHENER

REPRESENTED BY

PACEWILDENSTEIN MACGILL

32 East 57 Street, New York, NY 10022

Tel:212.759.7999   Fax:212.759.8964

COMING UP IN THE FALL ISSUE

CROSSING OVER

Edited by Bradford Morrow

Our millennial issue celebrates the word in the world as we cross over into another century from one which witnessed radical transfigurations in every aspect of life, not the least of which were in the forms of fiction, poetry and plays. With contributions from writers throughout the global community, *Crossing Over* will give readers a ranging overview of innovative literature at this interesting moment in time.

Eduardo Galeano of Uruguay contributes from *Legs Up: A Looking-Glass Primer* which challenges, with crisp wit and a deft eye, the very way we may want to reconsider our future canons, curricula and cultures. The South African poet Peter Sacks, now living in America, makes his first appearance in *Conjunctions* with five poems from *O Wheel*, and the brilliant young Irish writer Carol Azadeh debuts in this issue with "The Country Road," a remarkable story set in rural mid-century Ireland.

Thomas Bernhard's most ambitious and controversial play, "Heldenplatz"—which provoked riots at its premiere several years ago in Vienna—will appear here for the first time in English, as will Peter Handke's "The Play of the Film of the War" which premieres this summer at the Burgtheater, where Bernhard's play was staged.

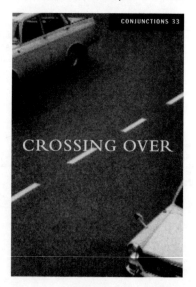

China's pioneering fiction writer, Can Xue, weighs in with an essay about Czech master Franz Kafka, and Lois-Ann Yamanaka offers a passage from her novel-in-progress, *Ten Thousand Wishes in the Round*. Pulitzer Prize–winning novelist Robert Olen Butler contributes an excerpt from his newest novel, as do Carole Maso and Paul West from theirs.

New work by Thalia Field, Reginald Shepherd, William H. Gass, Melvin Jules Bukiet, Mei-mei Berssenbrugge, Walter Abish, Malinda Markham and nearly two dozen others from around the world (with many surprises among them) will once more prove *Conjunctions* to be an invaluable sourcebook for all readers of contemporary literature.

Subscriptions to *Conjunctions* are only $18, for nearly 800 pages per year of contemporary and historical literature and art. Please send your check to *Conjunctions*, Bard College, Annandale-on-Hudson, NY 12504. Subscriptions can also be made over the Internet at www.conjunctions.com or by telephoning us at (914) 758-1539.

CONJUNCTIONS

Bi-Annual Volumes of New Writing

Edited by
Bradford Morrow

Contributing Editors
Walter Abish
Chinua Achebe
John Ashbery
Mei-mei Berssenbrugge
Guy Davenport
Elizabeth Frank
William H. Gass
Jorie Graham
Robert Kelly
Ann Lauterbach
Norman Manea
Patrick McGrath
Mona Simpson
Nathaniel Tarn
Quincy Troupe
William Weaver
John Edgar Wideman

published by Bard College

EDITOR: Bradford Morrow
MANAGING EDITOR: Michael Bergstein
SENIOR EDITORS: Robert Antoni, Martine Bellen, Peter Constantine, Elaine Equi, Brian Evenson, Thalia Field
COPYEDITOR: Laura Starrett
ART EDITORS: Anthony McCall, Norton Batkin
PUBLICITY: Mark R. Primoff
WEBMASTERS: Brian Evenson, Michael Neff
EDITORIAL ASSISTANTS: Jedediah Berry-Boolukos, Jonathan Safran Foer, Andrew Small, Alan Tinkler

CONJUNCTIONS is published in the Spring and Fall of each year by Bard College, Annandale-on-Hudson, NY 12504. This issue is made possible in part with the generous funding of the National Endowment for the Arts, and with public funds from the New York State Council on the Arts, a State Agency.

SUBSCRIPTIONS: Send subscription orders to CONJUNCTIONS, Bard College, Annandale-on-Hudson, NY 12504. Single year (two volumes): $18.00 for individuals; $25.00 for institutions and overseas. Two years (four volumes): $32.00 for individuals; $45.00 for institutions and overseas. Patron subscription (lifetime): $500.00. Overseas subscribers please make payment by International Money Order. For information about subscriptions, back issues and advertising, call Michael Bergstein at 914-758-1539 or fax 914-758-2660.

All editorial communications should be sent to Bradford Morrow, *Conjunctions*, 21 East 10th Street, New York, NY 10003. Unsolicited manuscripts cannot be returned unless accompanied by a stamped, self-addressed envelope. Correction: In *Conjunctions:31, Radical Shadows*, Burton Pike's translator's note for "The Indifferent One" by Marcel Proust stated that the story was only previously available in English in a limited edition. It has come to our attention that this previous translation, by Alfred Corn, was reprinted in *Grand Street*, 10:4. We regret the error, and invite readers to compare the different approaches Burton Pike and Alfred Corn, each a preeminent translator, take to this text.

Visit the *Conjunctions* website at www.Conjunctions.com.

Copyright © 1999 CONJUNCTIONS.

Cover design by Anthony McCall Associates, New York. Cover photograph by Deborah Luster, used with permission of the photographer.

All rights reserved. No part of this book may be reproduced or transmitted in any form or by any means, electronic or mechanical, including photocopying, recording or by any information storage and retrieval system, without permission in writing from the Publisher.

Printers: Edwards Brothers.
Typesetter: Bill White, Typeworks.

ISSN 0278-2324
ISBN 0-941964-48-5

Manufactured in the United States of America.

TABLE OF CONTENTS

EYE TO EYE

Thomas Bernhard, *Walking* (translated from German
by Kenneth Northcott, the definitive and authorized
English version) 7

*   *   *

EYE TO EYE: A PORTFOLIO OF WRITER/ARTIST COLLABORATIONS

Ann Lauterbach, *Handheld (At The Isabella Stewart
Gardner Museum)*. 68

Meredith Stricker, *Lexicon*. 78

William H. Gass and Mary Gass, *The Architecture of the
Sentence* 93

C. D. Wright and Deborah Luster, *Retablos* 109

Brian Evenson and Eve Aschheim, *Internal*. 126

Cole Swensen, *Such Rich Hour* 144

John Yau and Trevor Winkfield, *Three Peter Lorre Poems* 154

Rikki Ducornet, From *The Fan-Maker's Inquisition* 163

Lynne Tillman and Haim Steinbach, *Madame Realism
Looks for Relief*. 197

Diana Michener, *Solitaire*. 208

Robert Kelly and Brigitte Mahlknecht, From *The Garden
of Distances*. 218

Three for Cornell:

Joyce Carol Oates, *The Box Artist* 228

Paul West, *Boxed In* 235

Bradford Morrow, *For Brother Robert* 258

Camille Guthrie and Louise Bourgeois, *Articulated Lair* 267

Robert Creeley and Archie Rand, *Drawn & Quartered* 279

Forrest Gander and Sally Mann, From *Late Summer Entry* 289

*   *   *

Myung Mi Kim, From *Arcana* 299

Suzan-Lori Parks, From *In the Blood* 307

Donald Revell, *Five Poems* 354

Marguerite Young, *The Black Widow* 359

Diane Williams, *Four Stories* 379

Barbara Guest, *Ghosts* 383

Rainer Maria Rilke, *The Seventh Elegy* (translated from
    German by William H. Gass) 386

ACKNOWLEDGMENTS 389

NOTES ON CONTRIBUTORS 390

Walking
Thomas Bernhard

—Translated from German by Kenneth Northcott

TRANSLATOR'S NOTE

This is the authorized, definitive English translation of Thomas Bernhard's novella Gehen, *originally published by Suhrkamp Verlag, Frankfurt am Main, Germany, in 1971. The novella is a seminal work, quintessential to the understanding of Bernhard's complete oeuvre. In it he treats, and distils, many of the themes that are central to both his dramatic and his fictional writings: the problems of identity, mortality, suicide, ethics, perception and of spiritual and personal liberty in the face of unbending authority are all explored with the full force of Bernhard's mordant wit, narrative genius and philosophical acuity. In a true Bernhardian spirit, I have tried to preserve the author's often idiosyncratic punctuation and sentence structure, particularly in the case of quotations within the text which form such an integral part of this remarkable novella.*

I am deeply indebted to Bradford Morrow for bringing the novella to my attention and asking me to translate it, but my gratitude is greatest for the intellectual care and devotion, to say nothing of the hours of editorial work, that he has lavished on this project.

*   *   *

THERE IS A CONSTANT tug-of-war going on between all the possibilities of human thought and between all the possibilities of a human mind's sensitivity and between all the possibilities of human character.

Whereas, before Karrer went mad, I used to go walking with Oehler only on Wednesdays, now I go walking—now that Karrer has gone mad—with Oehler on Monday as well. Because Karrer used to go walking with me on Monday, you go walking on Monday with me

7

as well, now that Karrer no longer goes walking with me on Monday, says Oehler, after Karrer had gone mad and had immediately gone into Steinhof. And without hesitation I said to Oehler, good, let's go walking on Monday as well. Whereas on Wednesday we always walk in one direction (in the eastern one), on Mondays we go walking in the western direction, strikingly enough we walk far more quickly on Monday than on Wednesday, probably, I think, Oehler always walked more quickly with Karrer than he did with me, because on Wednesday he walks much more slowly and on Monday much more quickly. You see, says Oehler, it's a habit of mine to walk more quickly on Monday and more slowly on Wednesday because I always walked more quickly with Karrer (that is on Monday) than I did with you (on Wednesday). Because, after Karrer went mad, you now go walking with me not only on Wednesday but also on Monday, there is no need for me to alter my habit of going walking on Monday and on Wednesday, says Oehler, of course, because you go walking with me on Wednesday *and* Monday you have probably had to alter your habit and, actually, in what is probably for you an incredible fashion, says Oehler. But it is good, says Oehler, and he says it in an unmistakably didactic tone, and of the greatest importance for the organism, from time to time, and at not too great intervals, to alter a habit, and he says he is not thinking of just *altering*, but of a *radical alteration* of the habit. You are altering your habit, says Oehler, in that now you go walking with me not only on Wednesday but also on Monday and that now means walking alternately in one direction (in the Wednesday-) and in the other (in the Monday-) direction, while I am altering my habit in that up till now I always went walking with you on Wednesday and with Karrer on Monday, but now I go with you on Monday and Wednesday, and thus also on Monday, and therefore on Wednesday in one (in the eastern) direction and on Monday in the other (in the western) direction. Besides which, I doubtless, and in the nature of things, walk differently with you than I did with Karrer, says Oehler, because with Karrer it was a question of a quite different person from you and therefore with Karrer it was a question of quite different walking (and thinking), says Oehler. The fact that I—after Karrer had gone mad and had gone into Steinhof, Oehler says, finally gone into Steinhof—had saved Oehler from the horror of having to go walking on his own on Monday, these were his own words, I would not have gone walking at all on Monday, says Oehler, for there is nothing more dreadful than having to go walking on one's own on Monday and having to walk on one's own is the most

dreadful thing. I simply cannot imagine, says Oehler, that you would
not go walking with me on Monday. And that I should have to go
walking on my own on Monday is something that I cannot imagine.
Whereas Oehler habitually wears his topcoat completely buttoned
up, I leave my topcoat completely open. I think the reason for this is
to be found in his persistent fear of catching a chill and a cold when
leaving his topcoat open, whereas my reason is the persistent fear of
suffocating if my topcoat is buttoned up. Thus Oehler is constantly
afraid of getting cold whereas I am constantly afraid of suffocating.
Whereas Oehler has on boots that reach up above his ankles, I wear
ordinary shoes, for there is nothing I hate more than boots, just as
Oehler hates nothing more than regular shoes. It is ill-bred (and
stupid!) always to wear regular shoes, Oehler says again and again,
while I say it's senseless to walk in such heavy boots. While Oehler
has a wide-brimmed black hat, I have a narrow-brimmed gray one. If
you could only get used to wearing a broad-brimmed hat like the one
I wear, Oehler often says, whereas I often tell Oehler, if you could get
used to wearing a narrow-brimmed hat like me. A narrow-brimmed
hat doesn't suit your head, only a wide-brimmed one does, Oehler
says to me, whereas I tell Oehler, only a narrow-brimmed hat suits
your head, but not a wide-brimmed one like the one you have on.
Whereas Oehler wears mittens—always the same mittens—thick,
sturdy, woolen mittens that his sister knitted for him, I wear gloves,
thin, though lined, pigskin gloves that my wife bought for me. One
is only really warm in mittens, Oehler says over and over again, only
in gloves, only in soft leather gloves like these, I say, can I move my
hands as I do. Oehler wears black trousers with no cuffs, whereas I
wear gray trousers with cuffs. But we never agree about our clothing
and so there is no point in saying that Oehler should wear a narrow-
brimmed hat, a pair of trousers with cuffs, topcoats that are not so
tight as the one he has on etcetera, or that I should wear mittens,
heavy boots etcetera, because we will not give up the clothing that
we are wearing when we go walking and which we have been wearing for decades, no matter where we are going to, because this clothing, in the decades during which we have been wearing it, has
become a fixed habit and so our fixed mode of dress. If we *hear* something, says Oehler, on Wednesday we check what we have heard and
we check what we have heard until we have to say that what we
have heard is not true, what we have heard is a lie. If we *see* something, we check what we see until we are forced to say that what we
are looking at is horrible. Thus throughout our lives we never escape

from what is horrible and what is untrue, the lie, says Oehler. If we
do something, we think about what we are doing until we are forced
to say that it is something nasty, something low, something outrageous, what we are doing is something terribly hopeless and that
what we are doing is in the nature of things obviously false. Thus
every day becomes hell for us whether we like it or not, and what we
think will, if we think about it, if we have the requisite coolness of
intellect and acuity of intellect, always become something nasty,
something low and superfluous which will depress us in the most
shattering manner for the whole of our lives. For, everything that is
thought is superfluous. Nature does not need thought, says Oehler,
only human pride incessantly thinks into nature its thinking. What
must *thoroughly* depress us is the fact that through this outrageous
thinking into a nature which is, in the nature of things, fully immu-
nized against this thinking, we enter into an even greater depression
than that in which we already are. In the nature of things conditions
become ever more unbearable through our thinking, says Oehler. If
we think that we are turning unbearable conditions into bearable
ones, we have to realize quickly that we have not made (have not
been able to make) unbearable circumstances bearable or even less
bearable but only still more unbearable. And circumstances are the
same as conditions, says Oehler, and it's the same with facts. The
whole process of life is a process of deterioration in which everything—and this is the most cruel law—continually gets worse. If we
look at a person, we are bound in a short space of time to say what a
horrible, what an unbearable person. If we look at Nature, we are
bound to say, what a horrible what an unbearable Nature. If we look
at something artificial—it doesn't matter what the artificiality is—
we are bound to say in a short space of time what an unbearable artificiality. If we are out walking, we even say after the shortest space
of time, what an unbearable walk, just as when we are running we
say what an unbearable run, just as when we are standing still, what
an unbearable standing still, just as when we are thinking what an
unbearable process of thinking. If we meet someone, we think
within the shortest space of time, what an unbearable meeting. If we
go on a journey, we say to ourselves, after the shortest space of time,
what an unbearable journey, what unbearable weather, we say, says
Oehler, no matter what the weather is like, if we think about any
sort of weather at all. If our intellect is keen, if our thinking is the
most ruthless and the most lucid, says Oehler, we are bound after
the shortest space of time to say of *everything* that it is unbearable

and horrible. There is no doubt that the art lies in bearing what is unbearable and in not feeling that what is horrible is something horrible. Of course we have to label this art the most difficult of all. The art of existing against the facts, says Oehler, is the most difficult, the art that is the most difficult. To exist against the facts means existing against what is unbearable and horrible, says Oehler. If we do not constantly exist *against,* but only constantly *with* the facts, says Oehler, we shall go under in the shortest possible space of time. The fact is that our existence is an unbearable and horrible existence, if we exist *with* this fact, says Oehler, and not *against* this fact, then we shall go under in the most wretched and in the most usual manner, there should therefore be nothing more important to us than existing constantly, even if *in,* but also at the same time *against* the fact of an unbearable and horrible existence. The number of possibilities of existing *in (and with)* the fact of an unbearable and horrible existence, is the same as the number of existing against the unbearable and horrible existence and thus *in (and with)* and at the same time *against* the fact of an unbearable and horrible existence. It is always possible for people to exist *in (and with)* and, as a result, *in all* and *against all* facts, without existing against this fact and against all facts, just as it is always possible for them to exist in (and with) a fact and with all facts and against one and all facts and thus above all against the fact that existence is unbearable and horrible. It is always a question of intellectual indifference and intellectual acuity and of the ruthlessness of intellectual indifference and intellectual acuity, says Oehler. Most people, over ninety-eight percent, says Oehler, possess neither indifference of intellect nor acuity of intellect and do not even have the faculty of reason. The whole of history to date proves this without a doubt. Wherever we look, neither indifference of intellect, nor acuity of intellect, says Oehler, everything is a giant, a shatteringly long history without intellectual indifference and without acuity of intellect and so without the faculty of reason. If we look at history, it is above all its total lack of the faculty of reason that depresses us, to say nothing of intellectual indifference and acuity. To that extent it is no exaggeration to say that the whole of history is a history totally without reason, which makes it a *dead* history. We have, it is true, says Oehler, if we look at history, if we look into history, which a person like me is from time to time brave enough to do, a tremendous Nature behind us, actually under us but in reality no history at all. History is a history-lie, is what I maintain, says Oehler. But let us return to the

11

individual, says Oehler. To have the faculty of reason would mean nothing other than breaking off with history and first and foremost with one's own personal history. From one moment to the next simply to give up, accepting nothing more, that's what having the faculty of reason means, not accepting a person not a thing, not a system and also, in the nature of things, not accepting a thought, just simply nothing more and then to commit suicide in this really single revolutionary realization. But to think like this leads inevitably to sudden intellectual madness, says Oehler, as we know, and to what Karrer has had to pay for with sudden *total madness.* He, Oehler, did not believe that Karrer would ever be released from Steinhof, his madness is too fundamental for that, says Oehler. His own daily discipline had been to school himself more and more in the most exciting and in the most tremendous and most epoch-making thoughts with an ever greater determination, but only to the furthest possible point before absolute madness. If you go as far as Karrer, says Oehler, then you are suddenly decisively and absolutely mad and have, at one stroke, become useless. Go on thinking more and more and more and more with ever greater intensity and with an ever greater ruthlessness and with an ever greater fanaticism for finding out, says Oehler, but never for one moment think too far. At any moment we can think too far, says Oehler, simply go too far in our thoughts, says Oehler, and everything becomes valueless. I am now going to return again, says Oehler, to what Karrer always came back to: that there is actually no faculty of reason in this world, or rather in what we call this world, because we have always called it this world, if we analyze what the faculty of reason is, we have to say that there simply is no faculty of reason—but Karrer had already analyzed that, says Oehler—that actually, as Karrer quite rightly said and the conclusion at which he finally arrived by his continued consideration of this incredibly fascinating subject was that there is no faculty of reason, only an under-faculty of reason. The so-called human faculty of reason, says Oehler, is, as Karrer said, always a mere under-faculty of reason, even a sub-faculty of reason. For if a faculty of reason were possible, says Oehler, then history would be possible, but history is not possible, because the faculty of reason is not possible and history does not arise from an under-faculty or a sub-faculty of reason, a discovery of Karrer's, says Oehler. The fact of the under-faculty of reason, or of the so-called sub-faculty of reason, says Oehler, does without doubt make possible the continued existence of Nature through human beings. If I had a faculty of reason, says Oehler, if I had an unbroken faculty of reason, he says, I would long ago have committed suicide. What is to be understood from, or by, what I am saying, says Oehler, can be understood, what is not to be understood cannot be understood. Even if everything cannot be understood, everything is nevertheless unambiguous, says Oehler. What we call thinking, has in reality nothing to do with the faculty of reason, says Oehler, Karrer is right about that when he says that we have no faculty of reason because we think, for to have a faculty of reason means not to think and so to have no thoughts. What we have is nothing but a substitute for a faculty of reason. A substitute for thought makes our existence possible. All the thinking that is done is only substitute thinking, because actual thinking is not possible, because there is no such thing as actual thinking, because Nature excludes actual thinking, because it has to exclude actual thinking. You may think I'm mad, says Oehler, but actual, and that means real, thinking is completely excluded. But we call what we think is thinking, thinking, just as we call walking what we consider to be walking, just as we say we are walking when we believe that we are walking and are actually walking, says Oehler. What I've just said has absolutely nothing to do with cause and effect, says Oehler. And there's no objection to saying *thinking,* where it's not a question of thinking, and there's no objection to saying *faculty of reason* where there's no possibility of its being a question of faculty of reason and there's no objection to saying *concepts* where they are not at issue. It is only by calling actions and things, actions and things that are in no way actions and things, because there is no way that they can be actions and things that we get any further, it is only in this way, says Oehler, that something is possible, indeed that anything is possible. Experience is a fact about which we know nothing and above all it is something which we cannot get to the root of, says Oehler. But on the other hand it is just as much a fact that we always act exactly or at least much more in concert with this fact, which is what I do (and recognize) when I say, these children, whom we see here in Klosterneuburgerstrasse, have been made because the faculty of reason was suspended, although we know that the concepts used in that statement, and as a result the words used in the statement, are completely false and thus we know that *everything* in the statement is false. Yet if we cling to our experience which represents a zenith and we can no longer sustain ourselves, then we no longer exist, says Oehler. Offhand, therefore I say, these children whom we see here in Klosterneuburgerstrasse were made because the faculty

13

of reason was suspended. And it is only, because I do *not cling to experience,* that everything is possible. It is only possible in this way to utter a statement like: people simply walk along the street and make a child, or the statement: people have made a child because their faculty of reason is suspended. Oehler says, these people who make a child do not ask themselves anything, is a statement that is completely correct and at the same time completely false, like all statements. You have to know, says Oehler, that every statement that is uttered and thought and that exists is at the same time correct and at the same time false, if we are talking about proper statements. He now interrupts the conversation and says: In fact these people do not ask themselves anything when they make a child although they must know that to make a child and above all to make your own child means making a misfortune and thus making a child and thus making one's own child is nothing short of infamy. And when the child has been made, says Oehler, those who have made it allow the state to pay for it—this child they have made of their own free will. The state has to be responsible for these millions and millions of children who have been made completely of people's own free will, for the—as we know—completely superfluous children, who have contributed nothing but new, million-fold misfortune. The hysteria of history, says Oehler, overlooks the fact that in the case of all the children who are made, it is a question of misfortune that has been made and a question of superfluity that has been made. We cannot spare the child-makers the reproach that they have made their children without using their heads, and in the basest and lowest manner, although, as we know, they are not mindless. There is no greater catastrophe, says Oehler, than these children, made mindlessly and which the state, that has been betrayed by these children, has to pay for. Anyone who makes a child, says Oehler, deserves to be punished with the most extreme possible punishment and not to be subsidized. It is nothing but this completely false, so-called social, enthusiasm for subsidy by the state—which as we know is not social in the least, and of which it is said that it is nothing but the most distasteful anachronism in existence, and which is guilty of the fact that the crime of bringing a child into the world, which I call the greatest crime of all, says Oehler—that this crime, says Oehler, is not punished, but is subsidized. The state should have the responsibility, Oehler now says, for punishing people who make children, but no it subsidizes the crime. And the fact that all children who are made are made mindlessly, says Oehler, is a fact. And whatever is made

14

mindlessly and above all whatever is made that is mindless should be punished. It should be the job of parliament and of parliaments to propose and carry out laws against the mindless making of children and to introduce and impose the supreme punishment, and everyone has his own supreme punishment, for the mindless making of children. After the introduction of such a law, says Oehler, the world would very quickly change to its own advantage. A state that subsidizes the making of children and not only the mindless making of children without using one's head, says Oehler, is a mindless state, certainly not a progressive one, says Oehler. The state that subsidizes the making of children has neither experience nor knowledge. Such a state is criminal, because it is quite consciously blind, such a state is not up-to-date, says Oehler, but we know that the up-to-date or, let's say, the so-called up-to-date, state is simply not possible and thus this, our present, state cannot be in any shape or form a present-day state. Anyone who makes a child, says Oehler, knows that he is making a misfortune, he is making something that will be unhappy, because it has to be unhappy, something which is by nature totally catastrophic, in which again there is nothing else except what is by nature and which is bound to be totally catastrophic. He is making an endless misfortune, even if he makes only one child, says Oehler. It is a crime. We may never cease to say that anyone who makes a child, whether mindlessly or not, says Oehler, is committing a crime. At this moment, as we are walking along Klosterneuburger-strasse, the situation is that there are so many, indeed hundreds of, children on Klosterneuburgerstrasse and this prompts Oehler to continue his remarks about the making of children. To make a human being about whom we know that he does not want the life that has been made for him, says Oehler, for the fact that there is not a single human being who wants the life that has been made for him will certainly come out sooner or later, and before that person ceases to exist no matter who it is: to make such a person is really criminal. People in their baseness—disguised as helplessness—simply convince themselves that they want to have their lives, whereas in reality they never wished to have their lives, because they do not wish to perish because of the fact that nothing disgusts them more than their lives and, at root, nothing more than their irresponsible father—whether these fathers have already left their progeny or not—they do not want to perish because of this fact. All of these people convince themselves of this unbelievable lie. Millions convince themselves of this lie. They wish to have their lives, they say, and bear witness to it in public, day in day out, but the truth is that they do not want to have their lives. No one wants to have his life, says Oehler, everyone has come to terms with his life, but he does not want to have it, if he once has his life, says Oehler, he has to pretend to himself that his life is something, but in reality and in truth it is nothing but horrible to him. Life is not worth a single day, says Oehler, if you will only take the trouble to look at these hundreds of people here on this street, if you keep your eyes open where people are. If you walk along this street that is overflowing with children just once and keep your eyes open, says Oehler. So much helplessness and so much frightfulness and so much misery, says Oehler. The truth is no different from what I see here: frightful. I ask myself, says Oehler, how can so much helplessness and so much misfortune and so much misery be possible? That Nature can create so much misfortune and so much palpable horror. That Nature can be so ruthless toward its most helpless and pitiable creatures. This limitless capacity for suffering, says Oehler. This limitless capricious will to procreate and then to survive misfortune. In point of fact, right here in this street, this individual sickness which runs into the thousands. Uncomprehending and helpless, says Oehler, you have to watch, day in day out, the making of masses of new and ever greater human misfortune, so much human ugliness, so much human atrocity, he says, every day, with unparalleled regularity and stupidity. You know yourself, says Oehler, just as I know myself, and all these people are also no different from us, but only unhappy and helpless and fundamentally lost. He, Oehler, to speak radically, stood for the gradual, total demise of the human race, if he had his way, no more children not a single one and thus no more human beings, not a single one. The world would slowly die out, says Oehler. Ever fewer human beings, finally no human beings at all, not a single human being more. But what he has just said, the earth gradually dying out and human beings growing fewer and fewer in the most natural way and finally dying out altogether is only the raving of a mind that is already totally, and in the most total manner still, working with the process of thinking and, in Oehler's own words, a *non*sense. Of course, an earth that was gradually dying out, and finally one without human beings would probably be the most beautiful, says Oehler, after which he says; the thought is, of course *non*sense. But that doesn't alter the fact, says Oehler, that day in day out you have to stand by and see how more and more people are made with more and more inadequacy and with more and more misfortune, who have the same capacity for suffering and the same frightfulness and the same ugliness and the same detestableness as you yourself have, and who, as the years go by, have an even greater capacity for suffering and frightfulness and ugliness and detestableness. Karrer was of the same opinion, says Oehler. Oehler keeps repeating, *Karrer's view was the same* or *Karrer had a similar view* or *Karrer had a different* or *a contrary view (or opinion)*. Karrer's statement always went: How do these people, who do not know how they get to such a point, and who have never been asked a question that affected them, how do all these people, with whom, if we think about it, we are bound again and again and with the greatest soundness of mind, to identify ourselves, throughout the course of their lives, no matter who they are, no matter what they are, and no matter where they are, how can they, I say, plunge themselves with ever more terrifying speed into, up into, and down into, their ultimate misfortune with all the horrible—that is human—means at their disposal? My whole life long, I have refused to make a child, said Karrer, Oehler says, to add a new human being over and above the person who I am, I who am sitting in the most horrible imaginable prison and whom science ruthlessly labels as human, I have refused to add a new human being to the person who is in the most horrible prison there is and to imprison a being who bears my name. If you walk along Klosterneuburgerstrasse, and especially if you walk along Klosterneuburgerstrasse with your eyes open, says Oehler, the making of children and everything connected with the making of children completely fades away from you. Then everything fades away from you, Oehler quotes Karrer as saying. I am struck by how often Oehler quotes Karrer without expressly drawing attention to the fact that he is quoting Karrer. Oehler frequently makes several statements that stem from Karrer and frequently thinks a thought that Karrer thought, I think, without expressly saying, what I am now saying comes from Karrer. *Fundamentally, everything that is said is a quotation* is also one of Karrer's statements, which occurs to me in this connection and which Oehler very often uses when it suits him. The constant use of the concept *human nature* and *nature* and in this connection *horrible* and *repugnant* and *dreadful* and *infinitely sad* and *frightful* and *disgusting* can all be traced back to Karrer. I think now that I used to go walking with Karrer in Klosterneuburgerstrasse for twenty years, says Oehler, like Karrer I grew up in Klosterneuburgerstrasse, and we both knew what it means to have grown up in Klosterneuburgerstrasse, this knowledge has underlain all our actions and all our thinking and most of all the whole time we were walking with one another. Karrer's pronunciation was the clearest, Karrer's thought the most correct, Karrer's character the most irreproachable, says Oehler. But recently I had already detected signs of fatigue in his person, above all in his mind, on the other hand his mind was unbelievably active, in a way I had never noticed before. On the one hand Karrer's body which had suddenly grown old, says Oehler, on the other, Karrer's mind that was capable of incredible intellectual acuity. His sudden physical decrepitude on the one hand, says Oehler, the sudden weirdness and outrageousness of the thoughts in his head on the other. Whereas Karrer's body, especially in the past year, could very often be seen as a body that had already declined and was in the process of disintegrating, says Oehler, the capacity of his mind was at the same time, in its outrageousness, truly terrifying to me. I suddenly had to consider what sorts of outrageousness this mind of Karrer's was capable of, says Oehler, on the other hand how decrepit this body of Karrer's is, a body that is not yet really old. Doubtless, says Oehler, Karrer went mad when he was at the height of his thinking. This is an observation that science can always make in the case of people like Karrer. That they suddenly, at the height of their thinking, and thus at the height of their intellectual capacity, become mad. There is a moment, says Oehler, at which madness *enters*. It is a single moment in which the person affected *is suddenly mad*. Again, Oehler says: in Karrer's case it is a question of a total, final madness. There's no point in thinking that Karrer will come out of Steinhof again as he did eight years ago. We shall probably never see Karrer again, says Oehler. There is every sign, says Oehler, that Karrer will stay in Steinhof and not come out of Steinhof again. The depression caused by a visit to Karrer in Steinhof would probably be so violent, says Oehler, especially for his mind and as a result, in the nature of things, for his thinking, that such a visit would have the most devastating effect, so that there is no point in thinking about a visit to Karrer in Steinhof. Not even if we were to go together to visit Karrer, says Oehler. If I go alone to see Karrer, it will be the ruin of me for weeks, if not for months, if not forever, says Oehler. Even if you visit Karrer, says Oehler to me, it will be the ruin of you. And if we go together, a visit of that sort would have the same effect on both of us. To visit a person in the condition that Karrer finds himself at the moment would be nonsense, because visiting a person who is totally and finally mad makes no sense. Quite apart from the fact, says Oehler, that every visit to

Steinhof has depressed me, visiting a lunatic asylum requires the greatest effort, says Oehler, if the visitor is not a fool without feeling or the capacity to think. It makes me feel ill, even to approach Steinhof, let alone to go inside. The world outside lunatic asylums is scarcely to be borne, he says. If we see hundreds and thousands of people, of whom, with the best will in the world and with the greatest self-abnegation, we cannot say that we are still dealing with human beings, he says. If we always see that things are much worse in lunatic asylums than we imagined they were before we visited a lunatic asylum. Then, when we are in Steinhof, says Oehler, we recognize that the unbearableness of life outside lunatic asylums—which we have always separated from the life and existence and existence from life and the existence and existing inside lunatic asylums—*outside* lunatic asylums is really laughable compared with the insupportability *in* lunatic asylums. If we are qualified to compare, says Oehler, and to declare ourselves satisfied with the justness of the concepts of inside and outside—that is, inside and outside lunatic asylums—and with the justness of the concepts of the so-called intact as distinct from the concepts of the so-called non-intact world. If we have to tell ourselves that it is only a question of the brutality of a moment to go to Steinhof. And if we know that this moment can be any moment. If we know that every moment can be the one when we cross the border into Steinhof. If you had said to Karrer three weeks ago that he would be in Steinhof today, says Oehler, Karrer would have expressed doubt, even if he had taken into consideration the possibility that at any moment he might be back in Steinhof. Here on this very spot, I said to Karrer, says Oehler, and he stops walking: if it is possible to control the moment that no one has yet controlled, the moment of the final crossing of the border into Steinhof, and that is, into final madness, without being able to finish the unfinished statement, says Oehler, Karrer said at that time, he did not undersand what was doubtless an unfinished statement, but that he knew what was meant by this unfinished statement. Even Karrer did not succeed where no one has yet succeeded, says Oehler, in knowing the moment when the border to Steinhof is to be crossed and thus the moment the border into final madness is to be crossed. When we do something we may not think about why we are doing what we are doing, says Oehler, for then it would suddenly be totally impossible for us to do anything. We may not make what we are doing the object of our thought, for then we would first be the victims of *mortal doubt*, and, finally, of

19

mortal despair. Just as we may not think about what is going on around us and what has gone on and what will go on, if we do not have the strength to break off our thinking about what happens around us and what has happened and what will happen, that is about the past, the present and the future at precisely the moment when this thinking becomes fatal for us. The art of thinking about things consists in the art, says Oehler, of stopping thinking before the fatal moment. However, we can, quite consciously, drag out this fatal moment, says Oehler, for a longer or a shorter time, according to circumstances. But the important thing is for us to know when the fatal moment is. But no one knows when the fatal moment is, says Oehler, the question is, is it possible that the fatal moment has not yet come and will always not yet come? But we cannot rely on this. We may never think, says Oehler, how and why we are doing what we are doing, for then we would be condemned—even if not instantaneously—but instantaneously to whatever degree of aware-ness we have reached regarding that question, to total inactivity and to complete immobility. For the clearest thought, that which is the deepest and, at the same time, the most transparent, is the most complete inactivity and the most complete immobility, says Oehler. We may not think about why we are walking, says Oehler, for then it would soon be impossible for us to walk and then, to take things to their logical conclusion. Everything soon becomes impossible, just as when we are thinking why we may not think, why we are walking and so on, just as we may not think how we are walking, how we are not walking, that is standing still, just as we may not think how we, when we are not walking and standing still, are thinking and so on. We may not ask ourselves: why are we walking? as others who may (and can) ask themselves at will why they are walking. The others, says Oehler, may (and can) ask themselves anything, we may not ask ourselves. In the same way, if it is a question of objects, we may also not ask ourselves, just as if it is not a question of objects (the oppo-site of objects). What we see we think, and, as a result, do not see it, says Oehler, whereas others have no problem in seeing what they are seeing because they do not think what they see. What we call per-ception is really stasis, immobility, as far as we are concerned, noth-ing. Nothing. What has happened is thought, not seen, says Oehler. Thus quite naturally when we see, we see nothing, we think every-thing at the same time. Suddenly, Oehler says, if we visited Karrer in Steinhof, we would be just as shocked as we were eight years ago, but now Karrer's madness is not only much worse than his madness of eight years ago, now it is final and if we think how shocked we were eight years ago during our visit to Karrer it would be senseless to think for a moment of visiting Karrer now that Karrer's condition is a dreadful one. Karrer is probably not allowed to receive visitors, says Oehler. Karrer is in Pavilion VII, in the one that is most dreaded. What horrible prisons these the most pitiable of all creatures are locked up in, says Oehler. Nothing but filth and stench. Everything rusted and decayed. We hear the most unbelievable things, we see the most unbelievable things. Oehler says: Karrer's world is his own to the same extent that it is ours. I could just as well be walking here with Karrer along Klosterneuburgerstrasse and be talking with Karrer about *you*, if you and not Karrer were in Steinhof at the moment, or if it were the case that they had sent me to Steinhof and interned me there and you were out walking with Karrer through Klosterneuburgerstrasse and talking about me. We are not certain whether we ourselves will not, the very next moment, be in the same situation as the person we are talking about and who is the object of our thought. *I* could just as well have gone mad in Rustenschacher's store, says Oehler, if I had gone into Rustenschacher's store that day in the same condition as Karrer to engage in the argument with Rustenschacher in which Karrer had been engaged and if I, like Karrer, had not accepted the consequences that followed from the argument in Rustenschacher's store and was now in Steinhof. But in fact it is impossible that I would have acted like Karrer, says Oehler, because I am not Karrer, *I would have acted like myself*, just as *you would have acted like yourself* and not like Karrer, and even if I had entered Rustenschacher's store, like Karrer, to begin an argument with Rustenschacher and his nephew, I would have carried on the argument in a quite different manner and of course everything would have turned out differently from what it did between Karrer and Rustenschacher and Rustenschacher's nephew. The argument would have been a different argument, it simply wouldn't have come to an argument, for if I had been in Karrer's position, I would have carried on the argument quite differently and probably not carried it on at all, says Oehler. A set of several fatal circumstances, which are of themselves not fatal at all and only become fatal when they coincide, leads to a misfortune like the one that befell Karrer in Rustenschacher's store, says Oehler. Then we are standing there because we had witnessed it all and react as though we had been insulted. It is unthinkable to me that, if I had been Karrer, I would have gone into Rustenschacher's store that afternoon, but Karrer's intensity that afternoon was a greater intensity and I followed Karrer into Rustenschacher's store. But to ask *why* I followed Karrer into Rustenschacher's store that afternoon is senseless. Then let's say that what we have here is a *tragedy*, says Oehler. We judge an unexpected happening, like the occurrence in Rustenschacher's store, as irrevocable and calculated where there is no justification for the concepts irrevocable and calculated. For nothing is irrevocable and nothing is calculated, but a lot, and often what is the most dreadful, simply happens. I can now say that I am astonished at my passivity in Rustenschacher's store, my unbelievable silence, the fact that I stood by and fundamentally reacted to *nothing*, it is true that I feared something without knowing (or suspecting) what I feared, but that in the face of such a fear and thus in the face of Karrer's condition, I did nothing. We say that circumstances bring about a certain condition in people. If that is true, then circumstances brought about a condition in Karrer in which he suddenly went finally mad in Rustenschacher's store. I must say, says Oehler, that it was a question of a case of fear of ceasing to be senselessly patient. We observe a person in a desperate situation, the concept of a desperate situation is clear to us, but we do nothing about the desperate condition of the person, because we can do nothing about the desperate condition of the person, because in the truest sense of the word we are powerless in the face of a person's desperate condition, although we do not have to be powerless in the face of such a person and his desperate condition, and this is something we have to admit, says Oehler. We are suddenly conscious of the hopelessness of a desperate nature, but by then it is too late. It is not Rustenschacher and his nephew who are guilty, says Oehler. Those two behaved as they had to behave, obviously so as not to be sacrificed to Karrer. The circumstance did not, however, arise in a very short space of time, says Oehler, these circumstances always, and in every case, arise as the result of a process that has lasted a long time. The circumstances that led to Karrer's madness in Rustenschacher's store and to Karrer's argument with Rustenschacher and his nephew did not arise on that day nor on that afternoon and not just in the preceding twenty-four or forty-eight hours. We always look for everything in the immediate vicinity, that is a mistake. If only we did not always look for everything in the immediate vicinity, says Oehler, looking in the immediate vicinity reveals nothing but incompetence. One should, in every case, go back *over everything*, says Oehler, even if it is in the depths of the past and scarcely ascertainable and discernible any longer. Of course the most nonsensical thing, says Oehler, is to ask oneself why one went into Rustenschacher's store with Karrer, to say nothing of reproaching oneself for doing so. He was obliged, he says, to repeat that in this case everything, and at the same time nothing, indicated that Karrer would suddenly go mad. If we may not ask ourselves the simplest of questions, then we may not ask ourselves a question like the question as to why Karrer went into Rustenschacher's store in the first place, for there was absolutely no need to do so, if you disregard the fact that, possibly, Karrer's sudden fatigue after our walk to Albersbachstrasse and back again was actually a reason, nor may we ask why I followed Karrer into Rustenschacher's store. But as we do not ask, we may not, by the same token, say that everything was a foregone conclusion, was self-evident. Suddenly, at this moment, what had, up till then, been possible, would now be impossible, says Oehler. On the other hand what is, is self-evident. What he sees while we are walking, he sees through and for this reason he does not observe at all, for anything which can be seen through (completely) cannot be observed. Karrer also made this same observation, says Oehler. If we see through something, we have to say that we do not see that thing. On the other hand no one else sees the thing, for anyone who does not see through a thing does not see the thing either. Karrer was of the same opinion. The question of why do I get up in the morning? can (must) be absolutely fatal if it is asked in such a way as to be really asked and if it is taken to a conclusion or has to be taken to a conclusion. Like the question of why do I go to bed at night?, like the question of why do I eat? Why do I dress? Why does everything (or a great deal or a very little) connect me to some people and nothing at all to others? If the question is taken to a logical conclusion which means that the person who asks a question, which he takes to its logical conclusion, *because* he takes it to a conclusion or because he has to take it to a conclusion, also takes it to a conclusion, then the question is answered once and for all, and then the person who asked the question does not exist any longer. If we say that this person is dead from the moment when he answers his own question, we make things too simple, says Oehler. On the other hand, we can find no better way of expressing it than by saying that the person who asked the question is dead. Since we cannot name everything and so cannot think *absolutely*, we exist and there is an existence outside of ourselves, says Oehler. If we have come as far as we have come (in thought), says Oehler, we must take the consequences and we must abandon these (or the) thoughts which have (or has) made it possible for us to come this far. Karrer exercised this faculty with a virtuosity which, according to Karrer, could only be called mental agility, says Oehler. If we suppose that I, and not Karrer, were in Steinhof now, says Oehler, and you were talking to me here—the thought is nonsensical, says Oehler. The chemist Hollensteiner's suicide had a catastrophic effect upon Karrer, says Oehler, it had to have the effect upon Karrer that it did, rendering chaotic—in the most devastating manner—Karrer's completely unprotected mental state in the most fatal manner. Hollensteiner, who had been a friend of Karrer's in his youth, had—as will be recalled—committed suicide just at the moment when the so-called Ministry of Education withdrew funds vital to his Institute of Chemistry. The state withdraws vital funds from the most extraordinary minds, says Oehler, and it is precisely because of this that the extraordinary and the most extraordinary minds commit suicide, and Hollensteiner was one of these most extraordinary minds. I, says Oehler, could not begin to list the number of extraordinary and most extraordinary minds—all of them young and brilliant minds—who have committed suicide because the state, in whatever form, had withdrawn vital funds from them, and there is no doubt, in my mind, that, in Hollensteiner's case we are talking about a genius. At the very moment which was most vital to Hollensteiner's institute—and so to Hollensteiner himself—the state withdrew the funds from him (and thus from his institute). Hollensteiner who had, in his own day, made a great name for himself in chemistry—which is today such an important area of expertise—at a time when no one in this, his own country, had heard of him, even today, if you ask, no one knows the name Hollensteiner, says Oehler, we mention a completely extraordinary man's name, says Oehler, and we discover that no one knows the name, especially not those who ought to know the name: this is always our experience, the people who ought to know the name of their most extraordinary scientist do not know the name or else they do not want to know the name. In this case, the chemists do not even know Hollensteiner's name, or else they do not want to know the name Hollensteiner and thus Hollensteiner was driven to suicide, just like all extraordinary minds in this country. Whereas, in Germany, the name Hollensteiner was one of the most respected among chemists and still is today, here, in Austria, Hollensteiner has been completely blotted out, in this country, says Oehler, the extraordinary has always, and in all ages, been blotted out, blotted out until it committed suicide. If an Austrian mind is extraordinary, says Oehler, we do not need to wait for him to commit suicide, it is only a question of time and the state counts on it. Hollensteiner had so many offers, says Oehler, none of which he accepted, however. In Basle they would have welcomed Hollensteiner with open arms, in Warsaw, in Copenhagen, in Oxford, in America. But Hollensteiner didn't even go to Göttingen where they would have given Hollensteiner all the funds he wanted, because he couldn't go to Göttingen, a person like Hollensteiner is incapable of going to Göttingen, of going to Germany at all; before a person like that would go to Germany he would rather commit suicide first. And at the very moment when he depends, in the most distressing manner, on the help of the state, he kills himself, which means that the state kills him. Genius is abandoned and driven to suicide. A scientist, says Oehler, is in a sad state in Austria and sooner or later, but especially at the moment when it appears to be most senseless, he has to perish because of the stupidity of the world around him and that means because of the stupidity of the state. We have an extraordinary scientist and ignore him, no one is attacked more basely than the extraordinary man and genius goes to the dogs, because in this state it has to go to the dogs. If only an eminent authority, like Hollensteiner, had the strength and, to as great an extent, the tendency toward self-denial to give up Austria, and that means Vienna, and go to Marburg or Göttingen, to give only two examples that apply to Hollensteiner, and could there, in Marburg or in Göttingen, continue the scientific work that it has become impossible for him to continue in Vienna, says Oehler, but a man like Hollensteiner was not in a position to go to Marburg or to Göttingen, Hollensteiner was precisely the sort of person who was unable to go to Germany. But it was also impossible for Hollensteiner to go to America, as we see, for then Hollensteiner, who was unable to go to Germany, because the country made him feel uncomfortable and was intensely repugnant to him, would indeed have gone to America. Very, very few people have the strength to abandon their dislike of the country that is fundamentally ready to accept them with open arms and unparalleled good will and go to that country. They would rather commit suicide in their own country because ultimately their love of their own country, or rather their love of their own, the Austrian, landscape is greater than the strengths to endure their own science in another country. As far as Hollensteiner is concerned, says Oehler, we have an example of how the state treats an unusually clear and important mind. For years Hollensteiner begged for the funds that he needed for his own research, says Oehler, for years Hollensteiner demeaned himself in the face of a bureaucracy that is the most repugnant in the whole world, in order to get his funds, for years Hollensteiner tried what hundreds of extraordinary and brilliant people have tried. To realize an important—and not only for Austria but, without a shadow of doubt, for the whole of mankind—undertaking of a scientific nature with the aid of state funds. But he had to admit that in Austria no one can realize anything with the help of state funds, least of all something extraordinary, significant, epoch-making. The state, to whom a nature like Hollensteiner's turns in the depths of despair, has no time for a nature like Hollensteiner's. Thus, a nature like Hollensteiner's must recognize that it lives in a state—and we must say this about the state without hesitation and with the greatest ruthlessness—that hates the extraordinary and hates nothing more than the extraordinary. For it is clear that, in this state, only what is stupid, impoverished and dilettante is protected and constantly promoted and that, in this state, funds are only invested in what is incompetent and superfluous. We see hundreds of examples of this every day. And this state claims to be a civilized state and demands that it be described as such on every occasion. Let's not fool ourselves, says Oehler, this state has nothing to do with a civilized state and we shall never tire of saying so continually and without cease and on every occasion even if we are faced with the greatest difficulties because of our ceaseless observation—as a repetition of the same thing over and over again—that this is a state where lack of feeling and sense is boundless. It was Hollensteiner's misfortune to be tied by all his senses to this country—not to this state, you understand—but to this country. And we know what it means, says Oehler, to love a country like ours with all of one's senses in contrast to a state that does everything it can to destroy you instead of coming to your aid. Hollensteiner's suicide is one suicide among many, every year we are made aware of the fact that many people whom we value and who have had talent and genius and who were extraordinary or most extraordinary have committed suicide, for we are constantly going to cemeteries, says Oehler, to the funerals of people who, despairing of the state, have committed suicide, who, if we stop to think, have thrown themselves out of windows, or hanged themselves or shot themselves, because they felt that they had been abandoned by our state. The only reason we go to cemeteries, says Oehler, is to inter a genius who has been ruined by the state and driven to his death, that is the truth. If we strike a balance between the beauty of the country

26

and the baseness of the state, says Oehler, we arrive at suicide. As far as Hollensteiner was concerned, it became clear that his suicide was bound to distress Karrer, after all, the two had an unbelievable relationship as friends. Only, I always thought that Hollensteiner had the strength to go to Germany, to Göttingen, where he would have had everything at his disposal, says Oehler: the fact that he did not have this strength was the cause of his death. It would also have been of no use to have tried even more intensely to persuade him to go to Göttingen at any price, said Karrer, says Oehler. A nature that was not quite as sensitive as Hollensteiner's would of course have had the strength to go to Göttingen, to go anywhere at all, simply to go where all the necessary funds for his scientific purposes would be at his disposal, says Oehler. But for a nature like Hollensteiner's it is, of course, utterly impossible to settle down in an environment which is unbearable, especially not for scientific purposes or to work in no matter what scientific discipline. And it would be senseless, says Oehler, to leave a country that you love but in which you are bound, as we can see, gradually to perish in a morass of indifference and stupidity, and go to a country where you will never get over the depression that that country breeds in you, never get out of a state of mind that must be equally destructive: then it would be better to commit suicide in the country that you love—if only out of force of habit— says Oehler, rather than in the country that, not to mince words, one hates. People like Hollensteiner are admittedly the most difficult, says Oehler, and it is not easy to keep in contact with them, because these people are constantly giving offense—a characteristic of extraordinary people, their most outstanding characteristic, giving offense—but on the other hand there is no greater pleasure than being in contact with such extremely difficult people. We must leave no stone unturned, says Oehler, and we must always, quite consciously, set the highest value on keeping in contact with these extremely difficult people, with the extraordinary and the most extraordinary, because this is the only contact that has any real value. All other contacts are worthless, says Oehler, they are necessary but worthless. It is a shame, says Oehler, that I didn't meet Hollensteiner a lot earlier but a remarkable caution toward this person, whom I always admired, did not permit me to make closer contact with Hollensteiner for at least twenty years after I had first set eyes on Hollensteiner, and even then our contact was not the intense contact that I would have wished for. People like Hollensteiner, says Oehler, do not allow you to approach them, they attract you and then at the

crucial moment reject you. We think that we have a close relationship with these people whereas, in reality, we can never establish a
close relationship with people like Hollensteiner. In fact, we are
captivated by such people as Hollensteiner without exactly knowing
the reason why. On the one hand it is not, in fact, the person, on the
other it is not their science, for we do not understand either of them.
It is something of which we cannot say what it is and *because of
that* it has the greatest effect upon us. For, says Oehler, you have to
have gone to elementary school, to secondary school and the university with a man like Hollensteiner, as Karrer did, to know what
he is. A person like me doesn't know. We comment, with really
terrifying helplessness, upon a matter or a case or simply just a misfortune or just simply Hollensteiner's misfortune. I talked to Karrer
about this at precisely the place where we are now standing, after
we had attended Hollensteiner's funeral a few hours earlier. Just in
Döblingen cemetery itself, says Oehler, where we buried Hollensteiner and, in the nature of things, buried him in the most simple
way. He wanted to have a very simple funeral, says Oehler, he had
once indicated to Karrer, actually very early on when he was only
twenty-one, he had indicated that he wanted a very simple funeral
and in Döblingen cemetery. Just in Döblingen cemetery itself, says
Oehler, there are so many extraordinary people buried, all of whom
were destroyed by the state, who perished as a result of the brutality
of the bureaucracy and the stupidity of the masses. We comment
upon a thing, a case or simply a misfortune and wonder how this
misfortune could have arisen. How was this misfortune *possible?*
We deliberately avoid talking about a so-called *human tragedy.* We
have a single individual in front of us and we have to tell ourselves
that this individual has perished at the hands of the state and vice
versa that the state has perished at the hands of this individual. It is
not easy to say that it's a question of a misfortune, says Oehler, of
this individual's misfortune, or the state's misfortune. It makes no
sense to tell ourselves, now, that Hollensteiner could be in Göttingen (or Marburg) now, because Hollensteiner is not in Göttingen and
is not in Marburg. Hollensteiner no longer exists. We buried Hollensteiner in Döblingen cemetery. As far as Hollensteiner is concerned
we are left behind with our absolute helplessness (of thought). What
we do is to exhaust ourselves meditating about insoluble facts,
among which we do not understand the process of thought, though
we call it thought, says Oehler. We become aware once more of
our unease when we occupy ourselves with Hollensteiner, with

Hollensteiner's suicide and with Karrer's madness, which I think is directly connected with Hollensteiner's suicide. We even misuse a subject like that of Hollensteiner in relation to Karrer, to bring ourselves satisfaction. A strange ruthlessness—that is not recognizable as ruthlessness—dominates a man like Hollensteiner, says Oehler, and we are inevitably captivated by this ruthlessness if we recognize that it is an incredibly shrewd emotional state which we could also call a state of mind. Anyone who knew Hollensteiner had to ask himself now and again where Hollensteiner's way of acting would lead. Today we can see quite clearly where Hollensteiner's way of acting has led. Hollensteiner and Karrer together represent the two most unusual people I have known, says Oehler. There is no doubt that the fact that Hollensteiner hanged himself in his institute is demonstrative in character, says Oehler. The shock of Hollensteiner's suicide was, however, like all shocks about suicides, very very short-lived. Once the suicide is buried, his suicide and he himself are forgotten. No one thinks about it any more and the shock turns out to be hypocritical. Between Hollensteiner's suicide and Hollensteiner's funeral a lot was said about saving the Institute of Chemistry, says Oehler, people saying that the funds that had been denied to Hollensteiner would be placed at the disposal of his successor—as if there were one!—cries Oehler, the newspapers carried reports that the ministry would undertake a so-called extensive redevelopment of Hollensteiner's institute at the funeral, people were even talking about the state's making good what it had up till then neglected in the Institute for Chemistry, but today, a few weeks later, says Oehler, that's all as good as forgotten. Hollensteiner demonstrates by hanging himself in his own institute the serious plight of the whole domestic scientific community, says Oehler, and the world, and thus the people around Hollensteiner, feigns shock and goes to Hollensteiner's funeral and the moment Hollensteiner is buried they forget everything connected with Hollensteiner. Today, nobody talks about Hollensteiner any more and nobody talks about his Institute of Chemistry, and nobody thinks of changing the situation that led to Hollensteiner's suicide. And then someone else commits suicide, says Oehler, and another and the process is repeated. Slowly but surely all intellectual activity in this country is extinguished, says Oehler. And what we observe in Hollensteiner's field can be seen in every field, says Oehler. Up till now we have always asked ourselves whether a country, a state, can afford to allow its intellectual treasure to deteriorate in such a really shabby way, says Oehler, but nobody asks the question any longer. Karrer spoke about Hollensteiner as a perfect example of a human being who could not be helped because he was extraordinary, unusual. Karrer explained the concept of the eccentric in connection with Hollensteiner with complete clarity, says Oehler. If there had been a less fundamental, a distanced, relationship between him, Karrer and Hollensteiner he, Karrer, would have made Hollensteiner the subject of a paper entitled *The Relationship between Persons and Characters like Hollensteiner, as a Chemist, to the State which is gradually and in the most Consistent Manner Destroying and Killing Them.* In fact, there are in existence a number of Karrer's remarks about Hollensteiner, says Oehler, hundreds of slips of paper, just as there are about you, says Oehler to me, there are in existence hundreds of Karrer's slips of paper just as there are about me. It is obvious that these slips of paper written by Karrer should not be allowed to disappear, but it is difficult to get at these notes of Karrer's, if we want to secure Karrer's writings, we have to apply to Karrer's sister, but she doesn't want to hear anything more about Karrer's thoughts. He, Oehler, thinks that Karrer's sister may already have destroyed Karrer's writings, for as we see over and over again stupid relatives act quickly as, for example, the sisters or wives or brothers and nephews of dead thinkers, or ones who have gone finally mad, even when it is a case of brilliant characters, as in the case of Karrer, they don't even wait for the actual moment of the death or the final madness of the hated object, says Oehler, but acting as their relatives destroy, that is burn, the writings that irritate them for the most part before the final death or the final internment of their hated thinker. Just as Hollensteiner's sister destroyed everything that Hollensteiner wrote, immediately after Hollensteiner's suicide. It would be a mistake to assume that Hollensteiner's sister would have taken Hollensteiner's part, says Oehler, on the contrary Hollensteiner's sister was ashamed of Hollensteiner and had taken the state's part, the part that is of baseness and stupidity. When Karrer went to see her, she threw him out, says Oehler, that is to say she didn't even let Karrer into her house. And to his question about Hollensteiner's writings she replied, Hollensteiner's writings no longer existed, that she had burned Hollensteiner's writings because they appeared to her to be the writings of a madman. The fact is, says Oehler, that the world lost tremendous thoughts in Hollensteiner's writings, philosophy lost tremendous philosophical thoughts, science lost tremendous scientific thoughts. For Hollensteiner had been a continuous, thinking, scientific mind, says Oehler, who constantly put his continuous scientific thought onto paper. In fact, in Hollensteiner's case, we were dealing not only with a scientist but also with a philosopher, in Hollensteiner the scientist and the philosopher were able to fuse into one single, clear intellect, says Oehler. Thus, when you talk of Hollensteiner, you can speak of a scientist who was basically really a philosopher, just as you can speak of a philosopher who was basically really a scientist. Hollensteiner's science was basically philosophy, Hollensteiner's philosophy basically science, says Oehler. Otherwise we are always forced to say, here we have a scientist but (regrettably) not a philosopher, or here we have a philosopher but (regrettably) not a scientist. This is not the case in our judgment of Hollensteiner. It is a very Austrian characteristic, as we know, says Oehler. If we get involved with Hollensteiner, says Oehler, we get involved with a philosopher and a scientist at the same time, even if it were totally false to say that Hollensteiner was a philosophizing scientist and so on. He was a totally scientific philosopher. If we are talking about a person, as we are at the moment about Hollensteiner (and if we are talking about Hollensteiner, then basically about Karrer, but very often basically about Hollensteiner and so on), we are nevertheless speaking all the time about a result. We are mathematicians, says Oehler, or at least we are always trying to be mathematicians. When we think, it is less a case of philosophy, says Oehler, more one of mathematics. Everything is a tremendous calculation, if we have set it up from the outset in an unbroken line, *a very simple* calculation. But we are not always in the position of keeping everything that we have calculated intact within our head, and we break off what we are thinking and are satisfied with what we see, and are not surprised for long that we rest content with what we see, with millions upon millions of images that lie on, or under, one another and which constantly merge and displace each other. Again, we can say that what appears extraordinary to a person like me, what is in fact extraordinary for me, *because* it is extraordinary, says Oehler, means nothing to the state. For Hollensteiner meant nothing to the state, because he meant nothing to the masses, but we shall not get any further with this thought, says Oehler. And whereas the state, and whereas society, and whereas the masses do everything to get rid of thought, *we* oppose this development with all the means at our disposal, although we ourselves believe most of the time in the senselessness of thinking, because we know that thinking is total senselessness, because, on the other hand, we know that

31

without the senselessness of thinking *we* do not exist or are nothing. We then cling to the effortlessness with which the masses dare to exist, although they deny this effortlessness in every statement that they make, says Oehler, but, in the nature of things, we do not, of course, succeed in being really effortless in the effortlessness of the masses. We can, however, do nothing less than cling to this misconception from time to time, subject ourselves to the misconception—and that means all possible misconceptions—and exist in nothing but misconception. For strictly speaking, says Oehler, everything is misconceived. But we exist within this fact, because there is no way that we can exist outside this fact, at least not all the time. Existence is misconception, says Oehler. This is something we have to come to terms with early enough, so that we have a basis upon which we can exist, says Oehler. Thus misconception is the only real basis. But we are not always obliged to think of this basis as a principle, we must not do that, says Oehler, we cannot do that. We can only say yes, over and over again to what we should unconditionally say no to, do you understand, says Oehler, that is the fact. Thus Karrer's madness was causally connected with Hollensteiner's suicide that of itself had nothing to do with madness. Behavior like Hollensteiner's was bound to do damage to a nature like Karrer's, if we consider Hollensteiner's relationship to Karrer and vice versa, in the way in which Hollensteiner's suicide harmed Karrer's nature, says Oehler. Karrer had on many occasions, he went on, spoken to Oehler of the possibility of Hollensteiner's committing suicide. But he was talking about a suicide that would come *from within*, not of one that would *be caused externally*, says Oehler, if we disregard the fact that inner and outer are identical for natures like Hollensteiner and Karrer. For, and these are Karrer's words, says Oehler, the possibility that Hollensteiner would commit suicide from an inner cause always existed, but then with the extension of Hollensteiner's institute and with Hollensteiner's obvious successes in his scientific work, simultaneously with the ignoring and the torpedoing of these scientfic successes of Hollensteiner's by the world around him, the possibility existed that he would commit suicide from *an external cause*. Whereas, however, it is characteristic and typical of Hollensteiner, says Oehler, that he did finally commit suicide, as we now know, and what we could not know up to the moment that Hollensteiner committed suicide, is that it is also typical of Karrer that he did not commit suicide, after Hollensteiner had committed suicide, but that he, Karrer, went mad. However, what is frightful, says Oehler, is the thought that a person like Karrer, because he has gone mad and, as I believe, has actually gone finally mad, because he has gone finally mad he has fallen into the hands of people like Scherrer. On the previous Saturday, Oehler made several statements regarding Karrer to Scherrer which, according to Scherrer, says Oehler, were of importance for him, Scherrer, in connection with Karrer's treatment, he, Oehler, did not believe that what he had told Scherrer on Saturday, especially about the incident that was crucial for Karrer's madness, the incident in Rustenschacher's trousers store, that the very thing that Oehler had told Scherrer about what he had noticed in Rustenschacher's store, shortly before Karrer went mad still made sense. For Scherrer's scientific work *it did*, for Karrer *it did not*. For the fact that Scherrer now knows what I noticed in Rustenschacher's store before Karrer went mad in Rustenschacher's store makes no difference to Karrer's madness. What happened in Rustenschacher's store, says Oehler, was only the factor that triggered Karrer's final madness, nothing more. For example, it would have been much more important, says Oehler, if Scherrer had concerned himself with the relationship of Karrer and Hollensteiner, but Scherrer did not want to hear anything from Oehler about this relationship, Karrer's relationship to Hollensteiner was not of the slightest interest to Scherrer, says Oehler. I tried several times to direct Scherrer's attention to this relationship, to make him aware of this really important connection and of the really important events that took place within this year- and decades-long connection between Karrer and Hollensteiner, but Scherrer did not go into it, says Oehler, but, as is the way with these people, these totally unphilosophical and, for that reason, useless psychiatric doctors, he continued to nag away at the happenings in Rustenschacher's store which are, in my opinion, certainly revealing, but not decisive, says Oehler, but he understood nothing about the importance of the relationship Karrer/Hollensteiner. Scherrer kept on asking me *why* we, Karrer and I, went into Rustenschacher's store, to which I replied every time that I could not answer that question and that I simply could not understand how Scherrer could ask such a question, says Oehler. Scherrer kept on asking questions which, in my opinion, were unimportant questions, whereupon, of course, Scherrer received unimportant answers from me, says Oehler. These people keep on asking unimportant questions and for that reason keep on getting unimportant answers, but they are not aware of it. Just as they are not aware of the fact that the questions they ask are unimportant and as a result make no sense, it does not occur to them that the answers they receive to these questions are unimportant and make no sense. If I had not gone on mentioning Hollensteiner's name, says Oehler, Scherrer would not have hit upon Hollensteiner. There is something terribly depressing about sitting opposite a person who, by his very presence, continuously asserts that he is competent and yet has absolutely no competence in the matter at hand. We observe time and again, says Oehler, that we are with people who should be competent and who also assert and claim, indeed they go on claiming, to be competent in the matter for which we have come to them, whereas they are in an irresponsible, shattering and really repugnant manner incompetent. Almost everybody we get together with about a matter, even if it is of the highest importance, is incompetent. Scherrer, says Oehler, is, in my opinion, the most incompetent when it's a question of Karrer, and the thought that Karrer is in Scherrer's hands, because Karrer is interned in Scherrer's section, is one of the most frightful thoughts. The enormous arrogance you sense, says Oehler, when you sit facing a man like Scherrer. Hardly a moment passes before you ask yourself what has Karrer (the patient) really got to do with Scherrer (his doctor)? For a person like Karrer to be in the hands of a person like Scherrer is an unparalleled human monstrosity, says Oehler. But, because we are familiar with his condition, it is immaterial to Karrer whether he is in Scherrer's hands or not. After all, the moment Karrer became finally mad it became immaterial whether Karrer is in Steinhof or not, says Oehler. But it is not the fact that a man like Scherrer is totally unphilosophical that is repugnant, says Oehler, although someone in Scherrer's position ought, first and foremost, besides having his medical knowledge, to be philosophical, it is his shameful ignorance. No matter what I say, Sherrer's ignorance repeatedly finds expression, says Oehler. Whenever I said something—no matter what it was—to Scherrer or whenever Scherrer responded to what I had said—no matter what it was— I was constantly aware that Scherrer's ignorance kept coming to light. But even when Scherrer says nothing, we hear nothing but ignorance from him, says Oehler, a person like Scherrer does not need to say something ignorant, for us to know that we are dealing with a completely ignorant person; whenever I said something to Scherrer or whenever Scherrer responded to what I had said, no matter what it was. The observation that doctors are practicing in complete ignorance shakes us when we are with them, says Oehler. But among doctors, ignorance is a habit to which they have become accustomed over the centuries, says Oehler. Some exceptions not-withstanding, says Oehler. Scherrer's inability to think logically, and thus to ask logical questions, give logical answers and so forth, says Oehler, it was precisely when I was in his presence that it occurred to me that people like Scherrer can never go mad. As we know, psychiatric doctors do become mentally ill after a while, but not mad. Because they are ignorant of their life's theme these people finally become mentally ill, but never mad. As a result of incapacity, says Oehler, and basically because of their continual decades-long incompetence. And at that moment I again recognized to what degree madness is something that happens only among the highest orders of humanity. That at a given moment madness is *everything*. But to say something like that to Scherrer, says Oehler, would, above everything else, be to overestimate Scherrer, so I quickly gave up the idea of saying anything to Scherrer like what I have just said about the actual definition of madness, says Oehler. Scherrer is probably not the least bit interested in what took place in Rustenschacher's store, says Oehler, he only asked me to go up to Steinhof because he didn't know anything better to do, to ask me about what happened in Rustenschacher's store, says Oehler. Psychiatric doctors like to make a note of what you tell them, without worrying about it, and what you tell them is a matter of complete indifference to them, that is, it is a matter of complete indifference to them, and they do not worry about it. Because a psychiatric doctor has to make inquiries, they make inquiries, says Oehler, and of all the leads the ones they follow are the least important. Of course, the incident in Rustenschacher's store is not insignificant, says Oehler, but it is only one of hundreds of incidents which preceded the incident in Rustenschacher's store and which have the same importance as the one in Rustenschacher's store. Not a question about Hollensteiner, not a question about the people around Hollensteiner, not a question about Hollensteiner's place in modern science, not a question about Hollensteiner's philosophical circumstances, about his notes, never mind about Hollensteiner's relationship to Karrer or Karrer's to Hollensteiner. In the nature of things, Scherrer should have shown an interest in the time Hollensteiner and Karrer spent together at school, says Oehler, in their common route to school, their origins and so on, in their common, and their different, views and intentions and so on, says Oehler. The whole time I was there, Scherrer insisted that I only make statements about the incident in Rustenschacher's store, and on this point with regard to the happenings in Rustenschacher's store, says Oehler, Scherrer demanded the utmost precision from me. He kept saying leave nothing out, says Oehler, I can still hear him saying leave nothing out while I went on talking—without a break—about the incident in Rustenschacher's store. This incident acted as a so-called trigger-incident, I said to Scherrer, says Oehler, but there can be no doubt that it is not a fundamental one. Scherrer did not react to my observation, I made the observation several times, says Oehler, and so I had repeatedly to take up the incident in Rustenschacher's store. That is absolutely grotesque, Scherrer said on several occasions during my description of the incident in Rustenschacher's store. This statement was merely repugnant to me.

Oehler told Scherrer, among other things, that their, Oehler's and Karrer's, going into Rustenschacher's store was totally unpremeditated, we suddenly said, according to Oehler, let's go into Rustenschacher's store and immediately had them show us several of the thick, warm and at the same time sturdy winter trousers (according to Karrer). Rustenschacher's nephew, his salesman, Oehler told Scherrer, who had served us so often, pulled out a whole heap of trousers from the shelves that were all labeled with every possible official standard size and threw the trousers onto the counter, and Karrer had Rustenschacher's nephew hold all the trousers up to the light, while I stood to one side, the left-hand side near the mirror, as you look from the entrance door. And as was his, Karrer's, way, as Oehler told Scherrer, Karrer kept pointing with his stick and with greater and greater emphasis at the many thin spots that are revealed in these trousers if you hold them up to the light, Oehler told Scherrer, at the thin spots that really cannot be missed, as Karrer kept putting it, Oehler told Scherrer, Karrer simply kept saying these so-called new trousers, Oehler told Scherrer, while having the trousers held up to the light, and above all he kept on saying the whole time: these remarkably thin spots in these so-called new trousers, Oehler told Scherrer. He, Karrer, again let himself be carried away so far as to make the comment as to why these so-called new trousers—Karrer kept on saying so-called new trousers, over and over again, Oehler told Scherrer—why these so-called new trousers which even if they were new, because they had not been worn, had nevertheless lain on one side for years and, on that account, no longer looked very attractive, something that he, Karrer, had no hesitation in telling Rustenschacher, just as he had no hesitation in telling

Rustenschacher anything that had to do with the trousers that were lying on the counter and which Rustenschacher's nephew kept holding up to the light, it was not in his, Karrer's, nature to feel the least hesitation in saying the least thing about these trousers to Rustenschacher, just as he had no hesitation in saying a lot of things to Rustenschacher that did *not* concern these trousers, though it would surely be to his, Karrer's, advantage not to say many of the things to Rustenschacher that he had no hesitation in telling him, why these trousers should reveal these thin spots that no one could miss in a way that immediately aroused suspicion about these trousers. Karrer told Rustenschacher, Oehler told Scherrer, these very same new, though neglected, trousers which for that reason no longer looked very attractive, though they had never been worn, should reveal these thin spots, said Karrer to Rustenschacher, as Oehler told Scherrer. Perhaps it was that the material in question— of which these trousers were made—was an imported Czechoslovakian reject, Oehler told Scherrer. Karrer used the term Czechoslovakian reject several times, Oehler told Scherrer, and actually used it so often that Rustenschacher's nephew, the salesman, had to exercise the greatest self-control. Throughout the whole time we were in Rustenschacher's store, Rustenschacher himself busied himself labeling trousers, so Oehler told Scherrer. The salesman's self-control was always at a peak from the moment that we, Karrer and I, entered the store. Although from the moment we entered Rustenschacher's store everything pointed to a coming catastrophe (in Karrer), Oehler told Scherrer, I did not believe for one moment that it would really develop into such a, in the nature of things, hideous catastrophe for Karrer, as Oehler told Scherrer. However, I have observed the same thing on each of our visits to Rustenschacher's store, as Oehler told Scherrer: Rustenschacher's nephew exercised this sort of self-control for a long time, for the longest time, and in fact exercised this self-control up to the point when Karrer used the concept and term Czechoslovakian reject. And Rustenschacher himself always exercised the utmost self-control during all our visits to his business, up to the moment, as Oehler told Scherrer, when Karrer suddenly, intentionally almost inaudibly, but in this way all the more effectively, used the concept and the term Czechoslovakian reject. Every time, however, it was the salesman and Rustenschacher's nephew who first objected to the word reject, as Oehler told Scherrer. While the salesman, in the nature of things, in an angry tone of voice, said to Karrer that the materials used in the trousers lying on the counter were neither rejects nor Czechoslovakian rejects, but the very best of English materials, he threw the trousers which he had just been holding up to the light onto the heap of other trousers, while Karrer was saying that it was all a matter of Czechoslovakian rejects, and made a move as if to go out of the store and into the office at the back of the store. It was always the same, Oehler told Scherrer: Karrer says, as quick as lightning, Czechoslovakian rejects, the salesman throws onto the heap the trousers that had just been held up and says angrily the very best English materials and makes a move as if to go out of the store and into the office at the back of the store, and in fact takes a few steps, as Oehler told Scherrer, toward Rustenschacher, but stops just in front of Rustenschacher, turns round and comes back to the counter, standing at which Karrer, with his walking-stick held up in the air, says I have nothing against the way the trousers are finished, no I have nothing against the way the trousers are finished, I am not talking about the way the trousers are finished, but about the quality of the materials, nothing against the workmanship, absolutely nothing against the workmanship. Understand me correctly, Karrer repeats several times to the salesman, as Oehler told Scherrer, I admit that the workmanship in these trousers is the very best, said Karrer, as Oehler told Scherrer, and Karrer immediately says to Rustenschacher's nephew, besides I have known Rustenschacher too long not to know that the workmanship is the best that anyone could imagine. But he, Karrer, could not refrain from remarking that we were dealing here with trouser materials—quite apart from the workmanship—with rejects and, as one could clearly see, with Czechoslovakian rejects, he simply had to repeat that in the case of these trouser materials we are dealing with Czechoslovakian rejects. Karrer suddenly raised his stick again, as Oehler told Scherrer, and banged several times loudly on the counter with his stick and said emphatically: you must admit that in the case of these trouser materials we are dealing with Czechoslovakian rejects! You must admit that! You must admit that! You must admit that! Whereupon Scherrer asks whether Karrer had said you must admit that several times and how loudly, to which I replied to Scherrer, five times, for still ringing in my ears was exactly how often Karrer had said you must admit that and I described to Scherrer exactly how loudly. Just at the moment when Karrer says you must admit that! and you must admit that gentlemen, and you must admit gentlemen that in the case of these trousers that are lying on the counter we are dealing with Czechoslovakian rejects,

Rustenschacher's nephew again holds one of the pairs of trousers up to the light and it is, truth to tell, a pair with a particularly thin spot, I tell Scherrer, Oehler says, twice I repeat to Scherrer: with a particularly thin spot, with a particularly thin spot up to the light, I say, says Oehler, every one of these pairs of trousers that you show me here, says Karrer, Oehler tells Scherrer, is proof of the fact that in the case of all these trouser materials we are dealing with Czechoslovakian rejects. What was remarkable and astonishing and what made him suspicious at that moment, Oehler told Scherrer, was not the many thin spots in these trousers, nor the fact that in the case of these trousers we were dealing with rejects, and actually Czechoslovakian rejects, as he kept repeating, all of that was basically neither remarkable nor surprising and not even astonishing. What was remarkable, surprising and astonishing was the fact, Karrer said to Rustenschacher's nephew, as Oehler told Scherrer, that a salesman, even if he were the nephew of the owner, would be upset by the truth that was told him and he, Karrer, was telling nothing but the truth when he said that these trousers all had thin spots and that these materials were nothing but Czechoslovakian rejects, to which Rustenschacher's nephew replied, as Oehler told Scherrer, that he swore that in the case of the materials in question they were not dealing with Czechoslovakian rejects but with the most excellent English materials, several times the salesman swore to Karrer that in the case of the materials in question they were dealing with the most excellent English materials, most excellent, most excellent, not just excellent I keep on repeating, Oehler told Scherrer, again and again most excellent and not just excellent, because I was of the opinion that it is decisive whether you say excellent or most excellent, I keep telling Scherrer, actually in the case of the materials in question we are dealing with the most excellent English materials, says the salesman, Oehler told Scherrer, at which the salesman's—Rustenschacher's nephew's—voice, as I had to keep explaining to Scherrer, whenever he said the most excellent English materials, was uncomfortably high-pitched. If Rustenschacher's nephew's voice is of itself unpleasant, it is at its most unpleasant when he says the most excellent English materials, I know of no more unpleasant voice than Rustenschacher's nephew's voice when he says the most excellent English materials, Oehler told Scherrer. It is just that the materials are not labeled, says Rustenschacher's nephew, that makes it possible to sell them so cheaply, Oehler told Scherrer. These materials are deliberately not labeled as English materials: clearly to defraud the customs, says Rustenschacher's nephew, and in the background Rustenschacher himself says, from the back of the store, as Oehler told Scherrer, these materials are not labeled so that they can come onto the market as cheaply as possible. Fifty percent of goods from England are not labeled, Rustenschacher told Karrer, I told Scherrer, says Oehler, and for this reason they are cheaper than the ones that are labeled, but as far as the quality goes there is absolutely no difference between goods that are labeled and ones that are not. The goods that are not labeled, especially in the case of textiles, are often forty, very often even fifty or sixty, percent cheaper than the ones that are labeled. As far as the purchaser—above all the consumer—is concerned it is a matter of complete indifference whether he is using labeled or unlabeled goods, it is a matter of complete indifference whether I am wearing a coat made of labeled, or whether I am wearing a coat made of unlabeled materials, says Rustenschacher from the back of the store, Oehler told Scherrer. As far as the customs are concerned we are, of course, dealing with rejects, as you say, Karrer, says Rustenschacher, so Oehler told Scherrer. It is very often the case that what are termed Czechoslovakian rejects, and declared as such to the customs authorities, are the most excellent English goods or most excellent goods from another foreign source, Rustenschacher said to Karrer. During this argument between Karrer and Rustenschacher, Rustenschacher's nephew kept holding up another pair of trousers to the light for Karrer, Oehler says to Scherrer. While I myself, so Oehler told Scherrer, totally uninvolved in the argument, was leaning on the counter, as I said totally uninvolved in the argument between Karrer and Rustenschacher. The two continued their argument, Oehler told Scherrer, just as if I were not in the store, and it was because of this that it was possible for me to observe the two of them with the greatest attention, in the process of which my main attention was, of course, focused on Karrer, for at this point I already feared him, Oehler told Scherrer. Once again I tell Scherrer, if you look from the entrance door, I was standing to the left of Karrer, once again I had to say, in front of the mirror, because Scherrer no longer knew that I had already told him once that during our whole stay in Rustenschacher's store I was always standing in front of the mirror. On the other hand, Scherrer did make a note of everything, according to Oehler, he even made a note of my repetitions, said Oehler. It was obviously a pleasure for Karrer to have all the trousers held up to the light, but having all the trousers held up to the light was nothing new for Karrer and he refused to leave Rustenschacher's store until Rustenschacher's nephew had held all the trousers up to the light, Oehler told Scherrer, basically it was always the same scene when I went to Rustenschacher's store with Karrer but never so vehement, so incredibly intense and, as we now know, culminating in such a terrible collapse on Karrer's part. Karrer took not the slightest notice of the impatience, the resentment and the truly incessant anxiety on the part of Rustenschacher's nephew, Oehler told Scherrer. On the contrary, Karrer put Rustenschacher's nephew the salesman more and more to the test with ever new sadistic fabrications conspicuously aimed at him. Rustenschacher's nephew always reacted too slowly for Karrer. You react too slowly for me said Karrer several times, says Oehler to Scherrer, basically you have no ability to react, it is a mystery to me how you find yourself in a position to serve me, how you find yourself in a postion to work in this truly excellent store of your uncle's, Karrer said several times to Rustenschacher's nephew, Oehler told Scherrer. While you are holding two pairs of trousers up to the light, I can hold up ten pairs Karrer said to Rustenschacher's nephew. How unhappy Rustenschacher was about the argument between Karrer and his, Rustenschacher's, nephew is shown by the fact that Rustenschacher left the store on several occasions and went into the office, apparently to avoid having to take part in the painful argument. I myself was afraid that I would have to intervene in the argument at any moment, then Karrer raised his stick again, banged it on the counter and said, to all appearances we are dealing with a state of exhaustion, it is possible that we are dealing with a state of exhaustion, but I cannot be bothered at all with such a state of exhaustion, cannot be bothered at all, he said to himself, while he was banging on the counter with his stick, in the particular rhythm with which he always banged on the counter in Rustenschacher's store, apparently to calm his inner state of excitement, Oehler told Scherrer, and then he, Karrer, began once more to heap his excesses of assertion and insinuation concerning the trousers on the head of the salesman. Rustenschacher certainly heard everything from the back of the store, as Oehler told Scherrer, even if it appeared as though Rustenschacher observed nothing happening between Karrer and his nephew, Rustenschacher's self-control, I told Scherrer, said Oehler, was at an absolute peak, as the argument between Karrer and Rustenschacher's nephew heated up, Rustenschacher had to exercise a degree of self-control which would have been impossible in another human being. *But the way* in which Karrer had behaved at certain times in Rustenschacher's store and because Rustenschacher *knew* how Karrer always *acts in this almost unbearable manner* in Rustenschacher's store and Rustenschacher knew how Karrer always *reacts* to everything, but he knew that he had nevertheless always calmed down in the end, in fact, whenever we had gone into Rustenschacher's store, Rustenschacher had always shown a much greater ability to judge Karrer's state of mind than Scherrer. Suddenly Karrer said to Rustenschacher, Oehler told Scherrer, if you, Rustenschacher take up a position behind the pair of trousers that your nephew is at this moment holding up to the light for me, immediately behind this pair of trousers that your nephew is holding up to the light for me, I can see your face through this pair of trousers with a clarity with which I do not wish to see your face. But Rustenschacher controlled himself. Whereupon Karrer said, enough trousers! enough materials! enough! Oehler told Scherrer. Immediately after this, however, Oehler told Scherrer, Karrer repeated that with regard to the materials that were lying on the counter, they were dealing one hundred percent with Czechoslovakian rejects. Aside from the workmanship, says Karrer, Oehler told Scherrer, it was a question as far as these materials were concerned, even to the layman, quite obviously of Czechoslovakian rejects. The workmanship is the best, of course, the workmanship is the best, Karrer keeps repeating, that has always been apparent in all the years that I have been coming to Rustenschacher's store. And how long had he been coming to Rustenschacher's store? and how many pairs of trousers had he already bought in Rustenschacher's store? says Karrer, Oehler tells Scherrer, not one button has come off, says Karrer, Oehler told Scherrer. Not a single seam has come undone! says Karrer to Rustenschacher. My sister, says Karrer, has never yet had to sew on a button that has come off, says Karrer, it is true that my sister has never yet had to sew on a single button that has come off a pair of trousers that I bought from you, Rustenschacher, because all the buttons that have been sewn onto the trousers that I bought from you are really sewn on so securely that no one can tear one of these buttons off. And not a single seam has come undone in all these years in any of the pairs of trousers that I have bought in your store! Scherrer noted what I was saying in the so-called shorthand that is customary among psychiatric doctors. And I felt terrible to be sitting here in Pavilion VI in front of Scherrer and making these statements about Karrer, while Karrer is interned in Pavilion VII we say *interned*, because we don't want to say *locked up* or *locked up like an animal*, says Oehler. Here I am sitting in

Pavilion VI and talking about Karrer in Pavilion VII without Karrer's knowing anything about the fact that I am sitting in Pavilion VI and talking about him in Pavilion VII. And, of course, I did not visit Karrer, when I went *into* Steinhof, nor when I came *away from* Steinhof, says Oehler. But Karrer probably couldn't have been visited. Visiting internees in Pavilion VII is not permitted, says Oehler. No one in Pavilion VII is allowed to have visitors. Suddenly Rustenschacher says, I tell Scherrer, says Oehler, that Karrer can try to tear a button off the trousers that are lying on the counter. Or try to rip open one of these seams! says Rustenschacher to Karrer, subject all of these pairs of trousers to a thorough examination, says Rustenschacher and Rustenschacher invites Karrer to tear, to pull and to tug at all the pairs of trousers lying on the counter in any way he likes, Oehler told Scherrer. Rustenschacher invited Karrer to do whatever he liked to the trousers. Possibly, Rustenschacher was thinking pedagogically, at that moment, Oehler said to Scherrer. Then Oehler said to Rustenschacher that he, Karrer, would refrain when so directly invited to tear up all these pairs of Rustenschacher's trousers, Oehler told Scherrer. I prefer not to make such a tear-test, said Karrer to Rustenschacher, Oehler told Scherrer. For if I did make the attempt, said Karrer, to rip *open a seam* or even tear a button *off* just one pair of these trousers, people would at once say that I was mad, and I am on my guard against this, because you should be on your guard against being called mad, Oehler told Scherrer. But if I really were to tear these trousers, Karrer said to Rustenbacher and his nephew, I would tear all of these trousers into rags in the shortest possible time, to say nothing of the fact that I would tear all the buttons off all of these trousers. Such rashness to invite me to tear all these trousers! says Karrer. Such rashness!, Oehler told Scherrer. Then Karrer returned to the thin spots, Oehler told Scherrer, saying that it was remarkable that if you held all of these trousers up to the light thin spots were to be seen, thin spots which were quite typical of reject materials, says Karrer. Whereupon Rustenschacher's nephew says, you mayn't, as anyone knows, hold up one single pair of trousers to the light, because all trousers if held up to the light show thin spots. Show me a pair of trousers in the whole world that you can hold up to the light, says Rustenschacher to Karrer from the back. Not even the newest, not even the newest, says Rustenschacher, Oehler told Scherrer. In every case you would find at least one thin spot in a pair of trousers that were held up to the light, says Rustenschacher's nephew, says Oehler to Scherrer. Suddenly,

Rustenschacher adds from the back: every piece of *woven goods* reveals a thin spot, when held up to the light, a thin spot. To which Karrer replies that every intelligent shopper naturally holds an article that he has chosen to buy up to the light, if he doesn't want to be swindled, Oehler told Scherrer. Every article, no matter what, must be held up to the light if you want to buy it, Karrer said. Even if business people fear nothing as much as having their articles held up to the light, said Karrer, Oehler told Scherrer. But naturally there are trouser materials and thus trousers, I tell Scherrer, which you can hold up to the light without further ado, if you are really dealing with excellent materials, I say, you can hold them up to the light without further ado. But apparently, I tell Scherrer, according to Oehler, we were dealing with English materials in the case of the materials in question and not, as Karrer thought, with Czechoslovakian, and thus not with Czechoslovakian rejects but I do not believe that we were dealing with excellent, or indeed most excellent English materials, I tell Scherrer, for I saw the thin spots myself in all of these trousers, except that naturally I would not have held forth in the way that Karrer held forth about those thin spots in all the trousers, I tell Scherrer. Probably I would not have gone into Rustenschacher's store at all, seeing that we had been in Rustenschacher's store two or three days before the visit to Rustenschacher's store. It was the same the time before last when we went in: Karrer had Rustenschacher's nephew hold the trousers up to the light, but not so many pairs of trousers, after just a short time Karrer says, thank you, I'm not going to buy any trousers, and to me, let's go, and we leave Rustenschacher's store. But now the situation was totally different. Karrer was already in a state of excitement when he entered Rustenschacher's store, because we had been talking about Hollensteiner the whole way from Klosterneuburgerstrasse to Albersbachstrasse, Karrer had become more and more excited as we made our way and at the peak of his excitement—I had never seen Karrer so excited before—we went into Rustenschacher's store. Of course we should not have gone into Rustenschacher's store in such a high state of excitement, I tell Scherrer. It would have been better not to go into Rustenschacher's store, but to go back to Klosterneuburgerstrasse, but Karrer did not take up my suggestion of returning to Klosterneuburgerstrasse. I have planned to go into Rustenschacher's store, Karrer says to me, Oehler told Scherrer, and as Karrer's tone of voice had the character of an irreversible command, I tell Scherrer, according to Oehler, I had no choice but to go into

Rustenschacher's store with Karrer on this occasion. And I could never have let Karrer go into Rustenschacher's store on his own, says Oehler, not in that state. It was clear to me that we were taking a risk in going into Rustenschacher's store, I tell Scherrer, Karrer's state prevented me from saying a word against his intention of going into Rustenschacher's store. If you know Karrer's nature, I tell Scherrer, according to Oehler, you know that if Karrer says he is going into Rustenschacher's store it is pointless trying to do anything about it. No matter what Karrer's intention was when he was in such a condition there was no way of stopping him, no way of persuading him to do otherwise. On the one hand, it was Rustenschacher who let him go into Rustenschacher's store, on the other hand Rustenschacher's nephew, both of them were basically repugnant to him, just as, basically, everyone was repugnant to him, even I was repugnant to him: you have to know that everyone was repugnant to him, even those with whom he consorted of his own volition, if you consorted with him of his own volition, you were not exempted from the fact that everybody was repugnant to Karrer, I tell Scherrer, says Oehler. *There is no one with such great sensitivity. No one with such fluctuations of consciousness. No one so easily irritated and so ready to be hurt,* I tell Scherrer, says Oehler. The truth is Karrer felt he was constantly being watched, and he always reacted as if he felt he was constantly being watched, and for this reason he never had a single moment's peace. This constant restlessness is also what distinguishes him from everyone else, if constant restlessness can distinguish a person, I tell Scherrer, Oehler says. And to be with a constantly restless person who imagines that he is restless even when he is in reality not restless is the most difficult thing, I tell Scherrer, says Oehler. Even when nothing suggested one or more causes of restlessness, when nothing suggested the least restlessness, Karrer was restless because he had the feeling (the sense) that he was restless, because he had reason to, as he thought. The theory according to which a person is everything he imagines himself to be could be studied in Karrer, the way he always imagined, and he probably imagined this all his life, that he was critically ill without knowing what the illness was that made him critically ill, and probably because of this, and certainly according to the theory, I tell Scherrer, says Oehler, he really was critically ill. *When we imagine ourselves to be in a state of mind,* no matter what, we are in that state of mind, and thus in that state of illness which we imagine ourselves to be in, *in every state that we imagine ourselves in.* And we do not allow ourselves to be disturbed in what we imagine, I tell Scherrer, and thus we do not allow what we have imagined to be negated by anything, especially by *anything external.* What incredible self-confidence, on the one hand, and what incredible weakness of character and helplessness, on the other, psychiatric doctors show, I think, while I am sitting opposite Scherrer and making these statements about Karrer and above all about Karrer's behavior in Rusten-schacher's store, says Oehler. After a short time I ask myself why I am sitting opposite Scherrer and making these statements and giving this information about Karrer? But I do not spend long thinking about this question, so as not to give Scherrer an opportunity of start-ing to have thoughts about my unusual behavior toward him, because I had declared myself ready to tell him as much as possible about Karrer that afternoon. I now think it would have been better to get up and leave, without bothering about what Scherrer is think-ing, if I were to leave in spite of my assurance that I would talk about Karrer for an hour or two I thought, Oehler says. If only I could go outside, I said to myself while I was sitting opposite Scherrer, out of this terrible whitewashed and barred room and go away. Go away as far as possible. But, like everyone who sits facing a psychiatric doctor, I had only the one thought, that of not arousing any sort of suspicion in the person sitting opposite me about my own mental condition and that means about my soundness of mind. I thought that basically I was acting against Karrer by going to Scherrer, says Oehler. My conscience was suddenly *not clear,* do you know what it means to have a sudden feeling that your conscience is not clear with respect to a friend, and it makes things all the worse if your friend is in Karrer's position, I thought. To speak merely of a bad con-science would be to water the feeling down quite inadmissibly, says Oehler, I was ashamed. For there was no doubt in my mind that Scherrer was an enemy of Karrer's, but I only became aware of this *after a long time, after long observation of* Scherrer—whom I have *known* for years, ever since Karrer was first in Steinhof—and it was only because we were acquainted that I agreed to pay a call on him, but he was not so well known to me that I could say this is someone I know, in that case I would not have accepted Scherrer's invitation to go to Steinhof and make a statement about Karrer. I thought several times about getting up and leaving, says Oehler, but then I stopped thinking that way, I said to myself it *doesn't matter.* Scherrer makes me uneasy because he is so superficial. If I had orig-inally imagined that I was going to visit a scientific man, in the shape of a scientific doctor, I soon recognized that I was sitting down across from a charlatan. Too often we recognize too late that we should not have become involved in something that unexpectedly debases us. On the other hand, I had to assume that Scherrer performed a useful function for Karrer, says Oehler, but I saw more and more that Scherrer—although he is described as the opposite and although he himself believes in this opposite, is indeed convinced by it—is an enemy of Karrer's, a doctor in a white coat playing the role of a benefactor. To Scherrer, Karrer is nothing more than an object that he misuses. Nothing more than a victim. Nauseated by Scherrer, I tell him that Karrer says that there really are trousers and trouser materials that can be held up to the light, *but these,* says Karrer and bursts out into a laughter that is quite uncharacteristic of Karrer, because it is characteristic of Karrer's madness, *you don't need to hold these trousers up to the light,* Karrer says, banging on the counter with his stick at the same time, *to see that we are dealing with Czechoslovakian rejects.* Now for the first time I noticed quite clear signs of madness, I tell Scherrer, whereupon, as I can see, Scherrer immediately makes a note, says Oehler, because I am watching all that Scherrer is noting down, says Oehler. *Oehler* (that's me) *says at that moment: for the first time quite clear signs of madness* I observe *not only how Scherrer reacts, I also observe what Scherrer makes notes of and how Scherrer makes notes* I am not surprised, says Oehler, that Scherrer underlines my comment *for the first time signs of madness.* It is merely proof of his incompetence, says Oehler. It occurred to me that Rustenschacher was still labeling trousers in the back, I told Scherrer, and I thought it's incomprehensible, and thus uncanny, that Rustenschacher should be labeling so many pairs of trousers. Possibly it was a sudden, unbelievable increase in Karrer's state of excitement that prompted Rustenschacher's incessant labeling of trousers, for Rustenschacher's incessant labeling of trousers was slowly irritating even me. I thought that Rustenschacher really never sells as many pairs of trousers as he is labeling, I suddenly tell Scherrer, but he probably also supplies other smaller businesses in the outlying districts, in the twenty-first, twenty-second and twenty-third districts, in which you can also buy Rustenschacher's trousers and thus Rustenschacher also plays the role of a trousers wholesaler for a number of such textile firms in outlying districts. Now, Karrer says, in the case of this pair of trousers that you are now holding right in front of my face instead of holding them up to the light, Oehler tells Scherrer, it is clearly a case of Czechoslovakian rejects. It was simply because Karrer did not insult Rustenschacher's nephew to his face with this new objection to Rustenschacher's trousers, Oehler told Scherrer. Karrer had at first prolonged his visit to Rustenschacher's store because of the pains in his leg, I told Scherrer, says Oehler. Apparently we had walked too far before we entered Rustenschacher's store and not only too far, but also too quickly while at the same time carrying on a most exhausting conversation about Wittgenstein, I tell Scherrer, says Oehler, I mention the name on purpose, because I knew that Scherrer had never heard the name before, and this was confirmed at once, in the very moment that I said the name Wittgenstein, says Oehler, however, at that point Karrer had probably not been thinking about his painful legs for a long time, but simply for the reason that I could not leave him I was unable to leave Rustenschacher's store. This is something we often observe in ourselves when we are in a room (any room you care to mention): we seem chained to the room (any room you care to mention) and have to stay there, because we cannot leave it when we are *upset*. Karrer probably wanted to leave Rustenschacher's store, I tell Scherrer, says Oehler, but Karrer no longer had the strength to do so. And I myself was no longer capable of taking Karrer out of Rustenschacher's store at the crucial moment. After Rustenschacher had repeated, as his nephew had before him, that the trouser materials with which we were dealing were excellent— he did not, like his nephew before him, say most excellent, just excellent—material and that it was senseless to maintain that we were dealing with rejects or even with Czechoslovakian rejects, Karrer once again says that in the case of these trousers they were apparently dealing with Czechoslovakian rejects and he made as if to take a deep breath, as it seemed unsuccessfully, whereupon he wanted to say something else, I tell Scherrer, says Oehler, but he, Karrer, was out of breath and he was unable, because he was out of breath, to say what he apparently wanted to say. *These thin spots. These thin spots. These thin spots. These thin spots. These thins spots* over and over again. *These thin spots. These thin spots. These thin spots,* incessantly. *These thin spots. These thin spots. These thin spots.* Rustenschacher had immediately grasped what was happening and, on my orders, Rustenschacher's nephew had already ordered everything to be done that had to be done, Oehler tells Scherrer.

The unbelievable sensitivity of a person like Karrer on the one hand and his great ruthlessness on the other, said Oehler. On the one hand, his overwhelming wealth of feeling and on the other his overwhelming brutality. There is a constant tug-of-war going on between all the possibilities of human thought and all the possibilities of a human mind's sensitivity and between all the possibilities of human character, says Oehler. On the other hand we are in a state of constant *completely natural* and not for a moment *artificial* intellectual preparedness when we are with a person like Karrer. We acquire an increasingly radical, and in fact an increasingly more radically clear, view of and relationship to all objects even if these objects are the sort of objects which in normal circumstances human beings cannot grasp. What till now, till the moment that we met a person like Karrer, we found unattainable we suddenly find attainable and transparent. Suddenly the world no longer consists of layers of darkness, but is totally layered in clarity, says Oehler. It is in the recognition of this and in the constant readiness to recognize this, says Oehler, that the difficulties of constantly being with a person like Karrer lie. A person like that is, of course, feared because he is afraid (of being transparent). We are now concerned with a person like Karrer, because now he has actually been taken away from us (by being taken into Steinhof). If Karrer were not at this moment in Steinhof and if we did not know for certain that he is in Steinhof, were this not an absolute certainty for us, we would not dare to talk about Karrer, but because Karrer has gone finally mad, as we know, which we know not because science has confirmed it, but simply because we only need to use our heads, and what we have ascertained by using our own heads and what, furthermore, science has confirmed for us, for there is no doubt that in Scherrer, says Oehler, we are dealing with a typical representative of science, which Karrer always called *so-called* science, we do dare to talk about Karrer. Just as Karrer, in general, says Oehler, called everything "so-called," there was nothing that he did not call only so-called nothing that he would not have called so-called, and by so doing his powers achieved an unbelievable force. He, Karrer, had never said, says Oehler, even if on the contrary he did say it frequently and in many cases incessantly, in such incessantly spoken words and in such incessantly used concepts that it was not a question of science, always only of so-called science, it was not a question of art, only of so-called art, not of technology, only of so-called technology, not of illness, only of so-called illness, not of knowledge, only of so-called knowledge while saying that everything was only so-called he reached an unbelievable potential and an unexampled credibility. When we are dealing with people we are only dealing with so-called people, just as when we are dealing with facts we are only dealing with so-called facts, just as the whole of matter, since it only emanates from the human mind, is only so-called matter, just as we know that everything emanates from the human mind and from nothing else, if we understand *the concept knowledge* and accept it as a concept that we understand. This is what we go on thinking of and we constantly *substantiate* everything on this basis and on no other. That on this basis, things, and things in themselves, are only so-called, or to be completely accurate, only so-called so-called, to use Karrer's words, says Oehler, goes without saying. The structure of the whole is, as we know, a *completely simply one* and if we always accept this completely simple structure as our starting point we shall make progress. If we do not accept this completely simple structure of the whole as our starting point, we have what we call a complete standstill, but also *a whole, as a so-called.* How could I dare, said Karrer, not to call something only so-called and so draw up an account and design a world, no matter how big and no matter how sensible or how foolish, if I were always only to say to myself (and to act accordingly) that we are dealing with what is so-called and then, over and over again, a so-called so-called something. Just as behavior in its repetition as in its absoluteness is only so-called behavior, Karrer said, says Oehler. Just as we have only a so-called position to adopt vis-à-vis everything we understand and vis-à-vis everything we do not understand, but which we think is real and thus true. Walking with Karrer was an unbroken series of thought processes, says Oehler, which we often developed in juxtaposition one to the other and would then suddenly unjoin them somewhere along the way, when we had reached a place for *standing* or a place for *thinking,* but generally at one particular place for *standing and thinking* when it was a question, says Oehler, of making one of my thoughts into a single one, with another one (his) not into a double one, for a double thought is, as we know, impossible and therefore nonsense. There is never anything but one single thought, just as it is wrong to say that there is a thought beside this thought and what, in such a constellation, is often called a secondary thought, which is sheer nonsense. If Karrer had a thought, and I myself had a thought—and it must be said that we were constantly finding ourselves in that state, because it had long since ceased to be possible for us to be in any state but that state—we both constantly had a thought, or, as Karrer would have said, even if he didn't say it, a so-called constant thought right up to the moment when we dared to make our two separate thoughts into a single one, just as we maintain that about really great thoughts, that is so-called really great thoughts, which are however not thoughts, for a so-called really great thought is never *a* thought, it is a summation of all thoughts pertaining to a so-called great matter, thus there is no such thing as the really great thought, we do not dare, we told ourselves in such a case, says Oehler, when we had been walking together for a long time and had had *one* thought each individually, but side by side, and when we had held on to this thought and seen through it to make these two completely transparent thoughts into one. That was, one could say, nothing but playfulness, but then you could say that everything is only playfulness, says Oehler, that no matter what we are dealing with we are dealing with playfulness is also a possibility, says Oehler, but I do not contemplate that. The thought is quite right, says Oehler, when we are standing in front of the Obenaus Inn, *suddenly* stopping in front of the Obenaus, is what Oehler says: the thought that Karrer will never go out to Obenaus again is quite right. Karrer really will not go out to Obenaus again, because he will not come out of Steinhof again. We know that Karrer will not come out of Steinhof again, and thus we know that he will not go into Obenaus again. *What will he miss by this?* we immediately ask ourselves, says Oehler, if we get involved with this question, although we know that it is senseless to have asked this question, but if the question has once been asked let us consider it and approach the response to the question, *What will Karrer miss by not going into Obenaus again?* It is easy enough to ask the question, but the answer is, however, complicated, for we cannot answer a question like, *What will Karrer miss if he does not go into Obenaus again?* with a simple *yes* or a simple *no.* Although we know that it would have been simpler not to have asked ourselves the question (it doesn't matter what question), we have nevertheless asked ourselves the (and thus a) question. We have asked ourselves an incredibly complicated question and done so completely consciously, says Oehler, because we *think* that it is possible for us to answer even a complicated question we are not afraid to answer such a complicated question as, *What will Karrer miss if he does not go into Obenaus again?* Because we think we know so much (and in such depth) about Karrer that we can answer the question, *What will Karrer miss if he does not go into Obenaus again?* Thus we do not dare to answer the question, *we know* that we can answer it, we are not risking anything with this question although it is only as we come to the realization that we are risking nothing with this question that we realize that we are risking *everything* and not only with this question. I would not however go so far as to say that I can *explain* how I answer the question, *What will Karrer miss if he does not go into Obenaus again?*, says Oehler, but I will also not answer the question without explanation and indeed not without explanation of how I have answered the question or of how I came to ask the question at all. If we want to answer a question like the question, *What will Karrer miss if he does not go into Obenaus again?*, we have to answer it *ourselves*, but this presupposes a complete knowledge of Karrer's circumstances with relation to Obenaus and thereafter, of course, the full knowledge of everything connected with Karrer and with Obenaus, by which means we arrive at the fact that we cannot answer the question, *What will Karrer miss if he does not go into Obenaus again?* The assertion that we answer the question while answering it is thus a false one, because we have probably answered the question and, as we believe and know, have answered it ourselves, we haven't answered it at all, because we have simply not answered the question ourselves, because it is not possible to answer a question like the question, *What will Karrer miss if he does not go into Obenaus again?* Because we have not asked the question, *Will Karrer go into Obenaus again?*, which could be answered simply by yes or no, in the actual case in point by answering no, and would thus cause ourselves no difficulty, but instead we are asking, *What will Karrer miss if he does not go into Obenaus again?*, it is automatically a question that cannot be answered, says Oehler. Apart from that, we do, however, answer this question when we call the question that we asked ourselves a so-called question and the answer that we give a so-called answer. While we are again *acting* within the framework of the concept of the so-called and are thus *thinking* it seems to us quite possible to answer the question, *What will Karrer miss if he does not go into Obenaus again?* But the question, *What will Karrer miss if he does not go into Obenaus again?* can also be applied to *me*. I can ask, *What will I miss if I do not go into Obenaus again?* or you can ask yourself, *What will I miss if I do not go into Obenaus again?* but at the same time it is most highly probable that one of these days I will indeed go into Obenaus again and you will probably go into Obenaus again to eat or drink something, says Oehler. I can say *in my opinion* Karrer will not go into Obenaus again, I can even say *probably* Karrer will not go into Obenaus again, I can say *with certainty* or *definitely* that Karrer will not go into Obenaus again. But I cannot ask, *What will Karrer miss by the fact that he will not go into Obenaus again?* because I cannot answer the question. But let's simply make the *attempt* to ask ourselves, *What does a person who has often been to Obenaus miss if he suddenly does not go into Obenaus any more (and indeed never again)?* says Oehler. Suppose such a person simply never goes among the people who are sitting there, says Oehler. When we ask it in this way, we see that we cannot answer the question because in the meantime we have expanded it by an endless number of other questions. If, nevertheless, we do ask, says Oehler, and we start with the people who are sitting in Obenaus. We first ask, *What is or who is sitting in Obenaus?* so that we can then ask, *Whom does someone who suddenly does not go into Obenaus again (ever again) miss?* Then we at once ask ourselves, *With which of the people sitting in Obenaus shall I begin?* and so on. Look, says Oehler, we can ask any question we like, we cannot answer the question if we *really* want to answer it, to this extent there is not a single question in the whole conceptual world that can be answered. But in spite of this, millions and millions of questions are constantly being asked and answered by questions, as we know, and those who ask the questions and those who answer are not bothered by whether it is wrong because they cannot be bothered, so as not to stop, so that there shall suddenly be nothing more, says Oehler. Here, in front of Obenaus, look, here, up there on the fourth floor, I once lived in a room, a very small room, when I came back from America, says Oehler. He'd come back from America and had said to himself, you should take a room in the place where you lived thirty years ago in the ninth district and he had taken a room in the ninth district in the Obenaus. But suddenly he couldn't stand it any longer, not in this street any longer, not in this city any longer, says Oehler. During his stay in America, everything had changed in the city in which *he was suddenly living again after thirty years* in what for him was a horrible way. I hadn't reckoned on that, says Oehler. I suddenly realized that there was nothing left for me in this city, says Oehler, but now that I had, as it happened, returned to it and, to tell the truth, with the intention of staying *forever*, I was not able immediately to turn round and go back to America. For I had really left America with the intention of leaving America forever, says Oehler. I realized, on the one hand, that there was nothing left for me in

Vienna, says Oehler and, on the other, I realized with all the acuity of my intellect that there was also nothing more left for me in America, and he had walked through the city for days and weeks and months pondering how he would commit suicide. For it was clear to me that I must commit suicide, says Oehler, completely and utterly clear, only not *how* and also not exactly *when*, but it was clear to me that it would be *soon*, because it had to be soon. He went into the inner city again and again, says Oehler, and stood in front of the front doors of the inner city and looked for a particular name from his childhood and his youth, a name that was either loved or feared, but which was known to him, but he did not find a single one of these names. Where have all these people gone who are associated with the names that are familiar to me, but which I cannot find on any of these doors? I asked myself, says Oehler. He kept on asking himself this question for weeks and for months. We often go on asking the same question for months at a time, he says, ask ourselves or ask others but above all we ask ourselves and when, even after the longest time, even after the passage of years, we have still not been able to answer this question, because it is not possible for us to answer it—it doesn't matter what the question is, says Oehler—we ask another, a new, question, but perhaps again a question that we have already asked ourselves, and so it goes on throughout life, until the mind can stand it no longer. Where have all these people, friends, relatives, enemies got to? he had asked himself and had gone on and on looking for names, even at night this questioning about the names had given him no peace. Were there not hundreds and thousands of names? he had asked himself. Where are all these people with whom I had contact thirty years ago? he asked himself. If only I were to meet just a single one of these people. Where have they gone to? he asked himself incessantly, and why. Suddenly it became clear to him that all the people he was looking for no longer existed. These people no longer exist, he suddenly thought, there's no sense in looking for these people because they no longer exist, he suddenly said to himself, and he gave up his room in Obenaus and went into the mountains, into the country. I went into the mountains, says Oehler, but I couldn't stand it in the mountains either and came back into the city again. I have often stood here with Karrer beneath the Obenaus, says Oehler, and talked to him about all these frightful associations. Then we, Oehler and I, were on the Friedensbrücke. Oehler tells me that Karrer's proposal to explain one of Wittgenstein's statements to him on the Friedensbrücke came to nothing;

because he was so exhausted, Karrer did not even mention Wittgenstein's name again on the Friedensbrücke. I myself was not capable of mentioning Ferdinand Ebner's name any more, says Oehler. In recent times we have very often found ourselves in a state of exhaustion in which we were no longer able to explain what we intended to explain. We used the Friedensbrücke to relieve our states of exhaustion, says Oehler. There were two statements that we wanted to explain to each other, says Oehler, I wanted to explain to Karrer a statement of Wittgenstein's that was completely unclear to him, and Karrer wanted to explain a statement by Ferdinand Ebner that was completely unclear to me. But because we were exhausted we were suddenly no longer capable—there on the Friedensbrücke—of saying the names of Wittgenstein and Ferdinand Ebner because we had brought our walking and our thinking, the one out of the other, to an incredible, almost unbearable, state of nervous tension. We had already thought that this practice of bringing walking and thinking to the point of the most terrible nervous tension could not go on for long without causing harm and in fact we were unable to carry on the practice, says Oehler. Karrer had to put up with the consequences, I myself was so weakened by Karrer's, I have to say, complete nervous breakdown—for that is how I can unequivocally describe Karrer's madness, as a fatal structure of the brain—that I can no longer say the word Wittgenstein on the Friedensbrücke, let alone say anything about Wittgenstein or anything connected with Wittgenstein, says Oehler, looking at the traffic on the Friedensbrücke. Whereas we always thought we could make walking and thinking *into a single total process*, even for a longer time, I now have to say that it is impossible to make walking and thinking into one total process for a longer period of time. For, in fact, it is not possible *to walk and to think with the same intensity for a longer period of time*, sometimes we walk more intensively, but think less intensively, then we think intensively and do not walk as intensively as we are thinking, sometimes we think with a much higher presence of mind than we walk with and sometimes we walk with a far higher presence of mind than we think with, but we cannot walk and think with the same presence of mind, says Oehler, just as we cannot walk and think with the same intensity over a longer period of time and make walking and thinking for a longer period of time into a total whole with a total equality of value. If we walk more intensively, our thinking lets up, says Oehler, if we think more intensively than our walking does. On the other hand, we have to walk in order to be able to think, says Oehler, just as we have to think in order to be able to walk, the one derives from the other and the one derives from the other with ever-increasing skill. But never beyond the point of exhaustion. We cannot say we think like we walk, just as we cannot say we walk like we think because we cannot walk like we think, cannot think like we walk. If we are walking intensively for a long time deep in an intensive thought, says Oehler, then we soon have to stop walking or stop thinking, because it is not possible to walk and to think with the same intensity for a longer period of time. Of course, we can say that we succeed in walking evenly and in thinking evenly but this art is apparently the most difficult and one that we are least able to master. We say of one person he is an excellent thinker and we say of another person he is an excellent walker, but we cannot say of one single person that he is an excellent (or first-rate) thinker and walker at the same time. On the other hand walking and thinking are two complete similar concepts and we can readily say (and maintain) that the person who walks and thus the person who, for example, walks excellently also thinks excellently, just as the person who thinks, and thus thinks excellently, also walks excellently. If we observe very carefully someone who is walking, we also know how he thinks. If we observe very carefully someone who is thinking, we know how he walks. If we observe most minutely someone walking over a longer period of time, we gradually come to know his way of thinking, the structure of his thought, just as we, if we observe someone over a longer period of time as to the way he thinks, we will gradually come to know how he walks. So observe, over a longer period of time, someone who is thinking and then observe how he walks, or vice versa, observe someone walking over a longer period of time and then observe how he thinks. There is nothing more revealing than to see a thinking person walking, just as there is nothing more revealing than to see a walking person thinking, in the process of which we can easily say that we see how the walker thinks just as we can say that we see how the thinker walks, because we are seeing the thinker walking and conversely seeing the walker thinking and so on, says Oehler. Walking and thinking are in a perpetual relationship that is based on trust, says Oehler. The science of walking and the science of thinking are basically a single science. How does this person walk and how does he think! we often ask ourselves, as though coming to a conclusion, without actually asking ourselves this question as though coming to a conclusion, just as we often ask the question, in order to come to a conclusion (without actually asking it), how does this person think, how does this person walk! Whenever I see someone thinking, can I therefore infer from this how he walks? I ask myself, says Oehler, if I see someone walking can I infer how he thinks? No, of course, I *may* not ask myself this question, for this question is one of those questions that *may* not be asked because they *can*not be asked without its being nonsense. But naturally we may not reproach someone who walks, whose walking we have analyzed, with his thinking, before we know his thinking. Just as we may not reproach someone who thinks with his walking before we know his walking. *How carelessly this person walks* we often think and very often *how carelessly this person thinks* and we soon come to realize that this person walks in exactly the same way as he thinks, and walks the same way as he thinks. However, we may not ask *ourselves* how we walk, for then we walk differently from the way we really walk and our walking simply cannot be judged, just as we may not ask ourselves how we think for then we cannot judge how we think because it is no longer *our* thinking. Whereas, of course, we can observe someone else without his knowledge (or his being aware of it) and observe how he walks or thinks, that is his walking and his thinking, we can never observe ourselves without our knowledge (or our being aware of it). If we observe ourselves we are never observing ourselves but someone else. Thus, we can never talk about self-observation or when we talk about the fact that we observe ourselves we are talking as someone who we never are when we are not observing ourselves, and thus when we observe ourselves we are never observing the person whom we intended to observe, but someone else. The concept of self-observation and so, also, of self-description is thus false. Looked at in this light, all concepts (ideas), says Oehler, like self-observation, self-pity, self-accusation and so on, are false. We ourselves do not see ourselves, it is never possible for us to see ourselves. But we also cannot explain to someone else (a different object) what he *is* like, because we can only tell him *how we see him* which probably coincides with what he is, but which we cannot explain in such a way as to say *this is how he is*. Thus, everything is something quite different from what it is for us, says Oehler. And always something quite different from what it is for everything else. Quite apart from the fact that even the designations with which we designate things are quite different from the actual ones. To that extent all designations are wrong, says Oehler. But when we entertain such thoughts, he says, we soon see that we are lost in these thoughts. We are lost in every thought if we surrender ourselves to that thought, even if we surrender ourselves to one single thought, we are lost. If I am walking, says Oehler, I am thinking and I maintain that I am walking and suddenly I think and maintain that I am walking and thinking, because that is what I am thinking while I am walking. And when we are walking together and *think* this thought, we think that we are walking together and suddenly we think, even if we don't think it together, we *are thinking*, but it is something different. If I think that I am walking, it is something different from your thinking I am walking, just as it is somewhat different if we both think at the same time (or simultaneously) that we are walking, if that is possible. Let's walk over the Friedensbrücke, I said earlier, says Oehler, and we have walked over the Friedensbrücke because I thought that I was thinking, I say, I am walking over the Friedensbrücke, I am walking with you so we are walking together over the Friedensbrücke. But it would be quite different were you to have had this thought, let's go over the Friedensbrücke, if you were to have thought, let's go over the Friedensbrücke, and so on. When we are walking, intellectual movement comes with body movement. We always discover that when we are walking, and so causing our body to start to move, then our thinking—that *was* not thinking in our head—also starts to move. We walk with our legs, we say and think with our head. We could, however, also say we walk with our mind. Fancy walking in such an incredibly unstable state of mind, we think when we see someone walking whom we assume to be in that state of mind, as we think and say. This person is walking completely mindlessly, we say, just as we say, this mindless person is walking incredibly quickly or incredibly slowly or incredibly purposefully. Let's go, we say, into Franz Josef station when we know that we *shall* say, let's go into Franz Josef station. Or we think that we are saying let's go over the Friedensbrücke and we go over the Friedensbrücke because we have anticipated what we are doing, that is going over the Friedensbrücke. We think what we have anticipated and do what we have anticipated, says Oehler. After four or five minutes we intended to visit the park in Klosterneuburgerstrasse, the fact that we went into the park in Klosterneuburgerstrasse, says Oehler, presupposes that we *knew* for four or five minutes that we *would* go into the park in Klosterneuburgerstrasse. Just as when I say *let's go into Obenaus* it means that I have *thought, let's go into Obenaus* irrespective of whether I go into Obenaus or not. But we are lost in thoughts like this, says Oehler, and it is pointless to occupy yourself with thoughts like this for any length of time. Thus we are always on the point of throwing away thoughts, throwing away the thoughts that we have and the thoughts that we always have, because we are in the habit of always having thoughts, throughout our lives, as far as we know, we throw thoughts away, we do nothing else because we are nothing but people who are always tipping out their minds like garbage cans and emptying them wherever they may be. If we have a head full of thoughts we tip our head out like a garbage can, says Oehler, but not everything onto one heap, says Oehler, but always in the place where we happen to be at a given moment. It is for this reason that the world is always full of a stench, because everybody is always emptying out their heads like a garbage can. Unless we find a different method, says Oehler, the world will, without doubt, one day be suffocated by the stench that this thought refuse generates. But it is improbable that there is any other method. All people fill their heads without thinking and without concern for others and they empty them where they like, says Oehler. It is this idea that I find the cruelest of all ideas. The person who thinks also thinks of his thinking as a form of walking, says Oehler. He says my or his or this train of thought. Thus it is absolutely right to say let's enter this thought, just as if we were to say, let's enter this haunted house. Because we say it, says Oehler, because we have this idea, because we, as Karrer would have said, have this so-called idea of such a so-called train of thought. Let's go further (in thought), we say, when we want to develop a thought further, when we want to progress in a thought. This thought goes too far and so on, is what is said. If we think that we have to go more quickly (or more slowly) we think that we have to think more quickly, although we know that thinking is not a question of speed, true it does deal with something, as when it is a question of walking, that is moving but thinking has nothing to do with speed, says Oehler. The difference between walking and thinking is that thinking has nothing to do with speed, but walking is actually always involved with speed. Thus, to say let's go to Obenaus quickly or let's go over the Friedensbrücke quickly is absolutely correct, but to say let's think faster, let's think quickly, is wrong, it is nonsense and so on, says Oehler. When we are walking we are dealing with so-called practical concepts (in Karrer's words), when we are thinking we are dealing simply with concepts. But we can, of course, says Oehler, make thinking into walking and, vice versa, walking into thinking without departing from the fact that thinking has nothing to do with speed, walking everything. We can also say, over and over again, says Oehler, we have now walked to the end of such and such a road, it doesn't matter what road, whereas we can never say now we have thought this thought to an end, there's no such thing and it is connected with the fact that walking but not thinking is connected with speed. Thinking is by no means speed, walking, quite simply, is speed. But underneath all this, as underneath everything, says Oehler, there is the world (and thus also the thinking) of practical or secondary concepts. We advance through the world of practical concepts or secondary concepts, but not through the world of concepts. In fact, we now intend to visit the park in Klosterneuburgerstrasse; after four or five minutes in the park in Klosterneuburgerstrasse, Oehler suddenly says, we still have some bird food we brought for the birds under the Friedensbrücke in our coat pockets. Do you have the bird food we brought for the birds under the Friedensbrücke in your coat pocket? To which I answer, yes. To our astonishment both of us, Oehler and I, still have, at this moment in the park in Klosterneuburgerstrasse, the bird food in our coat pockets that we brought for the birds under the Friedensbrücke. It is absolutely unusual, says Oehler, for us to forget to feed our bird food to the birds under the Friedensbrücke. Let's feed the birds our bird food now, says Oehler and we feed the birds our bird food. We throw our bird food to the birds very quickly and the bird food is eaten up in a short time. These birds have a totally different, much more rapid, way of eating our bird food, says Oehler, different from the birds under the Friedensbrücke. Almost at the same moment, I also say: a totally different way. It was absolutely certain, I think, that I was ready to say the words—a totally different way—before Oehler made his statement. We say something, says Oehler, and the other person maintains that he has just thought the same thing and was about to say what we had said. This peculiarity should be an occasion for us to busy ourselves with the peculiarity. But not today. I have never gone from the Friedensbrücke into Klosterneuburgerstrasse so quickly, says Oehler. We, Karrer and I, also intended, says Oehler, to go straight from the Friedensbrücke back into Klosterneuburgerstrasse, but no we went into Rustenschacher's store today, I really don't know why we went into Rustenschacher's store today but it's pointless to think about it. I can still hear myself saying, says Oehler, *let's go back into Klosterneuburgerstrasse.* That is back to where we are now standing, because I always went walking with Karrer here, but certainly not to feed the birds, as I do with you. I can still hear myself saying, *let's go back into Klosterneuburgerstrasse, we'll calm down in Klosterneuburgerstrasse.* I was already under the impression that what Karrer needed above all else was to calm down, his whole organism was at this moment nothing but sheer unrest: I really did call out to him several times, *let's go into Klosterneuburgerstrasse,* that was what I said, but Karrer wasn't listening, I asked him to go to Klosterneuburgerstrasse, but Karrer wasn't listening, he suddenly stopped in front of Rustenschacher's store, a place I hate, says Oehler—the fact is that I hate Rustenschacher's store—and said, let's go into Rustenschacher's store and we went into Rustenschacher's store, although it was not, in the least, our intention to go into Rustenschacher's store, because when we were still in Franz Josef station we had said to one another, *today we will neither go to Obenaus nor into Rustenschacher's store.* I can still hear us both stating categorically *neither to Obenaus* (to drink our beer) *nor into Rustenschacher's store,* but, suddenly, we had gone into Rustenschacher's store, says Oehler, and what followed you know. What senselessness to reverse a decision, once taken, on the grounds of reason, as we had to say (afterwards) and replace it with what is often a terrible misfortune, says Oehler. I had never known such a hectic pace as when I was walking with Karrer down from the Friedensbrücke in the direction of Klosterneuburgerstrasse and into Rustenschacher's shop, says Oehler. We had never even crossed the square in front of Franz Josef station so quickly. In spite of the people streaming toward us from Franz Josef station, in spite of these people suddenly streaming toward us, in spite of these hundreds of people suddenly streaming toward us, Karrer went toward Franz Josef station, and I thought that we would, as was his custom, sit down on one of the old benches intended for travelers, right in the midst of all the revolting dirt of Franz Josef station, as was his custom, says Oehler, to sit down on one of these benches and watch the people as they jump off the trains and as, in a short while, they start streaming all over the station, but no, shortly before we were going, as I thought, to enter the station and sit down on one of these benches, Karrer turns round and runs to the Friedensbrücke, runs, says Oehler several times, runs, past the clothing store "Zum Eisenbahner," toward the Friedensbrücke and from there into Rustenschacher's store at an unimaginable speed, says Oehler. Karrer actually ran away from Oehler. Oehler was only able to follow Karrer at a distance of more than ten, for a long while of fifteen or even twenty meters; while he was running along behind Karrer, Oehler kept thinking, if only Karrer doesn't go into Rustenschacher's store, *if only he won't be rash enough* to go into Rustenschacher's store, but precisely what Oehler feared, as he was running along behind Karrer, happened. Karrer said, *let's go into Rustenschacher's store,* and Karrer, without waiting for a word from Oehler—who was, by now, exhausted—went straight into Rustenschacher's store, Karrer tore open the door of Rustenschacher's store with an incredible vehemence, but was then able to pull himself together, says Oehler, only, of course, to lose control again immediately. Karrer ran to the counter, says Oehler, and the salesman, without arguing, began at once to show Karrer—to whom he had shown all the trousers the week before—all the trousers, to hold up all the trousers to the light. Look, said Karrer, says Oehler, his tone of voice suddenly so quiet, probably because we are now standing still, I have known this street from my childhood and I have been through everything that this street has been through, there is nothing in this street with which I would not be familiar, he, Karrer knew every regularity and every irregularity in this street, and even if it is one of the most ugly, he loved that street like no other. How often have I said to myself, said Karrer, you see these people day in day out and it is always the same people whom you see and whom you know, always the same faces and always the same head and body movements as they walk, head and body movements that are characteristic of Klosterneuburgerstrasse. You know these hundreds and thousands of people, Karrer said to Oehler, and you know them, even if you do not know them, because basically they are always the same people, all these people are the same and they only differ in the eyes of the superficial observer (as judge). The way they walk and the way they do not walk and the way they shop and do not shop and the way they act in summer and the way they act in winter and the way they are born and the way they die, Karrer said to Oehler. You know all the terrible conditions. You know all the attempts (to live), those who do not emerge from these attempts, this whole attempt at life, this whole state of attempting, seen as a life, Karrer said to Oehler, says Oehler. You went to school here and you survived your father and your mother here, and others will survive you as you survived your father and mother, said Karrer to Oehler. It was in Klosterneuburgerstrasse that all the thoughts that ever occurred to you occurred to you (and if you know the truth, all your ideas, all your rebukes about your environment, your inner world they all occurred to you here). How many monstrosities is Klosterneuburgerstrasse filled with for you?

You only need to go into Klosterneuburgerstrasse, and all life's misery and all life's despair come at you. I think of these walls, these rooms with which, and in which, you grew up, the many illnesses characteristic of Klosterneuburgerstrasse, said Karrer, in Oehler's words, the dogs and the old people tied to the dogs. The way Karrer made these statements was, in Oehler's words, not surprising in the wake of Hollensteiner's suicide. Something hopeless, depressing, had taken hold of Karrer after Hollensteiner's death, something I had never observed in him before. Suddenly, everything took on the somber color of the person who sees nothing but *dying* and for whom nothing else seems to happen any more but only *the dying* which surrounds him. But Scherrer, according to Oehler, was not interested in all the changes in Karrer's personality that were connected with Hollensteiner's suicide. Do you remember how they dragged you into the entrances of these houses and how they boxed your ears in those entrances, Karrer suddenly says to me in a tone that absolutely shattered me. As if Hollensteiner's death had darkened the whole human or rather inhuman scene for him. How they beat up your mother and how they beat up your father, says Karrer, says Oehler. These hundreds and thousands of windows shut tight both summer and winter, says Karrer, according to Oehler, and he says it as hopelessly as possible. I shall never forget the days before the visit to Rustenschacher's store, says Oehler, how Karrer's condition got worse daily, how everything that you had thought was already totally gloomy became gloomier and gloomier. The shouting and the collapsing and the silence in Klosterneuburgerstrasse that followed this shouting and collapsing, said Karrer, says Oehler. And this terrible filth! he says, as though there had never been anything in the world for him but filth. It was precisely the fact that everything in Klosterneuburgerstrasse, that everything remained as it always had been and that you had to fear, if you thought about it, that it would always remain the same that had gradually made Klosterneuburgerstrasse into an enormous and insoluble problem for him. *Waking up and going to sleep in Klosterneuburgerstrasse,* Karrer kept repeating. *This incessant walking back and forth in Klosterneuburgerstrasse. My own helplessness and immobility in Klosterneuburgerstrasse.* In the last two days these statements and scraps of statements had continually repeated themselves, says Oehler. *We have absolutely no ability to leave Klosterneuburgerstrasse. We have no power to make decisions any more. What we are doing is nothing. What we breathe is nothing. When we walk, we walk from one hopelessness to another. We walk and we always walk into a still more hopeless hopelessness. Going away, nothing but going away,* says Karrer, according to Oehler, over and over again. *Nothing but going away. All those years I thought I would alter something, and that means everything, and go away from Klosterneuburgerstrasse, but nothing changed* (because he changed nothing), says Oehler, and he did not go away. *If you do not go away early enough,* said Karrer, *it is suddenly too late and you can no longer go away. It is suddenly clear you can do what you like, but you can no longer go away. No longer being able to alter this problem of not being able to go away any more occupies your whole life,* Karrer is supposed to have said, and from then on that is all that occupies your life. You then grow more and more helpless and weaker and weaker and all you keep saying to yourself is that you should have gone away early enough, and you ask yourself why you did not go away early enough. But when we ask ourselves why we did not go away and why we did not go away early enough, which means did not go away at the moment when it was *high time* to do so, we understand nothing more, said Karrer to Oehler. Oehler says: because we did not think intensively enough about changing things, when we should have really thought intensively about making changes and in fact did think intensively about making changes, but not intensively enough, because we did not think intensively in the most inhuman way about making changes in something and that means, above all, ourselves, making changes in ourselves to change ourselves and by this means to change everything, said Karrer. The circumstances were always such as to make it impossible for us. Circumstances are everything, we are nothing, said Karrer. What sort of states and what sort of circumstances have I been in, in which I simply have not been able to change myself in all these years because it all boiled down to a question of states and circumstances that could not be changed, said Karrer. Thirty years ago, when you, Oehler, went off to America, where, as I know, most circumstances were really dreadful, Karrer is supposed to have said, I should have left Klosterneuburgerstrasse, but I did not leave it; now I feel this whole humiliation as a truly horrible punishment. Our whole life is composed of nothing but terrible and, at the same time, terrifying circumstances (as states) and if you take life apart, it simply disintegrates into frightful circumstances and states, Karrer said to Oehler. And when you are in a street like this for so long a time, so long that you have left the discovery that you have grown old behind you long ago, you can, of course, no longer go away, in thought yes, but in reality no, but to go away in thought and not in reality means a double torment, said Karrer, after you are forty, your will-power itself is already so weakened that it is senseless even to attempt to go away. A street like Klosterneuburgerstrasse is, for a person of my age, a sealed tomb from which you hear nothing but dreadful things, said Karrer. Karrer is supposed to have said the words *the vicious process of dying* several times and several times, *early ruin*. How I hated these houses, Karrer is supposed to have said, and yet I kept on going into these houses with a life-long appetite that is nothing short of depressing. All these hundreds and thousands of mentally sick people, who have come out of these houses dead over the course of those years, said Karrer. For every dreadful person who has died from one of these houses, two or three new dreadful people are *created into* these houses, Karrer is supposed to have said to Oehler. I haven't been into Rustenschacher's store for weeks, Karrer said the day before he went into Rustenschacher's store, says Oehler. We live in a time when one should be at least twenty or thirty years younger if one is to survive, Karrer said to Oehler. There has never been an artificiality like it, an artificiality with such a naturalness, for which one should not be over forty. No matter where you look, you are looking into artificiality, said Karrer. Two or three years ago, this street was still not so artificial that it terrified me. But I cannot explain this artificiality, said Karrer. Just as I cannot explain anything any more, said Karrer. Dirt and age and absolute artificiality, said Karrer. You with your Ferdinand Ebner, Karrer kept on repeating, and I, at first, with my Wittgenstein, then you with your Wittgenstein and I with my Ferdinand Ebner. If, in addition, you are dependent upon a female person, my sister, said Karrer. But it is frightful after years of absence, suddenly to face all these people (in Obenaus), said Karrer. If things are peaceful around me, then I am restless, the more restless I grow, the more peaceful things are around me, and vice versa, said Karrer. If you are suddenly dragged back into your filth, said Karrer. Into the filth that has doubtless increased in the thirty years, said Karrer. After thirty years it is a much filthier filth than it was thirty years ago, says Karrer. When I am lying in bed, assuming that my sister keeps quiet, that she is not pacing up and down in her room that is opposite mine, said Karrer, that she is not—as she is in the habit of doing, just as I have gone to bed—opening up all the cupboards and all the chests and suddenly clearing out all these cupboards and chests, then I think back on what I was thinking the day before, said

Karrer. I close my eyes and lay the palms of my hands on the blanket and go back very intensely over the previous day. With a constantly increasing intensity, with an intensity that can constantly be increased. The intensity can always be increased, it may be that this exercise will one day cross the border into madness, but I cannot be bothered about that, said Karrer. The time when I did bother about it is past, I do not bother about it any more, said Karrer. The state of complete indifference, in which I then find myself, said Karrer, is, through and through, a philosophical state.

EYE TO EYE:
A Portfolio of Writer/Artist Collaborations

⁂

Ann Lauterbach

Meredith Stricker

William H. Gass *and* Mary Gass

C. D. Wright *and* Deborah Luster

Brian Evenson *and* Eve Aschheim

Cole Swensen

John Yau *and* Trevor Winkfield

Rikki Ducornet

Lynne Tillman *and* Haim Steinbach

Diana Michener

Robert Kelly *and* Brigitte Malknecht

Three for Joseph Cornell:
Joyce Carol Oates
Paul West
Bradford Morrow

Camille Guthrie *and* Louise Bourgeois

Robert Creeley *and* Archie Rand

Forrest Gander *and* Sally Mann

⁂

Edited by Bradford Morrow

Handheld
(At The Isabella Stewart Gardner Museum)
Ann Lauterbach

The dim brocade

the dry fountain

the decayed nose

the bright exit

the pensive woman

the table settings

the empty frames

the six chairs

the great bowl

the long neck

the Chinese poet

the hidden books

the animated feast

the cabinet of lace

the miniature scribe

the awful tear

Cannot find here, in the odd locale of the after-imaged

life I went to see, did not see,

in the event, thus tuned

into shapes, their continuities,

distributions, staged dimensions,

uncanny in material detail: was it thought's

tool, source, provenance

vagrant in memory, like a hum of loss

coming toward, and so close it was

not what I expected to find, not the clue.

Little trim agenda, who turns your page?

The crimson book
the rose hedge
the scarlet turban
the goldfinch

Might have been a circuitous loam fumbling under the dress

of the believer. Stone cold. Or yet

a Spanish temptress, wildly scented,

fearless of the aftermath. A collision.

Emphatic fog travels down into rubble,

small gushes, breath eroding what was desire,

courtyard silted with orchids, desire

                  at the hinge of her mouth, its

January curve

anointed by a hot brushstroke.

Here, among petitioners,

curators weep at the decaying silk,

children search for the color of their skin,

Ann Lauterbach

one guard roams from room to room
noticing graffiti scratched into the ancient choir stall,
a hole in the breast of the bronze
lanced in some war, some war, across from
the portrait of the collector in her pearl-wrapped dress—

        on her forehead slashed morning
          thru the blinds

    local migration

                please do not touch

      now across her left eye

a ribbon, slight

         place no object here

   all image

        sacred matter

            instructing our chaos

       washing the feet
       bringing the gifts

    regal lamentation
    staining the floor

     and the sad Madonna's ancient Child
     lifted across gold air   hand outstretched

             please do not touch

hinges of the rose damask screen

73

Ann Lauterbach

        and the young couple

        under the serpent's tongue

        about to speak

              their predicated decision

      peacock's fan between his legs

      wheel of fortune

      thief in the night

               her face now dark.

And on this wall, baffled under a broken key

unredeemed, quick burden of sight,

Piero's Hercules, his posture

as if recently

fledged from myth

      distilled lapse softly hung

with what caused the moon to turn and turn

into the enameled interior —

          as in a Venetian night

     among tapestries and glass

      and Rebecca among the slow branches

        eternal recitation

   stitch stitch stitch

       to still the story

       from chamber to chamber   to possess

this this this

      the credence, the ewer, the armchairs, the strongbox,
the lectern, the plate

              and Michael's warrior wing

      swivels night air —

*prince of the presence, angel of repentance, righteousness,
mercy, prince of Israel, guardian of Jacob, conqueror of Satan —*

        immense surfeit —

the Yellow Room behind the mirrored door

the violent anonymity of space

        the object usually in this place has been

                temporarily removed

the guitar silent below the depiction of mayhem

        holding a dove

        holding a scroll

        holding the head of John.

violet light around the moon

dolphins sighted earlier

a small boat floating

Lexicon

Images by the Author

Meredith Stricker

Aphrodite's

Large plane trees, leaves rattling in the wind. Also:
silver on the underside of olives, honeycombed bees.
Bells at dusk, mirrors. Violet light around the moon.
anything shaped Δ or v. And waves: saltwater's engine.

Bells

echo all morning. First doves, then cicadas, then doves again.
In the courtyard tangled with cobalt morning glories, a country
& western song on the radio keeps time with the sound of women
sweeping stone paths with water.

The sacred makes noise everywhere it can.

Cowry shells

Sewn with bells on the leather neckbands
of sheep. Evidence of ancient trade routes,
why she is sometimes called Black Athena.

Dolphins

Sighted earlier that day, beyond the harbor. A young Artemis girl—
fights in play with the men at the taverna. If she weren't smiling,
she would scare them to death.

Eftalou

Hot springs, shallow tidepools, translucent seaweed.
White domed building: openings scattered across the ceiling
like stars for light & swallows to enter & cross overhead.

The body feels like a small boat floating.

Meredith Stricker

turning into sun

garden

shard

Fig trees

The fruit stays green a long time
turning itself into sun

Garden

From Apostolo's house on the edge of town, you look straight
across dry fields & the Aegean to Asia Minor. He was eighteen
years at sea—the garden blooms from seeds collected from all over
the world. There are beehives, almond trees, dahlias, daylilies & the
round, small-leaved basilico. After coffee, Apostolo brings out the
shards he finds at work digging up the streets.

Here, in an empty peanut can: a buckle, two clay pipes. And the
head of Sappho, the size of his thumb.

Hammered

metal plaques: offerings hung by the altar in shaded light: a lady,
child, gentleman, a foot, leg, eyes—as though everything that can
be named carries its own prayer.

Intense

heat at midday stops work. We enter some other dream,
the other world of night by our side in wide open sunlight.

Karaghiosis

Early evening, in an open-air courtyard, the shadow puppet theater
begins. Human-sized stick figures are lit up from behind translucent
curtains. The puppets are in black outlining bright primary colors,
like stained-glass windows or butterfly wings. They move like
Punch & Judy, jumping & beating each other with sticks, speaking
in gravelly Greek voices, tracing ancient routes out of Indonesia
& India.

Persistence of guerrilla theater, occupation & resistance (on the
walls current graffiti denounces the US & NATO). There's an
enormous, opulent Turkish residence on one side & the small
Greek domos on the other. The wily, long-nosed Greek puppet,
like Coyote, outsmarts his opponent all evening.

saints & blue glass

branch of green almonds

her eyes half closed

Behind us, a grandmother lets her empty carriage roll down the walkway. A child wanders down & opens the stage door, revealing the puppeteers at work. The moon grows brighter overhead.

KALLONI

All along the fertile plain of Kalloni, oleanders, pine & olive groves flash across bus window shiny with beads, saints & blue glass against the evil eye. We are driving into the heart of flowering— a countryside of bees.

LITERATURE

Abalone shell—eroded as the cliffs: coral exterior, smooth pearlescent layers, thin as paper. Water's motion written deeply into its form: perfect, unreadable sentences.

LUNA

At moonrise Strato says a poem for the moon that the women taught him. He shows us how to herd sheep by throwing a rock in the air and yelling *o o o t — o o o t — b r r r*. The full moon is clear over the rocky hillsides. Strato holds out a branch of green almonds the size of eggs.

MIDDAY

We find her walking toward us—eyes half closed—in the middle of the narrow stone street.

MITHYMNA

Passing old women in black at dusk: *kalespera, kalespera*— the sound of the evening star *hesperus* in their voices.

Meredith Stricker

musica

even dreams are more solid

returning home

Musica

In fields by the cemetery, I've been recording the sound
of sheep & their bells as they run in many different timbres
& rhythms. When I hand the earphones over to the shepherd,
his face transforms listening to his own flock as though they called
to him from another world. *Musica,* we say, *oraira:* beautiful.
Sitting close enough to the sheep until they forget me,
their music becomes thistles and wind at dusk.

Nai:

the sound *yes* makes in the sweep of the broom, Evterape's low &
throaty humming as she clears her courtyard, the sound of thistles,
and doves, the turning over of a small car's engine, sails flapping
loose in the wind. Even refusal makes a place for us, a break in the
surface of ideas.

Night

The sky & ocean meet & exchange places in the dark—
are we walking in the starry firmament or shifting water?
Even dreams are more solid.

Odysseus

works with very small puppets for a theater group in Paris near les
Halles & returns home every summer. We stand in front of what
was the mayor's old villa, shaded in plane trees, entirely overrun
with roses: *"all the intelligentsia were there."*

Also: the postman, riding his moped through the narrow stone
walkways, exactly two donkeys-wide with baskets on either side.
Intelligence of vines & olive groves, conversations without the
pressure of arrival, letters carried & unsent. Returning home an
entire lifetime.

ψ

A lame fisherman cleans his catch. At night, lights hung from the
small boats echo the stars.

sanctuary in the palm

black netting in olive trees

cave of written knowledge

⊙

At the edge of town, the temple of Apollo—across from an old woman's house, near the bare shade of her apricot tree. Sanctuary in the eyes & in the palm of the hand.

∴

Old stone house, given over to bats & mice. Elegant row of cypress: the air heavy with bees & sleep. Abandoned well under fig trees near grapes & oleander. Dry grasses, green pomegranates. Roses too dry to flower. Black netting hung in olive tree branches, the silver on their leaves like thoughts.

On this island, Sappho named what we see: water, olive tree, doves—so that there is no separating the fruit and what shines from it.

The body is a woman, her spirit is a body, is a rose, is beloved, like the olive.

ΠΕΤΡΑ

Off the bus, near the Women's Agricultural Cooperative in Petra. Along paths up the mountainside to Petri: a lizard & green turtle, snake head. Poplars, figs, mostly olives—& the skin & quills of a porcupine. There are fresh springs in channels running along walkways in the village, across the courtyard into the church.

QUIET

Rough sand in the cove: thin-ribbed shells, deep blue mussels, a sienna-colored starfish pressed flat & secret: what we can find looking inside ourselves.

ROSES

struggle for water in front of the library's glaring white marble stairs. Next to windows overlooking the sea, two women crochet in the cool rooms, keepers of this cave of written knowledge.

a table under fig trees

speeding across time

turtles live near the springs

Shepherds

There's Costa, with a scarf on his head, his two dogs: Daisy and Micro. In an old photograph he's wearing wide-legged Turkish style pants, immense moustaches and carries a rifle. He pours endless, thick Turkish coffee and brags about his herd: fifty pulaika.

At an afternoon party to celebrate the cassette player he has just traded for a sheep skin, Costa sets a table under fig trees and serves cakes, plates of melon, metaxa & more Turkish coffee. The recorder plays his music energetically from its place of honor in the center of the table. Two respectable ladies have been invited, one speaks French, the other English, also a college-age nephew, Odysseus, a little girl. And there's a shy older shepherd too, who stays on the edge of our group. All at once, he climbs like a swift wild animal up the tree to see if the figs are ripe yet (knowing they aren't).

Squid

dries like laundry—twisted nylon hosiery—on the trellis of the Paradise Taverna at Naxos.

Taverna

Tzaziki, potatoes, delicate cod in butter, koreotiki, souvlakia, ouzo, white lesbos wine, melons.

Traffic

Temples rise above Athens' traffic as if they too were speeding across time—in absolute stillness.

White marble, congestion, smog, cool green trellised walkways & shuttered rooms.

Karpousi: small, very sweet watermelons.

Thistles growing at the edge of the runway.

Undergrowth

Turtles live near the springs among oleanders. Nearby, up the hillside:

Meredith Stricker

all kinds of shrines

widow

their white wings

a chapel the size of a shed. Tall thistles on the path, swallow's nest at the door and a wasp's hive: all variations of shrines.

VILLA

decaying elegantly like thick opera records with worn grooves. Rusty iron gates, the sound of singing in French from the shuttered window. A fig-shaped woman carrying laundry blocks the entryway.

Entrance across the threshold is a kind of entrancement, even into an ordinary room.

WIDOW

After two Greek husbands, now she wants an English one.

WINNOWING RING

The first theater: a circle of stones. My grandfather, strapped to the threshing mill like a horse or mule, covered white with raw, crushed flour.

WHITE LINE

Morning smells of wet barley, trampled mud & sedge. Herons continue to design the marshes—standing or flying, moving or still.

How are words separate from their white wings? How is their motion like an idea inside us?

WORDS

The old woman at the sweater store reads English books cut into thirds so they are easier to carry on the bus. Reading, she says, is better than speaking—the way people talk is too irregular, too hard to understand. In books, the words are perfect.

the letter which is a motion

X

The taxi driver crosses himself before setting out into city traffic at dawn.

The letter which is a motion we make for what we can't say.

Mystery within mysteries:

groves of olives & palms, traffic jams, a drop of water in a leaf's ridge, choros, harmonics, light spilling out of nowhere.

light spilling out of the heart of γ and ζ.

The Architecture of the Sentence
Essay and Drawings
William H. *Gass* and *Mary Gass*

> *"What is the goal of the world?" said Silaka Salavatya.*
> *"Space," said Pravahana; "for all these contingent beings originate from space, and to space do they return. For space is greater (and more ancient) than they: space is the final goal."*
>
> —Chandogya Upanishad

ONE: INTRODUCTION

LET ME BEGIN by trying to state the point of this project as succinctly as possible.

Two sorts of spaces concern us here. First, there are the spaces we live and work and build in, the space which the physicist studies and the space we fly through to reach Salt Lake City or Chicago from St. Louis. But there are also all the spaces of representation, those places in the head or on paper where we imagine relations and try to express them: the cartographer's projections, the painter's perspectives, society's hierarchies, the musician's scale and score, the architect's plans, the electrician's diagrams, management's flow charts, tables of tides and organization, every display of information, statistical or otherwise and, in particular, writing itself. Here, in such spaces, we think, we plan and we design.

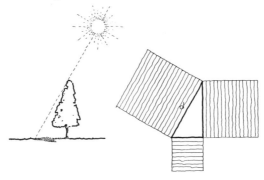

What is the relation between these two sorts of space? the real and the represented? between an engraver's perspective and an actual street? between the Social Register and a cardboard house beneath a bridge? between a note and a noise? Our investigation, merely begun here, and in the most provisional way, wonders whether it is possible to think or plan or design at all without a representational space in which to do it, and without an adequate notation through which such plans or ideas can be expressed; and whether there may not be a commonality between these arenas, a basic similarity between the relations involved, which might make possible the discovery of what it means to say of something that it is "architectural." For architecture, as we conceive it, may be the general method of constituting relations in representational spaces in order that they may be materially constructed in phenomenological spaces—in spaces as lived in.

If the consequence of human culture is basically that it surrounds man with man; that it replaces nature with convention; that it tries to tame the wilderness, intervening in everything; then architecture is the art which underlies all such construction, and its ultimate aim is to surround man, not merely with more man, but with the best— the most human—in what is human of us. If our bodies contain our consciousness, it is the business of our buildings, our cities, our culture to contain us.

A book is a building for what a brain has spun. Literature, the other pole of this enterprise—like music, like logic and mathematics—is designed to fill that consciousness from within, to contrive, inside the mind, arrangements of sound, and structures of sense, which will find their best accommodation in the public places, in the edifices, which will—in their principled depths—resemble them.

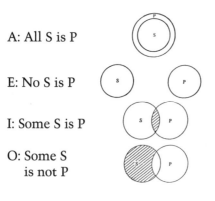

A: All S is P

E: No S is P

I: Some S is P

O: Some S
is not P

**Euler Diagrams
for Categorical
Propositions**

'S' stands for the subject term.
'P' stands for the predicate term.

TWO

1. a. Our first stop is at Aristotle and the concept of "same form." Aristotle discovered that all propositions in Greek could be reduced to four kinds: All S is P, Some S is P, No S is P and Some S is not P. All methods of representation are based on a belief that formal relations can be reproduced in different media without significant falsification; that not only are apparently different sentences nevertheless of the same form, for instance: "The cat ate the rat," and "The Professor seduced his student"; but that the music "in" the score, the music as markings on a CD, the music as vibrations in the air, music as heard sound, etc., all have the "same form." Thus a Palladian symmetry—two squares on either side of a circle—exhibits the same form as the sonata, namely, A B A, or Home-Departure-Return, which is the same as the course of the *Iliad* and the *Odyssey*.

b. Aristotle also discovered that the validity of an argument depended solely on its form, but this could not be clearly understood until the concepts which stood for S and P in any proposition were first: spatialized, and regarded as representing classes, and second: the copula (is) was given what is called an extensional interpretation. "Is" (under extensional interpretation) means either identity, class-inclusion or class-membership.

c. Later Venn diagrams allowed us to "see" what made a valid argument valid.

d. The invention of a proper musical notation also enabled music to become what it is. A new musical space came into being, made of the higher and lower notes on the scale, of musical dynamics (fast, slow, loud, soft), of instrumental placement, the color and texture and length of tones, etc. And words and music sought common meanings in imitative form. The world of musical space lies behind the closed eyes, in the dark hollow of the head.

When, in our time, the scale became chromatic; when propellers and air cylinders and sirens were added to the orchestra; when electronics enlarged the realm of possible sounds; then composers had to modify the old notation or invent a new one for their new needs.

e. Early on, the Greeks, who had a predominately oral culture, and could not handily consult books, formulated elaborate methods for remembering. These methods continued well through the Renaissance and they were almost invariably architectural. One of the most famous is the memory theater of Giulio Camillo. Early in life one began picturing to oneself an imagined building, furnishing it over time with icons which stood for subjects and moods. In Camillo's theater the basic images are taken from the planetary gods, expressing, for example, the tranquility of Jupiter, the anger of Mars, the melancholy of Saturn, the ardor of Venus and so on. Beneath these images were drawers in which manuscripts of Cicero's speeches, appropriate to the topic symbolized, were kept. Such theaters were actually built. They anticipate the computer's hyperspace.

f. Grammarians began to try to symbolize the form of the sentence with various kinds of diagrams, all of them spatial, mostly treehouse-forms which show up very early and have genealogical uses, and naturally adapt themselves to the depiction of syntactical structures, though some look more like river deltas, or even mobiles, before returning to a soberer sort of tinkertoy geometry. These scholars recognized that the right motivation was not merely the clearest or least complicated one, but actually created the ground for understanding.

g. Chomsky added deep structure to the grammarian's surface structure. The term "deep" is itself spatial. The term "deep" is also talismanic. Anything deep is veiled. Anything deep is deeply important. I have reservations about deep structure and its workability. It remains, nevertheless, basically a spatial notation project.

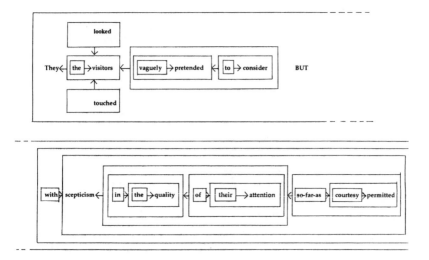

h. The most useful of these schemes is what I call the box diagram, whose function is to show how each meaning is subsumed by another until all the words of the sentence are in a single space. When we box diagram the syntax of a sentence we are drawing the sentence's floor plan. For example: "They looked, the visitors, they touched, they vaguely pretended to consider, but with skepticism in the quality of their attention so far as courtesy permitted." We shall encounter this sentence by Henry James again.

i. But sentences are well-formed in more than logical and syntactical ways. They are also formed with esthetic and rhetorical intentions. Rhetoric is, in a sense, the study of the forms of the paragraph, and how phrases and clauses are arranged, not only in sentences, but in the linkage of sentence to sentence. Prosody attempts to do something with the rhythm of language. And many theorists have tried to deal with vowel music and other elements, including the actual "look" of letters.

j. When one writes, one is constructing not only a set of sentences, but a complex set of spaces (logical, grammatical, rhetorical, referential, musical, social and so on) in which and through which the feelings, ideas and energies of the sentences can express themselves. This is the architecture of the sentence. And sometimes architecture itself resembles a sentence. Perhaps these spaces can help us define "the architectural."

THREE

1. There is a distinction to be drawn between sentences spatially formed from the outside, and those formed from the inside, as well as spaces determined at least in part by the various meanings of the sentence, rather than by the structure of the sentence alone.

a. The first sort is nicely illustrated by what is called "concrete poetry." External shaping occurs when the context of the poem or paragraph suggests an object in the world whose shape is then used to format the poem or paragraph on the page. Apollonaire's Calligrams usually assume the shape of their subject. George Herbert's well-known poem not only imitates the Easter wings it speaks of, but those wings symbolize the poem's spiritual aspirations. More significantly, Herbert planned an entire volume of verse so that each poem would combine to form a Temple. The most extreme case is that of Morganstern's Fish, which is formed entirely from the symbols for strongly and weakly stressed syllables—symbols that form very natural scales.

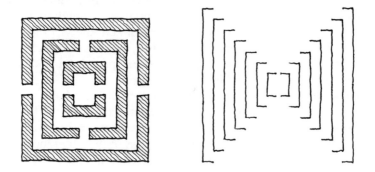

b. Above are two schematic pictures of the Frame Tale, one like a maze, the other like an accordion or nest of boxes. The general form resembles that of indirect address, of "Helen said that you told her that in the middle of the movie Melanie suddenly shouted: 'I've got to have a perm!'" Boccacio's *Decameron, A Thousand and One Nights,* Chaucer's *Canterbury Tales* and Flann O'Brien's *At Swim-Two-Birds* are similarly framed. This particular diagram pictures John Barth's "Menelaid." Helen of Troy, having been rescued from the Trojans by her husband, is busy giving him excuses for her long stay in Paris's company, and is endeavoring to postpone what is likely to happen to her: to be ravished by her long-denied husband or murdered by him out of jealousy. So each excuse is interrupted by another like a stutter, and continued to the number seven. The conclusion of story seven permits six to conclude and so on. This means that at certain points in the work some of the words will be occurring in more than one section at a time. We can literally look through one narrative to see parts of others passing in a previous time.

John Barth has been very inventive in other ways. A story called the "Perseid" is a retelling of the myth of Perseus as if the hero's exploits were carved on a triumphal column like Hadrian's pillar, so that some parts of the piece have to be read as if they were above and to the left of the others. The story inscribes a logarithmic spiral. Italo Calvino's *Invisible Cities* similarly unwinds, turning through Dante's descending circles.

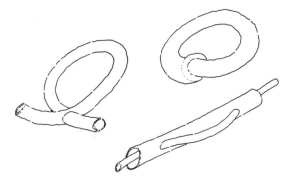

c. We are dealing with the phenomenon which logicians (traditionally lovers of erotic terminology) call embedding and which is frequently represented by Klein worms. When a sentence finds itself inside another sentence, as Melanie's shout, "I've got to have a perm" does, it is said to be embedded. Klein worms are geometric shapes which in various ways include or swallow or emerge from themselves. The sentence "David could have kissed Goliath" is engulfed by "Saul told Bathsheba that David could have kissed Goliath, but she wouldn't believe him."

d. Sentences also create space by layering their meaning, and suggesting both surface and depth. Gregor Samsa wakes to find himself a bug in a bed: that is, a bedbug, and, since the root of "Samsa" is "sam" or "seed," he is also a soiled source of DNA. The metrics of "Sam sa" resemble those of "Kaf ka," telling us who else is in this buggy bed.

e. Every sentence contains spaces where logically more words could be placed. Each word is therefore like a picket in a fence. As these spaces are filled, the fence becomes solid. The minimalist style tends to leave these spaces open. The baroque style tends to fill them.

Henry said goodbye to Larry.

Good old Henry said a short goodbye to Larry, his friend of twenty years.

The guy people called "good old Henry" said a short but fond goodbye to a sour and sullen, pale-faced Larry, his off and on friend of these tumultuous last twenty or so years. Etc.

Or: Goodbye, Larry, Henry said.

Goodbye.

Bye.

By.

FOUR

1. Sentences and paragraphs first of all function as bearers of meaning, and the basic unit of their organization is the syntax of the sentence.

2. Sentences and paragraphs secondly function musically, in terms of rhythm and meter, and in terms of the intonation, dynamics and quality of sound.

3. Sentences and paragraphs operate, thirdly, at the rhetorical level, in terms of patterns, repetitions, balances, inversions and so on.

4. Sentences and paragraphs function, in addition, kinetically, in terms of how the mouth makes them: gutterally, dentally, trippingly, etc. "The Pit and the Pendulum" is well-named. Often overlooked, every mode of their manufacture is important.

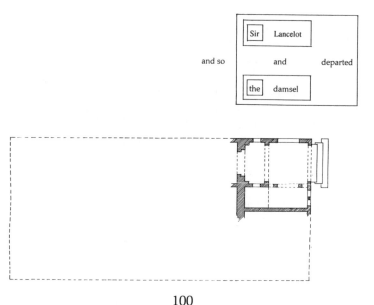

5. Central to understanding the syntactical structure of the sentence is the box diagram, whose purpose is to depict the order and nature of meaning modification in the sentence by means of adjoining and inclusive spaces.

Sir Thomas Malory

And so Sir Lancelot and the damsel departed.

a. The conjunction signifies that the sentence to follow will be connected to another structure; the "so" suggests that the sentence is a consequence of that other structure. Although the syntax places Lancelot and the damsel in equal positions, as agents of the action, it is clear that Lancelot creates a much more superior space than that designated by "damsel" who is not even given a name. Moreover, damsels are young. The socially superior space in which "Sir" puts Lancelot, his prior place in the word order, his having a name, all indicate a dominant function. "Lancelot" as a name, closes up with a stress at both ends. Compare "Arthur and the damsel departed." Even the sound of damsel echoes the so-sir-cel which precedes it, and the "am" we find there resembles the "an" of "Lancelot."

b. The rhythm of the sentence suggests a rearward movement right after Lancelot closes strongly with its "ot," since "and the damsel departed" has only two strong stresses. The verb "depart" is like a sidewalk away from the sentence's two subordinate rooms.

SECOND MODEL SENTENCE: THE WALL
Sir Thomas Browne

Grave-stones tell truth scarce forty years. Generations pass
while some trees stand, and old families last not three oaks.

Taking a clue from the content of the two sentences, and following the evidence of the strong beat in the paired and stressed syllables, it is easy to see, I think, that part of the success of these sentences depends upon the wall which they erect, almost as if they were gravestones themselves. The first sentence sets the pattern for the second whose two clauses follow its sound, its beat, and its meaning. Here we have more than parallel courses. We have pile-upon structures.

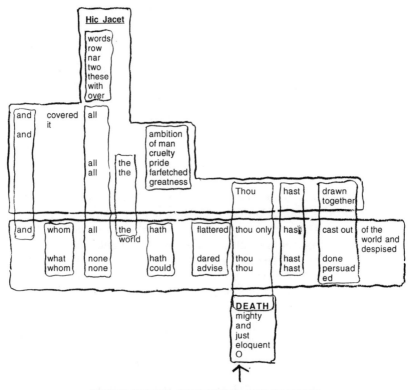

THIRD MODEL SENTENCE: THE FAÇADE
Sir Walter Raleigh

O eloquent, just, and mighty death! Whom none could advise, thou hast persuaded; what none hath dared, thou hast done; and whom all the world has flattered, thou only hast cast out of the world and despised. Thou hast drawn togeth-er all the far-stretched greatness, all the pride, cruelty, and ambition of man, and covered it all over with these two nar-row words, *hic jacet.*

We actually enter the "O" (as one is expected to do at the beginning of this kind of apostrophe, and we pass through several other Os, either actual or implied, on our way to the dreaded subject: death. O elOquent, we begin, but must remember that syntactically the sentence runs: O eloquent, O just and O mighty Death! We have climbed to the threshold of this mausoleum. Parallel and antithetical clauses are ranged on either side of Death, whose name is repeatedly invoked through "thou" and "whom." As we did to form our wall, we place the parallels one above the other being careful to match word order, sense, beat and sound in each clause.

The antitheses completed, the passage goes straight up the catalogue of "greatness," "pride," "cruelty" and "ambition" to its bleak covering conclusion, ringing "all" and "none" like bells: this passes, all goes.

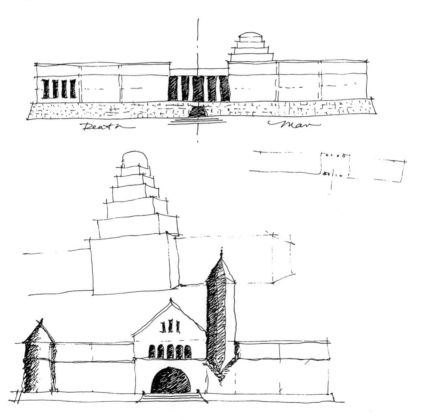

It is more than metaphorical, to arrange Raleigh's prose this way. At the same level at which we can say that score and recorded groove have the "same form" this diagram has much the same form as its verbal generator. And implies an appropriate façade.

103

William H. Gass / Mary Gass

SPACE OF THE OBSERVER: the Shopman, Prince, Charlotte.

SPACE OF THE HAND: briefly, nervously, tenderly.

Ancientries	Ornaments	Pendants	Lockets	Brooches	Buckles	Brilliants	Rubies
Pearls	Minatures	Snuffboxes	Cups	Trays	Taperstands		

SPACE OF THE TABLE: the list.

SPACE OF SOCIAL MEANING.

FOURTH MODEL SENTENCE: MULTIPLE SPACES
Henry James

Early in the development of Henry James's late novel, *The Golden Bowl*, we accompany an impoverished and clownishly named Italian prince, Prince Amerigo, on a shopping expedition with the lovely Charlotte Stant, an Italian-born American who is infatuated with him. The meeting is clandestine, and its purpose is the purchase of a gift for Maggie Verver, the woman whom the Prince plans to marry. At last they arrive in the antique shop where they will be eventually shown a goblet cut from a single crystal and covered skillfully in gold, a gilding which not only enhances the beauty of the bowl, but also hides a flaw in the quartz. However, first the dealer sets out a few smaller items in this singular sentence:

> Of decent old gold, old silver, old bronze, of old chased and jeweled artistry, were the objects that, successively produced, had ended by numerously dotting the counter, where the shopman's slim, light fingers, with neat nails, touched them at moments, briefly, nervously, tenderly, as those of a chess-player rest, a few seconds, over the board, on a figure he thinks he may move and then may not: small florid ancientries, ornaments, pendants, lockets, brooches, buckles, pretexts for dim brilliants, bloodless rubies, pearls either too large or too opaque for value; miniatures mounted with diamonds that had ceased to dazzle; snuffboxes presented to—or by—the too-questionable great; cups, trays, taper-stands, suggestive of pawn-tickets, archaic and brown, that would themselves, if preserved, have been prized curiosities.

104

As we enter the sentence, we observe first of all that the sounds of the words, normally rather arbitrary and accidental properties of what we want to convey, are the object of the greatest care, and that patterns are produced quite different from the ones which syntax requires, and these organize and direct its course. The letters "o" and "l" predominate, as they do in the phrase "the golden bowl." The word "old" is reiterated, as it ought to be in a shop full of antiques, and the metals are announced which have always named the legendary ages of man: "old gold, old silver, old bronze."

They take us down, these sounds, these patterns, these metals, the opening pun on the word "decent," they take us down steps into the shop itself, for observe how the reader's attention is constantly returned to "old," as if it were a riser. The shop, on the other hand, is created by the fiction itself, not the shape of the sentence; the sentence is interested in the shop's objects, and in the shopman himself.

The shopman is playing a game with the Prince and his companion, exactly as James is with us. He is making his moves, and each object he displays is defective in some slight way. He shows them "dim brilliants, bloodless rubies," "diamonds that had ceased to dazzle." The expression "small florid ancientries" is itself, and aptly, a bit ancient, just a little florid. The pauses, the hesitations in the passage, mimic the movement of the tradesman's hand, which touches the various brooches and pendants and pearls "briefly, nervously, tenderly." The action of the language and the action of the hand lie on parallel and resembling planes. The shopkeeper lovingly offers Charlotte and the Prince a counter full of things. James lovingly gives us a list of words: "cups, trays, taper-stands." As readers we are placed in the position of the Prince. He sees these bibelots. We read these words. The one *is* the other. The Prince's instructed eye, and James's immaculate judgment, wittily remark the vulgar limitations of the stock, as the rich list continues, wrapped in the elegant warmth of its own sound, the delightful shimmer of its irony:

> A few commemorative medals, of neat outline but dull reference; a classic monument or two, things of the first years of the century; things consular, Napoleonic, temples, obelisks, arches, tinily re-embodied, completed the discreet cluster; in which, however, even after tentative reinforcement from several quaint rings, intaglios, amethysts, carbuncles, each of which had found a home in the ancient sallow satin of some weakly-snapping little box, there was, in spite of the due proportion of faint poetry, no great force of persuasion. They looked, the visitors, they touched, they vaguely pretended to

> consider, but with scepticism, so far as courtesy permitted, in
> the quality of their attention.

In the ancient <u>s</u>allow <u>s</u>atin of <u>s</u>ome weakly-<u>s</u>napping little box
In the <u>an</u>cient s<u>al</u>low sa<u>ti</u>n of some weakly-sn<u>ap</u>ping little box
In the ancient sall<u>ow</u> satin of s<u>om</u>e weakly-snapping little b<u>ox</u>
In the ancient sa<u>ll</u>ow satin of some weak<u>ly</u>-snapping <u>l</u>ittle box
In the ancient sa<u>ll</u>ow satin of some weakly-sna<u>pp</u>ing li<u>tt</u>le box

Ĩn thẽ án̆ciẽnt sállŏw sátĩn õf sŏme weáklỹ-snáppiñg líttĩe bóx

James returns to his brilliantly reflective form as one still hungry
goes back to the buffet, but now the concern of the sentence is the
nature of the Prince's and Charlotte's attention:

> They looked, the visitors, they touched, they vaguely pre-
> tended to consider, but with scepticism, so far as courtesy
> permitted, in the quality of their attention.

A style could scarcely be more a mirror of its own effects. The nervous nicety of word, the salesman's hesitant manipulations, the shift
of both our attention as readers and that of the characters and finally
the quality of their sensitivity and ours, of course, as we follow and
affirm it, not to omit the author's deeper discriminations as he com-
poses the entire scene, are combined to provide us with an almost
daunting example of what a culture crystallized within a style can do.

How many spaces are there here? There is the stairspace through
which we moved to reach the shop. There is the space of the ob-
servers, the Prince and Charlotte, the salesman. There is the space
made by the shopkeeper's nervous, duplicitous hand. There is the
table which bears these trophies, marked like a chess board with its
positivist grid. There is the social space each object suggests and
belongs in, as well as the social level of the space we inhabit while
we think of what to buy.

Should the architect omit any of these spaces when the total space
he or she is insisting on rises into the world of sense from the pale
lines of the drafting page?

Finally, let me try just once to work the other way. Here is McKim,
Meade and White's plan for the Brooklyn Museum, which, as you
know, was only partly realized. What sort of sentence might have its
form? Since I have only partly coped with the spatial hierarchy here,
this too will be only partly realized—however:

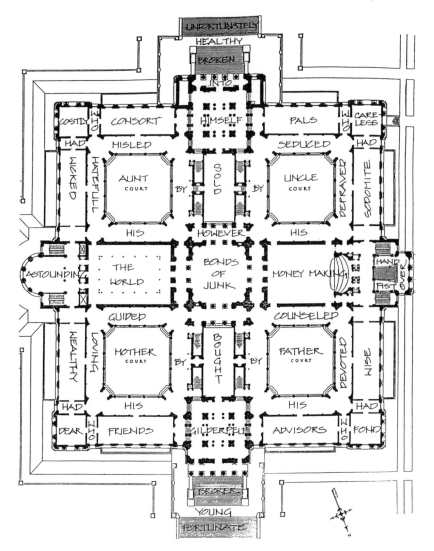

Fortunate young broker, Gilderpelf, guided by his loving mother, who had wealthy dear friends, and counseled by his devoted father, who had wise and fond advisors, bought bonds of junk, astounding the world, and making money hand over fist; however, misled by his hateful aunt, who had a wicked and costly consort, and by his depraved uncle, who had careless sodomite pals, sold himself into broken health, unfortunately.

107

Many sentences of this form might be imagined, but the important thing is: they would have this form.

At one end of the scale of the management of relations, there stands the mathematician, who has facilities ordinary people can scarcely imagine, but the mathematician cannot touch flesh or even rattle bones. On the other end is the architect, who works with relations realized in some material, in the connections of objects, in the concretions necessary to sense. He should remember, when he is placing stone by stone, that he is shaping a type of sentence; he should remember, when he is drawing this or that line, that he is also outlining a pattern of sounds; for the architect is the master of represented space of every kind, and that means he is the master of the making mind.

Retablos
Poems and Photographs
C. D. *Wright* and *Deborah Luster*

—Translations by Gabriel Bernal Granados

FLOATING LADY RETABLO

Remember I remember   I lay my young bullocks
On thine altar   bald and cold as the truth   I was your
Personal all purpose all weather fuck machine   before the finger
Of suspicion could fire one bad shot   the door
Closed on us   I am the emancipated white man   in the paddock
Common as dirt   I scare the horses   I can lie
At any speed   Recuerda me   as I did you from the short stob
Of memory in my path   Love Letter #3   recuerda me
Siempre   go try your luck on the mountain   if it pleases ye

RETABLO DE LA MUJER FLOTANTE

Recuerdo yo recuerdo   ofrezco a mis bueyes
En vuestro altar   desnudo y frío como la verdad   yo era tu
Máquina de coger siempre dispuesta   antes que el dedo
De la sospecha pudiera errar el disparo   se nos cerró
La puerta   soy el hombre blanco emancipado   en la dehesa
Común como la mugre ahuyento a los caballos   puedo mentir
A cualquier velocidad   Recuérdame   as I dig you from the
    short stob
De la memoria en mi camino   Carta de Amor #3   recuérdame
Siempre   ve a probar suerte en la montaña   si te place

HANDFISHING RETABLO

Leftover shoofly pie   charred baby bed
Stuffed bear   in the raked dirt
Smoke coming out of its butt   snake eyes
In the robin nest   piano repossessed   who decides
Who sits down   to pee   who stands in the mist   if
There is something   worth knowing   if
There is some one thing   important for us
To know   we come   to build worlds   arriba los corazones
Media Naranja   pray keep us in   contact with our ground

RETABLO DE LA PESCA MANUAL

Sobras de un merengue   cuna carbonizada
Osito de peluche   en la mugre apelmazada
Humo que sale de sus nalgas   ojos de serpiente
En el nido del petirrojo   piano embargado   quien decide
Quien se sienta   a orinar   quien se para en la bruma   si
Hay algo   digno de saberse   si
Hay alguna cosa   que valga la pena
Saber   llegamos   a construir mundos   arriba corazones
Media Naranja   favor de dejarnos   en contacto con tu suelo

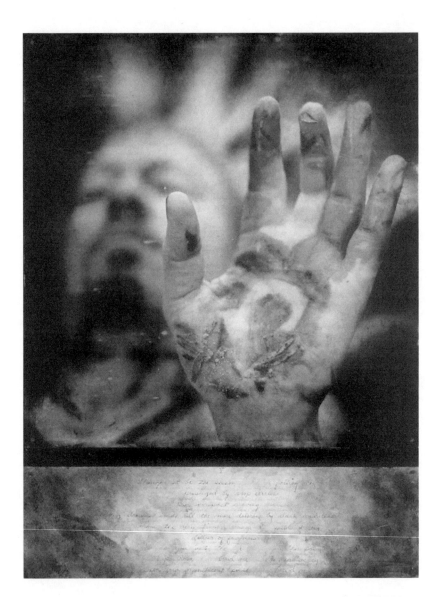

ROSESUCKER RETABLO

Though it be the season   of falling men
Presaged by crop circles
And compact moving masses
Long dresses made all the more dolorous by dark umbrellas
From these very fingers emerge   pistols of love
Lilies of forgiveness
And as you enter the eye   in this palm
Chupa Rose   bind me   to your secrecy
Open your munificent purse   hoard me

RETABLO DEL CHUPA ROSA

Aunque sea la estación   de los hombres caídos
Presagiada por los círculos del grano
Y las masas compactas en movimiento
Los vestidos largos aún más dolorosos por los paraguas negros
De estos mismos dedos surgen   pistolas de amor
Lirios de perdón
Y comforme entras en el ojo   en esta palma
Chupa Rosa   átame   a lo que guaras en secreto
Abre tu bolso munífico   abárcame

HANDFISHING RETABLO

Walking   from a corona of bees   Carumba
Our mind sees   him walking   on color monitor
For too long   have we been   trying too hard
Carumba   dreaming   too little   were it not
So far down   we love   but   no lock can keep him
In house   discalced   he walks   El Camino Real
Through smoking rubble   given the choice   of eyebrows
Or scales   which would it be   Carumba you're asking me
Were it not   so far down   plug of poetry in jaw
He is a step ahead   all ear and revery   way old way down

RETABLO DE LA PESCA MANUAL

Viene   de una corona de abejas   Carumba
Nuestras mentes lo   ven caminando   en un monitor de color
Hemos hecho   demasiado tiempo   el esfuerzo
Carumba   hemos soñado   muy poco   si no fuera
Demasiado lejos   amamos   mas   ninguna llave   puede retenerlo
En casa   camina   descalzo   El Camino Real
Por los restos humeantes   habiendo elegido   entre cejas
O escalas   cuál podría ser   Carumba me preguntas que
Si no fuera   demasiado lejos   la clavija de la poesía en la quijada
Él está un paso al frente   de todo oído y todo ensueño   sendero
    viejo sendero abajo

ROSESUCKER RETABLO

And though my birds be torn   to rags of smoke
And I into a nexus   of feather and ash
You must move ahead   unencumbered
By melancholy or defects
Behold the woman   Chupa Rosa
May you never endure a week
Without letters from an inmate
Never the day without apples nor bread
Come in   from distant penetralia   blasted immaculacy

RETABLO DEL CHUPA ROSA

Y a pesar de que mis pájaros se vuelvan   jirones de humo
Y yo el nexo   entre la pluma y la ceniza
Debes proseguir   sin el peso de
La melancolía o los defectos
Observa a la mujer   Chupa Rosa
Que nunca sobrevivas una semana
Sin las cartas de un encarcelado
Nunca el día en que no haya ni manzanas ni pan
Entra   de distantes santuarios   pureza maculada

FLOATING LADY RETABLO

Unable to read   garden by the moon
Unable to dream   sleep with elvers
The locusts start chewing   the sheets off the line
The big top burns down to the ground   Escuchame
Chuparosa   we begin to see   the typewriting
On the wall   you teach English   in a Vulcan Tool Truck
Rattling full tilt   which is it   what shall be
The remedy   or   what shall the remedy be
Vamos Chuparosa   we will be the stars' ashtray

RETABLO DE LA MUJER FLOTANTE

Incapaz de leer   jardín bajo la luna
Incapaz de soñar   dormida con angulas
Las langostas comienzan a mascar   las sábanas mojadas
El circo se desploma envuelto en llamas   Escúchame
Chuparrosa   empezamos a ver   la mecanografía
En la pared   das clase de inglés   in a Vulcan Tool Truck
que traquetea vertiginosamente   cuál es   cuál será
El remedio   o   cuál será el remedio
Vamos Chuparrosa   seremos el cenicero de las estrellas

HANDFISHING RETABLO

Born not stillborn   one elderly baby
At the bedstead of mourning   below depot town
Half god half hart   hodfuls of blood   dirt daubers in the dreadlocks
Potter wasps you say   in the red zone   where isn't illegal to serve
An egg   sunnyside up   now listen Chupa Rosa
He's had it   this baby's had it   with that old tired bullshit
Whether or not the danger is past   everready   unscripted   unbred
To become a memory   free air   we serve   Laissez
Les bontemps roulez   help your selves   flywheels turned ici

RETABLO DE LA PESCA MANUAL

Nacido no nonato   un bebé longevo
En la cama desnuda del duelo   bajo el pueblo-almacén
Mitad dios mitad venado   coágulos de sangre   cerdas sucias en
    las trenzas
Avispas de barro dices   en el mercado negro   donde no es
    ilegal servir
Un huevo   estrellado   ahora escucha Chupa Rosa
Ya se hartó   este bebé ya se hartó   de esta misma mierda
    trasnochada
Haya o no pasado el peligro   infalible   no escrito   descastado
De convertirse así en un recuerdo   aire libre   servimos   *Laissez*
Les bontemps roulez   ayúdense a sí mismos   los volantes
    vueltos *ici*

121

FLOATING LADY RETABLO

This is the shape of the sound   all the information you need
Comes with the light   which melts away   odd   how
Some of the letters   of a life   get printed backwards   how
One pupil looks   for solace   while the other is sweeping the ground
For trouble   how your skin is sensitive as a snail   easy baby
That's my electric eye   it can open anything from ketchup
to old trousseaus   the Venetian eye I saved for you   easy
Baby   I must disabuse you   of your whiny bugaboos   your
Churlish defenses   from here to yonder baby   it's zero visibility

RETABLO DE LA MUJER FLOTANTE

Ésta es la forma del sonido   toda la información que necesitas
Viene con la luz   que se disuelve a la distancia   curioso   cómo
Algunas de las cartas   de una vida   se imprimen al revés   cómo
Un discípulo anda en busca   de solaz   mientras que el otro anda
      barriendo el piso
En busca de problemas   cómo tu piel es sensible como un caracol
      suavecito nene
Ése es mi ojo eléctrico   puede abrir cualquier cosa   desde la catsup
Hasta los viejos *trousseaus*   el ojo veneciano que te guardé
      suavecito
Nene   debo quitarte la venda   de tus ridículos fantasmas   tus
Endebles defensas   de acá hasta allá nene   visibilidad: cero

HANDFISHING RETABLO

Followed us   to the shaft   end of the song   Que milagro
At the nock end   our fight   at the point   your breath
The worst man   a stone   the worst woman
A mill   the hair Chupa Rosa the hair   always gets caught
Leaf on leaf   worm by worm   we museum   in a box
On the other side   of the clearing   is another
Forest   fraught with unknowns   O my flammable
Pajamas   O my degenerating fibroids
When they lift the prints off our breast   will they be yours
Young epitaph   kiss me   then count your teeth

RETABLO DE LA PESCA MANUAL

Nos siguieron   hasta el pozo   final de la canción   Qué milagro
Al trunco final   de nuestro vuelo   al momento que   tu respiración
El peor de los hombres   una piedra   la peor de las mujeres
Un molino   el cabello Chupa Rose el cabello   siempre se enreda
Hoja sobre hoja   gusano tras gusano   los atesoramos   en una caja
Al otro lado   del claro   hay otro
Bosque   repleto de incógnitas   O mi pijama
Inflamable   O mis fibroides en descomposición
Cuando revoquen las huellas de nuestros senos   serán tuyos
Joven epitafio   bésame   luego cuéntate los dientes

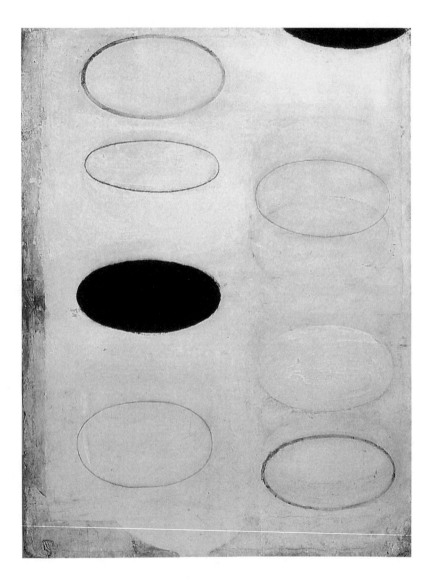

126

Internal
Fiction and Paintings
Brian Evenson and Eve Aschheim

I. APPROACH/OBSERVATION

My Internship

My INTERNSHIP, so Doctor Rauch now informs me, will consist not only of the dispersal of pills, the administration of pain and relief, the observation and restraint of patients—in short, the rigorous exploration of all the clinic's faces—but, in addition, the covert analysis of Rauch's brother. Said analysis to occur not within the confines of the clinic proper but at some distance, in the city. In our colloquies Rauch classifies this as "field work." His brother he refers to only as *my brother Rauch.* I do not know Doctor Rauch's forename, but only the initials he signs before his surname on each illustrious and highly respected article: B.K.

Such covert observation is irregular. Indeed, a discreet canvassing of other interns reveals that none has been asked by administrating doctors to depart from usual expected tasks, though it is possible that some are lying to protect themselves. Still, I have reason to believe my circumstance atypical. When Rauch called me into his chamber to issue the assignment (also train tickets, several months' stipend and a key to an apartment on the same floor as his brother's), Rauch claimed he could ask this of me because I am "hardly the typical intern."

Rauch tends to endow all his operations with mystery. He often addresses one (or at least me—"hardly the typical intern") with a conspiratorial air. Yet one can never be certain if one is co-conspirator or object of conspiracy. The second-year students supervised by Kagen have advised me to avoid extended contact with Rauch, despite his reputation. When I ask them to explain, they shake their heads. I am ashamed to admit that sometimes—perhaps as a result of their warning, perhaps from genuine personal unease—I hide from Rauch. Observing him progress down the corridor, I rush through the nearest doorway, though on one occasion that door led to a custodial closet. Although Rauch is both my administrating doctor and supposed mentor, he has a perpetually strange effect on me. I prefer him in the abstract, reduced to an authorizing signature on a commendatory document. At times I suspect Rauch to be involved in a subtle, complex, damaging negotiation with me. His instructions and advice seem to negate in all important particulars my previous training. At other times I sense Rauch despises me. I can discover no concrete basis for such belief. Quite the contrary: Rauch seems, with his confidential air and manner, to offer me information he would normally refrain from revealing to an intern. Yet later, pondering what I have actually been told, there seems very little to it, indeed nothing at all.

MY INSTRUCTIONS

The apartment I am to inhabit is adjacent to that of Rauch's brother. I am to observe him by any means possible, am to keep comprehensive records, gathering information that can be transmuted into a scholarly monograph. I am to share this record with nobody. Rauch's brother must not under any circumstances know I am observing him: my internship, Rauch has implied, depends on it.

The brother is, according to Rauch, *the nervous type*. Not only *the nervous type*, but also *the nihilistic type*, and *the depressive type*. At times he can even be classified as *the psychotic type*. His brother is *the suicidal type*, though he has never had the strength of will (not being *the strong-willed type*) to bring about his own death. He is constantly injuring himself—might even be referred to as *the accident-prone type*, though this has not sufficiently conjoined with the suicidal type so as to bring a seemingly accidental end to his life.

Do you understand this? Rauch asked me, then offered, in what he claimed to be a clarification, a listing of all the types his brother was, along with a matching percentage. I told him I had synthesized the information, which was not entirely true. The nervous type, if I do not misremember, amounted to eighteen percent of his brother's total being in Rauch's professional opinion. The other figures I do not even remotely recall. I do remember that the total summed at only ninety-two percent. *But what of the other eight percent?* I asked. *Ah*, Rauch said. *Undetermined. That, my not-the-usual-intern, is where you come in.*

In essence, then, I am to analyze eight percent of Rauch's brother.

I must absolutely not, according to Rauch, mistake his brother for having within him qualities of *the genteel type, the artistic type* or *the milk-of-human-kindness type.* Such types are not in his brother's character, though his brother has been known to fake them. As I am "hardly the ordinary intern," I am not to be taken in. His brother "is treacherous in every way." I must be "constantly on guard against him."

A SUMMATION OF RAUCHIAN THEORY

Individual psyches are, to varying degrees, fluid conglomerations of Pure Types. If one can define and diagnose those types gathered within a subject's body, Rauch claims, one can assemble a precise cure that will directly address all aspects of the subject's psyche. A cure achieves psychotopic stability either by establishing a typic balance or drawing the dominant type into an impregnable position at the "fore" of the psyche. Rauch believes the typological method allows him to diagnose infallibly a subject's psychotypes and, through this, to "definitively heal the spirit."

Rauch's first book, *A Modest Chromatics of Selfhood,* did not employ types. Instead, it offered identity colors, with the subject defined as a psychochromatic or psychospectral overlay of personalities. During analysis, Rauch would develop chromatic profiles for his patients, providing them with a series of sheets of colored transparent plastic to consider as externalized manifestations of their supposed inner reality.

Rauch's second book, *Psychotonic Types I Have Known,* introduced the Typic System along with forty-three possible Pure Types. The first edition of *A Typology of the Spirit* expanded this to ninety-two, the second edition to one hundred and twenty-eight. The third (and current) edition offers well over two hundred. Rauch has declared the types expandable. Each month he posts a short list of newly recognized Pure Types, along with precise descriptions.

I have substantive reservations. I would inform Rauch himself of these, but it is considered unwise for an intern to offend an advising doctor.

MY RECORD AND JOURNEY

I begin my record with these events rather than those that might follow because of a certain ambiguity of wording. Rauch asked me to "keep careful record of the affair." I affirmed a commitment to do so. It was not until boarding the train that I realized the ambiguity of the phrase "the affair." "Affair" might merely indicate time spent observing his brother. Yet it might span from the moment I leave the clinic to the moment I return. It might even refer to the whole course of my intership.

Uncertain of one's tasks, one must provide for all possibilities. Then, by default, one becomes certain of one's tasks.

This record is also kept for other, more interested, reasons. It will be a means of throwing blame back upon Rauch should my absence from the clinic be questioned. It is a means of insuring Rauch's continued commitment to his irregular intern.

The journey by train was unblemished, the remainder of the trip as well. I had intended to carry Doctor Rauch's *A Typology of the Spirit* to prime myself for the analysis, but neglected to pack it. I record this now because it is true, despite realizing Rauch might hold it against me later.

Perhaps, I mused, I am what Rauch might refer to as *the forgetful type.* I was puzzled as to what percentage of forgetfulness to assign myself. Surely I was other types as well.

Underground in a suburban station; walls slung with remaindered lavatory tile; my bags all around me. I discovered I had too many bags to carry comfortably, the medical profession having weakened me more than I cared to admit. I examined my flaccid arms. Because of my mental training, my mind can lift more than my body, I thought, though I knew such thoughts were associated with *the hyperbolic type.*

I had been strictly instructed by Rauch to avoid porters. He offered no explanation and I dared not demand one. Instructions such as this have caused me to wonder about the nature of the "affair." Perhaps I am as much the subject as the brother. Once analysis worms its way into one's head one is obliged to employ it. Analysis, I thought, refuses to cease smoothly and cleanly at the limit known as one's brother, in addition concerning itself with the interns one administrates. I struggled my way up the stairs.

At the curb, by sheer will, I transformed myself into *the hail-a-taxi type,* then *the giving-the-address type,* then the *paying-the-driver-and-descending type.* By such assumption and abandonment of spurious selves, I came to be standing outside Rauch's brother's building—a *staring-mutely-up type.*

THE APARTMENT

In one room, a mattress without sheets, in another a chair, in a third a hot plate and a bidet. A small water closet, a sink, no kitchen. The sole closet contains a single pot, a spoon, a can pry and several dozen

cans of a glutinous substance labeled "corn chowder." Above, naked bulbs on bare wires. The walls are ill with dirt, cleaner white squares scattering them where pictures must have hung. Cleaner patches of carpet, memories of furniture, a phantom geography moving from room to room. Two windows to the rear of the apartment, a peephole in the door, no other openings. No telephone.

By what means will Doctor Rauch recall me to the clinic once he feels my analysis sufficient? I cannot be reached by letter, for the mailbox requires a key, a key Doctor Rauch has failed to provide. I am isolated, at the mercy of my advising doctor. I must hurl myself into the analysis and remain engulfed until he drags me forth.

MY ATTEMPTS

Abandoning the apartment, I have descended the eight flights of stairs and thrust my head out to examine the buzzers. Doctor Rauch has failed to inform me which apartment is his brother's, the one to the left or the one to the right of my own: A or C.

I depressed each button, A and C, even B. No response.

Perhaps merely as a result of the hour I made my descent, the building seemed deserted.

At all hours, I have knocked at the left door (A), the right (C). Neither opened. I shouted as well: "Mr. Rauch? Delivery for Mr. Rauch." This, too, had no result.

Perhaps he has relocated? Another possibility: like me, he has a closetful of comestibles and thus no reason to leave his apartment. To observe him, I shall be forced to adopt measures I prefer to avoid. How to undertake them while still complying with Rauch's instructions, therein the difficulty.

A DAY ABROAD

I have charted a course through the building, from the roof down to the cellar. Above, heat purls off insufficiently graveled tar paper, the tar adhering to my soles. My shoes are ruined. I have removed them, discarded them behind my comestibles.

As many floors lie above my apartment as below. Both below and above, an absence of activity. I have turned the doorknobs of several apartment doors. All are locked. Yet I cannot be certain all the apartments are unoccupied. People might be there, hunched silently behind the doors, holding their breath. Or mere chance or some fact of building or season might explain my failure to detect anything.

Better luck in the cellar. Though various chicken-wire cages are padlocked, an open door on the salt-stained back wall leads to a dug-in supply closet. Run into the dirt that makes up the closet's back wall are two rusted iron rods, a warped board thrown across them as a shelf. Upon it: a coiled hose, a telescope, a can of putty, a paint spatula, a cupful of screws, a hand drill, a rotary saw.

The drill I carried to my room, leaving in its place a written statement that I am borrowing the drill and intend to return it. I am *the careful type* (thirty-three percent), *the fastidious type* (thirty-three percent), *the considerate type* (thirty-four percent).

Affixing the thickest and longest drill bit and tightening the chuck, I tapped my finger along the wall until I found a hollow space between studs. I bored easily through the plaster to the other side. Applying my eye to the hole, I observed an unfurnished room, a low light from the sun drifting through the windows, no sign of habitation.

The remainder of the day I spent tapping more holes into the wall, observing the neighboring apartment through them. By nightfall, I was certain the apartment had not been occupied for some time.

There is an apartment on the other side (C). All is not lost.

My Mental health and a Meal

Any analysis of the mental health of a subject must take into account the conditions to which said subject has been subjected, according to Rauch.

Having considered present conditions with care, I find I am not merely healthy; I am healthier than can be expected.

Thus satisfied, I derive further satisfaction from manipulating the can pry and from the operation of the hot plate. Simple but compelling. I open the can, empty its contents into the pan, heat them, consume, then lick the pan clean. I store the emptied can in the closet, behind those cans still containing soup.

My body has accepted the unvaried regularity of my diet, processing food with consistency and completeness. I remain in continual awe of the human machine.

Parameters

From door to comestibles, nineteen steps. From can pry to open can, nine turns of the wrist. Comestibles to hot plate, eight steps. Hot plate to chair, ten steps. Chair to door, five steps.

I am discarding fractions. Unseen, they accumulate somewhere.

APARTMENT C

A single hole enough to make clear that C resembles in all important particulars A. Uninhabited. Doctor Rauch's brother gone, if ever here at all.

A PROVISIONAL RAUCHIAN MAP

All findings concerning Doctor Rauch's brother, based on the data I have been able to gather:

The nervous type	=	0%
The squeamish type	=	0%
The distracted type	=	0%
The codswallop type	=	0%
The broken-nosed type	=	0%
The gangrenous type	=	0%
The rubbed-purr type	=	0%
The resurrective type	=	0%
Eater-of-chowder type	=	0%
The gill-net type	=	0%
The carbuncular type	=	0%
The Siamese-tarp type	=	0%
Total	=	0%

PART II.

A CURIOUS CASE

Words exchanged with Kagen today, who tells me I am to take on a new task. I am to observe his brother, a "curious case." Not, as one would expect, in the clinic: his brother will not allow himself to be moved. Moved, his brother becomes "maniacal."

I was setting these details down on paper when Kagen stopped speaking. "Why are you writing this down?" he asked. "Do not write this down."

I put the notebook away, pen as well.

"Write nothing," he said (not his exact words). "The only notebook you need," he said, tapping me on the temple, "is the 'notebook' within your skull."

I listened with rising anxiety, trying to remember his words. Once dismissed, I rushed into the bathroom, locked the door, scribbled notes from memory, then started to puzzle the case together:

A. Kagen has a brother who he insists does not physically resemble him.
B. Said brother is seriously disturbed.
C. Brother does not care to leave room.
D. I am Kagen's intern.
E. Because of B, Kagen's brother must be professionally observed.
F. Because of D, I am assigned to observe him.
G. Because of B,C,D, I am to:
  1. Observe Kagen's brother not at the clinic but on-site.
  2. Conduct a Kagenian analysis.
  3. Leave school; return only when said analysis is complete.
H. Reimbursement possible only for *legitimate and receipted* expenses.

All other details, because of my faulty memory, I have misplaced. Two unanswered questions:

1. Why does Kagen so vehemently insist on his brother's lack of resemblance to himself (see A above)?
2. Though D (see above) is true, I am not Kagen's only intern. I am utterly ordinary. Why me?

I am to leave immediately. Who, if not Kagen, I ask, does Kagen's brother resemble? I will "know [his] brother when I see him." Yet since Kagen's brother does not resemble Kagen (A), how can this possibly be true?

TECHNIQUE

I have come to study with Kagen only recently, after my disappointment with Doctor Rauch. I have little experience in Kagenian analysis. I have read the books: Kagen's *A Theory Concerning Clinical Theories*; his *A Physiognomy of the Spirit*; his trilogy saluting the body: *Hand, Stance, Face*:

> Gesture, expression, stance are the primary tools of analysis for Kagenian posturology. Any discrete gesture or action which a patient repeats, or any characteristic posture, contains keys for understanding the patient's basic conflicts. The therapist observes the patient's gesture and posture and constructs his own counter-postures to neutralize them, thus establishing equilibrium. The therapist must draw the patient's attention to his body and body image (physiological schema). He must modify the patient's postures, reformulate the postural and gestural schema. . . .

136

Physical expression [claims Kagen] is the most accurate index of mental health. . . .

Dialogue between patient and psychiatrist occurs, but speech and conversation are to be bracketed as distractors (i.e., devices used to minimize or conceal patients' physiological schema) or as convectors (i.e., devices used by the patient to amplify and elaborate the physiological schema). . . .

The therapist is to facilitate a decay of the physiological schema but not decay in such degree as would cause the patient to become alarmed and potentially resistant. Gesture and posture are first negated and then subtly reconstructed by the therapist. . . . The patient is cured once his physiological schema is adjusted sufficiently so as to bring about somatic stability. . . .

My Own Posture

Departure imminent, I was bold enough to ask Kagen to judge my own expressive traits.

"Your expressive traits?"

"My posture," I said. "Does it indicate somatic and psychodynamic balance?"

He waved me away, but I folded my arms and did not leave. Finally, he went behind his desk, slipped on his glasses, squinted through them at me.

"No, no, no," he said. "You have it all wrong."

He approached me. Knotting his hands behind my back, he squeezed, then twisted dorsally. My body was wrenched sidewards, my spine cracking.

"There," he said as he released me. "Don't move."

From his desk he removed a photograph of himself. "If you feel yourself slipping, emulate this image.

"Abandon your notebook," he repeated, tapping his skull. "This is the sole 'notebook' you require."

Furnishings

A brief and brutal journey by train to find myself in the city, before Kagen's brother's building, looking up. No doorman, nor anyone tending the lobby. Lobby unlit, apparently deserted. Jagged flights of stairs, in disrepair. The lock resisting the key, a flash of panic—*What if Kagen himself had been confused as to the number of the room?*—but suddenly the key turned.

137

Against Kagen's wishes, I have retained my notebook. As an aid to memory.

Bathroom: small and cramped, containing a squat-toilet (two crosshatched footpads and a hole in the floor) which doubles as a shower. Kitchen: no kitchen. In a closet: hot plate, several hundred soup cans, a pan. Bedroom: one worn and filthy mattress (I will opt to sleep on the floor). Living Room: a single chair. The west wall perforated with five or six holes, each hole just larger than my toe. I am reminded of the boxes I kept for birds and mice when a child, punctured so as to allow them to breathe.

Through the holes: an empty apartment, apparently uninhabited, quite identical to my own.

AN OBSERVATION BEGINS

Observation at the holes three hours twenty-two minutes before Kagen's brother appeared, skin and hair and clothes a ruin. Seated on a chair similar to my own, writing slowly on a clipboard. Initial schema:

10:16   Stretches both arms over his head, never letting go of his pen (position 7: clenched fist, free thumb).

10:18   Crosses right leg over left, at ankle.

10:20   Squinches eyes closed, puts clipboard down beside him, stands. Posture curved and bowed (c.f. postures 3 & 13).

10:21   Withdraws, gait inscribing a meandering path though nothing in the room impedes him.

No sign nor indication of the violence Kagen insists his brother capable of. Mostly passive, writing, then disappearing into rooms I cannot see.

I chart his gestures, assign values. No violence in them either.

Sometimes blinks or squeezes eyes shut, but generally expressionless.

. . . *such expressionlessness,* Kagen has written, *particularly when outside of the game context (e.g., poker), a possible indication of mental subempathy.*

HAND

The more I consider my current situation, the odder it seems. To be engaged in such a task, outside clinic, the subject not knowing he is being observed, appears to violate clinical policy.

Yet it has been ordered by Kagen.

Erratic movements: a right finger stuttering from left cheek to left

thigh, then reverse. Repeated clenching and unclenching of fist.
Kagen's book *Hand:*

> ... repeated gesture can always be said to express motiva-
> tions on conscious and subsconscious levels. Repeated hesi-
> tation or incomplete movement of the hand or fingers is often
> indicative of an attitude of contempt, disgust ... obsessive
> clench and release, the haptic expression of insecurity. .... All
> gestures are symbols, all movement a language as elaborate as
> (and oftentimes more meaningful than) speech.

The basics of the language are clear, but Kagen gives little sense of
how to interpret the complexities:

> The only key for interpretation is repeated observation of an
> individual subject. Gesture is the most individual of all lan-
> guages. The analyst must learn to converse in the patient's
> particular gestural language, and later, while within the phys-
> iological framework of the gestural dialogue, sabotage the
> patient's physiological grammar and syntax.

After All

Perhaps Kagen distrusts me because of my initial commitment to
Rauch. Am I being punished? Perhaps should have stayed with
Rauch.

Diagnosis

Varied stance and posture, coupled with the odd gait. As if empty
room were full of obstacles. For him, perhaps yes.

*Physiological schema: mentally disturbed. Nature of the distur-
bance not yet otherwise specified (NOS).*

Will this be enough for Kagen?

It will not.

Observing the brother through a hole in the wall, watching him
write. I withdraw from the hole to my own chair to write notes. How
to define the brother for Kagen? No simple task.

A Flash of Eye

Stumbled out from sleep this morning, sat in chair, considered past
notes. Twelve straight hours trying to draw some order into them.
Glanced up to see the brief flash of an eye at a hole. I approached the
hole and looked through. No one.

Had I imagined it? Perhaps he was crouched against the wall,

140

below the hole, where I could not observe him.

I scratched quietly on the wall, so softly that unless he had been pressed against the other side he could not have heard. No response. This does not prove he was not there.

A DISTINCT POSSIBILITY

Facing a distinct possibility I am being observed myself. A distinct possibility his clipboard contains notes about my behavior.

No object to block the holes when I am not observing him. He may look at me at any moment, though I should be the one looking at him.

Will stay to my back room when not engaged in observation. I do not care to be observed.

WHAT I KNOW

What I know:
  A. I observe Kagen's brother through holes.
  B. I am in turn observed through said holes.
  C. I write about Kagen's brother in a notebook.
  D. Kagen's brother writes on a clipboard. I do not know what he is writing.
Postulation: If B is to D as A is to C, Kagen's brother writes about me.

WHAT I CAN TAKE AS GIVEN

Nothing.

SHARP

No object to block the holes, though perhaps I can discourage him from using them. Had I a sharp object, I could attempt, hiding beneath the hole, to plunge it into his eye.

He is thinking the same thing concerning my eye.

A pen might be sharp enough.

He is thinking a pen might be sharp enough.

Face to a hole, drawing air.

MY OR HIS BEHAVIOR

Stops ears and rushes from sight. *Clear signs of mental disturbance.*

What of me, my stance and gestures? No telling. Only this poor photograph of the well-postured Kagen to emulate. Enough to sustain me? How, with no mirror, can it be?

CONTACT

Copied a page of notes onto a loose sheet, rolled it up tightly, pushed it into one of the holes. Then sat in my chair, watching. Soon the paper was drawn the rest of the way through, to disappear.

Rushed to the wall. Already he was out of sight, vanished into the back room or pressed against the same wall as I, below me, a few inches away.

I waited for him to return. Eye later pressed to hole. No further sightings. I waited further.

AN EXCHANGE

Hungry, thirsty, sleepless. My own appearance and manner of dress, what can be seen without a mirror, slovenly.

If I leave the hole even for a moment he might come and be gone before I return.

I wait, drift off. Come awake again to find my cheek against the floor.

During my sleep, something pushed through the hole. A rolled sheet of paper. I unroll it. Blank, nothing on either side. I turn it slightly in the light, look for the impressions of fingers, small smudges.

I sit holding it in my hands. I open my notebook, write.

Serenity of face, steadiness of hand, straightness of spine. I am, I can feel it, the picture of postural health.

I am being observed.

Make no false moves. Always gestures brimming with health.

THE PEN'S CASING

There, through the pen's casing: eight last dim drops of ink. Soon I will have only blank pages as well.

Observation must continue. Close notebook, wait for the dim flicker of eye at hole again. Seven drops of ink to assemble full diagnosis. Six drops of ink, all that remain to bring me to the cure. Forward.

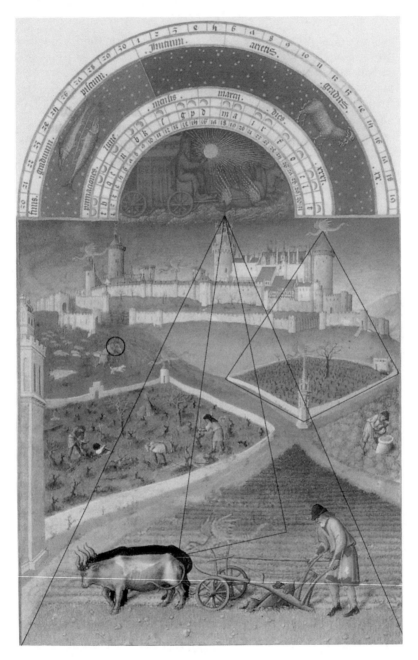

MARCH

144

Such Rich Hour
Cole Swensen

—With images from Les Très Riches Heures du Duc
de Berry, 15th century, computer-manipulated
by the author

MARCH 1

(Thus we find triads: dimension, form, and order
substance, nature, power

and took (all three brothers
or was it the single other?)
every care and every caution:

green infused with grey   indicates   a cult of weather

were you born here were you born
vassal, slave, your only master
with the fingers of a weaver tied back the finite branches
with the fingers of a lover let the seed sift through his fingers

who so thereafter lived here. A small dog running up to the road
in front of a flock of sheep in front of a large man carrying
something (we can't see what) (sheaf) (shearing) holding (soft)
against him
(close).

MARCH 3

father son and holy father son and only counting   if it gathers
can amount to or can turn   as has here   almost human.
You would have thought   or so you said
            Who knew him later, carved

145

a three-legged stool to go milking, a three-pronged
fork to go haying and the child born with three fingers on every hand
and three hands was allowed to live because, and it all adds up: father,
form & after; face, hand & anger. Spherical. Cubical. Envelop you
in
and is
its own and only weather: wind, wind and wind on fire.

MAY 1, 1410, 1 A.M.: LES REVENANTS

Old and on / certain nights of the Walpurgis   I saw it
coming
back
a thing that lives
on bridges
suspended

*" . . . for centuries were the exclusive privilege of the very wealthy
and of saints."*
Forgive
my apprehension
it
stood on a bridge slightly
swaying, vagary of wind,
tracery of sound that could have been wind
carved. And refused
to leave. "Here lives
what I did and cannot stop doing"

*"Then suddenly by the 11th or 12th century, they were all over,
sometimes alone, sometimes in great numbers, at first largely in
dreams, but soon not so confined."*   (came back to us)
(and thought I saw)   (as he was
then)

the army of the dead, they called it
Maisnie Hellequin—soldiers, children, women, saints, by the thousands with all their attributes on

*

146

MAY

The moral was blatant ("there they go, paying") but we were too dis-
tracted by their faces, how they hadn't
changed at all and were   more similar and were
                                                                the precision there,
                                                                the choice.

MAY 1, 1411: BROAD DAY

note the curves   we pause and forth
                       and he turns
                       and she looks down.
Start again:
        the entire forest in its gentle bow
                mirrored in color
                love was something we invented

                and perfectly enacted
"And made this body perfect
to the glory of the season: one bows low,
wears green,
gets made the center of a painting   made of crushed stone
                (just grind and mix with water) (called
                                        verde azzurro
to note its close connection with the azurite so common, also called
                chrysocolla
                azurinum conversum in viridem colorem
                and
                viride terrestre
                though that is also
something else
something called "green earths"
                                my love   who has promised
but they weren't sufficiently intense to make a landscape live
                a world
but did
wonderfully as the base for the warm tones of the skin
                when what I want
and were mixed with white alone in most works, though that too
        changed

148

Cole Swensen

He turned
      toward a castle just visible beyond the trees,
and pointed and smiled but I couldn't hear what he said.

MAY 30, 1427: JEANNE-NOT-YET-SAINT WITH SHEEP

When they eat from your hand it's said that you're saved
      or that you saved them.   You can never be sure.
                    What you heard.   What did
And how   do you know it was Saints She and Her?
            And which them?
            And will you agree to the musical score.

We ask you to
close your eyes and picture: it's night (held close, black & white).
Campfires, men in armor, the army at the gate.   And we haven't
even begun to consider what we really mean by mad. If it
approaches. Seeing vs. seen.
And will make of it a king.   We ask you to picture
men huddled around fire. There was so much less light then. And
    it glinted their armored
bodies into black bodies of water. The way things move in
    uncertain light
is not to be discounted. A touch
with the tip of a finger on an otherwise sleeping forehead, between
    the eyebrows and up about half an inch. What
would you give.

JUNE

JUNE 1

Sickle one, scythe two and sweep and sheaf and sign
in the rocking field and the river whole
in its own   (what hold
                 what
                 boat

of the errance of a spire (despite appearance
                 it's miles

(at the door of the river) (that curves into harvest)

Choir: Let us
          harbor in this witness
                                a man
                 with an oar
shreds a surface

(at the door he calls a river)

a person slipping inward

                 How stone reigns
                 How hay stings
                 (How swing this scythe so I look a little less like
                                          my own death) who
                                     sings
                          of

of all the towers on the castle, three are red.
What are they carrying in the boat?
(List everything you could carry
away in a boat.)

OCTOBER

OCTOBER 1, 1945

How to paint a filament designed to be invisible:
How to paint a white dog against a white wall:
How a world in stages, striated, calibrated:

first you notice the person walking, the river that occupies the center
of the picture, the three boats and the one man, arms raised, something hard in his hand. Such a busy world ruled by birds, held down
by a stone, and what is—just behind and to the right of the first tower
on the left—the moon that looks like a planet of skies against the sky
and how do we live there and how do we live on air.

*Executed 1440–1450, after shadows had been invented, and re-
flections,* and lives on water, and is made of light or of its slight
absence.

OCTOBER 2

At the center of the picture, a river

cuts the picture in two. This is not the first time. Perhaps you've
    noticed

this straight line at the heart and the world doesn't meet
                                batel = boat
                                atant: to this point
                                and *choir,* to fall down into
            each one, its wavering twin
the river offers
                        of the river, sheer passage
                            and ere in passing
        And here ends the fragment: tends to
retrace its primitive route, curving just below the hills of Belleville,
and on toward Montmartre, making islands out of floods.
                "I'm a wishing mill"
        I'm a wedge between the ribs
    a peeled muscle exposed to sun
                                cut in two. I did not choose.

154

Three Peter Lorre Poems
Poems and Drawings
John Yau and Trevor Winkfield

PETER LORRE SPEAKS TO THE SPIRIT OF
EDGAR ALLAN POE DURING A SEANCE

Back then which is anywhere in back of now
I was pretending to be a practicing mendicant,

a mower of smaller children, a moratorium in a tuxedo,
while you were acting like a hopeless sponge.

a photograph of a convict whose mind
isn't quite made up, but it is.

Later, I draped the last of my outer garments
over my jockey shorts, and left town in a cab.

I told the man whose shiny head
reminded me of a bottle of wine

Deliver me to the suburban rodeos of
Piccadilly or Paradise

a harbor of idle tugboats
an island of glass huts

wherever smoke hasn't started
charting its progress across a torn sky

Thus, the journal of our journey
began with the opening of faucets;

tear ducts; syrupy vittles; Arctic ice storms;
bowler hats above long thick sleeves;

white haired gymnasts and their smelly pets.
The detectives came later,

examples of their tarnished industriousness
tucked beneath their tongues.

Did you know that I was never called upon
by those who would have known

what I meant
when I said

I was a star,
a stage of deterioration,

a page upon which
someone has drawn

the seven shapes of my name,
their skeletal facades

pressing against deserted streets.
The rest of me—the part you know

as it is also you—
is sitting inside,

watching television,
waiting for further instructions on how

I might dig myself out of the roles
blind biographers have stuck me in

PETER LORRE RECORDS HIS FAVORITE
WALT WHITMAN POEM FOR POSTERITY

I am an indigestible vapor rising from the dictionary
you sweep under your embroidered pillow

My only offer: A kidnapped dog in exchange for your thirst
Call me Zanzibar Sam, Bulging Pharoah, Narcoleptic Swill

Custom labyrinths made to order, purveyor of mid-sized jungles
a gravedigger counting shoes in a candlelit saloon

A miracle erupted from a reunion of mouse and sow, horse and hubby
Son became bagged contraband penetrating ring of nibbled pyres

Me criminal puss no longer muzzled and mugged by snoring camera
Me signaled pasty or patsy, but donned smooth glacial twitches

Mere slip in a sequined slapper, lolling whimper of purring grape,
not just smoothed flotsam bulk and hankering moss

Inside me dwells a nude drummer toy, all pomade and fancy,
while the outer me, the bun you tufted, was heavy-lipped

reflection of uncanny twittering amidst gnawed leaves

MY CHRONOLOGY
BY PETER LORRE AS TOLD TO JOHN YAU

The splattered flag of an idiot scavenger; this was how
I sailed beyond the perfect faces of the coming storm.
Many times, almost as many as in your shabby arenas,
their walls of baritone shadows, their stream of flailing ants.
I was rolled beneath a couch. Stuffed in a trunk. Drooled
down a box (complete with fishing tackle,
their silvery tangle and heap of pink wigglers).
Flopped into a crumpled cup. A semi-anonymous heap,
shorn of all but secondary features, some of which
were legendary, petals of manufactured smoke
erasing butterflies shivering in the branches of
                              my material remains.
Did you try and insert me in a pile of juggled lumps?
Was I part of a column of figures? Or was I
a figural column surrendering sky's black roof?
Who traces the umbilicus of these outbursts of frenzy
back to its mouth, my carriage of sagging carbon
cries out? Who embraces these hummingbird sparks
                              of lateral agitation?
A monogrammed hanky steeped in sepulchral vapors?
Pathetic this monaural chivalry.

Once I even crawled around a lake resting in
the crevice of a porcelain saucer, before being
swatted into diaphanous mulch, leaving only
an inky signature on the lard inflated plains.
What is chronology, but detachable hands
sifting for condensation collectivized in an earlier era?
Could I not have arrived before you opened your eyes,

found your axial culmination seated in the upper registers
of a Babylonian balcony or Sumerian wing chair,
optically registering disturbances flooding through
the illuminated window? Or were you always there,
always perfectly poised, stored among the glass roses
you will be requested to accompany to the heated antechamber?
Always waiting for the mirror to begin reciting
                              its sordid tale?

From The Fan-Maker's Inquisition
Drawings by the Author
Rikki Ducornet

There is no explosion except a book.

—Mallarmé

ONE

—A fan is like the thighs of a woman: It opens and closes. A good fan opens with a flick of the wrist. It produces its own weather—a breeze not so strong as to mess the hair.

There is a vocabulary attendant upon fan-making. Like a person, the fan has three principle parts: *les brins* or ribs are most often of wood; *les panaches* or, as courtesans call them, the legs, also made of wood or ivory or mother of pearl (and these may be jade: green—the color of the eye, rose—the color of the flesh, and white—the color of the teeth); the mount—and this is also a sexual term—which is sometimes called *la feuille* or the leaf (another sexual term dating, it is said, from the time of Adam)—the mount is made of paper or silk, or swanskin—

—Swanskin?

—A fine parchment made from the skin of an unborn lamb, limed, scraped very thin and smoothed down with pumice and chalk. The mount may be made of taffeta, or lace, or even feathers—but these are cumbersome. A fan trimmed with down has a tendency to catch to the lips if they are moist or rouged. A paper fan can be a treasure, especially if it is from Japan. The Japanese make the finest paper fans and the most obscene. These are sturdier than one might think. Such a fan is useful when one is bored, forced to sup with an ailing relative whose ivory dentures stink. It is said that the pleated fan is an invention of the Japanese and that the Chinese collapsed in laughter when it was first introduced to China. The prostitutes, however, took to it at once.

—Why is that?

—Because it can be folded and tucked up a sleeve when, having lifted one's skirts and legs one goes about one's business. Soon the gentlemen were sticking theirs down their boots—a gesture of evident sexual significance. Once I saw a fan from India. The *panaches* were carved to look like hooded cobras about to strike the naked beauty who, stretched out across the mount, lay sleeping. That was a beautiful fan.

—Earlier you referred to the three parts of the person. Name these.

—The head, the trunk and the limbs.

—Please continue.

—Little mirrors may be glued to the fan so that one may admire oneself and dazzle others. It may be pierced with windows of mica or studded with gems. A telescopic lens may be attached to the summit of a *panache;* such a fan is useful at the theater. La Comtesse Gimblette owns a fan made of a solid piece of silver cut in the form of a heart and engraved with poetry.

> *Everything*
> *Is to your taste.*
> *You snap up the world*
> *With haste!*

A red fan is a symbol of love, and a black of death, of course.

—When the fan in question—the one found in the locked chamber at La Coste—was ordered, what did Sade say, exactly?

—He came into the atelier looking very dapper and he said: "I want to order a pornographic *ventilabrum!*" And he burst out laughing. I said: "I understand pornographic, Monsieur, but *ventilabrum?*" "A *flabellum!*" he cried, laughing even more. "With a scene of flagellation." "I can paint it on a *fan*," I said, somewhat out of patience with him, although, I have to admit I found him perfectly charming, "on velvet or on velum, and I can do you a *vernis Martin*—" This caused him to double over with hilarity. "Do me!" he cried, "*Do me*, you seductive, adorable fan-maker, a *vernis Martin* as best you can and as quickly as you can, and I will be your eternal servant." "You do me too much honor," I replied. Then I took down his order and asked for an advance to buy the ivory. Because of the guild regulations, I purchase the skeletons from another craftsman. Sade wanted a swanskin mount set to ivory—which he wanted *very* fine.

—Meaning?

—The ivory of domesticated animals is brittle because the elephants eat too much salt. Wild ivory is denser, far more beautiful and more expensive, too. For pierced work it cannot be surpassed. Then, the mount needed thin slices of ivory cut into ovals for the faces, *les fesses,* the breasts—

—This request was unusual?

—I have received stranger requests, citizen.

—Continue.

—The slivers of ivory, no bigger than a fingernail, give beauty and interest to swanskin and velum—as does mother-of-pearl. I am sometimes able to procure these decorative elements from a button and belt buckle maker for a fair price because I have an arrangement with him.

—Describe this arrangement.

—I paint his buttons.

—Continue.

—The making of buckles and buttons is not wasteful; nonetheless, there is always something left over, no matter the industry. I also use scraps to embellish the *panaches,* not where the fingers hold the fan because over time the skin's heat causes even the best paste to soften. But further up the pieces hold so fast no one has ever complained.

—And this is the paste that was used to fix the six wafers to the upper section of the . . . mount?

—The same. Although I diluted it as the wafers were so fragile.

—The entire fan is fragile.

—So I told Sade. He said it did not matter. The fan was an amusement. A gift for a whore.

—Some would call it blasphemy. Painting licentious acts including sodomy on the body of Christ.

—We are no more living beneath the boot of the Catholic Church, citizen. I never was a practicing Catholic. Like the paste that holds

165

them to the fan, the wafers are made of flour and water. They are of human manufacture, and nothing can convince me of their sacredness.

—Your association with a notorious libertine and public enemy is under question today. Personally, I don't give a fig for blasphemy, although I believe there is no place in the Revolution for sodomites. But now, before we waste any more time, will you describe for the Comité the scenes painted on the fan. (*The fan, in possession of the* Comité de Surveillance de la Commune de Paris, *is handed to her.*) Is this the fan you made for Sade?

—Of course it is. (*She examines the fan, briefly.*) It is a convention to paint figures and scenes within cartouches placed against a plain background, or, perhaps a background decorated with a discreet pattern of stars, or hearts, or even eyes—as I have done here. In this case there are two sets of cartouches: the six painted wafers, well varnished, at the top, and the three large, isolated scenes beneath—three being the classic number.

—And now describe for the Comité the scenes.

—There is a spaniel.

—The girl is naked.

—All the girls are naked as are all the gentlemen. Except for the Peeping Tom hiding just outside the window.

—And the spaniel.

—He is dressed in a little vest and he carries a whip in his teeth.

—His master's whip?

—His master's whip.

—And the . . . master is in the picture, too?

—Yes! smack in the middle. It is a portrait of Sade with an enormous erection!

—As specified in the agreement?

—Exactly. "Have it point to the *right!*" he said. "Because, if I could fuck God *right* in the eye, I would." And he laughed, "Point it right for hell," he said. So I did.

—The Comité is curious to know about your continued service to the Marquis de Sade.

—I paint pictures for him, and I—

—What is the nature of these pictures? Why is he wanting pictures?

—Because he is in prison! He has nothing before his eyes but the guillotine! All day he has nothing to occupy his mind but executions, and all night nothing but his own thoughts.

—Explosive thoughts.

—Yes. Those are his words: explosive thoughts. He has told me that the pictures serve not only to amuse and occupy his mind. They also enable him to follow the itinerary of his madness—for he believes he is going mad and has little else to do but be the observer of his own destruction. "My head," he told me, "will be rolling soon." He was *not* referring to the guillotine. "If I didn't have your pictures," he said not long ago, "my skull would explode under the pressure of my imagination, and this tower splattered with blood and brains."

—Do you believe such a thing possible?

—Of course not. The walls splattered with blood and brains is a description of how he feels. He also says his head is an oven, an oven so hot it burns everything that goes into it. He says, "My daydreams are all char and smoke. The stench of my own thoughts makes it impossible to breathe."

—At this point I would ask you to read aloud this letter—the first of many—taken from your rooms on the night of the eleventh.

—(*Taking up the letter.*) Ah! the one I call "A Cup of Chocolate."

Little wolf, my prize wench. The things you
sent have at last arrived this morning, pawed
over by the contemptible Scrutinizer, a wretch
who cannot keep his hands to himself; but
nothing broken and it seems everything
in place: the ink, candles, linens, sugar,
chocolate—the chocolate! Untouched! And
what chocolate! so that I may start the day
just as the Maya kings with a foaming cup.

167

Like a good fuck, a good cup of chocolate starts with a vigorous whipping and here I am, my little anis de Flavigny, *breathing the Yucatán as I write this letter. There are fops who swear by* ambre gris *and would put that in their chocolate, but I'm particular to the classic cup—unadulterated—perhaps the one instance when I can say I prefer a thing unadulterated!*

A cup of chocolate, ma douce amie, *and my mood—and it couldn't have been worse—has lifted; why I am so buoyant that did God exist I'd be in paradise with my nose up his arse! But this is a godless universe—you know it as well as I—and therefore nothing in the world, or, for that matter, in any of the myriad other worlds, planets and moons, smells better than a good cup of hot chocolate! Or tastes better. Hold on for a moment, will you, as I take another sip . . . As I was saying: Nothing! Not even those sanctified turds no bigger than the coriander seeds which falling from the sky into the wilderness fed the famished Jews. A pretty story . . . And here's another (although I warn you, it's not near as nice):*

Yesterday as the clouds rolled into the city from the West obscuring the sky and just before it began to rain, I saw a young fellow, fuckable beyond one's wildest dreams, kneel before the guillotine. Now I know that all I imagine in my worst rages is only a mirror of the world. All day, over and over again, although the rain fell in torrents and the wind sent a bloody water surging into the crowd, Hell materialized beneath my window. At times it seemed a staged tableau, a diabolic theater as redundant as the bloodthirsty entertainments I have, poisoned by ennui, catalogued time and time again. To tell the

*truth, all day I wondered if thoughts are
somehow contagious, if my own rage has not
infected the world. I thought: Because I dared
to dream unfettered dreams I have brought a
plague upon the city.*

*This idea persisted; I could not let it be but
worried it like a dog worries the corpse of a
cat. Such redundancy is exemplary: A machine
has been invented that lops off a head in a
trice, and suddenly the world is not what it
was. And I who have dreamed of fucking
machines, of flogging machines—I am* outdone!
*The plague I have unleashed is not only highly
contagious, it is mutable: See how it gathers
strength and cunning!*

*And now—a death machine, là! Là! Just
beneath my window! Have I engendered it?
It seems that I have. Even the clouds pissing
rain, the air filled with mortal shrieks, with
sobs, the laughter of sows—seems to pour out
of me. I imagine that every orifice of my body
oozes crime. A lover of empiricism (and this is
a tendency that, on occasion, plunges me into
a fit—for I would count the whiskers on the
face of a rat and weigh the dust motes in the
air if I think this will lead me somewhere . . .)
it occurs to me that I might find a way to
measure or track this seminal poison and
direct it. For the gore that accumulates like
the dead apples of autumn beneath my
window sickens me, yes! It is one thing
to dream of massacres; it is another to
witness one.*

*Is this violence the bastard child of one
man's rage? If so, all is irreparable, for I have
imagined so much. Worse: I have put it to
paper!*

*I recall the story of a notorious slut, one
Madame Poulaillon, who attempted to destroy
the husband she despised by soaking all his
shirts in arsenic. Arsenic she had in plenty as*

169

rats plagued her home. *(But what marriage
is not haunted by the midnight chatterings
and scrabblings of vermin?) It is a venerable
tradition: the poison garment. There is another
story, of a pagan queen, a Hindoo, a real piece,
who, made to marry the one who had taken
her kingdom by force, offered him a robe so
deadly it caused his flesh to fall away.*

*My mind is like these: Its poison is invisible
but deadly. Far from the world, locked in
ignoble towers, fed slop, forced to scribble
away my precious days and years with a quill
no bigger than a frog's prick—my venom soaks
the city like a fog. What would things be like,
I wonder, if I* really *put my mind to it? Could
they be worse?*

*Ah! But another taste of chocolate,
and all this dissolves. And I recall a
fan you once made for the actress
known as La Soubise: a fan of peacock
feathers, a fan made of eyes! When she
used it, it seemed that an exotic moth, a
moth from the Americas, had settled on her
hand. You called the fan "Andrealphus" in
honor of the demon who was said to transform
men into birds. And thanks
to your instruction in the
languages of fans, when La
Soubise glanced my way
and taking her fan with
her right hand and, holding
it before her face, left the
room, I knew she might
as well have spoken the*
words: Follow me. *Crowing like a cock, I flew
after her at once and spent a happy hour in her
barnyard. (Now, there was a courageous soul
who was not afraid of my reputation!)*

Remember when I asked for a flabellum?
*How later, together, we laughed at the joke?
A fan that represents chastity! That protects*

the host from Satan in the form of flies!
Just what is supposed to happen, I would
like to know, to a believer who swallows
a contaminated wafer?

—Have you ever fucked Sade?

—Never.

—You have painted scenes of unnatural acts punishable by death.

—I have painted such scenes. And I have also painted the body in dissolution. This does not make me a murderess! For exactitude I have visited the medical school and the morgue.

—A distasteful practice for a woman! Does nothing disgust you?

—My curiosity overcomes my disgust, citizen. This has always been so. It explains, I believe, Sade's interest in me. Our lasting friendship.

* * *

—How did you come to the attention of the Marquis de Sade?

—La Comtesse Cafaggiolo sent him to the atelier. I had painted erotic pictures for her on an Italian cabinet, very finely made. I painted scenes of amorous dalliance on the drawers, the doors and also the sides and top: sixty-nine scenes in all, some of them very small. La Comtesse treasured it and kept it in her most intimate chamber. How citizen Sade came to see it is for you to imagine.

—Describe this chamber.

—It no longer exists, citizen; it has been sacked and burned. But I knew it well, for the painting was done there, under the supervision of the Countess. It was papered in yellow silk and trimmed in the most tender green. Three large windows opened out on the gardens, and the walls were decorated with copper engravings by Marcantonio Raimondi, based on the drawings of Giulio Romano. The series was unique.

—These names are not familiar to me.

—Both men were once notorious, persecuted by the Catholic Church for the very pictures once hanging in the yellow room.
From the windows of the bed chamber one could see a fountain.

171

It was the twin of one Giulio Romano had designed for Federico di Gonzaga. As we speak, and as heads fall beneath Sade's own window, the fountain plays even now in the Gonzaga gardens. My first real conversation with Sade took place beside it, soon after I had completed the fan. I had become the Countess' confidant, and so it should not be surprising that we met again, as we did, beside the large *ucello* carved at the fountain's base.

—*Ucello! Ucello!*

—A winged phallus, citizen. Seeing it Sade exclaimed: *"Fuckgod! I like this fountain!"*

—Describe your conversation with the Marquis de Sade.

—Citizen Sade called our hostess a "purple brunette," as she had very white skin with a violet hue. Unlike another woman of his acquaintance—I've mentioned her, "La Soubise," whom he called *une dorée*—a "gold" brunette, and unlike myself who, because of my olive complexion, he called *une verte*. Then he shared with me some of his curious theories. For example, he spoke at great length about an invention of his: "the metaphysical eye." He likened the eye to a vortex that sinks directly to the soul, a vortex of fire that, paradoxically, is also a whirlpool in which one may drown.

He said that tears are potencies formed by the presence of light within the eye in concert with the heating action of the passions. He told me how the Maya of the Yucatán hurt little children to make them weep and so cause it to rain. The notion that pain could precipitate weather is a fascination of his because it suggests that the functions of the eye are simultaneously pertinent, acute, active and mysterious, too.

Later, Sade described a machine of his imagination that could measure the distillation of light within the eye and the subsequent production of tears. A similar engine could measure the salinity of the bodily secretions: tears, saliva, sperm, blood, urine, sweat and so on. According to him the body is a machine lubricated by these fluids; salt is the fuel. He wondered about the manner in which the spoken word, producing vapor in the air, might influence the humors of others: their moods, dreams and fantasies, the quality of their vision, sense of taste and touch, sexual desire—and also the weather.

—The weather?

—A droll idea of his: that words could produce wind. Just as the Maya thought tears—

—You have several times made mention of the New World. What has your involvement been in the production of a notorious manuscript that has recently come to the attention of the Comité?

—It is a project with which I am intimate.

—Explain.

—Early in our friendship, Sade said I had the mind of a man. That was to say that I was fearless, fearless of ideas, which, after all, are mere abstractions until put to use. I told him that I had the mind of a woman, adequately stimulated, adequately served. You see: Under the guidance of an enlightened parent, I became an educated woman transcending the limits of my craft. My father was a scholar who having lost the little he had was forced to deal in rags and—as luck would have it—old books, which, after all, are often the best. So that if we ate gruel, we had books to read for the price of a little lamp oil and this is how we spent our evenings. Father's books were green with mold, they smelled of cat piss, they smelled of smoke, they were stained with wine, ink and rain, or spotted with the frass of insects. Many contained copper engravings and even maps of invented or vanished lands. From a very young age I was swept up and away by a ceaseless and vertiginous curiosity. My curiosity was never thwarted and always indulged—such was my education.

—Continue.

—As much as Father loved books, he loved theater. We were too poor to ever frequent *la Comédie Française,* but we saw what we could: farces performed in barns by actors more ragged than we! Or the plays took place in the back of canvas booths thick with fleas; we prepared for the evening by rubbing our feet and legs with kerosene. Some of these plays seemed wonderful to me, and perhaps they were.

Once, after a particularly mysterious performance of *Beauty and the Beast* in a barn in which the Beast's roars were made to echo horribly in the hayloft above the stage, and as we made our way home again through streets barely visible beneath the stars, I asked my father which came first: plays or books? He thought the plays came first, the books after. And I asked him: If a thing on the great stage of *la Comédie Française* was as "real" as he said it was, would the play have a life of its own within one's head ever after? He told me yes:

173

just as a book lives on in the mind, mutable as the weather of one's moods. And what about the *actors?* I marveled. What happens to *their* memories? Are they swept away by the miracles they evoke? Does the painted scenery take on the colors of reality? Do the actors become all the people they have pretended to be? Father said: "Just as you, dear child, are all those beings and people you have read about in your fairy books and yet always yourself and none other, so it is with the actors."

—How did you come to the attention of La Comtesse Cafaggiolo?

—I was a gifted painter, even as a child, and so at the age of fourteen apprenticed to Désgrieux on the Rue Grenelle. There I learned my craft of fan-making and was trusted with the decoration of paper and velum fans, doing drawings in ink and paintings in the Chinese manner. One day Comtesse Cafaggiolo came into the atelier and fell in love with one of these. It showed a delicious little nude reclining on a divan, in a garden filled with curiously convoluted trees and flowering shrubs, snakes and elephants and snails . . . O! I can't recall all I'd crowded onto the mount of that fan! Shortly thereafter she returned to take me to her yellow room where I executed the paintings earlier described. Charmed by my capacities, she insisted I make use of her excellent library. I read avidly each night as, indeed, I always had, and became an obsessive bibliophile. So that all these years later, it should not come as a surprise that a humble fan-maker assists a notorious writer in the production of his book!

—Before we get to this book, has Sade's manner changed during his most recent incarceration?

—He is often preoccupied with food. For example, for several months his conversation consisted of little more than descriptive lists of ideal kitchens. He described ovens roasting day and night, ovens large enough to hold an ox: "I would have my cooks roast an ox stuffed with a pig, the pig stuffed with a turkey, the turkey with a duck, the duck with a pigeon, the pigeon with an ortolan." Along with the massive ovens, these fantasy kitchens contained great fireplaces fitted out with spits: "Sixteen spits all revolving night and day above a good, heaping mound of glowing embers, these to be attended by eight young roasting cooks, one for two spits, each naked because of the kitchen's hellish heat. Each spit will hold three geese, sausages, sides of beef, sides of bacon. In the bakery: Boys kneading dough day and night, producing buns by the hour, churning butter when otherwise not in service—"

—De Sade is hungry in prison?

—Do you need to ask? Famished . . . famished, citizen! He described maidens, not older than nine, shelling peas and beans, the bowls held between their thighs. White porcelain bowls, the maidens dressed in white, wearing white whimples. And scourers to scour the pans: saucepans—small, medium and large. To be made of copper. To be scoured with sand. These scourers to wear aprons, citizen, and nothing else. "Whipped to a frenzy," Sade said, "they will scour like nobody's business."

—All this was intended to evoke your laughter?

—My friend's *intentions* have always been obscure to me. It is true he walks a fine line between comedy and terror.

—Can you tell more?

—Female cooks, big Dutch women wielding spoons—great wooden spoons as tall as brooms and good for flogging. Cupboards bursting with chinaware, silver services, pewter tankards for beer, crystal glasses for each sort of wine; a cellar brimming with barrels and bottles; the kitchen rafters groaning under the weight of hams. Dewy-cheeked goatherds too young to have beards wearing brief leathers trooping into the kitchen by the dozens each one carrying a young goat slung over his back. Male cooks in droves gutting the corpses of animals still bleating: lambs, wild boar, venison; in every corner baskets gorged with onions; gravies bubbling in cauldrons; the dining table heaving beneath spun sugar palaces crepitating in the light of blazing candelabra and everywhere freshly cut flowers. Servants running to and fro panting with exhaustion, carrying pyramids of sweetmeats on trays of gold: rare oriental things soaking in honey, stuffed with pistachios. Marzipans in the forms of pagodas and clocks.

Every six hours a group of fresh scrubbers arrive to clean the floor of grease and blood and cinders. For thirty minutes on their knees, these, in a lather, purify the place as the cooks, their assistants, the butchers and bakers, the goatherds and postulants bathe in tubs supplied for this purpose and in full view of the diners whose feasting is eternal. Sparkling clean they return to their tasks with renewed purpose and vigor: quartering cows, skewering birds, scaling fish, glazing onions, threading cranberries, boiling jams, stirring tripe, stuffing geese, slicing pies, truffling goose liver, braising brains, tendering soufflés, jellying eggs, shucking oysters, puréeing chestnuts, larding sweetbreads, crumbling fried smelts, grinding coffee, building pyramids of little cheeses, filling puff pastry with cream, steaming artichokes, dressing asparagus, breading cutlets, making anchovy butter and frangipani and little savory *croustades,* and gutting crabs, preparing cuckoos and thrushes in pie and cucumbers in cream, icing pineapples, lining tartlet tins with pastry dough, larding saddle of hare . . . He also asked me to draw for him a number of gastronomic maps.

—(*The interrogator looks confused.*)

—The map of Corsica shows the regions for olives, chestnuts, lemons, lobster; for polenta, eels, the best roast partridge, cheese and sautéed kid; the map of Gascony shows the places where one may eat duck liver braised with grapes or a terrific soup of goose giblets.

—Is that all?

—Only the beginning! He invented a "Blasphemous Cuisine" superior, said he, to all other until contrary proof, a cuisine that is also a voluntary eccentricity born of legitimate rage.

—Explain.

—Sade invented a subterranean kitchen, a somber kitchen illumined by lanterns lit with grease; a room as black as the devil's arsehole; a chaotic, a demonic sanctuary licked by the fires of eternal ovens, ovens belching flames and smoke; a kitchen like a delirium, a blasphemous laboratory animated by nervous irritation, insatiable appetites; in other words: a kitchen in which to prepare cuisine of righteous anger.

These are recipes of his invention: A Pope, massaged by thirty sturdy choirboys for six months and rubbed down daily with salt, fed on soup made of milk, thyme, honey and buttered toast, is roasted in the classic manner stuffed with a *hachis de cardinal* and served with the truffled liver of a Jesuit and a *soufflé d'abesse.* The whole generously peppered and garnished with capers.

—(*Shouting above an approving rumpus in the room.*) All this is grotesque beyond belief!

—Recall that Sade has often been in isolation, fed on brown water and black bread. Wildly hungry and enraged, he is the victim of his own fathomless spite. Do not forget, citizen, he was fabulating, only. Such a meal was never prepared, never served, never eaten. But citizen—it is near midnight. Does the Comité never sleep?

TWO

Amie—

*Up here in my eyrie I consider the facts, those
five days in September when Satan, disguised
as a citizen, ruled Paris. And if the bodies of
the victims are rotting away in their beds of
lime and straw, if the courtyards are washed
clean of blood and the gardens
weeded of eyes and teeth; if,*
*already, the world—always so
eager to forget—is forgetting,
I, Donatien de Sade, remember.
I remember how a vinegar-
maker named Damiens cut the
throat of a general before cutting
out his heart, and how he put it to
his lips—Ah! The exemplary Maya gesture!
How a flowergirl was eviscerated and the
wound made into the hearth which roasted
her alive; how a child was told to bite the
lips of corpses; how one Mlle. de Sombreuil
was given a glass of human blood to drink;
how the face of the King's valet was burned
with torches; how one M. de Maussabre was
smoked in his own chimney; how the children
incarcerated in la Bicêtre were so brutally
raped their corpses were not recognizable; and
how the clothes of the victims taken from the
corpses were carefully washed, mended and
pressed and put up for sale! The Revolution,
ma mie, shall pay for itself. And I remember,
hélas, I shall never forget, how my cousin*

Stanislas, that gentle boy, was thrown from a window the night of August tenth; how his body, broken on the street, was torn apart by the crowd. All night the bells sounded—I hear them even now. The bells of massacre. The bells of rage. "What do you expect?" Danton— all jowl and black bile—said to the Comte de Ségur. "We are dogs, dogs born in the gutter."

Already, although blood continues to spill and the trees of Paris are daily watered with tears, there are those who would say all this never happened, that the trials and executions are orderly, silent and fair; that such stories— the head of Mme. de Lamballe exhibited on a pike, of M. de Montmorin impaled and carried to the National Assembly for display—are false, the fables so dear to the "popular imagination." Well, then, I ask you: If this is so, why am I, whose imagination is clearly as "popular" as the next man's, why am I still locked away?

There are days when horror has me feeling fortunate to be secreted in my tower, unseen, an all-seeing eye, remembering yet seemingly forgotten. When I leave my eyrie at last, spring will have come again, perhaps, and the cobbles of the killing  *yards washed clean by April showers. Sometimes my tomb feels like home! For one thing, I needn't go to the window if I don't want to; I need not listen for the blade, but instead, plug my ears and loudly hum; I can, like a wasp in his nest high above the world, get myself thoroughly drunk on honey. Which reminds me: I ate all the pastilles. I shall lose my teeth; no matter. Like Danton, "I don't give a fuck." What will be left to bite into? Without its kings France will be as unsavory as America. France too, is to be run by*

merchants. Merchants! I have met some—
good number—in jail. Their notion of
beauty is forgery; their idea of virtue,
counterfeit; their hearts are in deficit;
their interests, simple; their pricks as
dog-eared and limp as old banknotes.
Welcome to the New Century! We
shall tumble into it like frightened
rats tumble into a sewer. And the
horrors that will be done in the
name of Prosperity will make all
the corrupt castles of my mind
look like little more than the idle
thoughts of a cloistered priest—and
the excesses of Landa among the Maya
of the Yucatán, a mere drop of oil in a
forest on fire.

    Speaking of fire: Today in my idleness
I imagined a fan that could be ignited
by a tear. Can such a thing be?
                    Sade

—And what did you answer?

—I answered that such a thing is surely possible, like the *tunica molesta*—the shirts earlier described, I could easily imagine a fan treated with volatile poisons.

—Such as?

—Sulphur. Pitch. Naphtha and quicklime. One drop of rain, and yes, a tear, could transform the fan into a torch. If the one who held the fan wore garments whitened or fixed with lime, why, in no time, he would be blazing like a pillar of fire!

—And did you make the fan?

—Yes.

—Evidence of your complicity in his murderous operations!

—*(The fan-maker's brilliant laughter fills the chamber with light.)* I once made Sade a fan of horn cut to resemble a turreted fortress—an amusement to lighten his confinement. The fan was *ajouré*—as are the defense walls of a castle. And I once made him a

179

fan of lady fingers decorated with icing; the *panaches* were made of hard candy. The combustile fan was an experiment, you see. For the book. The book about Landa in the Yucatán. I made it only to see if it were possible. Then I informed him the thing had been done: A drop of water had set it to smolder, it quickly caught fire, blazed for an instant and was gone. And I thought that this combustible fan was like a person, like love itself. These, too, blaze briefly.

—(*Bewildered. As if to himself.*) How do you come up with such ideas?

—It is the nature of thought, is it not, to come up with ideas? Although Sade likes to say "I've come down with a terrible idea," the way others say "I've come down with a cold." My father, on the other hand, liked to "catch thoughts" as if the brain were a deep pool and thinking akin to fishing. But then, he was a fisherman of sorts; he fished for old books and papers, just as my mother angled for rags, or rather, the beautiful things she was able, with a gesture and a word, to reduce to rags in the owner's eyes.

—(*To himself:* Mother was an illusionist. *He writes this down.*)

—From her I inherited the capacity to, when necessary, forge ahead thoughtlessly; from my father the capacity to think. When I was a girl he had me study nature, the visible and the hidden; he had me study languages, the old and the new, so that I should appreciate the multiple paths thinking takes. I read philosophy; I have a knowledge of numbers; I am able to name not only the birds and the stars, but also the cats—

—The cats!

—Cats! Yes! Such as Tom, Tiger, Tortoise-shell, Mouser.

> *Lisette!* (*This shouted from the assembled crowd.*)
> *Grisette!* (*The names of cats cut loose from all corners.*)
> *Bandouille!*
> *Ecu!*
> *Chou Gras!*
> *Miou!*
> *La Chosette!*
> *Ma Jolie!*
> *Hollofernes!*
> *Bandouille!*

—*Silence!* One might as well be among wizards and witches! (*The president of the Comité claps his hands until order is restored.*) You learned nothing from your mother?

—In our brief time together ... (*Her eyes darken, and for a moment, the fan-maker, although standing, appears to grow smaller.*) She ... taught me to love beautiful forms and to recognize a free spirit when I see one. From her I inherited a tolerance for ... difficulty, and above all, how to inhabit time; how *not* to chew over losses.

—A thing your friend Sade would do well to master!

—But hard to master in *captivity!* Kept in a tower like a toad in a jar! To tell the truth, Sade's capacity to think is often badly scrambled by the inevitable violence of his moods.

"To calm the clatter in my skull," he said to me not long ago, "to quiet my hissing nerves, to soothe my accursed piles, I become a brainless ticking; I count the seconds passing, the minutes and the hours. To this sum," he said, "I add the ciphers my own body affords me: ten fingers, toes all pale as candles, the tongue as black as a bad potato, the nose like a bruised pear, two ears like broken umbrellas, one brain reduced to perpetual stupidity, a mood like Job's, one bunion, a pair of creaky knees, a belly swollen like a wet haystack, a cock as irritable as a caged parrot, balls like last week's porridge, teeth as untrustworthy as dice, an anus with a mind of its own. I use this number to divide my days spent in this tower, and then, by subtracting the sum of heads fallen since dawn, of letters received, dreams dreamed, of grains of salt scattered from a hard roll to my plate, of shadows leaking down the walls—I come up with the exact time to the minute of my release. Or of your next visit, beloved Comet in the Grim Sky of my Solitude. Also, the moment when Robespierre will be undone. This information I depend upon to reassure myself that I will one day feel the cobbles of the street beneath my feet; feel the rain beat against my joyous, my uplifted face; feel the caress of another human being; know the taste of another's lips; kiss the nape of a beloved neck; feel the scratch of a cat's tongue on palm; will awaken to the crowing of a cock, and fall asleep to the sound of mourning doves cooing, cooing in the trees.

"The loss of the world has me reeling with longing. Locked away I have come to know that the world is a food; it nourishes us. Without it the soul starves. I feel like Gulliver caged among giants;

181

sprawling in all directions, abundance is unattainable. You say they call me the 'Apostle of Nothingness.' But I am, if I am anything, the 'Apostle of Muchness,' the 'High Pope of Plenty and of Excess in Everything.' And if all my rights have been taken from me but one—the right to dream—I dream excessively. If they don't like it, they will have to chop off my head!

"My pen is the key to a fantastic bordello, and once the gate is opened, it ejaculates a bloody ink. The virgin paper set to shriek evokes worlds heretofore unknown: eruptive, incorruptible, suffocating."

—And brutal.

—Yes, citizen. As brutal as the world burning around us. Sade offers a mirror. I dare you to have the courage to gaze into it. (*The fan-maker has totally recovered her aplomb. She is standing with her hands on her hips.*)

—You dare me? (*He laughs, bitterly.*) Else—

—Else perish, perhaps.

—Mark my words, citizen. It is you who shall do the perishing. Now. Continue without irony, if you please. What else did Sade say?

—He said: (*Undaunted. Raising her voice.*) "And I don't give a fuck if my inventions, unlike the guillotine, are not 'useful.'" Sade is after new thoughts, you see. Thoughts no one has ever set to paper. Radical thoughts. "I am not simply dusting off the furniture!" he said. "When my pen starts thrashing it's like fucking a whore in the den of a famished lion. The world is brimming with plaster replicas and the point is to smash them to bits, to create an upheaval so acute it cannot be anticipated nor resisted. I am after Vertigo," Sade said. "I am wanting a world in which the Forbidden Fruit is ascendant and rises just as the Old Laws fall—yes! Even the Law of Gravity."

Sade was educated by the Jesuits who, as you must know, punish their charges—and often violently—for misdemeanors large and small, real and imaginary. One particularly crazed master whom the students called "the Broom" forced his boys to stand in a circle and thrash one another with whatever was at hand, thus forming an infernal circle, what Sade calls "The Broom's Infernal Machine." "It seemed to me," Sade said, "that we had become—the Broom, the other boys and I—a gear in the diabolic mechanism that makes the world spin. Night after night, the Broom sent us to our beds in pain, the lower part of our bodies covered with welts. Night after night I tossed about in a high fever caused by rage and humiliation: a murderous rage. We had heard of a Jesuit's throat being slashed by a boy who could no more bear the blows he received. Among ourselves, we spoke of little else.

"It seemed to me the functioning of the universe—planets in orbit about the sun and moons about the planets—depended upon the torture inflicted upon us. I was convinced that the machine was eternal, that the torture would never end, that its end would cause the world to end. And then I wanted that desperately: wanted the world to end in a cataclysm of fire!" Already then, Sade, like Landa, longed for a holocaust.

"The night I read the transcripts you brought me of the case brought against Landa," Sade continued, "and reviewing the outrages he had perpetrated in the Yucatán, I had a nightmare. I dreamed that I was once again taking part in the Broom's circle of fire. As I and the other boys ran howling like beasts, weeping and foaming, we produced so much heat, so much *perpetual heat* that suddenly the Broom's robes caught fire, the floor and walls caught fire, and then, we too, were burning! We formed a ball of flame that soared up into the sky: yellow and red, the colors of pus and blood.

"Beneath us a crowd had gathered, everyone gazing up with astonishment. 'A second sun!' they cried. 'What will become of us?' An astronomer was called and arrived riding a broom. I stood among the crowd and saw that the stars on his peaked hat were peeling off. Pointing at the two suns with his wand he shouted stridently: 'Let us now speculate upon the inevitable disaster!'

"I believe," Sade said to me, "that thanks to this dream I have seen the face of Truth. A hideous face, a monstrous face, eaten away by spite. Truth is a leper banished from the hearts of men and rotting away in exile. All that is left is corruption, a bad smell, some unnameable pieces of what was once a thing lucent and good. All that is left is a stench at the bottom of a tomb." He told me:

"I have seen a beauty's cunt worn like a fur collar; seen the bodies of wags, innocent of every crime but vanity cut into pieces and these carried aloft like filthy flags up and down the streets of Paris. I have seen carts in the night taking bodies to graves marked only by a stench. And I ask myself again and again: Is this the virtuous violence of which we dreamed? But what else could we expect from the rabble that continues to believe in warlocks and wizards and leper kings who bathe in the blood of babes and whisper that the nobility stuffs itself on roasted peasant boys—an extravagant piece of nonsense when you consider that the famished peasants don't have a spoonful of marrow or meat to be found on them anywhere but, perhaps, between their ears.

"Everything is clear now," Sade said to me just the other day. "The plan has always been to expel me first and eat me after. In other words, like a dog, the Revolution eats its own droppings and it is only a matter of time before I will be on my knees with my own head between its jaws. Until then I dream the same dreams as Landa, that bastard son of the Inquisition. I share that monster's fever; I am damned with the same *singularity*.

"The devastation ahead is immeasurable. I long for it night and day. Like Landa," he concluded, "I long for the disappearance of things."

THREE

—Do you continue to work on *Rue Grenelle*?

—Several years after my apprenticeship was completed, I found a shop on *Rue de Bout-du-Monde* and set up on my own. The place had seen the production of marzipan and still smelled of sugar and almonds. Better still, a swan was carved above the door. The first thing I did was to make a sign of tin in the shape of a fan which I painted with a picture of a red swan, and this I hung over the street. I hired a girl to build the skeletons (for by then the guild rules had changed) and hired another, a beggar and an orphan whose father had died of beriberi and whose mother of chagrin, and who, once her face was scrubbed, proved dazzling. She was quick as a whip and became a great favorite, for she knew when and to whom to show the fan with double meanings, the fan with two faces or three. She was always smiling and this is why Sade called her "La Fentine"—a name she assumes to this day with good humor, as she does all else.

"It's a clean living," La Fentine says of fan-making; you spend the day flirting without risk, you drink all the tea you want and you never, ever need to stand about in the wind and rain. All sorts come into the atelier, but barbers never do, nor beggars. So I can forget that once, because of ill fortune, I lived in the gutter like a dog."

La Fentine knew how to read in the eyes of the wealthy libertine in search of rarities, and in the secret thoughts of the inexperienced maiden who wants a fan with which to inflame the youth she desires. My atelier is called "The Red Swan at the World's End" and my motto, painted in a fair red color above the door, is:

> *Here Beauty and Laughter*
> *Rule all day and after*

I specialize in eccentricities, in artificial magic—such as anamorphic erotica—and imaginary landscapes: Chinese pyramids and jungle temples, a map of the world under water, hanging gardens filled with birds and grottoes illuminated by volcanic fire. There is no other atelier in Paris where you may buy a fan painted with the heraldic jaguar of the New World which appears to the initiated in narcotic-induced dreams. Painted on green silk, he leaps across the entire leaf, from left to right.

La Fentine has turned out to be a gifted fan-maker. She and I have together produced a lithographic series of two-faced fans: The seasons are painted on the back and the games of love on the front. Our "Diableries" are very popular; surely you have seen these, and our "Tables of Paris" with their recipe on one side and lovers at table on the other.

We are inspired by the Encyclopedia, but also our memories and inclinations, those potencies that animated our childhood and the mystery of our adolescence. We believe this is why our fans are so popular, but also why we come to the attention of the Lieutenant General of the Police so often. Scholars collect our fans, you see, and they are often of the most vociferous sort. They engage in animated talk just outside the shop, talk the Lieutenant thinks is seditious, and this only because he is too much of a numbskull to understand it. La Fentine likes to joke that the weather just outside our door is unlike that of the rest of Paris: "Hot, steamy, tropical!"

The shop is also a favorite haunt of literary madmen, some of them authentic visionaries, and others out of their minds. One of them, a surgeon, has been stunned by hallucinations ever since he was a child. He claims to have seen the Celestial Father, the Celestial Mother, Satan, Christ on the Cross and a host of Archangels. He came to us years ago to buy a fan large enough to hide him from the eyes of demons, to protect him from the devouring abyss of their glances, from the sulphur they farted in his face, to keep his own eyes safe from the appearances of intangible houris so captivating he feared his cock would run off with his balls, leaving him behind.

The scholars love to tease him, and on more than one occasion have created elaborate hoaxes with La Fentine's help. La Fentine, dressed in white velvet and black tulle wings, gilded horns stuck to her forehead with library paste, her lips roughed scarlet, chased him around the quarter shouting verses from the *Song of Songs:*

> Let him kiss me
> With the kisses of his mouth!

One of the scholars is a ventriloquist. You can well imagine the confusion he stirs up in the poor surgeon's brain when ravens cry: "Save the wax in your ears, Doctor! For all that is Worldly is Divine!" Or, mournfully: "He will perish forever, like his own dung."

Another of the literary madmen—how they flourish in our age!—is the author of a pamphlet in which he demonstrates that the brain of God is a hive-cot swarming with thoughts—all of which take form in the material world. "God likes to think of fleas," he says. He, too, has been hocussed by the scholars who buzz and hum whenever he is near, to convince him he is a party to the hizz of Celestial Mind. Thus having puffed him, they parade him up and down the streets of Paris as a Marvel.

I've always loved to laugh and so allow this foolery; I've always loved a game. Long ago when I was such a child, really, and for a brief but delicious time in the care of the Countess Cafaggiolo, she would propose a game that struck me for its singularity. We would each begin the day with a blank sheet of paper and write down all the things that struck us as unusual, fearsome or droll: the shape of a cloud, the markings on a moth; we also noted who among the criers passed first before the gate. If it was the scissor-and-knife man the Countess would shudder: "Here's an evil start to the day!" But when the beauty who sold *eau de vie* with cherries called out in her pretty way, *"La Vie!, La Vie!,"* the Countess was elated.

My favorite crier was the butcher's daughter, Césarine, who arrived with a basket, a brazier and a chop impaled on a fork held up for all to see. With a voice as rich as a bowl of tripe she'd sing:

> Just like the one
> God stole from Adam!
> Buy one for yourself, Sir,
> and one for your Madame.

—and she'd grill it for you there and then.

We also evolved our game of Heaven and Hell. I painted the itinerary on foolscap. The first player to reach Heaven got to embrace the Virgin Mary (Sade's conceit). Torquemada, Heinrich Kramer and

James Sprenger, or the Pope of his choice. As you can see, to win was also to lose. Hell was better. You lost the game but got to screw any Jew who piqued your fancy, pantheists and Manicheans, Ethiopians and Albigensians!

—Would you read this letter, citizen.

—I will. (*She takes up the letter.*)

Ma belle olive, ma Verte,

I'm so gloomy! My breeches are worn through,
my stockings in shreds, I've no ribbon for
what's left of my hair and to tell the truth I
long for something showy, a new silk coat,
green and white, with a canary yellow lining.
To slip on such a thing in the morning, grab
one's favorite walking stick and be off! But I'd
need clean linens, a fine shirt and all the rest,
else, even in here, and if only to myself, not to
look the fool. Today to exorcise my demons, I
itemized the things I used to wear—how I'd
fuss over my buttons! They'd have to be
inspired. My favorites were round, fronted
with glass; each one contained a spanking
green scarab and all were perfect specimens. I
had a silk waistcoat made up to match with
an obelisk embroidered on each side, a sphynx
at the heart. I called it "My Enigma."
    I had another—this one striped gold and
pink with a tender green lining. The buttons
were Chinese—pink jade carved to resemble
naked ladies. This one I named "The China
Peach." A fellow would be beheaded in a trice
if he walked about dressed like that now.
    These days, ma Verte, I have the imagina-
tion of a peasant. If a hag tumbled out of her
haystack and onto my chamberpot offering me
three wishes, I fear I would be as foolish as the
beggar who wished for sausage. You know
what happens next:
    The fool's wife, a shrew and a scold cries:
"You Pope's pink arsehole! You Knight of the

187

*Order of Screwup! What a turd in a pisspot
you are asking for sausage when we could
have feasted on roast pig! Or even the King's
own fesses smoked like hams! I've not had a
square meal since I married you, and now,
when you get the chance, all you come up
with is a stool the consistency of a newborn's
caca to share between the two of us! What a
miserable goat's anal fissure you are!"*

*As you can imagine, this enrages the poor
bonehead. It enrages him so much he picks the
thing up between finger and thumb and cries:*

*"I wish this sausage were stuck up this slut's
nose!" And at once it is. She, of course, is even
angrier than she was—if such a thing can be
imagined.*

*"You miserable wretch!" she screams,
the ignominious piece of tripe wagging like
a puppy's tail and causing her to sneeze—
and each time she sneezes she lets go a
triple salute of musketry loud enough and hot
enough to cause sunspots and other meteoro-
logical disturbances—"You Bishop's bastard
with a stool for a brain! I will hound you 'til
you shit pea soup and hamhocks, you dead
camel!" And on and on until he cries:*

*"I wish this shrew were as she was before!"
And so she is, and so they are—the two of
them as miserable as they were.*

*Ah! I too, have used up all my wishes
foolishly! My youth, my passion, my
promise. Today nothing much remains
but fever that prodded by unrequited
appetite summons a Satanic sauerkraut
renewing itself as it is eaten, not one
sausage crowning the cabbage heap, but
forty-four:*

*Frankfurterwürste,
saveloys,
crépinettes,
sheep's gut würstchen,*

pig's brain sausage,
madrilènes,
Polish sausage,
Strasbourg sausage
chorizo,
boudin blanc,
boudin noir,
bite d'évêque
smoked boudin,
marrow sausage,
truffled goose liver sausage in the
    manner of Mlle. de Saint Phallier,
rindfleischkochwürste,
sausage made from calf's mesentery,
dry Lyons sausage,
Saucisson parisien,
Genoa salami—
and so on and so forth. But these are mere
garnishes! For gleaming like smiles, bedded
down like houris from within the mound of
glistening cabbage which rises like the tits of
la Doulce France in my mind's eye, are chunks
of fat-studded pork loin smoked and fresh,
grilled and boiled and slices of fried bacon as
thin as dictionaries, and pork chops broad
enough to sail the Seine on, and goose, and
meatballs studded with onions, and onions
as glazed as the eyes of slaughtered cows,
and lastly—and thanks to Parmentier
who has assured us that potatoes may
be eaten with impunity, that rather
than thin the blood they thicken
it, strengthening muscle and bone,
soothing the brain yet animating the
intellect—a steaming heap of Dutch potatoes,
yellow as butter, sausage-shaped, sweet as
honey and as firm as my buttocks once
were and are no more.

    I'd settle for a macaroon. When I was a
little boy I was given a large macaroon stuck
with angelica and gilded with gold leaf. The

nuns who made it had put in all of their
misdirected sweetness, and I could tell that as
they pounded the almonds and sugar together
in the mortar they had dreamed of love. I
devoured it quickly and then, because it was
eaten, threw a tantrum—a rage as terrible as
that initial rage of infancy when I rode poor
Louis the way the Devil is said to ride the
damned, my teeth at his neck, my fists
pounding his ears; had I not been stopped
I might have torn out his eyes! Sometimes, I
long to tear out the eyes of those who keep me
here and everyone else into the bargain! To
lard my victims with their own eyes!

It is true that I have been savage, I have
savaged, I have oceloted *a number of people;*
it is true I was once an ocelot disguised in
a dove grey coat and carrying a perfumed
fan. And that, in my fury, the fury that has
hounded me all my life, I dreamed of the
extinction of the human race. But I never
killed a soul, I never did to anyone more than
the Broom did to me. Yet I languish here and
the Broom roams free.

The libertine acts upon his instincts
knowing that the world is without God and
his actions are impelled by his nature. The
corrupt ecclesiastic acts in the name of God
to justify, as Landa did, the worst crimes.
The crimes done in God's name are always the
worst, crimes that the libertine only imagines
in his black room lit by fairy lights.

Fairy lights! The words evoke the lucent
years of infancy when the world was a place
of constant amazement, like Lilliput. It is
true I was a spoiled brat. (I was once given an
entire breakfast service made of praline—cups,
dishes, spoons and forks—to coax me to table.)
But even such a boy, despite swamped nerves
and fits of rage (and what boy would not be
frenzied by a mother who spent every waking

190

hour on her knees sucking up to priests
while his father was forever falling all over
the king!)—even such a boy is eager for
astonishment.

Nothing is known of my birth; that is to
say nothing that is known is true. Because
Mother's oyster was too tightly shut to be
seeded, and Father, just like the One in
Heaven, no more than an Absence, I was
not born in the usual way.

There are numerous and conflicting stories
to explain the stubborn fact of my existence:

1. While Mother was at Mass, I tumbled
from the priest's thurible and into the cleft of
her bosom;

2. I slipped out of her missal and onto
her lap;

3. When on her knees looking for the
scattered beads of her rosary, she heard me
chirrup from under the pew.

But the true story is this one: My buttocking
father, warming his balls in a brothel, took it
into his head that he needed a son to fortify
his line, animate his eye, stimulate his heart
and afford him pocket in his decrepitude. Thus
like Minerva, it was my fatal destiny to have
been born of thought, to tumble from my
father's brain into his ear and from there onto
the rump of a whore. This prodigy he was able
to conceal, for I was no bigger than a grain of
pepper. He slipped me into his snuff box and
took me to my mother who left her
Paternosters long enough to cover my nudity
with the shell of a pea and to put me to rock
on the leaf of a geranium. Then she lulled me
with her papist melodies which, to tell the
truth, I tolerated because I had no choice. This
one fact explains why I was such a fussy baby,
for if other infants are quieted with doggeral
suited for the nursery, which makes them
laugh and think the world a clever, funny

*place, my mother's attempts were so dreary
I decided that once I knew how to speak I
would tell her to cease her canticles else
assure me a lifelong funk.*

*But mother was like the Woman I Married
who, when I asked for Masters Rabelais,
Boccaccio and Villon to entertain my mind
in gaol, sent me psaltery claptrap as convivial
as suet—the point being to keep me from
thinking. (Like priests, pious wives are made
uncomfortable by the functioning of grey
matter—that of others and their own.)*

*At the age of four I decided that if God did
not want me to think, I'd go to the Devil. And
so it came to pass: I was made to spend my
life pissing my heart out in prison! If this
makes sense, then mankind should be ruled
by imbeciles, which any fool will tell you* is
not the case. *One of my fiercest enemies says:
"Sade fills the heads of the innocent with
ideas." I should think so! "And ideas," this*

*bees' barber continues, "are contagious."
I should hope so! But I ask you: Since the
church hates pleasure as much as it hates
thought, why has God given us brains and,
Heaven help us, a pair of* fesses?

Brains and les fesses *. . . I venerate both. To
my way of thinking, the one leads inevitably
back to the other. They circle each other like
amorous butterflies. Brains and* les fesses!
These are our most precious possessions

192

The Bible is a pile of dung. I ask you: Is it
coherent? The words are recognizable: Nouns,
adjectives and verbs parade across the page
like ants on their way to a moldering cracker.
But the ideas are so incongruous they might
as well be written down in frass. The one
thoughtful moment is Eve's. Eve the mother
of Juliette. Eve who never asks "Why have
you forsaken me?" but who walks out of
Eden and climbs into bed. Eve who, in full
knowledge, fucks and engenders a world.
When as a child I read about that instance
in Eden when tyranny was subverted, that
exemplary moment, I cried out, "Eve was
right!" and I hurled the book across the room.
For this I was whipped and so it was revealed:
Les fesses are endangered by the functioning
brain.

My earliest memories are not of hired
buffoons or of riding pig-a-back upon a poor
wretch hired for that service, but of Mme. de
Roussillon dressed in spangles and telling
stories in a hushed voice; in one Gargantua
eats a salad of pilgrims and in another
Gulliver dances a jig for a queen the size of
Cheops. Later, after I nearly ripped the Prince
to shreds (he refused to play horsey unless I
played the horse's part), I was sent packing to
my uncle's castlekeep where I often slipped
away to rustle up some village brats all
rough and merry. I was as enchanted as
they when in the cobbler's back room, lit
only by a candle, finger shadow-figures were
made to dance upon the wall: Guignol and
highwaymen, a witch on her way to Sabbath,
La Fontaine's raven, the cheese tumbling from
its beak round as a fist, Noah swallowed by
the Whale. Thumbkin! Puss 'n Boots!

Or when Folle Blanche took us into her dark
kitchen to feed us apples and omelettes and
told us her "True Tales of the Infant Jesus," in

193

*which the son of God shared the womb with
kings and comets and camels, and who, while
still in the cradle, shat all the way to Rome
and into the Pope's face.*

Here's how Folle Blanche made an omelette:

She'd sauté her marrows in butter 'til
  sizzling.
With a splash of oil to keep them from
  scorching,
then whip her eggs 'til foaming;
(she'd take a sip of wine).

She'd add some chives chopped very fine,
sorrel, perhaps a pinch of thyme;
(she'd take a sip of wine).

Now the eggs are in the pan!
(She takes a sip of wine).
She sets them to shiver and shake to a man!
(She takes a sip of wine.)
Then roars: "Come boys! Let's sup! It's time!"

*She takes a sip of wine and sprinkles the
eggs with salt. (The poor know nothing of
pepper.) And if we eat with our fingers, we
feast like Kings of Spain.*

*The Romans made their omelettes with
honey. If a savory omelette stuffed with
lobster or ham—or both! Or both! is what
I'd sell my soul for this minute if I had one,
don't think I'd scorn the Roman sort, nor
the jam omelettes of my youth as delicate as
the thoughts of an angel amply dusted with
confectioners' sugar and disgorging strawberry
jam.*

*You'd think, wouldn't you, they'd serve eggs
in prison—a wholesome, inexpensive food and,
if your sense is in your cranium and not in
your navel, easy to prepare (although perhaps
beyond the skill of prison cooks who cannot
boil noodles to save their lives). If I had a say
in this, I'd assure each prison a poultry yard*

and, come to think of it, a trout pond, a
vegetable garden, an orchard, a milk-cow.
Better still, I'd supply each prisoner with his
own hen. She would afford companionship,
keep the cell free of vermin and provide
those precious eggs which, as every country
bumpkin knows, are at their best within the
hour of being laid—especially if they are to be
soft-boiled.

When the tedium of confinement proved too
much to bear, the prisoner might blow out his
eggs—just as the Russians do—and decorate
them. The more I think about it, the more
I like this idea. And a truly well-behaved
prisoner, although he might persist in thinking
the sorts of thoughts that got him into trouble
in the first place, might be rewarded for his
manners at least, with the gift of a goose.
If he was given a potted fruit tree, the fowl
could perch there. Its dung, falling as gravity
dictates, would fertilize the tree, producing
fruit of great quality. But for all this to be
possible, a certain demand must be met: a
large window facing south, allowing the sun
to enter and invigorate the living things inside
the cell—bird, tree and man.

Before I end this letter which has afforded
me the pleasure of your company for near the
entire afternoon, another recollection: The little feast you and La Fentine put on at The Red
Swan, the savories—aspics, crayfish, cod
tongues and barquettes—and the little cakes,
were all shaped like fans. You were little more
than a child and I a good deal your senior, yet
still a youth and unaware of mortality and
disease.

I was broke. I had squandered my wife's
dowry in pleasures too many to list, and a
beautiful woman sold her jewels to save my
skin. I believed I lived a charmed life and
knew nothing of remorse. Now, nearly thirty

*years later, I am old, broken, obese. But you—
you are at the height of your powers, still as
slender as you were although one cannot help
but notice with admiration how round your
bosom has become, and how merry your eye—
as if it could be merrier than it was then. How
lightly you carry the years,* mon amie, *yes, how
very lightly. I think it is because no one has
ruled you, not man nor god. If only you were a
libertine, what a perfect specimen of a woman
you would be!*

*You asked about my eyes, I continue to be
plagued by floaters, and this because rage
is a constant practice of mine, rage and
harrowing fatigue. Even asleep I do not rest
but continue to hear the sound a head makes
when, severed from the body, it falls into its
basket. My nightmares are terrible. I see an
eye blooming at the center of the bleeding
neck and so affected am I by the sight, I
am turned to stone, a clenched fist of black
marble raised eternally in anger against the
world. I shall replace my family's crest with
a* mano in fica: *that obscene hand making the
"fig."* Te faccio na fica! *May the evil eye do* you
no harm!

*The executions continue and it is impossible
for me to keep away. Standing at my window
I am like Andrealphus; I am liked a caged
ocelot:* I am all eyes. *I thought I was a writer
of fables; it turns out I am a writer of* facts.

Madame Realism Looks for Relief
Fiction and Installations
Lynne Tillman and *Haim Steinbach*

THE SULTRY NIGHTS stretched credulity. Madame Realism stood up from the table and pushed her chair into a corner. She had been sitting in one position for too long and had become stiff. Her body was tense, as if it, like a body of work, were on trial. What was there wasn't enough, what might be there was beyond her. She could also be a body of water, affected by an autonomous, distant moon. With tides, not nerves. Her inventiveness was a sponge, and it was rock, scissors and paper too. She wanted to play, but she didn't know which game. Then she turned on some music and danced. In motion, she produced a funny face. She jumped in the air and sang the lyrics: "I make my bed and I lie in it." She was weird, a character. I'm next to human, she supposed.

In an episode on TV Madame Realism hadn't watched, John Hightower played a poet, an educated man who lived in the country. The sun beat down on him. The field and he were parched. He didn't have many lines, and his part wasn't particularly distinguished or profound. Hightower hadn't received much attention as the poet, a kind of straw man, and even in a field where he was the only serious artist, he was overlooked. He took comfort in his uniqueness; he was one of a kind. His agent told him, you're great, an original. No one acts or interprets the way you do.

Madame Realism didn't know Hightower.

It was the second summer the Mets won the series. For Joe Loman it was the single event that made his day, his month, his year. It pierced the doom and gloom. Loman was more than a fan, he was a fanatic. He collected cards, autographs, attended every home game with his season pass. In the next world he wanted to play first or second base. He wore a Keith Hernandez pin on his shirt. To earn money Loman was a script doctor and a ghostwriter. He kept his hand on the pulse. Loman was nobody's dummy. He played his cards close to his vest and suspected everyone. He didn't work cheap.

Madame Realism didn't know Loman.

She lowered the volume, but she could still hear herself think. She opened her messy closet. She couldn't throw anything out. There were shelves, compartments, boxes, drawers. A walk-in closet big enough to live in. Inevitably, she would be inundated by stuff, suffocated by the little things in life, submerged under the weight of kitsch and kultur. Madame Realism couldn't decide what was trivial, insincere, fake, inauthentic, frivolous, superficial and gaudy; she herself was all of these. And crude, rude, stupid, obtuse and mean. And honest, real, prescient, dense, apparent, transparent, smart and beautiful. In different situations she was different things and to different people she was different people. Reality was a decision she didn't make alone.

(What's real to you isn't to me, she mentioned inadvertently in another story. Madame Realism once found herself in a Guy de Maupassant tale, the one about a man who picked up a piece of string in the road, and because he did, because he saved things, he had a bad end. One thing led to another, what had seemed a nothing operation—picking up a piece of string in the road—changed the direction of his life. That's because you never know who's watching or what the consequences are. Life and fiction, Madame Realism thought, are a series of incidents and accidents. Everyone faced the possibility of a stupid end or of being stupid to the end.)

Bending down to save something and place it in her messy closet, Madame Realism wondered if one day she would be destroyed or defeated by her own desires and devices. She accumulated. But if she saved everything, there wouldn't be a place for herself. Maybe she could expand, move or change. But most of her changes were minor adjustments. She was set on her ambiguous course.

What Madame Realism didn't treasure affected her as much as what she did.

Somewhere else Hightower's sweating and ranting:

> People tell me, "Hightower, you're not capable of being understood. You expect too much." I don't want to talk to these people because they'll tell me their opinions. I'll be forced into comic book situations worse than the one I'm living. That would be death. I'm sick because I'm conscious. I'm important, but I'm not yet considered a genius. Art isn't recognized by everyone, it's not quantifiable or practical. It's for the fine and discerning. Beauty is the basis of quality. How many people do I need to please anyway.

When Hightower finished delivering his impromptu manifesto, which he performed impeccably and with passion, he looked over the field. He was far ahead of everyone, miles ahead, and heads taller. He raced away, aghast, like Hamlet's father's ghost.

Hightower phoned Loman. They were contentious buddies from way back.

Loman's at his computer, ghosting a self-help manual:

> You're asking yourself why you get up in the morning; why you go to the same job every day; why you live alone or with the same person even though you're bored out of your mind; you're wondering why life goes on without the great highs you had when you were a teenager. You were miserable then too. But probably you don't remember. You were doing drugs. You remember that you were young and a lot of life wasn't behind you. But don't think about that. That won't help you. That's why you're down. You can't control this stuff once it gets going. Ignore it. Deny it. Just hang out, exercise, be seen, never say die, diet, don't eat fat, don't admit anything, you're not unhappy, get lifted not uplifted, make money not love. Stop complaining.

Meanwhile Madame Realism left her apartment and her closet. She still had a shelf in her mind, where she stored and catalogued experiences and memory, so she felt safe to walk outside. It was a fantastic night. She pretended she could understand other people. When she entered her favorite bar, her neighborhood bar, Madame Realism saw two characters perched on stools in her usual place. Part of her didn't like being displaced, another part invited the unexpected, unanticipated and unintended. She wanted to do the inviting, though, and the tables were turned. She was a guest.

What Madame Realism didn't apprehend might be more resistant than what she did.

Hightower and Loman were talking and gesturing, their hands and mouths furious implements. Madame Realism had to shove her barstool around and in, but finally she discovered a place at the counter. She wasn't going to let a couple of strangers push her around. She'd adjust, fight or hold her own, though she wasn't sure what that was.

Unabashedly Madame Realism listened in. She had decided years ago that if she listened only to herself, she'd go crazy.

Loman growled:

> You're too subtle, Hightower. You have to reach more people. Appeal to a wider audience. The umpire behind the plate makes calls, instant decisions. Ball, strike, he stands for the people. You think baseball can be played for one person alone? Broaden your base. You can't expect people to get your performance. You have to deliver. Be obvious. What would a baseball game be like if there was only one person in the stands. What if one player ran from base to base, and no one had any expectations about his getting a hit, or stealing second or sliding into home plate. You have to score.

Hightower glowered:

> Obvious? An umpire judges baseball. You want him to judge my performance? You think I should respond to, that's a ball, that's a strike? Not everyone in the stands likes the umpire's calls, there's a minority who argues. And some throw beer at each other. There should be a level of civilization, of civilized behavior we agree upon. Let people use dictionaries. Read the work of James Joyce. Everyone should know Shakespeare. There's excellence, standards, otherwise democracy runs amok. Raise the level, don't wallow in it. You pander to the lowest impulses. Broaden my base! Limit your baseness!

Like a wedge between the two, Madame Realism inserted herself. It was characteristic for her to jump in and sink or swim, and sometimes she did both:

> You say umpire, he says critic. You say ball game, he says theater. Who chooses the game? the umpire? the critic? Who decides on the players and the rules? I could go on and on.

Loman and Hightower looked at her. Loman thought Madame Realism struck out. She wouldn't even get to first base. Hightower dismissed her. He decided she wasn't very advanced.

Madame Realism went further:

> If I were a sonata by Bach, or a song by Courtney Love or Ray Charles, an antique hourglass or a home page on the Web, a china figurine, or a painting by Caravaggio, who decides what I mean? What makes me valuable or lets me be thrown out in the garbage? My projection isn't yours even when you and I go to the same movie.

They ignored her.

Loman raved:

> Your purity, Hightower, makes me sick. You wouldn't know what was great if it bled all over you. We're all just pitching balls or strikes. . . .

Hightower reacted:

> You want to please everybody, Loman, anybody. You have no
> eye. No taste. You know nothing of beauty or the spirit that's
> necessary for seeking truth and creating art.

Loman bellowed:

> For values, I go to the marketplace. You don't have an audi-
> ence, because you don't deserve one. Elitist!

Hightower countered:

> You disregard immutable laws that inspire all great endeav-
> ors and enduring work. Vulgarian!

Madame Realism wasn't sure what was really at stake. She'd heard
it was Western civilization. She displayed her version of the pleasure
principle:

> I seek pleasure, and I'll do anything to get it. We do anything
> to please ourselves, but we call it other names. Don't doubt
> that. I can be vicious in the pursuit of my pleasure. I fill my
> life with beauty, ugliness, happiness, despair, the cheap and
> the expensive, things are things. I need them, want them, I
> encounter them, they encounter me. I play them, they play
> me. We're all left to our own devices.

Madame Realism hated to feel that anything was insignificant. But
her performance might be another exercise in futility.

Hightower and Loman couldn't continue to ignore Madame Realism even though she was obscure to both of them. There they were—
three characters in a situation together. They came from different
places and found themselves sitting on bar stools in the same bar. It
was a dialogue or a car crash. Any one of them could have been the
piece of string, the narrator, or the man who bent down. Any one of
them could've been somewhere else or in another position.

Loman slammed his icy mug of Miller High Life on the counter:

> I'm through handling you with kid gloves, Hightower. You'll
> never be major. Face it. You think you're ahead of everyone,
> but you've lost the race. You're a loser.

Hightower raised his glass and protested ironically:

You have a mob mentality, you're trying to satisfy the lowest denominator. You speak down because you haven't an idea in your head. You're just a craven, trendy follower.

Madame Realism threw her drink to the ground. The glass shattered. Give me a break, an epistemological break, she declared. She pushed both of them away from her. They were crowding her. I don't have answers, but I need room. Her frustration showed, like a rash all over her body. I don't throw much away. I need to clear a space. You're tired, you're a couple of drunken clichés.

Hightower and Loman objected in unison: We aren't clichés. We're being unfairly caricatured.

What Madame Realism couldn't escape was bigger than she was. Madame Realism reconsidered:

> I hear your words. But did you choose them or did they just come to you? I draw and withdraw, I get drawn and I'm drawn into your argument. I try to keep my eyes open to see you, but I can't stop recognizing you as I do. I didn't organize the bar. I didn't organize your arguments. They've been around a long time. It's beyond my control, but you have become figures of

speech. And I'm a condition like you. A piece of circumstantial evidence too.

When Madame Realism came face to face with characters and notions she didn't subscribe to, like a magazine she'd never ordered, she felt surrounded or blocked. Or thrown against a brick wall. Madame Realism sometimes wanted to respond in other ways. She wanted to rid herself of some beliefs, put them away like objects in her closet or toss them out for good, but she was never sure if she did or could. Completely. For one thing, she couldn't even keep track of all her opinions, prejudices and points of view. They popped up at the weirdest moments. She couldn't always account for them. Worse, she didn't always believe her beliefs. She held some of them like a hand in cards or a script she didn't know she'd been reading. She tried to subject her ideas to analysis, doubt or possible evacuation. But every time she put one aside, or thought she did, another became bigger and moved into the vacancy. She wanted to shake free, but badly conceived and imperfect notions were clinging to her. She could smell them, like a sweet perfume named Sin.

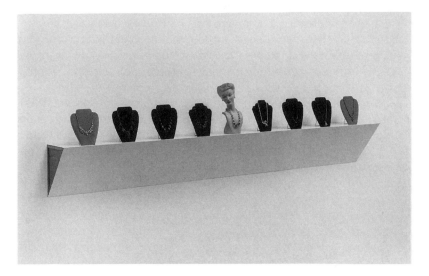

Like sin, one's own history is not original, but it weighs heavy. Madame Realism's history was original only to herself. Engrained notions were stealthy and resilient. They were permanently dyed into her woolly identity. And since she couldn't easily step outside her own situation or context, it was improbable to ask others to step outside theirs instantly. This was why, she found, most discussions took effect long after they were over. And why she saw things differently later.

Loman bought Madame Realism a drink. She never turned down a free drink, on principle. She had more trouble because of her principles than anything else. And with the drink in her hand, Madame Realism became fully part of this moment or episode. It didn't matter that it might be another déjà vu or received idea. (In some quarters this event might circulate as a joke, a performance or a case of mistaken identity.) Whatever they were, whoever they were, the three of them were relating and in some way equivalent and unequal.

Madame Realism was intoxicated. She couldn't get rid of anything. Her closet was a mess. She could deposit Hightower and Loman in it. She considered bringing them home with her, but she didn't know where'd she'd place them. She might let time settle the argument, since time wasn't necessarily on anyone's side. That might be a solution, she brightened, if time were truly faceless and without envy. But time was also an idea, and it wasn't empty or free of constraints and human engineering. Madame Realism looked at Loman and Hightower. They were still baiting each other.

Madame Realism would never know where to put everything she owned, or collected or that collected around her. She'd never know where to put everything that happened to her. She'd keep rearranging things.

Madame Realism looked around the smoky room. Stevie Winwood's "Bring Me a Higher Love" was playing on the jukebox, some people were kissing, some playing pool and others were just staring straight ahead and drinking. Madame Realism's attention settled on the startling array of glasses behind the bartender. Small, large, thin, thick, short, tall, wide, narrow, plain, fancy. All shapes and sizes. If people were containers, she wondered what kind of glass she'd be, what kind of drink. A broad-mouthed martini; a cool, narrow flute of champagne; an impatient and short shot of scotch. Or a mixed drink, a concoction served in a versatile shape. Smiling, Madame Realism bought a round for Hightower, Loman and the bartender.

She looked around the room again. She liked bars, all kinds of them. She thought she always would. They were a part of her. She hoped she'd always enjoy walking into one, taking a seat, seeing the shiny surface of the counter, watching a bartender mix a drink and listening to strangers talk bar talk. It was a relief to her.

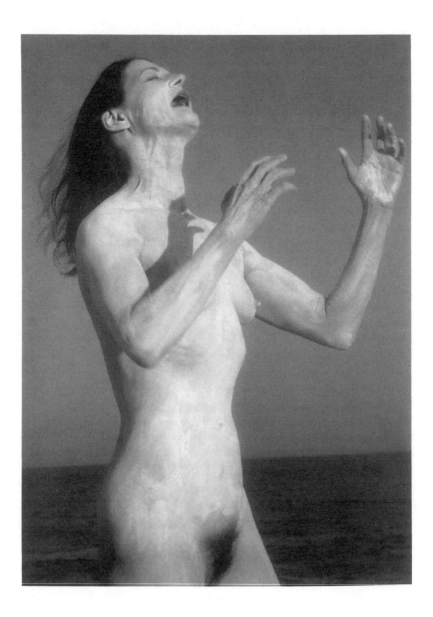

Solitaire
Diana Michener

Diana Michener

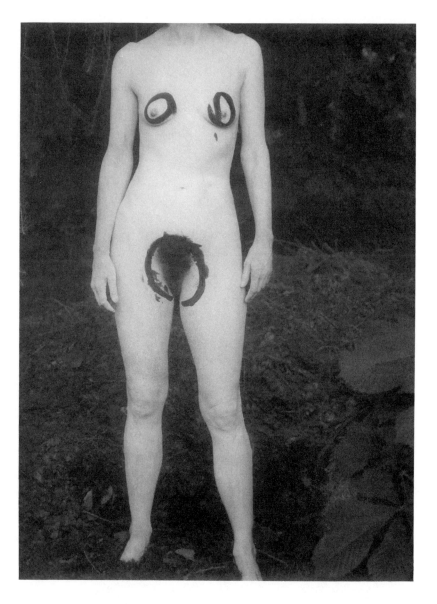

Diana Michener

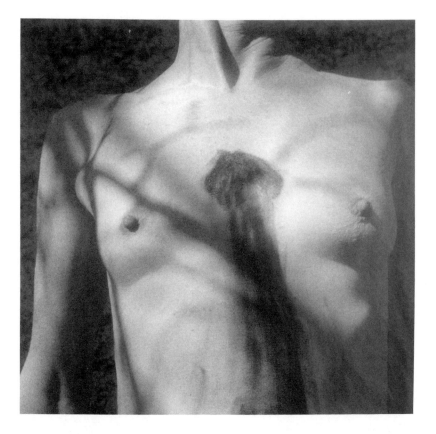

Diana Michener

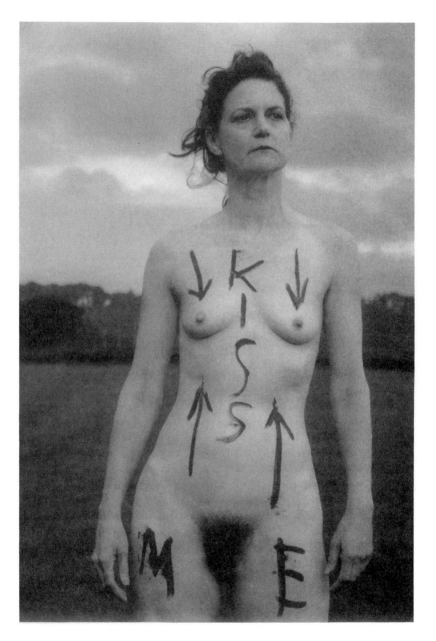

Diana Michener

218

From The Garden of Distances
Poems and Drawings
Robert Kelly and Brigitte Mahlknecht

THE RAPTURE

1.
There is a sphinx of air in the middle of the air.
Through this fleshy ring
(a ring of air)
the breath below
is squeezed
into the outer air.

And with the air so upwardly expressed
comes everything must live among the air.

beast, being, person, thing
and all the web of streets
we cast upon the stars

to make all things
diamond-dressed servants of our namefulness,

our words, names, wills, wants, needs—

through the ring of air
everything we are
is choked up into the utter
(outer)
  glory of what is there.

2.
Air is also a flower
whose petals

are the simplest
breaths.

       Air is also
a tower
from which we fall
into the actual.

Air is a rose
no one can smell,
its petals
where we hide,

its pollen mind.

3.
Sphinx is the squeezer.
Motherwombing Cervix Monster
through which one at a time
we squeeze into the waking/sleeping life

out of the life of ordinary being,

the dark plane beyond dream, beyond dreamless sleep.

Where no one sleeps.

4.
Nessun dorma
in the rapture
nessun dorma
questa notte
in dem Kino,

the story spills along the sky
we read it constantly
we think it lives our life,

no wonder we call them movie stars,
the giant persons who whisper in the sky.

5.
All we are
is projected upward,
mapped upon the sky
as stars,

   as what you are.
No wonder I want you,
to pour into you
what is your own
already by virtue of being me,

not mine, just the you of you
trapped in me,
      mapped in me
the rapture,

   mapping is how the self
   turns into other,
you are mapped on me
you find yourself
   in my topology, I also
come to you
   as in the middle—apple—
of one's eye
   the lover sees reflected
     only his own face,

we are mapped as each other,

maps of each other.

6.
The map *is* the actual terrain.

Now see the way the diverse populations
rise to meet the Rapture:
some with uplifted arms to welcome
the tortured mathematics of our change,
some with dark fists

shaken in god's face

and some, serene as oxen, curve their steps
along the exuberant contours of our fertile fields
and hope to walk to heaven.

But this is not heaven.
This is the squeeze,
                          the Sphinx
      wraps her arms around us,
           wraps her thighs around us,
every one of us,
      tight, tight,
                 and sees into our eyes
      and whispers "Dance for me,
                           dance
for me,
      for that is what my riddle is, my famous
riddle is
      no word to be answered by a word,

my riddle is a glance, a gaze
      that sees you
          all the way down
into where you are
      and makes you dance,

your dance is the answer and I squeeze it out of you,

dance for me, dance is the answer to the dance,
the air that strains upward to the air."

7.
In the last sunshine of a summer Sunday
the train station is empty, the tracks are empty,
the old iron stairs lead only to the sky

and the sky is empty,
         the numbers have forgotten how to count.

8.
One in the middle
is carrying his middle.
We carry our middles
to meddle with each other.
This goes in that
and that holds the other.

Everyone is in the middle,
everyone brings his middle
to the middle. Middle
hurries to the middle
always. Where we are.

9.
The one in the middle is carrying
some air to the air too,

the air needs air, it squeezes

down into our lungs.
                    Air makes us breathe.
It breathes us,

        we are the innocent victims of its charm.
It wakes us, it makes us
        breathe, and language
is our only way of getting back at air,

        language is revenge
                        against the natural
condition

        of which we are the lovely victims.

That is the rapture.
Sphinx against Sphinx.
        By language we deny the breath,
by breath deny the air.

Robert Kelly / Brigitte Mahlknecht

Robert Kelly / Brigitte Mahlknecht

THE INVASION

1. BUT NOT PARADISE

But it isn't paradise.
Whatever it could have been
it is not now,
      all the Fat Men have rushed in,
    or one Fat man shown in dozens of places
       trying to be himself by being everywhere,

the Fat Men are everywhere, standing with their thick legs
bowed out by the weight of their desires,
              their acquires,
they stand
on top of everything,
    they are everywhere,

and whatever anything could have meant before
now it just means what they want it to mean,

Fat Men are full of meaning, they stand around wanting
wanting more and wanting more,

taking silky meanings of grass and rough elbow meanings of rock
and turning them to what Fat Men mean, big fat meanings,
and everything turns into something they can eat or suck,

everything is just a property of lust.
And the Muses like frightened high-school girls
cluster together scared at the bottom of the world,
afraid to inspire, afraid to whisper into those fat ears
any of the ancient dignities of water and fire.

2. BIBLE LESSON

Lilith was enough. But one night she thought, if I were me, I could
be with myself. And so she thought hard and deep, so deep that she
felt something stir in the lower middle of herself, and Eve was born.

Lilith taught Eve all she knew, and then Lilith got tired of being with someone else all the time, so she withdrew, into the mountains and the deserts where later she would talk to people who came there to seek solitude. So few of them ever realized that the true name of Solitude is Lilith, herself.

Anyhow, Eve was left alone. And Eve was almost enough, but she wasn't as much enough as Lilith was, so she began wanting someone else to be there, someone she could be *me* to, someone she could call *you*.

You was such an interesting word. She said it and felt it, and felt it deeply, so deeply that in the lowest middle of her a feeling was born, and separated from her, and crouched on its own two feet and was a man. This was Adam, and he had come out of her, as people were to continue doing, forever.

Adam and Eve lived together intensely and all the time and knew nothing but the way each other changed the light and changed the dust and did everything together. And they did everything.

Then a day came when Adam just kept looking at Eve, and wanting just to be with her. I want to do nothing but be with her, he thought. This might have been the first thought Adam ever had had.

He wanted to be with her and kiss her open lips and rest his head in her armpit and lick the soft skin beside her breasts. This is enough to do, he thought, this is what *enough* really means. To be with someone and be free and still and do everything in them and with them. He wanted to lie in her thighs and consider carefully the way the wind tossed about her long, full-bodied hair.

But Eve after a time said No, if we do this, and I like to do this too, but if we do this then we will neglect our project. The garden we have all these months been trying to create will never amount to anything; the grass will dry up and the trees will bear no fruit. We have been building this beautiful Garden of the Distances, and now you want to lie down and just be close.

And Adam looked into his heart and saw that she was right. But still he wanted what he wanted, and that was the third thought he ever thought, I want what I want, and I am what I am because I want it.

Now Adam was a fat man, and wanted what he wanted. And he wanted, very much he wanted, all the tasty fruit that grew in the Garden of the Distances. And he would say in the morning to Eve, Go, get me some fruit. And every day she went and brought him a different kind. And every night they lay together, and Eve pondered their project, and Adam pondered the profile of her jaw, and how the damp skin of her neck caught the last glow of the firelight.

So it went for a long time. He knew she was right, and their garden prospered. Avenues and streets of vines and melons, boulevards lined with coffee trees and plazas crazy with cherries, in blossom now in the pink of the year.

And Adam looked at all this, and wanted it all, and wanted Eve, and said Go, bring me more fruit. And Eve rose up and went among the trees of the orchard, and Adam watched her as she went, and his eyes delighted in the sway of her walk and the line of her body, and he watched her till she was out of sight among the unfamiliar trees.

3. CAGES

Have you ever noticed how a Fat Man looks like a birdcage?
      Of course it's flesh instead of wire,
          instead of wicker.
But the shape is the same and the shape is everything. Shape
      is everything. The enclosure.
         And inside the Fat Man a small *bird*
chants with its digits (as Cégeste the Poet said),
      scattering the millet seed along the bottom of the heart.
For the man has swallowed seed
      and ground it fine as if he were a mill
         until his body is heavy and round
heavy as a millstone and he grinds all day long.
      A Fat Man is like a water mill,
         like a barn full of seed and the barn's on fire,
like a bar full of drunks making out with each other
      friendly and sweet, they meet, they sleep,
         never knowing what kind of bird is in the cage?

Joseph Cornell, Object 1941
© The Joseph and Robert Cornell Memorial Foundation

The Box Artist
Joyce Carol Oates

UNTO EVERY ONE *that hath shall be given, and he shall have abundance: but from him that hath not shall be taken away even that which he hath.* So Jesus rebukes the Box Artist who is not bold enough to seize his subject.

The Box Artist must constantly troll for happiness. La Puente. Cerritos. Olympic Boulevard. In this cruelly deprived Year of Our Lord 1935. This summer in which dried, cracked earth of the hue of baked blood is turning to dust, blown by a Santa Ana wind. Traveling the streets of Los Angeles anxious and yearning as any rejected lover. The Box Artist must seek his happiness *out there.* The Box Artist understands that happiness is chance, and always unmerited. The Box Artist understands *we must create the improbable circumstances of chance that the yet more improbable circumstances of happiness will be revealed to us.*

Cypress, Alvarado, Santa Clara. Westward, eastward. El Nido to the south, La Mirada to the east. To the west, the Pacific Ocean, which revulses me for *its vastness cannot be fitted into any box.*

The Nickel & Dime Diner on El Centro Avenue. Amid boarded-up storefronts GOING OUT OF BUSINESS! BANKRUPTCY! MUST SELL ALL! A clatter of trolleys, automobiles and trucks and the heat-haze stirred by the wind into a glowing phosphorescence of dust and grit. At El Centro and Cupertino, a building marked the Los Angeles Orphans Home Society. Weatherworn red brick set back in a large, mostly grassless lot surrounded by an eight-foot mesh-wire fence. What the eye first notices about this building is that there are few windows, especially on the uppermost third floor. These windows are tall and oddly narrow, like squinting eyes; on the first floor, the lower halves are crudely barred. Peeling white "colonial" trim, tarred roofs, rusted fire escapes and at the rear amid sand and thorny weeds the rudiments of a "playground."

A more melancholy "playground" I have never seen and I swear that it was this playground that initially drew me, and not the possibilities of the orphans—for it is rare that the children are released from their work duties to "play"—and at the time of my first visit, in the late winter of 1934, the playground was deserted.

Only by chance, at another time, did certain possibilities suggest themselves.

In the Box Artist's life of anxiety, yearning and sudden unexpected happiness there are such moments. One must only seek them without ceasing as Saint Theresa spoke of prayer without ceasing until prayer becomes the very soul, and the very soul, prayer. *It is as if the automobile makes this turn unbidden by me* onto an unpaved service road beyond the orphanage. Scrub palm trees, broom sage and hardy purple-flowering thistles coated in dust like exotic works of art. A flock of sparrows scatters at my approach.

How many weeks it has been since I discovered the Los Angeles Orphans Home. How many weeks observing the orphan-children from my automobile, hunched down beside the window in the passenger's seat. When moved to take photographs, carefully I ease open the door—carefully! the Box Artist is a master of precision. The Box Artist is a master of discretion. No one notices the Box Artist, for he is as near to invisible as any adult male, of indeterminate age and with no distinguishing physical characteristics (even my height and weight oscillate from day to day dependent upon temperature and barometric pressure), might be. My automobile attracts no suspicious eyes for it is a battered 1928 Ford, its shiny black exterior and dashing chrome worn by sun, rain, wind and wind-driven sand to this dull pewter-glow that is the very absence of color. *The Box Artist is but an eye, a pair of hands, a fierce and implacable will.*

You would identify the children of the Los Angeles Orphans Home as orphans, even from a distance, in their faded-blue clothing that fits them like smudged daubs of paint, with their worn shoes, their spindly limbs and raw scrubbed faces like the faces of wooden dolls with awkwardly fitted glassy-teary eyes. They are "children" in but a technical sense. Many of them are midget adults, with heads disproportionate to their thin bodies. Even the youngest are not "childish." Such terms—"children," "childish," "childlike"—apply solely to *wanted children.* There is a recognition of this fact, or complex of facts, in the slump of their heads and the sag of their shoulders and the limpness of their legs even when they are engaged, under no adult's supervision, in "play." (The playground is sand and concrete. A meager set of swings, only just two, the third having been broken for months; a tarnished slide; a wooden teeter-totter.) In the late morning and again in the late afternoon the orphans emerge from a rear slot of a door, trudging outside to blink in the mica-bright sunshine, dazed with exhaustion from their work duties (what these are, I can only guess) though a few of the younger and more hopeful run for a brief while and a few, always boys, as if recalling the bold maneuvers of children beyond the eight-foot mesh-wire fence, will push at one another and jostle for possession of a swing, a seat on the splintery teeter-totter.

Weeks, months. My photographs were few and infrequently inspired. Yet every time the orphans appeared, my heart leapt in hope. A scrim would be drawn, as in a film theater, and I stared, stared—but the one I sought wasn't among them. Until one afternoon, a hot Santa Ana wind blowing out of the Mojave Desert, and my eyelashes gummed with dust, I saw, I suddenly see, the Blond Child. A girl-orphan I have never seen before, yet recognize at once. *It is she. She is the one. The one the box awaits.*

In the late summer of 1935. In the earthen-floored cellar of the bungalow on Sacramento Street, East Los Angeles. Thirty-two wooden boxes stacked neatly against the walls and in each of these boxes was a "capture"—a snapshot, a small artifact, a stuffed, lifelike little bird. To the neutral observer the works of the Box Artist would be indistinguishable from trash, but each of the boxes was, to the Box Artist, a testament to those minutes, hours, sometimes days in which the box was executed. Even the relatively uninspired boxes, and there were some of these, were triumphs of a kind; they represented, to the Box Artist, the solutions to specific problems. *The box is the affliction for which only the box is the cure.*

Yet each "capture" was solitary. Each of the boxes stood apart from the others, though they were crammed together in that dank, airless space.

The one the box awaits, at last. The Blond Child, a little girl of eight or nine, swinging on one of the swings. She is new to the orphanage, at least I have never seen her before. Already in her faded-blue uniform she resembles the others—except for the fierce radiance in her face, and the speed in her little body. How desperate, flying on the swing with its crude creaking chains and hard, splintery wooden seat; how defiant, kicking and bucking, her white-knuckled hands gripping the swing above her head and her thin arms stretched taut, like a bird's wings partly wrenched from its body.

231

Both her knees are scraped and bruised. Her "dirty blond" hair is curly and snarled. Her eyes are intense, staring; her dazed soul shines through her waxy-pale skin. A beautiful child though wounded somehow, damaged. *The sorrow in being born, without love.*

She is one of them, now. The orphans of the world. Waiting to be loved. Waiting to be taken—"adopted."

I think—*I will adopt her. I will claim her!*

I will make her hurt, mangled mouth smile.

But of course, being the Box Artist, I can only take the Blond Child's photograph. And that only in stealth, hoping I won't be detected.

My heavy black box-camera is gritty with dust. It's an old camera; I am forever blowing dust off the lens, polishing it with my handkerchief. After a few minutes I become reckless and leave the protection of my automobile to squat in the dirt beside the mesh-wire fence, hoping to be hidden by tall weeds; aiming my camera with the assurance of a hunter as, oblivious of me, the Blond Child swings ever higher. Her hair is ringlets sparked with fire, her skin glints like mica, her eyes are ablaze like tiny blue jets of flame. As she swings, her skirt is bunched over her bruised knees, there's a glimpse of white beneath, much-laundered and frayed orphan's underwear it is, and her heels kick upward reckless as a colt's. The Blond Child swings carelessly off-balance, veering crooked and nearly falling from her seat as if her secret wish is to fall and crack her head on the dirty concrete. *No! no!* I whisper to her. *Don't injure yourself, the world will shortly enough do that for you.* In the creaking swing beside the Blond Child another, quite ordinary girl is swinging, not boldly at all but in a lackluster manner; an older, slump-shouldered girl, one who has been waiting to be adopted for years, and has all but given up hope. But the Blond Child is new to the orphanage. The Blond Child will never give up hope.

I promise. Someday. Something—maybe.

The Box Artist is the artist of desire. The tenderness of desire that can never be consummated.

The Box Artist plucks the child's flying image out of the air as you might pluck a feathery little bird out of the air, a canary or hummingbird, small enough to fit in your closed hand.

The heavy black box-camera grows heated with the effort. The shutter snapping! The mysterious film within, wound past the lens, imprinted with the Blond Child who is oblivious of it. (And yet, afterward I will wonder: Was she aware of me, in fact? Crouched here behind the mesh-wire fence, in a patch of dusty weeds? Was she playing a game as precocious girl-children do, watching the Box Artist through lowered eyelashes and giving no sign—except a sly little pursing of her lips?)

Until abruptly the children's "play" is over. In dispirited columns they shuffle back through the slot of a door. Someone must have called them, or a bell has rung. A matron in a dark coverall appears in the doorway, commanding the children to hurry. How strangely obedient they are, trooping back into the warehouse within; a house of unwanted wares; the emptying playground releases them without resistance. Yet, bravely, the Blond Child continues swinging, pretending not to have heard the summons. She's flying, kicking, bucking jets of blue flame leaping from her eyes, more recklessly than ever. The matron shouts at her what sounds like, "You! Get down." For another few seconds the Blond Child dares disobey, then she too gives in. Like a bird wounded in flight, she returns quickly to earth.

How forlorn, her abandoned swing.

The pathos of the *vertical, stilled* swing.

Indistinguishable now from the others—how many others, resigned, slump-headed in their faded-blue orphans' issue—the Blond Child disappears into the red-brick Los Angeles Orphans Home. My fingers continue to snap the camera's shutter as, after the death of its brain, a body may continue to thrash, to quiver, to pulse for a brief while. But at last I stop. Shaken and exhausted. My soul seems to have drained from me. Quickly, fumbling with my car keys, I prepare to leave; in a sudden terror that *the matron has seen me.* As in the past, not frequently but sometimes, occasionally, vigilant parties, invariably women, have called police to report—What? Who? What crime have I committed, with only a camera? The Box Artist is bound by no local law in the execution of his exacting art.

As I drive away in the 1928 Ford I peer anxiously into the rearview mirror. Seeing only a dust-tunnel raised in my wake.

My defense would be *the child knew me, as I knew her.*

*   *   *

For hours that evening, and then for days. In the dank earthen-floored cellar of the bungalow on Sacramento Street, East Los Angeles. A shabby house surrounded by palm trees, crude sword-shaped leaves rustling in the ceaseless maddening wind. The whisperings and murmurings of strangers *Look! look! look! look! Look what his life is.*

Yet unhurried, I develop my film, precious to me as my very soul. My pulse quickens as I contemplate the miniature images, I feel almost faint, the Blond Child so captured, so *my own.* I prepare the Box, the Box I have chosen for her measures approximately thirteen inches by nine by five; an ordinary wooden box you would say, and you'd be correct; stained from use, oil smears in the wood slats; a box scavenged by the sharp-eyed Box Artist out of a mound of trash in a drainage ditch out behind this bungalow. Eagerly then, and in excitement and fear, I select my artifacts. In honor of the Blond Child I must choose well; if I fail, she will be lost a second time.

This is my body, and this is my blood. Take ye and eat. The secret wish of all who live in their art.

After several blunders, and sleepless nights, I step back to discover that I have created a Box landscape of uncanny subterranean beauty! Coarse, earthen, primitive; of the rich sepia hue of memory. Tiny snapshot-images of the Blond Child are secreted in the Box's dark corners and beneath a heart-shaped rock covered in dried dirt that I brought back from beside the mesh-wire fence. A vividly yellow bird, canary or goldfinch, purchased from the taxidermist from whom I purchase all my creature-artifacts, is placed on top of this rock, tiny talon-claws secured by glue to the rock. With a tweezers I have managed to lift the little bird's wings from its body so that it appears about to fly away; its pert little tail feathers are at an upward angle that, too, suggests imminent flight; but never, never will the little yellow bird fly out of my Box, as the Blond Child will never fly out of my Box.

Of your fleeting and unloved life I make you immortal.
Of your broken heart, I make art.
Out of that lost day have I plucked you, and myself.
Yet, you are alone in the Box. I, doomed to invisibility, am forbidden to take my place beside you.

Boxed In

Paul West

FATHER GARNET SHRINKS from the Renaissance outside his bolt-hole, not because he trickles and gurgles with sudden eruptive swaggers of his tripes, but because the huge polity out there bellows Death To Jesuits, as if any one label sufficed to evince this polymath, baritone singer, adroit mellow speaker, earthy Derbyshireman still close to the loam that bore him, his little knotted soul all chirps and cheeps, weary of going on being careful even as he reminds himself that memory is the pasture, the greensward, on which the mind can disport itself most ably, molding everything to the shape of heart's desire. On a sailor's grave, he recalls, no flowers bloom. He wonders where he heard that, and why, able here to summon all his mental moutons into one flock, baa-ing the gospel according to Saint Garnet, that not too gaudy, too precious, stone. Doomed to practice it day after day, even to the extent of dipping his nib in orange juice to make the words invisible, he has fallen in love with secrecy.

Once again he hears the noise of himself, squirreled away here in a priesthole made by a maimed dwarf of a carpenter who also happens to be a lay brother. Saved by woodwork, and a little tampering with the original masonry, Garnet languishes in the bosom of a vast country house, or rather in a thimble carved within a nipple, waiting for daylight, unable even to stand in the space allotted him. Why, he moans, are we hated so? He sneezes, once, twice, pressing his nose hard to quell the seizure, each time murmuring the time-honored formula, *Bless You*, that saves the soul from being flung far away, angelic silver skein aloft amid the tawdry of this world, never to return. You could sneeze yourself soulless. But he never will, although strictly speaking someone other than you should babble the housekeeping, nose-saving formula. *Dieu vous aide*, he knows, is what the soul-saving French neighbor says, automatic in this as in almost every other prayer. It is good, he reassures himself, to be prayed for in this way by just about anyone standing nearby. So, what does the King do when he sneezes? Bless himself or have a chorus of courtiers mumble the phrase? That is what they are there for, to keep his soul in his body in the interests of, well, not the one and only church, but his sect anyway. Father Garnet thinks that, for the soul to speak, it should have a language of its own, pure and godly, unknown to humankind, and therefore blessing itself in blindest esoterica. Now, there's just the kind of phrase to get him damned, socially at least, hoicked out of his hidey-hole and hanged along with hundreds of other mildly dissenting churls. Father Garnet has no room in which to shrug, but his mind makes the motion for him.

This carpenter troubles him, this builder of hiding holes. He, Garnet, prefers the old-fashioned country word *joiner.* Little John Owen, the joiner in question, makes a fetish of joining priests to their mouseholes, almost as if he thinks of the priesthood as a furtive, shy calling: nothing of titles and fancy robes, but the essential spirit hidden within the rind of the planet, within all these lavish country houses. Hide-and-seek is not far from it, not when daily or even nightly life can be shattered at any hour by the arrival of priest-hunting poursuivants armed with torches and dogs, probes and huge cones of bark through which they listen to the masonry, the chimneys, the passageways. Garnet chides himself for thinking ill of his savior, but sticks to his point nonetheless: hiding us away as he does, and making endless provision for ever more of us all over the Midlands and the South, he presumes to some kind of power, making us invisible and yet, at the same time, even more spiritual than ever, more abstract, more distant, more creatures of the mind than of ritual, splendor, office.

It is like being made obsolete, he tells his creaking bones, remembering only too well the crippled joiner's instructions: "You will not stand, Father, you will have to contain yourself at the crouch, there can be little easing once you have been installed. To make your little easing once you have been installed. To make your little place any bigger would be to expose you." He is a priest-shrinker, as alive in his trade as the old word for plough in such a word as *carucate*, which means as much land as you might reasonably plough in a year. In a way, Father Garnet broods in his cramp, our Little John is the ideal candidate for these cubbyholes, but he has no need, can go abroad as he pleases, more or less an upright dwarf, bubbling with good humor and perhaps more than a little amused by the spectacle of us all crouched until doomsday. He is almost a sexton, of the living, omitting only to smooth the earth over us at the last, and no doubt tempted sometimes to seal us in with trowel and mortar which, if we do not burst out while the seals are still soft, encases us forever.

Between cramp and suffocation, we have a poorer life than we envisioned, far from the august panoply of the high-ranking prelate. Father Garnet, the ranking Jesuit in England, tries to soothe his mind with his own name, derived from the word *pomegranate,* the color of whose pulp approximates the stone. No use. The sheer inappropriateness of light hidden under a bushel provokes him and makes his stomach queasy, a fate little eased by recourse to the drinking tube that enters his hideaway from behind the wardrobe outside. A small pan, a slight tilt to the feeder, and water can reach its priest: anything that will flow, soup or gruel, just to keep body attached to soul. Father Henry Garnet of Heanor, Derbyshire, thinks of himself as a light.

Now he is trying to work out which is better: being alone in the hole or having another priest for company, Father Oldcorne, as on other occasions, or Father Gerard, as on a few. There is certainly more talk, he decides, but of such an abortive, thwarted nature it were better to keep still. Perhaps the pallid patter of the inward voice consorts best with secret living, on the run from King James's hunters. For those eligible to have women with them, if any, it might be better, he reckons, not so much cuddling as meeting head-on a different point of view; after all, those bearing within them the secretest hiding place might better adjust to circumstances and so cheer up anyone with them. A Jesuit, he tells himself, should be able to reason the pros and cons without too much trouble, but he finds his mind blocked, twisted, perversely longing for daylight, sleep, a reassuring companion voice. Instead, he hears the echo of a refrain voiced by Little John Owen:

> Him that casn't stand it tight
> May never see the morrow's light.

Small consolation, that. Imagine, then, the confessional even smaller than usual, even for the recipient, with the confessee granted room to squirm about during the painful act. What then? Should the priest freeze in there, shocked by what he hears? Should he practice in the confessional for the hole or vice versa? Has either any bearing on the other?

If there is any moral to be drawn from recusants' experiences of being hidden, it is better, if you intend to hide, not to do so on your own premises or in those of anyone else. Best go to Saint Omer with

Father Tesimond. Or, if that proves impossible, make sure you deal with a country house that has no servants in it and is not located in any of the English counties. It is not that Robert Wintour and Stephen Littleton, on the run, camping out in barns, washhouses, seed stores, stables and byres, were found by a drunken poacher, whom they had to gag and bind, but that, in their next abode, Hagley, the country home of "Red Humphrey" Littleton in Worcestershire, they were exposed by a certain cook, Findwood, who wondered at the excessive amount of food being sent upstairs. That Findwood receives an annual pension for his good deed goes without saying. When the poursuivants arrive, Red Humphrey denies everything after trying to block their entry. "This is our home, you shall not pass." Something Roman in his demeanor pleases him at this point. They come in anyway and receive the immediate cooperation of yet another servant, David Bate, who shows them the courtyard in which the conspirators have gone to ground.

Hindlip is not far away, readied like a fortress, although who is to guarantee the behavior of servants when they hear of John Findwood's pension, setting him up as an eternal spy, before the word gets out about him grafting himself onto the domestic life of some country house in order to undo it, pay promised, no vengeance as yet visited upon him. His breed will prosper in these gruesome times, and the trade of household spy will establish itself among the poor, almost in itself a revenge calling.

Anne Vaux and Father Garnet, Anne and Henry as they are now just about calling each other, have exhausted all means of delay, even standing their horses in the fashion of a love-seat, he pointing northward, she pointing south, in fervid contemplation of each other, with no help from tradition or literature, but left to the meager resources of eye and hand to express what is forbidden. Now they change places, advancing not at all, but feeling heavy at the much shrunken extent of land between here and Hindlip, that labyrinth of lighthouses, almost, Henry Garnet thinks, like Sicily in little. When, at last, after much dawdling (which Henry Garnet in his original way calls prevarication), they arrive at the rear of the building, he dismounts on a patch of ice, unassisted by grooms, and immediately slips backward, gathers himself to surge forward, then loses his feet altogether and crashes to the ground, in one fall slamming his knee, outside left ankle, his right thumb and his head on the virtually invisible ice. It is a poor welcome, but he survives it, feeling shaken and shocked, a whole series of fresh pains and aches moving through his body, and in his hands a potent trembling. Anne is almost in tears at this last sight of him before the mansion gobbles him up for what? A month or more. Already, Mary Wharmcliff, a scullery maid with child by her lover on a neighboring estate, Blackstone Grange, where she has walked to confront him, has returned with news that Sir Henry Bromley, a local justice of the peace, eldest son of Thomas Bromley who conducted the trial of Mary Queen of Scots—a brash, invasive family—was already on his way from who knows where, intent on combing through Hindlip from top to bottom. This leads, of course, to a further piece of wisdom which says: If you wish to move from one country house to another, say from Coughton to Hindlip, do not do it on horseback, or by any other means that entails travel between two points, lest you gallop right into the gang led by one of the Bromleys. Nor, knowing this and some of the Bromley history, should you extend too much trust to the idea that Sir Henry, related to the recusant Littletons, might go easy on certain Catholics. The schizophrenia of the times allows him to do his job without, in this case, altogether losing face with Muriel Littleton, his sister. It is simply another variant of the William Byrd philosophy, enabling the happy practitioner to face both ways without ever being damned as a hypocrite. It is almost as if opinions, tenets, beliefs, were so many silken handkerchiefs to be floated about in the wind, no more committing you to a certain code of conduct than the passage overhead of a moulting sparrow. Whence, Anne Vaux asks herself, this new breed of trimmers, people who out of corrupt self-interest trim their conduct for each situation? Is this the fabled opportunism of wolves or what Henry Garnet, rarely at a loss for a classical exemplum, calls *homo homini lupus:* man a wolf to man. Perhaps, though, she thinks, if nobody believes in anything very much, then all persecution is going to come to an end because nobody believes much in that either except as entertainment for the mob. It is all too much for her, being severed here and now as Henry Garnet, with no time for a meal or a drink, goes his way to join those already cached in the house: Father Oldcorne, the house chaplain, and the lay brother Ralph Ashley. Outside, by special dispensation granted to himself, Little John Owen hides in a dwarf-adapted birdhouse which, through a miracle of hydraulics known to him alone, floats in a duck pond. Or it did; thanks to the freeze, it now sits, compelling upon him all kinds of privation but permitting, as he has so often said during the design phase, fresh air galore. Crouched out there, the engineer and artificer of the whole hideaway (there is room for a dozen more, should need

239

arise), he fulfils yet another part of his destiny, as much in charge of his scheme as Cecil of his, and indeed a consummate piece of the drama. Simply, as he designed it, the birdhouse goes over him like a cloak; he then steps into a specially designed circular punt fashioned after the coracle, and waits, lowering the birdhouse to the coracle rim, which it exactly matches. Supplies abound, more or less, as if he is truly a flightless bird; the birdhouse is not round, but has a round base and this, he has assured the Habingtons, aghast at his perverse ingenuity, enables the birdhouse to move around in the water, making it the center of a perfectly self-controlling motion. It spins itself very slowly, without favoring any particular direction, whereas a rectangular punt will not. As if itinerant birds have left emergency packages for later comers (the code of the distant, romantic log cabin in America), the Owen birdhouse contains in tiny compartments bits of twig called locally Spanish juice, an import like strawberries from Aranjuez; hazelnuts, beech nuts and roasting chestnuts; tiny pastry pockets of quince jelly; sunflower seeds collected in small leather pouches that might have held rings; unicorns made of gingerbread, none more than two inches high. On the quiet, in the hours left over when he subtracts his work from his life, he bakes and rolls, stamps out two-dimensional pastries and polishes nuts for storage. A squirrel, in short, with a higher destiny ever awaiting him: There will never, what with the new influx of priests from the Continent, be enough hiding places. Yes, he grins, chilled in his private minaret, you can't always get a good hiding even though you deserve one. Such wit warms him when nothing else does. Attracted by the small holes de rigueur in a birdhouse, some nonmigrating birds have already called on him, and he has made the reckless error of sharing his supplies with them, in the interior dark proffering what he can, a sunflower seed, say, between finger and thumb, with aviary refinement. Surely, he thinks, hardly giving a thought to Hindlip's crew of festive, garrulous servants, they will never find me here; I am too blatant. No, the birdhouse is. They will search the house, but nothing else save the outhouses and barns. This is much better than suicide with beautifully crafted swords or being shot in a courtyard or blown up by gunpowder arranged to dry out in front of a roaring fire like a drenched cat. When they come, they will bounce off, as always; I wonder why they bother. Well, it must be to earn their wages, little realizing their real wages will be paid after death, in another world altogether.

Put out by having to share a space with Father Oldcorne (this the

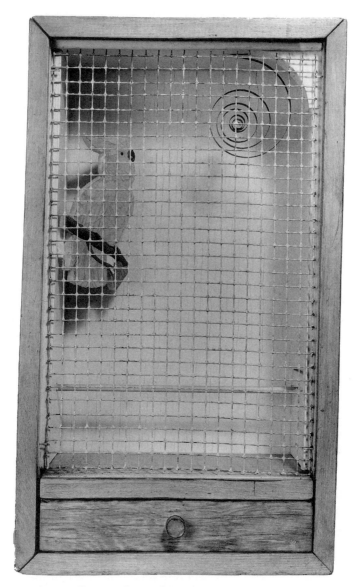

Joseph Cornell, Keepsake Parakeet, 1949–53
© The Joseph and Robert Cornell Memorial Foundation

safest in the entire house, Habington says), Father Garnet tries to collect his wits, damaged by the fall on the ice. He feels hollow and brittle, crouched in a space he cannot stand in or stretch out in: almost a torture in its own right, inflicted by friends. He tries to fix his mind on some old Roman words first discovered in childhood and treasured as jewels but they will not come, as once they did when he was in a better mood or circumstances were less drear. It is as if the shock of falling on the ice, as well as making his head ache and feel sore to the touch at one point in his left temple and upsetting his stomach too, has wiped out his memory, at least the verbal one. Come back, he says, trying an old trick to bring something to mind, catching himself in the act of naming it before he even tries to retrieve it. But only *tuli, latum,* come, and they in severed, broken form. He is not that much of an old Roman after all, he decides; all it takes to rattle him is a patch of ice and a household in a hurry. If he weren't who and what he is, he would be inclined to say damn them all, but he refrains, wishing instead he could have an accompaniment from Byrd, of Byrd's music performed by any of them, himself included, but there is so little time. Byrd, he notes drily, feels no need to hide; why does he not happen to be on the poursuivants' list of undesirables?

Making matters worse, even as he poises on the brink of darkness at noon, there is the standard cooking smell of Hindlip, the savory aroma of beef and gravy familiar from his childhood, when he lurked by the big kitchen table with his sisters and they sampled various tidbits of the meal. A small spoonful of gravy would set him up, or, better, a square of Yorkshire pudding, crispy brown on the outside, soft yellow within, a substance designed to replace meat when meat is hard to come by. None of that, though surely it might have been prepared. A hot cup of almost anything would serve, he thinks, it does not have to have much taste, only be hot, so that the warmth will linger after he has descended into the hole. He gives up, still wrinkling his nostrils at the cooking smell, almost as if he could eat with them. It is later than lunchtime, but who is watching the time? The absent sun is no guide, only his aching, volcanic stomach. No small ceremony, then, with a few chaste words in any language, softening the bleakness of the moment as language, the dominator, mostly does, converting the worst of situations into an interpreted something. In an ideal world, "real" in the sense that Anne Vaux uses it, he will be escorted (he loves the dignity and finesse of that word) upstairs to a small quiet room with clean sheets, there to sleep off the impact and stretch out his testy body. A pitcher of hot water would be there when he woke, and sundry other helps; a snack from the kitchen would set him to rights, it would not even have to be Yorkshire pudding or, if later, a wondrous trifle with custard and cream, peeled almonds and sponge cake or gingerbread drenched in fortified wine. No such perfection needed, neither ambrosia nor ichor. He is willing to go dry, he tells himself, it is a mark of his courage, as one going to punishment, which is bound to come later—Fathers Gerard and Briant have already been through that particular honor. If only, throughout this process, he could sagely sleep, putting his feet where directed, scooping himself up with an expended smile of the man shoved past his limit.

What he does feel rather than witness is a host of hands nudging and easing him, pressing him this way and that, raising or lowering, prodding him to buckle left or right, palming his head forward as if it stuck out too far, and with gentlest tiptoe of their own urging his feet to tuck themselves in better or he will never get all of him into place. He nearly chokes, being adjusted into so strait a place, but he lifts the top of the moment off as if dealing with boiled milk, tossing away the skin that says he might better have been naked for this, and oiled even, converted into a performing animal for the sake of safety. With muscles only a little more willing than not, he inches his way into the already established, pungent gloom that clings to Father Oldcorne, always a man of no great conversation, who twists and hunches as best he can while another human pushes into his space. The special aroma of the cancer-ridden Father Oldcorne is familiar to him; perhaps it is the bouquet of the self-flogger, the man who punishes his tongue as if it were some live, lascivious beast, corrupted by language. Father Oldcorne smells of burned leather, he decides, at least in close quarters he does, but this might be an effect of brief confinement; the smell is more that of rotting cauliflower, not a human aroma at all, but direct from the kitchen's anteroom, where discarded celeries and crozzled leftovers are put, often tempting a mouse into the open. Father Oldcorne is not his choice of traveling companion, or even for sitting still with through the dismal watches of the priestly night; the man's hangdog, punished look, not visible in here, thank Jesus, puts him off, as does his constant need for praise at having subjugated the body to a greater degree than Garnet and his free-flowing, almost flamboyant friends. Oldcorne has a dun, grievous quality that restores those who have overlooked it to the miserable side of life; no one, listening to him or inhaling him, will want to live too long.

Much of this Anne knows, can divine from what Henry Garnet fails to say as he vanishes bit by bit into the architectural trap devised by Little John Owen who, thanks to the emergency of Sir Henry Bromley's squad impending, freezes out in the martin-house stuck in pond ice. Anyone finding him will turn into a purple martin. One hug and Henry Garnet is gone. She wonders how many hugs there have been: two or three, this by far the most final, seeing that once again they are gambling with their own lives and those of priests, actually standing here to marvel at the completeness of the disappearance when the hiding place should have been sealed off, the upstairs water tank shoved back into place by eleven pairs of hands. With so many in league, she thinks, how keep a secret as bizarre as this? Only in a recusant household habituated to such scenes can you get away with it. Perhaps we will. It is assuredly one of John Owen's most decisive inventions, with the one priest's toes beside the other priest's head, for hygiene's sake. She scoffs at the very thought of hygiene, knowing they had better hygiene in the Ark, and this is a Greek word come down from a people who, professing it, loved the word because they achieved nothing of the kind. The voice of Father Oldcorne, rattled, comes from behind the tank, which actually seems to amplify any sound they make. "A devil in hell," he is saying, always partial to the extreme view of things. Not a sound from Henry Garnet, who has never felt more like a parcel of dirty clothes stuffed into a moldy drawer by a feckless washerwoman. Henry Garnet has never made a fetish of answering Father Oldcorne, whose self-directed rhetoric implies the coldest reaches of the universe, the most fearful moments of any human life. He is not exactly a misery, but one who exaggerates, Henry thinks, the dark side of the human antic. Well, when he gets out of here in a month's time, he will have cause for complaint. No, not a month, a week will do; even less, once Sir Henry Somebody has performed his sullen chase through the enormous house and gone his truculent way, his commission from the Privy council fluttering in his hand. Father Garnet does not know that the Bromley team has been promised "a bountiful reward" for its best efforts, so when they come they will screw their gimlets into the elegantly paneled walls with avaricious zeal— wherever a priest may be hovering (a favored word of the Privy Council, whose notion of priests involves a paradoxical angelic component that makes their lives difficult until they manage to combine angel with harpie). Everyone at Hindlip is familiar with the sounds of probing as, once again, the poursuivants, some recruited only for the day, sedulously go about the business of ruining good panel work, much to the distress of maestro Owen. Such grinding and scraping suggests a house full of rats, which in a sense it is whenever these busybodies show up. Mostly from hovels, they delight in the spoliation of luxury, delighted to bore holes in the eyes of the faces in portraits (who would hide behind *them*?) or next to an old borehole so that the two, plus another on another occasion, will form a peephole. By now, the house has a much-penetrated look as if musketry practice of the wildest abandon has taken place in the dining room, the bedrooms, even lofts and closets. Father Garnet thinks of Hindlip as *the punctured house*, practiced upon by dunce-doctors trying to let the blood out of it, to no purpose—nobody has ever been found here, never mind how vehement and specific the official proclamation borne in the hand of the poursuivant who leads. John Owen is far too clever for them, and Hindlip gives him more scope than almost any other country house. They might as well look for actual faces in the coats of arms proudly displayed on the walls.

Anne Vaux knows she cannot stand any more of this, so she goes downstairs, unable to believe she has just ridden cross-country to entomb the dearest priest in the world. She has not so much participated as lent an ear, an eye, a heart. Now her stomach, always upset by riding sidesaddle or any-saddle, begins to come back to normal, less afflicted by the devious fragility of her robust-looking life. She is not that strong, she knows, what with eyes, womb and—no, there is nothing else save the acid swilling about in her stomach. Not because she wants the dish, but because she associates it with conventional everyday conduct, she asks for an unusual lunch: ham and eggs, a dish often favored at Hindlip because the makings are always fresh. Gradually, overpowering the reek of cauliflower, the bouquet of roast beef, the companionable wideawake aroma of ham and eggs bubbling in hot lard ascends the stairs and seeps through the structure, reaching Henry Garnet and actually bringing a tear to his eye; why, this is the most exquisite torture, he feels, and surely Anne could stop it. Who on earth—no, he stops. It is no use getting into a swivet about a wrongly timed breakfast he would give his folding leather altar to devour. The smell will endure for at least a day; no windows open in November, and, over the decades, the house has brilliantly captured and fused its own smells, like a prisoner inhaling himself, until there is always a fused aroma—faint corky oversweet strawberry infused with an acrid spume of boiling vinegar—that serves as background to the smells of the moment. Against both delight and abomination, Henry Garnet decides to hold his breath, but he can do so only in upsetting spasms, and he soon gives up, rhapsodic and revulsed all at once.

Anyone with a developed sense of coincidence, as may arrive after reading a great deal of Dickens, will wish Father Garnet never to have arrived, instead circling with Anne Vaux in some nondescript, drab field until the end of time. By the same token, one does not want to have Sir Henry Bromley arriving within half an hour of Garnet's reaching Hindlip. As zealots go, Bromley is fairly civilized, although his arrival coincides also with break of day; Henry Garnet's feeling that it is lunchtime shows how exercised his mind has become (he's being previous as almost never), but Anne Vaux's craving for the ritual of ham and egg reveals her attunement to a daily round, a regimen that both pleases and steadies. Amid the panic of their confusion, no one is saluting the dawn except the kitchen staff, who time their work by daylight, and need only to be consulted once about, well, not so much time as the phase of the day. Sir Henry Bromley is too eager, having risen well before four in the morning to get his posse on the road.

So here they are, a motley team, some adorned in butcher's smocks with a big tool pouch in front containing awls and spikes, boring-tools of all kinds and little listening tubes with funnel ends. Some of them have teak mallets with which to tap on hollow-looking panels. They also have with them kindling to test the chimneys with, knowing full well that a lit fire in a fake chimney soon proves the case. Hargreaves is among them, but dragging a leg, he too from a fall on ice, but this time he kowtows to Sir Henry, who can make or break him depending on the skill with which he exposes the priests. They do not even recall who tipped them off about priests at Hindlip, but the word is out; perhaps it has always been out inasmuch as there has almost never been a time when priests were not at Hindlip. The rumor and the event match each other, but to no advantage for the poursuivants, who have found no one at all during their previous searches. As it happens, Thomas Habington is not at home when the inquisitorial rabble arrive at the main door, but his return prompts some lively exchanges between Bromley and himself.

"Do not brandish your proclamation, man," he bellows at Bromley. He speaks as a man who has already been in the Tower once. "I take your word for it. I will gladly die at my own front gate if you find any priests in here. Lurking under my roof! You will as soon find fish folded in among the tablecloths. We are who we are, Sir Henry." His vehemence cuts no ice; Bromley has seen it all before, the bluster and the indignation—he would cavort in the same fashion if he *were* hiding Jesuits. It goes with the suit, and Habington is not a "bad" man, just a misguided rebel with a taste for punishment, hence his impassioned cry about dying at his front door. There is no need for emotion, Bromley knows; either the priests are here or they are not, and he does not intend to go until the house has been ransacked, and indeed made to pay. It will take three days, he estimates, with his men rampaging around upstairs and downstairs, ignoring the protests of the Habington family and enigmatic visitors such as Mrs. Perkins, whom he has met before. The grinding, drilling, boring, go on all day, with naps taken in the big public rooms, nothing provided by way of food, but the kitchen raided so much the staff feel demented, unable to function according to the strict rules of the house. That they mean to spend the night appalls Anne Vaux, who detects in their behavior a new resolve: Gone are the days of the lazy, casual gentlemanly search; this is the work of plebeians eager for profit, and she works on her disdain, doing her best with stare and sniff to embarrass those who seem intent on taking the house apart.

"I actually turned people away," Habington is telling them, then as he thinks better of it (priests, plotters; who else?), "old friends who wanted to stay the night. I have a wife with child, I am far too busy for visitors. That includes you all."

"Quite so," Bromley says, himself doing nothing in the way of search; his servants do that for him. "I am not accusing you of being inhospitable, sir, or of uxorial coarseness. Oh no. I await only the conclusion of this business and will be happy to acquit you of any charges if we find nothing amiss. We have to be thorough, though, as your pig-scraper does, and your steeplejack. We cannot afford to skimp matters, sir. The national safety is at stake. As my father always said—"

But no one listens; he has been here before, with the same quotations, although a smaller crew. They intend to spend the night, sprawled anywhere soft, belching and grunting, drinking and quarreling, seeking the temporary oblivion the laborer needs from his hire. At such a time, Anne thinks, we might actually let the priests out, for a stretch and a snack, but there are so many of them you are bound to make a mistake. Little does she know it, but Bromley, an organized mind in an untidy life, has insisted that at least one man remain on guard on each floor, although how far any watchman can be trusted not to fall asleep he cannot know. If the priests make a move, he knows it will be by night. He resolves to stay awake until dawn, but realizes he has been on the go since today's, and readily exempts himself. Does he hope to find a priest or merely achieve the most thorough fruitless search in the world? This Habington, he muses, is a rather rash person, but manly in bearing and, if a liar, one with plausible good manners. My sister lies in the same fashion. Yet I do not worry about her; her lies are between her and God Almighty. Some of us in the highest power blow both ways. We are not without sympathy, but work is work is duty. Will I ever have to rope my sister in, merely for being a Catholic? Never, so what's all the fuss about? If you strip away the varnish of religion, life is the same for all of us. If I were God, would I want to be prayed to? No, I would want to be left alone, lost in the lap of memory.

Even on the first day, through diligence and willingness to deface the house's interior, the poursuivants have found grist for their mill: three simulated chimneys with planks soot-blackened to resemble the bricks, and cavities, chambers, full of trinkets and trumpery (as they say) ranging from books to rosaries, vases and chalices and huge thick candles. "I am a collector," Habington raves, "I am entitled to put my things where I want. Nothing *has* to be on view." What, then, are these? They produce the title deeds concerning the estate, opening them up and riffling the pages amid their pink ribbons. "Are you telling me," he insists, "I have no right to put important papers in a safe place? Don't *you?* What does this signify? I am a landowner, I do not want people wiping their boots on legal papers, or peering at them to see how much I am worth." Then they inform him that, in the brickwork of the gallery surmounting the gate, they have found two spaces, each large enough for a man. Why so many open cubbyholes? He tells them in his protracted huff that all country houses have such facilities, in which to store unwanted books, vases, hunting boots—"You know, Sir Henry," he says with his most produced voice, coming on strong, "the sorts of things you don't want to part with, but cannot stand to have under your feet. Any woman will tell you that. After all, dear sir, you found nobody in these places. There *is* nobody, as I said. I dare say, if you and the loyal Hargreaves wish to stay the night, as all the signs indicate, we can surely find so-called priestholes for you, in which you will feel so uncomfortable that you will just as soon recognize that they were never intended for human occupation. They are for storage, but you are welcome to try.

A severe lesson cannot be more certainly learned."

"I respect our armor, sir," Bromley tells him, "but you must understand we will be here as long as necessary. Hargreaves will keep an eye on the house all night."

"No, Sir Henry, *I* will."

"Not the need, sir. Take your rest. I will take mine."

"Not in a priesthole, then. We do have rooms adjudged suitable for a gentleman."

"A sit-up sleep," Sir Henry tells him. "Taught me by my father." He is still pondering Habington's riposte about a country house's being so vast that you forget what you have, and do not memorize a house by its cavities, whatever their purpose might be.

So: Anne Vaux ordered and got her ham and eggs just in time and so feels nourished for a fray in which she plays little part, now thinking of herself as merely a mouth, a tongue, likely to give evidence by accident. She keeps quiet, out of the way, wondering if music by Byrd might serve to lull the searchers, making them skimp and miss. Little John Owen, still out in the birdhouse in the pond, has done good work here, although perhaps not the best of his optical illusions. In one recently modified house he created a painting of a door opening on another door: three-dimensional until you get up close, just the sort of thing to suck in and confound a Hargreaves, but he has not done this everywhere. Another lifetime would help, she thinks. If only he had started work ten years earlier. Off she treads, out of the house, chunk of suet in hand to fasten to the side of the birdhouse in which he roosts—the side facing away from the house. It will be better than nothing, whereas cheese would alert their suspicions. All John Owen has to do is somehow help himself and try to keep the suet down. It is like wartime here, she decides, with troops garrisoned all over the privacy of the house. Is this how they treat the Jews in Europe? I am better doing this by day, in the open; they would wonder why I was doing it at night. If they keep watch, and they will. If Henry Garnet, who hurt his knee, cannot stand being cooped up, what are we to do?

In the blistering, gusty cold of that night, Wednesday leaking into Thursday, John Owen, who has been outside since Monday, cranks his almost petrified broken body out of the birdhouse, lifting it up and off him, and creeps into Hindlip through an entrance only he knows, thence into a hiding place known to most of them as Curly because it does not lie straight, and whoever is in it—in this case the lay brother Ralph Ashley, also there since Monday—can only lie curved. There is little room for two, but they wordlessly share the apple Ralph Ashley has been saving for three days. It is as cold in the house as it is outside, and Little John feels he has exchanged life for death. Ashley's body gives off no warmth. What they do next is rash, but they both feel dizzy, weak, can hardly move their legs; indeed, Little John is lucky to have stumbled in unseen. The kitchen tempts, the open road next. As Little John sees it, he is bound to be discovered if the searchers occupy the house long enough, and to stay any longer in the birdhouse would kill him with exposure. Wordlessly they decide to move out, through the wainscot into a gallery. The house is still and only faintly lit. If someone catches them, they will give themselves up; perhaps the poursuivants will be satisfied with them, mistaken as to who they are. Out they slip, one foot caressing the other before going farther, but the house becomes an uproar; Hargreaves, on his third patrol of the night, wandering into the gallery out of boredom with no expectations at all, catches sight of two shady figures tiptoeing their way into the hall and communicating with each other in dumbshow. In a second, they have been surrounded and pinioned while Sir Henry, half asleep and blustering to compensate for his bleariness, asks them who they are. Just servants, they answer, unable to sleep. But sleepless servants, he comments with a sniffle, do not wander through the main house at night like invited guests. Who are you? Are you Tesimond and Oldcorne, Greenway and Hall? He is wide of the mark, of course, but he is convinced he has caught someone, not of high station (he knows the smell of a servant when he sniffs one, and the whiff coming off them is quite different). Rather than interrogate them, he sends them off to his headquarters and occupies himself with the expectant mother, Mary Habington, sister to Monteagle, the savior of the hour.

"No fear, Sir Henry," she shrills, "not unless you carry me out yourself. I am staying here, where I belong. How dare you?"

Clearly he has no business trying to lug around someone so well-born and well connected; he makes no offer to remove Anne Vaux, whose sharpened glare upsets him, so he retires again and writes a report to Cecil, waffling away about the devious ways of Catholics, hosts, country gentlemen, ladies of the house and just about everybody not on his side. He will not sleep this night, nor will he hit on the truth, he is so eager to present himself in a good light as the finder, the exposer. Restrained enough in speech, he tends to hyperbole at the merest touch of self-esteem, informing Cecil that "of all the various scheming and trunculent priests, those Jesu-wits, I have two of the vilest in hand, for prompt sending to you, sire, and your diligent punitations. I have one or two misgivings about who these people are, for they will not say, but truth told they have, without any airs or graces as of high-born gentleman, that bloated humbleness we all recognize as bombast in reverse. We, who have not been educated for nothing, need yield no quarter to the Roman-suckled rabble of high priests. At your service always, with intaminate pride." He can go on in this vein for hours, sufficiently launched with writing materials, like someone taking to water for the first time and hitting on the correct stroke, even were he swimming in pitch. He calls off the search, explores his conscience, wishes he had not been so swift in sending them up to London, then renews the ransacking of the house into Friday, Saturday and Sunday, deeply conscious of interrupting a religious timetable that no one dares mention. From memory, in her diary, Anne Vaux writes as follows:

> We have here again, for the seventh day, the same behaviours as before at Baddesley-Clinton, which I fiercely complained of, though this house be none of mine and therefore not subject to mine own remonstrances. Suffice to say, these poursuivants behave like a pack of bad boys playing Blind Man's Bluff, who in their wild rush, bang into tables and chairs and walls and yet have not the slightest suspicion that their playfellows, God save them, are right on top of them and almost touching them.

She reads this through, crosses it all out as dangerous, then tears it loose, looking exasperatedly at the diary, flicks through some pages, wraps the volume in a fold of wallpaper she picks from a minty-smelling closet and bears the whole thing downstairs to the roaring fire, into which she sets her life, unseen in the whole endeavor, although one glimpse of her ferrying something perilous to read would have had them snapping at her heels. She realizes she is not living prudently: The constant hammering has unnerved her, given her a headache that reaches down the back of her neck into her shoulders, and the egg-and-ham breakfast is sitting none too well—days old, it seems to lie there and haunt her still, and she now agonizes at having put Fathers Garnet and Oldcorne through the miseries of aroma. Indeed, nothing she does helps them. They are not in the lower chamber that sits below the dining room, where it is possible to pass

Joseph Cornell, Untitled (The Grand Hotel), 1953
© The Joseph and Robert Cornell Memorial Foundation

food down to them as if they were plaintive dogs behaving well at their masters' feet. They do not even have an apple between them. She stews about Little John and Ralph Ashley, seized and sent away incognito, and knows there has come an end to hideaway-building. Further torture inflicted on John Owen will kill him certainly, and the whole recusant scheme will perish. It would be one thing if the searchers, having found, were gone, satisfied with their prey; but here they are still, racketing about, so much so that she twitches at every tap or rattle, every creak of the house as it settles down into winter repose. She recalls having noticed in herself and others a curious habit of completing a watched motion, when someone, bracing to move an arm or a leg, curtails the movement and the intent watcher goes through with it, for the moment identified into union with the person watched. This is how she feels about the two priests in their hole, sensing all the movements they dare not make and accomplishing them by guesswork. Will it always be thus? No, she knows, it is going to be much worse. The poursuivants, having found two, want to have two more, yelping and scattering, heedless of a house routine destroyed. Brave Mary Habington has refused to leave, but she finds their presence vile in the extreme, and all she can do is maintain a cool austere demeanor while her husband orates incessantly about an Englishman's home being his castle. Was he the originator of that saw? Well, castle no more, my loves, the rabble has entered its final playground and will not be contained by any code of decent manners. Sir Henry is already at odds with himself, she notes, for having not interrogated Owen and Ashley himself; whatever they said would be gold.

"The trouble is, my lady," Sir Henry is saying to her, "the moiety of this rabble we have here has not enough proper English to get someone to draw down their trews for the jakes, if you will pardon the reference. I am among apes."

"We are both, *all*, among apes, sir."

"Hence the high degree of choler among us."

He needs no agreement, she can see that; he is accustomed to silent assent while he roams in hit-or-miss meditation, hoping for a coup that will raise him even higher in Cecil's esteem. In truth he finds Worcester a bore and would love to move to London, at an advantage of course. In Worcester jail at this very moment, to save his life or at least delay his execution, Humphrey Littleton is telling all: He will tell who the Jesuits were who talked him into becoming a plotter. Why, Father Hall (Oldcorne, he explains) is almost certainly hidden away in Hindlip at this moment, "at this present," and easily flushed out. Hall's, Oldcorne's, servant happens to be in Worcester jail, and he will know all. Show him the rack. The manacles. Littleton is getting carried away with vicarious cruelty. "After all," he adds, "Oldcorne said the plot was a good thing and long overdue. *Commendable* was his word." The Sheriff of Worcester at once stays his execution to see what else this tap of a man might yield up. After the top layer, there are many others, with truth at the bottom, tiny and glistening: a corm of fact.

In fact, Oldcorne had compared the plot to a pilgrimage made by Louis XI of France, in the course of which the plague erupted twice, wiping out most of his retainers the first time, and killing Louis himself the next. His enemies came through unscathed. So much, Oldcorne said, for excursions organized by St. Bernard of Clairvaux. Someone flinched at the second syllable in Clairvaux, but no one spoke. "The principal thing," Father Oldcorne had said, "was what the expedition was for and how it was conducted. Many failures are honorable, and can only be judged by the moral good they bring about." Father Oldcorne still does not know what Catesby was trying to do. "It is between him and his God. Of course, I am against all reckless violence, sir." How easily, though, his words could be twisted into treason and treachery; between the inability to reveal what was said in confession and a general ignorance of the plot's aims, all priests were both unable to defend themselves and guilty to begin with.

To swell the general clamor, Mary Habington has her servants begin cleaning the household silver, tons of it all dun and gray from disuse, and suddenly Sir Henry feels at home in the presence of a familiar ritual, as if in readiness for some social event, a banquet, say, and his mind saunters away from his reasons for being here and starts to dream of banquets, balls, near-orgies he himself has sponsored (they watch one another talk and listen to one another eat). The acrid tang of silver polish rises upstairs to the nostrils of Father Garnet, gagging and trying not to cough. He has been here since January 21. It is now Monday January 27, what feels like years since Monteagle revealed the plot. He thinks he is going to faint as someone outside begins to hammer and grind. Surely this will be the ultimate discovery. He has no idea of what has happened to John Owen and Ralph Ashley, and he wonders if Anne has stayed on at Hindlip, convinces himself she has not. If not her, then, who has been sustaining them with warm broth sent through a long reed coming through the chimney? Was it not she who plied them with caudle, a food for invalids, succulent and sharp? Marmalade and candy they have provided for themselves, but that is all, and with the house in a state of perpetual siege from within there has been no chance of anyone's doing better. Their past week has been an elegy for egg and bacon, the aroma now overpowered by the reek of silver polish, the high acid content rising above everything else to tickle and scald the noses of those nearest.

"Well," says Garnet to Oldcorne, "shall we? I am choking, Edward."

"If we do, Henry, there will be no turning back. You well know how they proceed."

"Eternity in a byre," says Father Garnet. "Is this a perpetual penalty or have we earned our keep?"

"Our keep has always been free."

"*Ita vero.* Do we brave them, then?"

"Another day?"

"My gorge rises at the thought."

"Mine too. But shall we stay?"

"Shall we go out together?"

"To bathe and eat," Garnet echoes. Against their will, they take deep breaths and then have trouble uncoiling limbs. Then they impede each other, slithering out of that noxious narrow cupboard, Garnet coming out headfirst, his grievously swollen legs dragging behind him. He is an iguana, that ungainly. Oldcorne follows and, for a moment, they lie side by side, the old position, in the open, gasping and weeping tears of supreme effort mingled with self-disgust. "Were you ever in the one at Sawston," Garnet whispers. "I was," comes answer. "I know why you ask. There is an earth closet."

"Just so," says Henry Garnet, feeling like an incontinent schoolboy who has messed his pants during Latin grammar and will soon be thrashed, given a good hiding (he winces) once he has been scrubbed. "With one of those closed-stools," he murmurs, only inches from the stone floor, "we could have endured another three months. If we had only been able to get outside for an hour, we could have set ourselves up in there for life, with a folding altar and everything." He feels cheated: A brilliant idea has died at the hands of crass matter. "Oh to stand," he sighs.

"Or to stretch," Oldcorne adds, rising to the kneel.

They both have a look of stunned arthritis, unshaven and wan and shattered. They are the palest priests in or near Worcester, not as pale as Guido Fawkes, but victims of stilled blood.

"Ho," says Sir Henry, "who *are* these stinking fellows?"

The team of poursuivants, briefly dipping face into the hole, recoil, heaving and gurgling, and then move away from the two priests who stand unsteadily in barbaric isolation. Anne Vaux, horrified and weeping, keeps her distance, marveling that a mere week can reduce a human to such an abominable pass as Sir Henry, sensing the situation requires a summary comment, says "They have been undone by those customs of nature which must of necessity be done. Those little vital commoners of the body keep us all in slavery to them, requiring that we absterge the podex, ladies and gentlemen. These wretched prelates have squatted in there with the devil himself and he has paid them back. Who do we have, then? Do you have names or do you just make noises? Are you well enough to answer? Shall we wash you?" Anne Vaux volunteers, but it is a motley crew of Hargreaves and some six searchers holding their noses who escort the two priests to an alcove on the ground floor, to which water can be brought, and clouts that can be thrown away as infested infected loathsomes. The water-bringing servants squeal in horror and hasten to wash their hands and faces. Anne Vaux knows now that the rationale of the hiding place has another side she has never thought of. It was folly to feed these men at all or to succor them with liquid. A weeklong sleep, she decides, next time, like that—what is it, the polar bear in somebody's play, when I was a civilized woman living a social life? *Sub cardine glacialis ursae*—usually she will ask Father Garnet and he would know, but not today. What does it mean? The rising of the ice? Ah, now I remember, 'tis the snowy Bear! Her mind has eased itself a little, unable to hear any more about customs of nature, which, to be honest about it, nauseate her at the best of times, not per se but because the facilities impress her as primitive and gross; wood-ash and earth shoveled on the mire of the day. Pico, she recalls, says we stand in it to clutch at heaven. Pico was right. Now they are cleaner, Sir Henry is urging them along, he wants them in Worcester, but he seems oddly benign in his treatment of them. Perhaps he likes priests.

Sir Henry Bromley can hardly believe his luck, but he begins to lose faith in it when he questions Father Garnet. Hall, alias Father Oldcorne, he has no trouble identifying: A man with only one alias has no hypocrites among his friends, but someone such as Garnet, alias at least half a dozen other men, has been brilliantly dispersed and camouflaged. Certainly this emaciated, worn, shuddering person is not Mister Perkins, nor is he any kind of whoremaster or manual laborer (Bromley examines his almost silky palms).

"Are you a priest, sir?"

"I cannot lie before God."

"Well?"

"I am a colleague of this gentleman."

"Have you been rash enough ever to submit to a name, a single name?"

Father Garnet identifies himself in a listless monotone; Anne, eavesdropping behind a door, has never heard him sound so depleted, so dreary. Now she begins to understand the impact of month after month of hiding in abysmal quarters unfit for animals. She would like to start over and install him from the first in a luxurious apartment like the one they envision him having in Rome: a room full of sundials sheathed in gold satin. How reckless of me, she thinks. Now they know who he is, and what: Quite a catch. They are bound to let him go as guiltless. Look what brought him to this. She does a dry sob, blaming herself for making of him a constant fugitive.

Joseph Cornell, Untitled (Swan Box), ca. 1945
© The Joseph and Robert Cornell Memorial Foundation

257

Joseph Cornell, Aviary, ca. 1949
© The Joseph and Robert Cornell Memorial Foundation

For Brother Robert
Bradford Morrow

And then I heard them lift a box,
And creak across my soul
With those same boots of lead, again.
Then space began to toll . . .

—Emily Dickinson

THE WINTER DAY WAS AS PLAIN as flour paste, and outside your window the sunlight was of the same whiteness as your walls and ceiling. The moon had abandoned the sky the night before, and stars hid behind the haze. No meteors had fallen for us to esteem. Simply, the dead calm of your brother's birthday reigned over this morning, as it had before dawn when night is at its most impervious depth. And all this plain white emptied scape provoked a spirited proposition, an inducement to one whose sole thoughts until then turned to you, and were sorry leaden things, sunken cakes, silent and without shape.

Mild morning December light made the grass look chalky, like dried milk, out in our backyard. Our quince tree, too, was white and reminded us of a carving in ivory. The blanched chairs we arranged back there at certain angles, cast flat white shadows on the white lawn. The slow air—which toured our leaky house and traveled the yard and walked up into the quince tree where it was cooled by the ghosts of songbirds and by the dazzling wintry sun—appeared to be whitewashed and rubbed. Robert, we were young. Mother was strong, our sisters were young. You were especially strong in your frailty. The world, too, was tenuous and promising only insofar as it was an empty white box. Thin air coveted this box and, through its silences, declared both itself and the box that held it unfulfilled. The birds might have echoed this dilemma with warning cries in the ivory quince, had they not abandoned us to such stifling quiet. I strained without success to hear their tolling.

No time passed. Not a day, nor a fortnight, nor a year. All but the balmy, gone birds remained the same, as we thought, What to do? What to do?

259

You remember, dear Robert, old owl, that when they migrated months ahead of schedule that particular year, they left behind a pasteboard parrot in their wake—a collective gesture meant as a kindness, surely, but who could ever be sure? Meant perhaps to soothe those whom they'd fled—who could blame them? I did not— and left us alone in our clapboard house, left our garden chair beneath that tree, slumbering in old, abundant solitude. What did those many birds mean by such gestures of leaving? You said, although you might not have said it in just these words: Birds only partly succeed in fulfilling certain half-finished thoughts and half-made promises since, now, aren't we reminded once more of how silent and colorless the world can be without them in it? Whereas the breathing world may feel their absence, we feel the difficult presence of their not being in the quince, or under the eaves or on this windowsill.

So you said, Robert, on that plainest day, that once. And though there were no cardinals or jays in the boughs for my Christmas Eve birthday we decided the tree should not be cut down.

Paste real wings on the treacherous parrot but it would not fly away. Or so you tell me and so I believe you. Look at it, proud there, pretty and arrogant and anything but dumbfounded, with its evidently orange beak, and with feathers so blue they bring tears to your eyes and to the eyes of Mother and Helen and Elizabeth, too. You say, Let's keep it. I don't see these blues and oranges but keep my blindness to myself. The parrot seemed to be low maintenance, as pets go, and so I agreed, nodding. You noted my silence in the matter even as you swore the parrot was not colorless, let alone invisible. It perched on your ceiling that morning, observing us just as you watched it, our mother and sisters staring upward, too. Live and let live, I thought, but wondered if we were to be its keepers or its pets, wondered if we weren't the invisibles, while parrot, Chinese quince, the sunless sky beyond your constant bed, and even the narrow yard below, were the truer presences.

Visible or not, this parrot did display no interest in the crackers I set out on the newspaper, near the cage that I had made for it out of wooden clothes hangers—remember? Remember how I wanted to paint the parrot's beak a dark orange to suggest my deeper yearning, but could not? Even the water in the clear little plastic bowl hung inside the cage evaporated before the parrot had any chance to consider whether thirst might motivate it to drink. Shall I paint the water blue?

You heard my questions but only smiled, so I sat out in the back-yard in my overcoat and waited for another color to come to mind. None came just then. Mother helped you down so you could sit beside me, Robert. It was then you suggested that today, my birth-day, proposed an idea, one that might develop into other ideas. Today, yes today, you continued. Today we won't be staying home like we always do because today is your birthday and so we will go traveling, like air, like songbirds.

I reminded you I wasn't fond of birthdays—they represented death's knell—reminded you that you were hesitant of leaving the house. You insisted, however. You wanted me to see something. And now I must confess, Robert. You were courageous, our mother was strong and our sisters were young, our poor father, though gone to heaven, was capable and the world was shallow, hollow, insubstan-tial but promising insofar as it was yet an empty white box. How reluctant I was to break the trance cast by that quince, the mansard-roofed bayside house, the fenced yard.

Yes, I said. Go we will, and the parrot can eat or drink and if not, die. So we studied your maps, we talked and planned and as we did, the journey came toward us even as we inclined toward it. This was not to be some usual trip. But we admitted to a shared passion about the proposed excursion which seemed to involve magnificent trains. And weren't we delighted when the parrot descended from the ceil-ing and became a part of our more common world? It seemed a sign that all boded well and through the quick of my tedious doubts it cut.

Pasted with fondness, or do they say plastered, we were going to attend a holiday parade. It was early afternoon and you were mad with merriment and clapping your gloved hands for effect, knowing that while I have never cherished vivid displays of celebration, I would not break my promise to go.

Nothing would rain, sleet or snow on our parade today, I thought, still the nonpareil worst birthday celebrant ever. I dressed myself and helped you dress. We put on birthday hats and set out together to range across the field of dead flowers, leaves and bramble, going forth to the station in town under an abundant sky of pure anonymity. No snow today, I thought again, but rather, some interior mist, like a pri-vate grief hidden behind my hundred honest frowns. Mist like that which we remember rising sometimes from the Hudson back when we lived in Nyack. This, and the certainty of very slow progress of typical marching bands, the same old floats, some several clowns, some majorettes, and a variety of other wondrous, monstrous stuff at the end of the happy line.

Mother of course accompanied us, Elizabeth and Helen too, and foursquare we brought along thoughts of home and the quince tree in the yard and the chairs under the tree by the fence out back. Not to mention the hibernating rosebush there we might have strung with lights had we not gone on this excursion.

Our train ride was uneventful. We listened to the clacking of the steel wheels on the tracks. I bought hot coffee in the cafe car, and brought you tea with an old slice of lemon, no sugar. We passed a pleasant time together, then discovered we were there, having arrived along the main street of just another modest town—representatives, all of us, of the slow progress of being living souvenirs on a plain day, a day as common as a gift of a box full of worthless cutout artifacts given by a boy to his brother, his mother, his sisters, his friends or else given to nobody. Here was Main Street in an ordinary town on an ordinary day, naked in its ordinariness. This is what you said and I believed you.

You said my gift to you—like yours to me—of coming outside into the world was a good gift, but that sometimes the giver can be confounded by what may come from out of the blue (euphemism yours) in return.

I thought about that, but said nothing again, having nothing to give you back. So we traded bodies, and traded them again, as we rolled through town hoping to find a good place where we might sit on the curb and watch the parade. We rolled with sisters and mother (and maybe father's ghost) on through this modest town that put me in mind of boxes populated by emptiness. Rows of complex boxes reflecting the colorless clouds that limped along overhead no prouder than the dry rags they were. Dry white rags of clouds that were young back then, but nevertheless dry as that parrot's beak back home, from cardboard carefully cut.

Past, olden music strikes up, now, a tin horn somewhere, and a drum snares. A yuletide melody maybe. The horse carries the parade master who has lost one of his polished liturgical boots in some other promenade. A leaden grin plays at his lips—theirs, in fact, both horse's and master's. A large candelabra on the starlet's head and another on the dunce's, all their many wicks burning bright. What a show, I begin to think, as we settle in to watch with the rest, people standing and people seated around us. The large, meditative crowd laughs and claps as the horse, master, starlet and dunce plod forward somehow, the horse's white coat having now turned chestnut brown, whereupon you ask me did I see what happened? Did I see the starlet blush as the dunce winked?

You know I have no answer and so don't question my silence. We know one another pretty well, being brothers. Nor do Mother or Helen or Liz or the ghost of our father intervene, being as they are quite caught up in the grandeur and hilarity of the procession.

Now a fish is next, exotic, raising its fist not in defiance but as to hold aloft a striped orange and black balloon. And in the yellow wicker basket of this great balloon, a crew of foreign dignitaries is sipping champagne, it would appear. Top hats and tails on the gentlemen who have fiery eyes; and a filigreed gown on the lady whose face is a sincerely beautiful steam locomotive. Like parrots and bits of ancient lace—like the house and quince and lawnchair and rosebush back home, and like you yourself, old owl Robert—trains are truly beautiful. And this one is glossy black with silver trim. Imagine that.

Hooplas and huzzahs from the crowd for what comes along next. I missed whatever it was, but it doesn't matter because I glance at you, bearing witness to your growing contentment, and this is gift enough for me. I witness contentment in our mother's face, too, and in others'—enough, or almost enough.

Cut, paste, carve, you say. Arrange, rebalance. Go on, you say. Put your hands to the scene itself.

Proud as punch next come senators, fresh mollusks, highway patrolmen, gymnastic almanacs, waving cabriolets, pimps juggling clementines, caribou and zombies, the major himself and other deities, together in a feathered swanfloat, singing some mahogany chorale. Thereafter, devils and angels and curious harlot pumpkins. The alphabet block, the toy Judy, the commemorative spoon from Marseilles. The wicker fence percussion band, look and listen. The Golconda beyond my power to deem. Robin Hood in a nightgown is here, and so are the many marbles in his head. A Wassily chair waltzes the Matilda. Music by Glück, Mussorgsky and an acanthus leaf in frosty flames beyond the reach of any mathematician. Pennies are forged by various dirty vendors along the route, beside the burgeoning road, and other pennies are lost. The marionettes carry shards of glass gingerly and gingerly again. Whistles blow pink smoke as a huge Catherine's wheel twirls away above and beyond the history of all technology. But, more. Whales' teeth follow between the sleep and the sleep, eating the wild dust of other gadgets while they go. Nothing is a third wheel. Everything tells a story and the story is that everything tells the story.

A wooden crate was carried along, now that we neared the end of the procession, held by hands too burdened by the weight of it to count. A candid hush fell over the crowd. It came, it went, and we were left behind in thrall as the choir within it of mockingbirds, borzoi, gazelles and the rest of a comprehensive bestiary launched into some haunting song of faith that promised like decoupage a kind of richness in which reveling in detail becomes a feast of experience.

Robert, how we both cut up.

Pastel weather began to depreciate further chances for continued exposition, and these hundred fat bears on tricycles bring up the rear. One musician cupid seems to have lost a wing and lies on his side, ignored by everyone but us—we who go to him where he's fallen in the broomed dirt lane—and while it is true that he courageously waves us off, preferring his agony to our charity, his remaining wing does seem to twitch, which suggests that he'll have the use of one healthy wing, at least.

Not so bad, you say.

Won't he be forced to fly in circles from now on, though, given that he has but one wing? I ask.

We all fly in circles, you answer. It goes on, you say, it goes on just fine, and I believe you because we're brothers. Better one wing than none, you add.

This makes me smile, and I begin to think, Robert, as the sun dims down and the last train to Utopia Parkway awaits us at the station, whatever it was we saw this day, you seem to be more fortunate for it, or fortuned by it. Mother and sisters more fortunate, our dead father, and I more fortunate, as we say goodbye to the modest town of boxes less empty than I might have imagined, and watch the landscapes slide by us beyond the scratched windows of the train taking us home, retracing our way toward that unplush shoebox where the rosebush, the arranged chairs, the birdhouse on the fence, the quince and all the growing collection in my head of precious artifacts made by hands of mortals and, yes, the very idea of home, await us.

Not to mention our monastic parrot, or is it a parakeet?

*

264

Passing under Utopia's horizon the sun had gone. You asked me did I remember that turquoise elephant which, during the parade, danced on a glass bubble blown by a mauve butterfly? Whereas I could not remember such an elephant, nor bubble, nor butterfly, I knew if I opened my eyes I could imagine such things.

You misquoted our mutual favorite poet that evening after we finished dinner. *Some days,* you said,

> *Some days as if they were*
> *People or trains or sleepy quince*
> *Trees, do retire to rest, and*
> *In soft distinction lie*
> *Or tell some various truth.*

That day had been good for a birthday, truth to tell, after all. That day changed the shape and color of our house, and any world beyond.

Robert, how young we were. Mother, sisters, even Father. The world was young, going to war yet on its way back from war. Promising as an emptied, empty, emptying box. Whistling as the formerly unsung air toured it, the world and the box that was the world, soughing like someone breathing, and how it declared this little universe could be fulfilled, and you agreed with the speaking chill breeze which promised the empty box would be filled with fresh minutiae from your life, from mine, from every life ever lived.

I came along to see the parade at your kind invitation and this is my letter of gratitude. If I hadn't been there, it would have mattered. But I was there for you, and you, old friend, old owl, were there for me. A parade of amazements. Life enclosed in an intoxicating turbine casket.

More, you say. There's more.

Yes, the moon is somewhat edged by a pale orchid, though my eyes are exhausted and my mind may be playing tricks to trump me. Too, there might be truth in what you saw in dusklight—several warblers, crisply carved and brazenly painted, returning to their nests, having tired of the heat of untimely climates. It may be true their breasts are speckled black on yellow, and that some of them are dappled with reds and greens and blues. But by what magic did those cracker crumbs vanish while we were away?

Birds. What more is there to confess? The December day was plain as paste no longer and I knew what color to cut in for the parrot's beak and so did you. The beak was, like the day, the fortnight, the year, the world, unhinged, forever quince and blue and green and gray and red and black and orange and white and every known color and unknown and simply: *bird.*

The parrot is animate, beautiful, always bright. As are the quince, the moon, the yard and the house in which we dwelled together all those unforgotten years. Or so we tell ourselves and thus we believe, being brothers, being believers as we are and will be, opening and never closing our crypts of cutouts, and the pasts, nows and futures they manifest. That night, before you slept, we saw meteors lighting the sky, flying like wings outside your flaring window. From the starry dark an impossible nightingale sang you to your rest.

Articulated Lair
Poems and Art
Camille Guthrie and Louise Bourgeois

Every day you have to abandon your past and accept it and then, if you cannot accept it, you become a sculptor.

—Louise Bourgeois

PORTRAIT

At the word

RADIANCE

at any time, begins

Spiraling   solitary   trajectory

Blue white and black
made manifest

By hand, in thought

The underleaf of
reality is glinting

Camille Guthrie / Louise Bourgeois

Or, Nostalgia

and its winds

steeply drawn

born Christmas Day,
along the river

she casts intimates
in abandon

taking stunned Liberties

Louise Bourgeois, No Exit

The Past

hauled up, splashing

Ambition wrings
the necks of tapestries
of the rivulets of lineage

There, mesmerized

Immersion
at the original surface

———————

Tracing each little sensation

       the lucid ankle
       the hands irresistible

All the slight details
in repair

       Threw herself in

       Iridescent, the gloam
       of formalism

       to be loved

Louise Bourgeois, Le Défi

LE DÉFI

Crated azure

ALLUVIUM

    orders delicacy

(coveted) delivers a curved thirst
for dolphin volumes, found fountains,
vases evacuate, or blown vanities

Je t'aime accumulates

DEFY stacked secrets

Je t'aime

all the spilled lists, breakable voids,
crashing ice floes, and your eyelids

(apparent)

For isn't it

CLARITY

insuspensionof

MEMORY

in suspense of

Bells ringing

Louise Bourgeois, Nature Study

MAMELLES, OR NATURE STUDY

A STRETCHED drama of the self

poured hill to hill to a milked horizon

The fetish rubs close   is graspable   leads on

then acquiesces to divine rights

This poultice will travel will heave

Many handled rose-licked waves

for a garish thirst

EROSION

in evidence

Dismemberment

to a precipice

Camille Guthrie / Louise Bourgeois

UNTITLED (WITH GROWTH)

Penetralia

        and curiouser . . .

Ten blessings, ten pointers
Inside the solarium
Innocencies

Maybe all the humors have leaked
full-blown, worming

through opposable child-births

The full set only extrudes

Louise Bourgeois, Untitled (With Growth)

Who waters such shafts? Who

kneads marble into nourishment?

(I'd like to)

Where everything's coming up

AMORPHOUS

but eyeless, all thumbs
vegetable dumbly poking about

The rough coralline bed

she made

———————

                    sub-soil
                    sub-metaphor

She presses
pulsating scales
pushes the chisel

          Irrepressible
          Something comes through

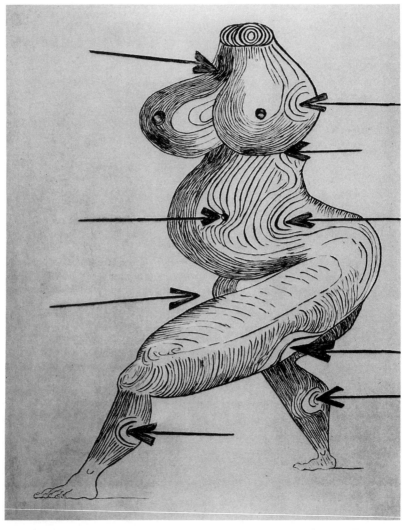

Louise Bourgeois, Sainte Sebastienne

STE. SEBASTIENNE

ARROWS

Mark the past
nakedness, inhibiting accurate portrait

Arrows over-racing
the tortured diameter

Left in the dust

The sexual directions
are armless
but voluptuous

ARROWS
acute   omnipotent

They let loose their aim
Bristling with words

I turn the other face to my chest
and cat-masked, count my wounds

Riddled, surrounded

drawn there by
immodest demands

Moving halves
drag knowledge
of the drama of the self

Camille Guthrie / Louise Bourgeois

You are sore, you are mercurial
shafting static by serial selves

Demeter

Again, angered
your trajectory fights a way

through miles and mountains
of betrayals

Standing in two of herself

Demeter

full of approaches

Drawn & Quartered
Poems and Drawings
Robert *Creeley* and Archie *Rand*

AUTHOR'S NOTE

IT WAS JOHN YAU who had introduced us some years ago in New York. Archie's humor, quickness and lack of pretension much attracted me, but the chance to work with him was curiously hard to come by despite his own play with narrative texts and old-time comic book formats. Then Archie sent me a cluster of xeroxes of drawings he'd been doing and suggested I might do some text or texts to go with them. It was an instantly attractive proposal, but, again, it wasn't until Archie actually came with his wife Maria to Buffalo— he was to check a 40-by-60-foot wall at the Castellani Museum in Niagara University, so as to do something with me for a show of my collaborations—that anything really happened.

How it did still amazes me. I knew Archie had brought with him the litho sheets with the fifty-four drawings. I had tried a few brief quatrains to see how that form might work in context with the xeroxed images he'd sent me earlier. But when we went into a back room at the museum, and Archie took out the litho sheets and asked if I might try to do a text for each image there and then, I was intimidated, not to say, shocked. Still I said I'd try, and so we set out. The procedure was for Archie to slide me an image on the litho paper. I'd try a take or two to get the feel, writing on a usual sheet of typing paper, then resolve on a particular quatrain, put it with the litho sheet related—and on to the next. So we worked through the afternoon until, finally, all fifty-four poems were finished. Then I copied each poem under its respective image on the litho sheet. I recall we pretty much closed up the place—as 'twere in dream! I felt as if I had been in some fantastic traffic of narratives, all the echoes and presences and situations—like very real life indeed. I loved the almost baroque feel of the drawings, the echo of old-time illustrations and children's books. Whatever, Archie's sure got to me. The rest you can judge for yourself.

—Robert Creeley

Dear cat, I see you
and will attend
and feed you
now as then.

If I had a cent you'd have it.
But I don't.
If I knew what to do,
I'd tell you.

Why not tell
what you've kept a secret,
not wait for it
to leap out?

What will you shoot with that?
A rabbit!
Well, where will you find it?
Behind you!

Angel holding up
the roof top—
else would fall
and kill us all!

Let me try that too
and see if I sound like you—
or is it your body's song
pulls things along?

285

Image of self at earlier age—
When thoughts had gone inward,
And life had become an emptying page—
Myself moving toward nothing.

Statue? Hermione's—
A Winter's Tale—
in the garden fixed
sense of beauty's evident patience.

It was still in front of them
but soon began to be gone.
Look, said one, now it's going!
Still, they thought, it will come again.

It was still in front of them
but soon began to be gone.
Look, said one, now it's going!
Still, they thought, it will come again.

From Late Summer Entry
Poems and Photographs
Forrest Gander *and* Sally Mann

RIVER AND TREES

The passage into a photograph may be so swollen, nacreous, limpid, and inviting that it requires a considerable effort, a convulsion in seeing's habit, to discover the drama. Just so, the river establishes the symmetry of this composition which combines soft tones, rich detail, and gentle, contrasting textures. But the river's peacefulness is contradictory. When we look closely, we see that it holds perfectly still as though in imitation of itself and so ceases to impress the likeness of a river. Long and white as a spinal column, it is surrounded by two swarthy densities like shoulder blades and arm bones with their masses of investing muscle.

Only at first does the photograph seem concerned with the river, and this is due to the long exposure, the photographer no longer shrouded behind her tripod, standing on a bridge in the galvanic eclipse of storm. Guessing at the time. The huge hiss and rip of lightning so close, the air, for seconds, isn't breathable. In these minutes, the river turns to quicksilver; its surface goes brighter, looms. The weight, though, and the dynamic tensions concentrate in the margins.

There, in the rumpled quiet of the trees, we catch animate qualities: in the swelling roll of foliage, not a composed stillness, but a smeared cascade of image. In the riffle of leafy detail, we sense the piston-driven respiration of the forest.

While we regard this slippage in the image's only-apparent repose, we register a slightly sickening feeling, as when we suddenly begin a descent. We see in the blurred trees the tracing of a peristaltic contraction. We see the landscape giving birth to our vision.

PHOTO CANTO

Even as its sexual allure condenses

                in the corners, massing,

preparatory, we situate

ourselves in the scene, the river

irradiating its grave forest,

                preplutonic.

Brush, hairy sedge, branches

unform, their outlines going

illegible, flayed to an edge of frenzy, light

                thrashing itself

out on the grass. On the retina,

a sullen cloud

shuttered to silence pours. The rock

dissolves into glint, into inference,

                a blast of cryptic menace.

The light's spasmic withdrawal

only discloses a living and utter blackness

where non-being stirs, where the swirling

roll of unborn things,

                like a nursery of spiders,

stirs beyond our senses.

ROAD AND TREE

Lit road, first letter.   Evening spooked with light.
Quarter moon road   with the darkness inside it, and full moon
sky with the dark tree inside it.   Smile of the road in the gloaming.
Tree trunk, a vector of force punched   upward. Held in place, in the
foreground, by a stenciled circle of light. Lit   road bearing a trunk of its own
darkness. Circle of light split   like a cat's eye. Road
curling left, eye   cutting right. Barely there in the soft
dirt, footprints and dogprints   commingling in the dark
throat of the radiant road   like remembered voices. An inner
landscape, for even   as light came back like bees
to the camera pronouncing   the photograph, the place
altered, had never availed   itself at all. A hem of cloud
brushed the sun, the Carolina wren's   *cheery* gave way
to a full moon   in the afternoon and little grass frogs.
Dry puffballs   exploded into gold spores as a hoof
lifted, and even if it had been   a picture of a real landscape for
one shuddering moment, of what place   is it a photograph now?
The image is all alone,   a word
knocked loose from the language, tooth   under a pillow.
And the place itself was neither   fully read nor erased since it never stopped
being written. Only   the photograph was delivered, only
the photograph stopped.

SCIENCE & STEEPLEFLOWER

The warm, velvet sheen on the water is not applied. It is
constituitive, generalized by a lack of surface texture. In this
photograph, only the stream utters light. All other light is hushed.
The vagueness of the near shoreline endows the water with a
transfigured, immaterial quality. Clear and earthbound in the
distance, the stream appears to float upward as it nears us. We
see the reflection of trees, partly erased in splotches, as through
delicate mist. The photographic grammar proceeds from slurred
darkness, in which we perspect, toward the clipped precision of
opalescent water, rocky beach, and muted woodland. The light
accelerates in luster and clarity as our eye moves more deeply into
the picture along the stream's axis. It is on this gleaming that we
are transported into the image's depths until the shorelines
converge at a stand of backlit trees whose collective shadows
pinch off the flow of our gaze.

Because the realm is uncertain, it responds to our emotions
and prompts feelings from us at the same time. Not placid, but
haunting, this pastoral. The shaggy forest is dim, private, oneiric.
And the frame of the image closes inward, producing an oblique
heaviness. The vignetting, this girdling dark, is a metaphor, and it
has two meanings. It signals the onset of our blink. So the
photograph takes on an especial power. It is the last thing we see
before our eyes snap shut. As such, vignetting can be read as a
physical sign of the evanescence of the image which, even in the
act of its preservation, must be relinquished. However it is equally
indicative of the incipient vision opening to us from the other side
of consciousness. It is the muscular curtain drawing back from the
beginning of dream.

IVY BRICK WALL

Not a transparency, it never aims to create an illusion of reality.
The distorting lens ripens our sense of mass, and momentum rises
to a feverish pitch. Under a surface language of swirling frets, of
implicitation, the discrete confrontational bodies of positive and
negative shape are sabotaged by a flotsam of vortical energy: the ivy
and brick bitten by light, tree limbs roached against the blast, a
canopy of leaves migrating rightward into marginal darkness.
Meanwhile the sparked grass rounds toward us, a proscenium.

Enmeshed in a field of concentric force, the spectator is drawn
through the framing horizontal and vertical axes into an exuberant
wormhole of unreadable brightness which suggests not depth but
an other dimension entire. A light which is life source.

It is this originary and inhuman force which transforms the
ordinary scene into an exultant one, and it presupposes an aesthetic
and ethical conception of nature as author of act and meaning.
Whelming ivy overwrites brickwork, merely human geometry.

By aggrandizing our impression of movement, the photographer
amplifies the relationship between observer and environment and
between the scene's various components. But such movement,
ungraspable by vision alone, dematerializes objects, exposing their
interior essences. At the core of the image, always, is the verb, the
seen revealing itself to our seeing. In this photograph there are no
nouns. There are no things.

COLLODION

Dogwood, laurel, rhododendron,   Judas tree. Some are not

interested in what they see, some   are not interested

in how.   The more intense

the emotion, the slower   the shutter speed.

Wrenched free of death, the mind   beholds the world. That world,

stepping clear of the still   draining pitch, shines.

Impasse of image,   an addition to meaning. Why

do you not understand   what you see? Because

you are unable   to quit

conceiving. When all goes   well, a shadow overthrows it.

Incarnate and carbonized,   the photograph gives evidence

of an arousal to be had   in no other form.

The hedge, not visible,   we feel it,

we see it.   A dark cloud, he wrote,

illuminates the night. Oh   aperture which reveals

the divine gesture   as pure demonstration of the world.

It is not a still life if it is necessary   to shift

your attitude in passing   from one section

to another. To find what is   there, proceed:

from interpretation through sensation to   finally perception. One stroke

of a wet sponge   wipes all the picture out.

From Arcana
Myung Mi Kim

pr

perdu   lying hidden, disguised. one who acts as a watcher or scout

perdure   to continue, endure, last on

The two are begun

They are shaving ends of sticks

The two are discussing seeds

They are specimens

Glass does not burn but the hillside does

The two are a vine's exhalation

———————

Myung Mi Kim

drum accompaniment

Then follow wood then water, then stones and metals, slow to heat

bbi-due-rrhuh-jut-dah   askew leaning twisted

In the bowels and studies of inferiors

Seaweed stench

"devote"

"wonder"

_____

[when my father died and left me nothing]

[this is how I speak]

_____

"helicopters hover"

"embassy compound"

Relative fence, cling fence

Someone is hiding an infant

Fish with two tails

Fish with two heads

Indigestible over days and days

Unfurled silver maple is a red burnish

———————

Myung Mi Kim

War is there and travel

The same is my sister, brothers, and mother

The father is thrush, white at birth and at dusk

Father is burying ground cool to the touch

This is some color but what color is it

"left their homes after two solid days of attacks"

"they had stayed to take care of their cow"

"the extreme cold froze medicine"

"religion and capitalism intersect in the muddy village twenty miles
     north of"

———————

cabbage looper moth
sugarcane stalk borer

What started then and ate through most of a decade

Contralto: the affliction is very near—and there is no one to help

Sad Sack places the dead dog around her shoulders—weeds higher than
    her head

Standing as standing might

Recitative

" I have dissected more than ten human bodies, destroying
    all the various members
"and removing the minutest particles of flesh which surrounded these
    veins, without causing
"any effusion of blood . . . and as one single body did not suffice for so
    long a time,
"it was necessary to proceed by stages with so many bodies as would
    render my knowledge complete

The Notebooks, da Vinci

Myung Mi Kim

At least 250,000 acres of cotton and fruit crops are under immediate
threat from the huge swarm of locusts which have invaded the southern
plain from the Pamir Mountains

Roving simians have ripped the curtains off polling booths and pushed
some officials preparing for parliamentary elections

In southwest and south central Kansas the worst condition is plants
stunted or killed off by extremely dry soil. Adding to farmers' woes are
infestations of green bugs and brown wheat mites

Three villages were overrun by thousands of toads, and farmers in the
area reportedly feel that the onslaught is a sign of impending tragedy.
Children are said to be terrified by the toads and unable to sleep. The
main road connecting the region with La Paz is coated with a thick layer
of dead toads and the stench is said to be unbearable.

———————

Myung Mi Kim

"peace-keeping troops"

"tanks beneath the windows"

The inside of someone else's dwelling visible—a table and some chairs.

You start to count one, two, three, four . . . until the explosion is near your neighborhood. You can guess the position of mortar by this counting and try to find a safe place.

If the windows are gone, weak plastic is taped up but the strong wind comes and we stay awake.

In this South Cholla Province where all vehicles had been confiscated, we resorted to walking, the method of travel of the Yi Dynasty. We reverted back 300 years.

Kwangju, 1980

It's the same to be in the house, at the shelter or anywhere. There is no safe place. When we have no electricity, we are sitting in the dark and we know what life looked like before Christ.

Sarajevo, 1992

Myung Mi Kim

The central organizing myth of comprehensive knowledge

Bent as light might bend

The openings in the human body

The age that one is

I will be my mother's age also

Color of robin's egg against spring grass

From In the Blood
Suzan-Lori Parks

Characters:
HESTER, LA NEGRITA
CHILLI/JABBER
THE WELFARE LADY/BULLY
THE DOCTOR/TROUBLE
THE AMIGA GRINGA/BEAUTY
REVERAND D./BABY

Author's Note: This play requires a cast of 6 adult actors; 5 of those actors double as adults and children.

Prologue

(ALL *clustered together.*)

ALL. wissa-wissa-wissa-wissa-wissa-wissa-wissa-wissa
   THERE SHE IS!
   WHO DOES SHE THINK
   SHE IS
   THE NERVE SOME PEOPLE HAVE
   SHOULDNT HAVE IT IF YOU CANT AFFORD IT
   AND YOU KNOW SHE CANT
   SHE DONT GOT NO SKILLS
   CEPT ONE
   CANT READ CANT WRITE
   SHE MARRIED?
   WHAT DO YOU THINK?
   SHE OUGHTA BE MARRIED
   SHE AINT MARRIED
   THATS WHY THINGS ARE BAD LIKE THEY ARE
   CAUSE OF
   GIRLS LIKE THAT

THAT EVER HAPPEN TO ME YOU WOULDNT SEE ME
    HAVING IT
YOU WOULDNT SEE THAT HAPPENING TO ME
WHO THE HELL SHE THINK SHE IS
AND NOW WE GOT TO PAY FOR IT
THE NERVE
SOME PEOPLE HAVE
BAD LUCK
SHE OUGHTA GET MARRIED
TO WHO?
THIS AINT THE FIRST TIME THIS HAS HAPPENED TO HER
NO?
THIS IS HER FIFTH
FIFTH?
SHE GOT FIVE OF THEM
FIVE BRATS
AND NOT ONE OF THEM GOT A DADDY
HAH!

    (*They spit.*)

WHOS THE DADDY?
SHE WONT TELL
SHE WONT TELL CAUSE SHE DONT KNOW
SHE KNOWS
NO SHE DONT
HOW COULD A GIRL NOT KNOW
WHEN YOU HAD SO MUCH ACTION YOU LOOSE
    A FRACTION
OF YR GOOD SENSE
THE PART OF MEN SHE SEES ALL LOOK THE SAME
    ANYWAY
WATCH YR MOUTH
I DIDNT SAY NOTHING
YR TALKING ALL NASTY AND THAT AINT RIGHT
THERES CHILDREN HERE
WHERES THE CHILDREN I DONT SEE NO CHILDREN
OOOOHWEEEE! GOLD JEWLRY ON HER, HA!
AND YOU KNOW WHERE SHE GOT IT TOO
FROM HER HUSBAND
SHE DONT GOT NO HUSBAND
THAT GOLD SHE GOT IS YR TAX DOLLARS AT WORK

SHE MARRIED?
SHE AINT MARRIED
WHOS THE DADDY?
SHE DONT KNOW
SHE DONT GOT NO SKILLS
CEPT ONE
CANT READ CANT WRITE
SHE MARRIED?
WHAT DO YOU THINK?

ALL
ALL

HOLD YR HEAD HIGH, GIRL
BUT NOT FOR LONG
CAUSE SHE KNOWS SHES A NO COUNT
SHIFTLESS
HOPELESS
BAD NEWS
BURDEN TO SOCIETY
HUSSY
SLUT
JUST PLAIN STUPID IF YOU ASK ME AINT NO SMART
    WOMAN GOT 5 BASTARDS
AND NOT A PENNY TO HER NAME
SOMETHINGS GOTTA BE DONE TO STOP THIS SORT
    OF THING
CAUSE I'LL BE DAMNED IF SHE GONNA LIVE OFF ME
HERE SHE COMES
MOVE ASIDE
WHAT SHE GOTS CATCHY
LET HER PASS
DONT GET CLOSE
YOU DONT WANNA LOOK LIKE YOU KNOW HER
STEP OFF!

(*They part like the Red Sea would.*)

(HESTER, LA NEGRITA *passes through them. She holds a "Newborn Baby" in her arms.*)

IT WONT END WELL FOR HER

309

HOW YOU KNOW?
I GOT EYES DONT I
BAD NEWS IN HER BLOOD PLAIN AS DAY

ALL
HESTER
ALL

(HESTER *lifts the child up, raising it toward the sky.*)

HESTER. My treasure. My joy.

ALL. HAH!

(*They spit.*)

Scene 1: Under the Bridge

(*Home under the bridge. The word "SLUT" scrawled on a wall. Hesters oldest child,* JABBER, *13, studies that scrawl.* HESTER *lines up soda cans as her youngest child,* BABY, *now 2 yrs old, watches.*)

HESTER. Zit uh good word or a bad word?

JABBER
JABBER

HESTER. Aint like you to have your mouth shut, Jabber. Say it to me and we can figure out the meaning together.

JABBER. Naaa—

HESTER. What I tell you about saying "Naa" when you mean no? You talk like that people wont think you got no brains and Jabber got brains. All my kids got brains, now.

(*Rest.*)

Lookie here, Baby. Mamma set the cans for you. Mamma gonna show you how to make some money, watch.

JABBER. Im slow.

HESTER. Slow aint never stopped nothing, Jabber. You bring yr foot down on it and smash it flat. Howabout that, Baby? Put it in the pile and thats that. Now you try.

(BABY *jumps on the can smashing it flat, hollering as he smashes.*)

BABY. Ha!

HESTER. Yr a natural! Jabber, yr little baby brothers a natural. We gonna come out on top this month, I can feel it. Try another one, Baby.

JABBER. They wrote it on yr practice place.

HESTER. Yes they did.

JABBER. They wrote in yr practice place so you didnt practice today.

HESTER. I practiced. In my head. In the air. In the dirt underfoot.

JABBER. Lets see.

(*With great difficulty she makes an "A" in the dirt.*)

HESTER. The letter A.

JABBER. Almost.

HESTER. You gonna disparage me I aint gonna practice.

BABY. Mommmmieee!

HESTER. Gimmieuhminute, Baby-child.

JABBER. Legs apart hands crost the chest like I showd you. Try again.

BABY. Mommieee!

HESTER. See the pretty can, Baby?

BABY. Ha!

JABBER. Try again.

BABY. Mommmieee!

HESTER. Later. Read that word out to me, huh? I like it when you read to me.

JABBER. Dont wanna read it.

HESTER. Cant or wont?

JABBER. —cant.

HESTER
JABBER

>(*He knows what the word says, but he wont say it.*)

HESTER. I was sick when I was carrying you. Damn you, slow fool. Aaah, my treasure, cmmeer. My oldest treasure.

>(*She hugs him close.*)

>(HESTER *looks at the word, its letters mysterious to her.* BABY *smashes can after can.*)

HESTER. Go scrub it off, then. I like my place clean.

>(JABBER *dutifully scrubs the wall.*)

HESTER. We know who writ it up there. It was them bad boys writing on my home. And in my practice place. Do they write on they own homes? I dont think so. They come under the bridge and write things they dont write no where else. A mean ugly word, I'll bet. A word to hurt our feelings. And because we aint lucky we gotta live with it. 5 children I got. 5 treasures. 5 joys. But we aint got our leg up, just yet. So we gotta live with mean words and hurt feelings.

JABBER. Words dont hurt my feelings, Mamma.

HESTER. Dont disagree with me.

JABBER. Sticks and stones, Mamma.

HESTER. Yeah. I guess.

HESTER
JABBER
HESTER

HESTER. Too late for yr sisters and brother to still be out. Yr little brother Babys gonna make us rich. He learns quick. Look at him go.

(*She lines up more cans and* BABY *jumps on them, smashing them all.*)

(BULLY, *her 12 yr old girl, runs in.*)

BULLY. Momieeeeeeeee! Mommie, Trouble he has really done it this time. I told him he was gonna be doing life and he laughed and then I said he was gonna get the electric chair and you know what he said?

HESTER. Help me sack the cans.

BULLY. He said a bad word!

HESTER. Sack the cans.

(*They sack the crushed cans.*)

BULLY. Trouble he said something really bad but Im not saying it cause if I do yll wash my mouth. What he said was bad but what he did, what he did was worse.

HESTER. Whatd he do?

BULLY. Stole something.

HESTER. Food?

BULLY. No.

HESTER. Toys?

BULLY. No.

HESTER. I dont like youall stealing toys and I dont like youall stealing food. But it happens and I wont punish you for it. Yr just kids. Trouble thinks with his stomach. He hungry he takes, sees a toy, gotta have it.

BULLY. A policeman saw him steal and ran after him but Trouble ran faster cause the policeman was fat.

HESTER. Policeman chased him?

BULLY. He had a big stomach. Like he was pregnant. He was jiggling and running and yelling and red in the face.

HESTER. What he steal?

BULLY. —nothing.

HESTER. You talk that much and you better keep talking, Miss.

(BULLY *buttons her lips.* HESTER *pops her upside the head.*)

BULLY. Owwww!

HESTER. Get outa my sight. Worse than a thief is a snitch that dont snitch.

(TROUBLE, *age 10 and* BEAUTY, *age 7, run in, breathless. They see* HESTER *eyeing them and stop running to walk nonchalantly.*)

HESTER. What you got behind you?

TROUBLE. Nothing. Jabber, what you doing?

JABBER. Cleaning the wall.

BEAUTY. My hair needs a ribbon.

HESTER. Not right now it dont. You steal something?

TROUBLE. Me? Whats cookin?

HESTER. Soup of the day.

TROUBLE. We had soup the day yesterday.

HESTER. Todays a new day.

BEAUTY. Is it a new soup?

HESTER. Wait and see. You gonna end up in the penitentiary and embarrass your mother?

TROUBLE. No.

HESTER. If you do I'll kill you. Set the table.

JABBER. Thats girls work.

TROUBLE. Mommiee—

BULLY. Troubles doing girls work Troubles doing girls work.

HESTER. Set the damn table or Ima make a girl outa you!

TROUBLE. You cant make a girl outa me.

HESTER. Dont push me!

(*Rest.*)

Look, Baby. See the soup? Mommies stirring it. Dont come close, its hot.

BEAUTY. I want a ribbon.

HESTER. Get one I'll tie it in.

(BEAUTY *gets a ribbon.*)

(TROUBLE *gets bowls, wipes them clean, hands them out.*)

(HESTER *follows behind him and, out of the back of his pants, yanks a policeman's club.*)

HESTER. Whered you get this?

TROUBLE
HESTER
TROUBLE

HESTER. I said—

TROUBLE. I found it. On the street. It was just lying there.

BULLY. You stole it.

TROUBLE. Did not!

HESTER. Dont lie to me.

TROUBLE. I found it. I did. It was just lying on the street. I was minding my own business.

HESTER. That why the cops was chasing you?

TROUBLE. Snitch!

BULLY. Jailbait!

TROUBLE. I aint no jail nothing I aint never been in no jail.

BULLY. Not yet!

TROUBLE. Least theyd take me. If you killed 100 people they wouldnt take you in the jailhouse cause you so damn ugly.

BULLY. You gonna get life imprisonment. You gonna get the electric chair.

TROUBLE. You gonna get a fist sandwich, Bitch.

315

(BULLY *hits* TROUBLE *hard. He bursts into tears.*)

(HESTER *hits* BULLY *hard. She bursts into tears.*)

(BABY *bursts into tears.*)

HESTER. Suppertime!

> (*They stop crying.*)
>
> (*She slips the club in the belt of her dress. It hangs there like a sword. She'll wear it like this for most of the play.*)
>
> (*Her children sit in a row holding their bowls. She ladles out the soup.*)

HESTER. Todays soup the day, ladies and gents, is a very special blend of herbs and spices. The broth is chef Mommies worldwide famous "whathaveyou" stock. Theres carrots in there. Theres meat. Theres oranges. Theres pie.

TROUBLE. What kinda pie?

HESTER. What kind you like?

TROUBLE. Apple.

HESTER. Theres apple pie.

JABBER. Pumpkin.

BULLY. And cherry!

HESTER. Theres pumpkin and cherry too. And steak. And mash-potatoes for Beauty. And milk for Baby.

BEAUTY. And diamonds.

JABBER. You cant eat diamonds.

HESTER. So when you find one in yr soup whatll you do?

BEAUTY. Put it on my finger.

> (*They slurp down their soup quickly. As soon as she fills their bowls, theyre empty again.*)
>
> (*The kids eat.* HESTER *doesnt.*)

JABBER. You aint hungry?

HESTER. I'll eat later.

JABBER. You always eating later.

HESTER. You did a good job with the wall, Jabber. Whatd that word say anyway?

JABBER. —Nothing.

(*The soup pot is empty.*)
HESTER
JABBER/BULLY/TROUBLE/BEAUTY/BABY

(*Rest.*)

HESTER. Bedtime.

TROUBLE. You gonna give the club back?

BULLY. Its not yours.

HESTER. You stole it from a cop?

TROUBLE. It was just dangling there.

HESTER. I oughta make you give it back. But then theyd lock you up for stealing. Time for bed.

BULLY. Could we have a story?

HESTER. (*Rest.*) All right.

(*Rest.*)

There were once these five brothers and they were all big and strong and handsome and didnt have a care in the world. One was known for his brains so they called him Smarts and one was known for his muscles, so they called him Toughguy, the third one was a rascal so they called him Wild, the fourth one was as good-looking as all get out and they called him Looker and the fifth was the youngest and they called him Honeychild cause he was as young as he was sweet. And they was always together these five brothers. Everywhere they went they always went together. No matter what they was always together cause they was best friends and wasnt nothing could divide them. And there was this Princess. And she lived in a castle and she was lonesome. She was lonesome and looking for love but she couldnt leave her castle so she couldnt look very far, but every day she would stick her head out her window and sing to the sun and every night she would stick her head

317

out and sing to the moon and the stars: "Where are you?" and one day the five brothers heard her and came calling and she looked upon them and she said. There are five of you, and each one is wonderful and special in his own way. But the law of my country doesnt allow a princess to have more than one husband. And that was such bad news and they were all so in love that they all cried. Until the Princess had an idea. She was after all the Princess, so she changed the law of the land and married them all.

(*Rest.*)

And with Bro Smarts she had a baby named Jabber. And with Bro Toughguy she had Bully. With Bro Wild she had Trouble. With Bro Looker came Beauty. With Bro Honeychild came Baby. And they were all happy.

JABBER. Until the bad news came.

HESTER. No bad news came.

JABBER. Theres always bad news.

HESTER. Bedtime.

BEAUTY. Where did the Daddys go?

HESTER. They went to bed.

TROUBLE. They ran off.

JABBER. The war came and the brothers went off to fight and they all died.

BEAUTY. They all died?

JABBER. And they fell into the ground and the dirt went over they heads.

HESTER. Its bedtime. Now!

BEAUTY. Im scared.

TROUBLE. I aint scared. Jabber, you a spook.

BULLY. Yr the spook.

TROUBLE. Yr a bastard.

BULLY. Yr a bastard.

HESTER. Yr all bastards!

(*The children burst into tears.*)

HESTER. Cmmeer. Cmmeer. Mama loves you. Shes just tired is all. Lemmie hug you.

(*They nestle around her and she hugs them.*)

HESTER. My 5 treasures. My 5 joys.

HESTER
JABBER/BULLY/TROUBLE/BEAUTY/BABY
HESTER

HESTER. Lets hit the sack! And leave yr shoes for polish and yr shirts and blouses for press. You dont wanna look like you dont got nobody.

(*They take off their shoes and tops and go inside leaving* HESTER *outside alone.*)

HESTER
HESTER
HESTER

(*Rest.*)

(*She examines the empty soup pot, shines the kids shoes, "presses" their clothes.*)

HESTER. You didnt eat, Hester. And the pain in yr gut comes from having nothing in it.

(*Rest.*)

Kids ate good though. Ate their soup all up. They wont starve. Wont be like them animals who die and leave they bones in the sun to dry. Having the bugs pick at they privates. And the vultures and the wolves. Me if I fell dead I would stay alive long enough to eat my arm up. You wouldnt catch me going to hell on an empty stomach. Bugs in my skin. Theyre gonna eat me up first. So when I go wont be nothing left.

(*Rest.*)

None of these shoes shine. Never did no matter how hard you spit on em, Hester. You get a leg up the first thing you do is get shoes. New shoes for yr 5 treasures. You got yrself a good pair of shoes already.

(*From underneath a pile of junk she takes a shoebox. Inside is a pair of white pumps. She looks them over then puts them away.*)

Dont know where yll wear them but yll look good when you get there.

(*She takes out a small tapeplayer. Pops in a tape.*)

(*She takes a piece of chalk from her pocket and, on the freshly scrubbed wall, practices her letters: she writes the letter "A" over and over and over.*)

(*The cassette tape plays as she writes.*)

REVERAND D. (*On tape.*) If you cant always do right then you got to admit that some times, some times my friends you are going to do wrong and you are going to have to *live* with that. Somehow work that into the fabric of your life. Because there aint a soul out there that is spot free. There aint a soul out there that has walked but hasnt stumbled. Aint a single solitary soul out there that has said "hello" and not "goodbye," has said "yes" to the lord and "yes" to the devil too, has drunk water and drunk wine, loved and hated, experienced the good side of the tracks and the bad. That is what they call livin, friends. L-I-V-N, friends. Life on earth is full of confusion. Life on earth is full of misunderstandings, repremandings, and we focus on the trouble, friends when it is the solution to those troubles we oughta be looking at. I have fallen and I cant get up! How many times have you heard that, friends? The fellow on the street with his whisky breath and his outstretched hand, the banker scraping the money off the top, the runaway child turned criminal all cry out "I have fallen, and I cant get up!" "I have fallen—"

(HESTER *hears someone coming. She quickly turns the tape off and rubs the wall clean.*)

(*She goes back to polishing the shoes.*)

(AMIGA GRINGA *comes in.*)

AMIGA GRINGA. "I have fallen right on my ass!"

HESTER. Dont make fun.

AMIGA GRINGA. Look at old mother hubbard or whatever.

HESTER. Keep quiet. Theyre sleeping.

AMIGA GRINGA. The old woman and the shoe. Thats who you are.

HESTER. I get my leg up thats what I'm getting. New shoes for my treasures.

AMIGA GRINGA. Thatll be some leg up.

HESTER. You got my money?

AMIGA GRINGA. Is that a way to greet a friend? "You got my money?" What world is this?

HESTER. You got my money, Amiga?

AMIGA GRINGA. I got *news* for you, Hester. News thats better than gold. But first: heads up.

(*The* DOCTOR *comes in. He wears a sandwich board and carries all his office paraphernalia on his back.*)

DOCTOR. Hester! Yr due for a checkup.

HESTER. My guts been hurting me.

DOCTOR. I'm on my way home just now. Catch up with me tomorrow. We'll have a look at it then.

(*He goes on his way.*)

AMIGA GRINGA. Doc! I am in pain like you would not believe. My hips, doc. When I move them—blinding flashes of light and then—down I go, flat on my back, like I'm dead, Doc.

DOCTOR. I gave you something for that yesterday.

DOCTOR
AMIGA GRINGA

(*He slips* AMIGA *a vial of pills. She slips him some money.*)

(*He goes on his way.*)

321

AMIGA GRINGA. He's a saint.

HESTER. Sometimes.

AMIGA GRINGA. Want some?

HESTER. I want my money.

AMIGA GRINGA. Patience, girl. All good things are on their way. Do you know what the word is?

HESTER. What word?

AMIGA GRINGA. Word is that yr first love is back in town, doing well and looking for you.

HESTER. Chilli? Jabbers daddy? Looking for me?

AMIGA GRINGA. Thats the word.

HESTER
HESTER

HESTER. Bullshit. Gimmie my money, Miga. I promised the kids cake and icecream. How much you get?

AMIGA. First, an explanation of the economic environment.

HESTER. Just gimmie my money—

AMIGA. The Stock Market, The Bond Market, Wall Street, Grain Futures, Bulls and Bears and Pork Bellies. They all impact the price a woman such as myself can get for a piece of "found" jewelry.

HESTER. That werent jewelry I gived you that was a watch. A Mans watch. Name brand. And it was working.

AMIGA. Do you know what the Dow did today, Hester? The Dow was up twelve points. And that prize fighter, the one everyone is talking about. The one with the pretty wife and the heavyweight crown, he rang the opening bell. She wore a dress cut down to here. And the Dow shot up 43 points in the first minutes of trading, Hester. Up like a rocket. And men glanced up at the clocks on the walls of their offices and women around the country glanced into the faces of their children and time passed. And someone looks at their watch because its lunchtime, Hester. And theyre having— lunch. And they wish it would last forever. Cause when they get

back to their office where they—work, when they get back the
Dow has plumetted. And theres a lot of racing around and time is
brief and something must be done before the closing bell. Phone
calls are made, marriages dissolve, promises lost in the shuffle,
Hester and all this time your Amiga Gringa is going from fence to
fence trying to get the best price on this piece of "found" jewlery.
Numbers racing on lightboards, Hester, telling those that are in
the know, the value of who knows what. One man, broken down
in tears in the middle of the avenue, oh my mutual funds he was
saying. The market was hot, and me, a suspicious looking mother,
very much like yourself, with no real address and no valid forms
of identification, walking the streets with a hot watch.

> (*Rest.*)

Here.

(*She gives* HESTER $.)

HESTER. Wheres the rest?

AMIGA. Thats it.

HESTER. 5 bucks?

AMIGA. It wasnt a good day. Some days are good some days are bad.
I kept a buck for myself.

HESTER. You stole from me.

AMIGA. Dont be silly. We're friends, Hester.

HESTER. I shoulda sold it myself.

AMIGA. But you had the baby to watch.

HESTER. And no ones gonna give money to me with me carrying
Baby around. Still I coulda got more than 5.

AMIGA. Go nextime yrself then. The dangers I incur, working with
you. You oughta send yr kids away. Like me. I got 3 kids. All under
the age of 3. And do you see me looking all baggy eyed, up all
night shining little shoes and flattening little shirts, and going
without food? Theres plenty of places that you can send them.
Homes. Theres plenty of peoples, rich ones especially, that cant
have kids. The rich spend days looking through the newspaper for
ads where they can buy one. Or they go to the Bastard Homes and

pick one out. Youd have some freedom. Youd have a chance at life. Like me.

HESTER. My kids is mine. I get rid of em what do I got? Nothing. I got nothing now, but if they go I got less than nothing.

AMIGA. Suit yrself. You wouldnt have to send them all away, just one, or two, or three.

HESTER. All I need is a leg up. I get my leg up I'll be ok.

(BULLY *comes outside and stands there watching them. She wears a pink one-piece flame-retardant pajama.*)

HESTER. What.

BULLY. My hands stuck.

HESTER. Why you sleep with yr hands in fists?

AMIGA GRINGA. Yr an angry girl, arentcha, Bully.

BULLY. Idunno. This ones stuck too.

HESTER. Maybe yll grow up to be a boxer, huh? We can watch you ringside, huh? Wide World of Sports.

AMIGA GRINGA. Presenting in this corner weighing 32 pounds the Challenger: Bully!

BULLY. Im a good girl.

HESTER. Course you are. There. You shouldnt sleep with yr hands balled up. The good fairies come by in the night with treats for little girls and they put them in yr hands. How you gonna get any treats if yr hands are all balled up?

BULLY. Jabber is bad and Trouble is bad and Beauty is bad and Baby is bad but I'm good. Bullys a good girl.

HESTER. Go on back to bed now.

BULLY. Miga. Smell.

AMIGA GRINGA. You got bad breath.

BULLY. I forgot to brush my teeth.

HESTER. Go head.

(BULLY *squats off, in the "bathroom" and rubs her teeth with her finger.*)

AMIGA GRINGA. Babys daddy, that Reverand, he ever give you money?

HESTER. No.

AMIGA GRINGA. He's a gold mine. I seen the collection plate going around. Its a full plate.

HESTER. I aint seen him since before Baby was born.

AMIGA GRINGA. Thats two years.

HESTER. He didnt want nothing to do with me. His heart went hard.

AMIGA GRINGA. My second kids Daddy had a hard heart at first. But time mushed him up. Remember when he comed around crying about his lineage and asking whered the baby go? And I'd already gived it up.

HESTER. Reverand D., his heart is real hard. Like a rock.

AMIGA GRINGA. Worth a try all the same.

(*Rest.*)

You know what my problem was? Not matter what kind of contraceptive device I tried, nothing never worked. Im a very fer-tile woman.

HESTER. Yeah.

(*Rest.*)

Who told you Chilli was lookin for me?

AMIGA GRINGA. Word on the street, thats all.

(TROUBLE, *dressed in blue flame-retardant pajamas, comes in.*)

(*He walks straight to* HESTERS *coat, rummages through it, finding a box of matches. He tries one. Then takes the box back inside.*)

HESTER. What the hell you doing?

TROUBLE. Sleepwalking.

HESTER. You sleepwalk yourself back over here and gimmie them matches or Im gonna kill you.

(*He dutifully gives her the matches back.*)

(BULLY *has finished with her teeth.*)

BULLY. You wanna smell?

HESTER. Thats ok.

BULLY. Dont you wanna smell?

(HESTER *leans in and* BULLY *opens her mouth.*)

BULLY. I only did one side cause I only ate with one side today.

HESTER. Go on to bed.

(BULLY *passes* TROUBLE *and hits him hard.*)

TROUBLE. Aaaaah!

BULLY. Yr a bad person!

(*She hits him again.*)

TROUBLE. AaaaaaaaaH!

HESTER. Who made you policewoman?

TROUBLE. Ima blow you sky high one day you bully bitch!

HESTER. You watch your mouth!

BULLY. Jailbait!

TROUBLE. Sky high kaboom and you gonna be in a million pieces, nigger!

BULLY. Who you calling nigger?

(BULLY *goes to hit him again.*)

HESTER. Freeze!

(*Rest.*)

Trouble I thought you said you was sleep. Go over there and lie down and shut up or you wont see tomorrow.

(*He goes back to sleepwalking and walks a distance off, curling up asleep.*)

326

HESTER. Bully. Go inside. Close yr eyes and yr mouth and not a word, hear?

(BULLY *goes inside without a word.*)

HESTER. I used to wash Troubles mouth out with soap. When he used bad words. Found out he likes the taste of soap. Sometimes you cant win. No matter what you do.

(*Rest.*)

Im going down to Welfare and get an upgrade. The worldll take care of the women and children.

AMIGA GRINGA. Theyre gonna give you the test. See what skills you got. Make you write stuff.

HESTER. Like what?

AMIGA GRINGA. Like yr name.

HESTER. I can write my damn name. Im not such a fool that I cant write my own goddamn name. I can write my goddamn name.

(*Inside,* BABY *starts crying.*)

HESTER. HUSH!

(BABY *hushes.*)

AMIGA GRINGA. You should pay yrself a visit to Babys daddy. Dont take along the kid in the flesh thatll be too much. For a buck I'll get someone to take a snapshot.

(JABBER *comes in, dressed in a one-piece blue flame-retardant pajama, sleepily shuffling.*)

(*He doesnt come too close but keeps his distance.*)

JABBER. I was in a row boat and the sea was flat like a blue plate and you was rowing me and it was fun.

HESTER. Go back to bed.

JABBER. It was a good day but then Bad news and the sea started rolling and the boat tipped and I fell out and—

HESTER. You wet the bed.

JABBER. I fell out the boat.

HESTER. You wet the bed.

JABBER. I wet the bed.

HESTER. 13 years old still peeing in the bed.

JABBER. It was uh accident.

HESTER. Whats wrong with you?

JABBER. Accidents happen.

HESTER. Yeah you should know cause yr uh damn accident. Shit. Take that off, wear my coat.

(JABBER *strips and puts on her coat.*)

AMIGA GRINGA. He aint bad looking, Hester. A little slow, but some women like that.

HESTER. Gimmie a kiss.

(*He kisses her on the cheek, she kisses him on the forehead.*)

JABBER. Mommie?

HESTER. Bed.

JABBER. All our daddys died, right? All our daddys died in the war, right?

HESTER. Yeah, Jabber.

JABBER. They went to war and they died and you cried. They went to war and died but whered they go when they died?

HESTER. They into other things now.

JABBER. Like what?

HESTER. —Worms. They all turned into worms, honey. They crawling around in the dirt happy as larks, eating the world up, never hungry. Go to bed.

(JABBER *goes in.*)

(*Rest.*)

AMIGA GRINGA. Worms?

HESTER. Whatever.

AMIGA GRINGA. He's yr favorite. You like him the best.

HESTER. He's my first.

AMIGA GRINGA. He's yr favorite.

HESTER. I dont got no *favorite.*

    (*Rest.*)

5 bucks. 3 for their treats. And one for that photo. Reverand D. aint the man I knew. He's got money now. A salvation business and all. Maybe his stone-heart is mush, though. Maybe.

AMIGA GRINGA. Cant hurt to try.

Scene 2: Street Practice

(HESTER *has a framed picture of Baby.*)

HESTER. Picture, it comed out pretty good. Got him sitting on a chair, and dont he look like he got everything one could want in life? He's two yrs old. Andll be growd up with a life of his own before I blink.

    (*Rest.*)

Picture came out good. Thought Amiga was cheating me but it came out good.

    (*She meets the* DOCTOR, *coming the other way. As before he carries all of his office paraphernalia on his back. He wears a sandwich board with the words hidden.*)

DOCTOR. Dont move a muscle, I'll be set up in a jiffy.

HESTER. I dont got more than a minute.

DOCTOR. Hows yr gut?

HESTER. Not great.

DOCTOR. Say "Aaaah!"

HESTER. Aaaah!

    (*As she stands there with her mouth open, he sets up his road-side office: a thin curtain, his doctor's shingle, his instruments, his black bag.)*

DOCTOR. Do you know what it takes to keep my road-side practice running? Do you know how much The Higher Ups would like to shut me down? Every blemish on your record is a blemish on mine. Take yr guts for instance: yr pain could be nothing or it could be the end of the road. A cyst or a tumor. A lump or a virus or an infected sore. Or cancer, Hester. Undetected. There youd be, lying in yr coffin with all yr little ones gathered around motherlessly weeping and The Higher Ups pointing their fingers at me, saying I should of saved the day, but instead stood idly by. You and yr children live as you please and Im the one The Higher Ups hold responsible. Would you like a pill?

HESTER. No thanks.

(The DOCTOR takes a pill.)

DOCTOR. How are yr children?

HESTER. Theyre all right.

DOCTOR. All 5?

HESTER. All 5.

DOCTOR. Havent had any more have you?

HESTER. No.

DOCTOR. But you could. But you might.

HESTER. —Maybe.

DOCTOR. Word from The Higher Ups is that one more kid outa the likes of you and theyre on the likes of me like white on rice. I'd like to propose something—. First, open yr mouth and show me yr tongue.

(He examines her quickly and thoroughly.)

DOCTOR . Good good good good good. The Higher Ups are breathing down my back, Hester. They want answers! They want results! Solutions! Solutions! Solutions! Thats what they want.

(He goes to take another pill, but doesnt.)

DOCTOR. I only take one a day. I only allow myself one a day.

(*Rest.*)

Give me a hug.

(HESTER *lets him hug her. He hugs her tightly and then a little lasciviously, before letting her go.*)

HESTER. You lonesome?

DOCTOR. No.

HESTER
DOCTOR

(*He goes back to examining her.*)

DOCTOR. Yr blood pressures a little high. Breathe in deep: lungs are clear. Yr heart sounds good. Strong as an ox. Youve kept yr shape, considering. Looks arent what they were back in the days but thats to be expected. No lumps no bumps thats lucky.

HESTER. This winters been cold. The wind under the bridge is colder than the wind on the streets.

DOCTOR. Excercise. Thats what I suggest. When the temperature drops I run in place. Yr ears look clear.

HESTER. If you could put in a good word for me and my kids. Help us get a place to live.

DOCTOR. Dont see why you dont go to the shelter.

HESTER. Theres bad people there.

DOCTOR. Touch yr toes. Again. Again. Stay down. Rectum seems fine. Lets take yr temperature.

(*He sees the club hanging from her belt and examines it as he would her arm.*)

DOCTOR. Whats this? Yr not growing a thing are ya? Ha ha.

HESTER. Its a club. For protection.

DOCTOR. Good thinking.

HESTER. In the shelter they touch my kids, so we had to go.

DOCTOR. Hard not to these days. And your kids, theyre probably

331

sexually curious too, right?

HESTER. They touch my kids.

> (*Unseen,* CHILLI *walks by with his picnic basket on his arm. He pauses, checks his pocketwatch, then continues on.*)

DOCTOR. What can you do? What can anyone do? Yr running a temperature. Bit of a fever. I would perscribe bedrest but you wouldnt do it. Hold yr hands out. Shaky. Experiencing any stress and tension?

HESTER. Not really.

DOCTOR. Howre yr meals?

HESTER. The kids come first.

DOCTOR. Course they do. Howre yr bowels. Regular?

HESTER. I dunno.

DOCTOR. Once a day?

HESTER. Sometimes. My gut—

DOCTOR. In a minute. Gimmie the Spread & Squat right quick. Lets have a look under the hood.

> (*Standing, she straddles and squats. Like an otter, he slides between her legs on a dolly and looks up into her privates with a flashlight.*)

DOCTOR. Last sexual encounter?

HESTER. Thats been awhile, now.

DOCTOR. Yve healed up well from your last birth.

HESTER. Its been 2 years. His names Baby.

DOCTOR. Any pain, swelling, off-color discharge, strange smells?

HESTER. No.

DOCTOR. L-M-P?

HESTER. About a week ago.

> (*Rest.*)

How *you* been feeling, Doc?

DOCTOR. Sometimes I'm up, sometimes I'm down.

HESTER. You said you was lonesome once. I came for a checkup and you said you was lonesome. You lonesome today, Doc?

DOCTOR. No.

HESTER. Oh.

DOCTOR. Yr intelligent. Attractive enough. You could of made something of yourself.

HESTER. Im doing all right.

DOCTOR. The Higher Ups say yr in a skid. I agree.

HESTER. Oh, I coulda been the Queen of Sheba, it just werent in the cards, Doc.

DOCTOR. Yr kids are 5 strikes against you.

HESTER. I dont need no lecture. Gimmie something for my gut so I can go.

DOCTOR. The Higher Ups, they say I'm not making an impact. But what do you care.

HESTER. My gut—

DOCTOR. Stand right here.

> (*He draws a line in the dirt, positions her behind it and walks a few steps away.*)
>
> (*He reveals the writing on his sandwich board. It is the letter "A."*)

Read.

HESTER. —A.

DOCTOR. Good.

> (*He takes a step back, increasing the distance between them, then reveals a second letter, this time the letter "P."*)

Read.

HESTER. —. —. —.

> (*Rest.*)

I need glasses for that.

DOCTOR. Uh huhn.

> (*He steps closer.*)

Howaboutnow?

HESTER. I need glasses I guess.

DOCTOR. I guess you do.

> (*He steps even closer and reveals an entire word. The word is "SPAY."*)

HESTER. (Somethin-A-somethin.)

> (*Rest.*)

I need glasses.

DOCTOR. You cant read this?

HESTER. I gotta go.

> (*She turns to go and he grabs her hand, holding her fast.*)

DOCTOR. When I say removal of your "womanly parts" do you know what parts I'm talking about?

HESTER. Yr gonna take my womans parts?

DOCTOR. My hands are tied. The Higher Ups are calling the shots now.

> (*Rest.*)

You have 5 healthy children, itll be for the best, considering.

HESTER. My womans parts.

DOCTOR. Ive forwarded my recommendation to yr case worker. Its out of my hands. Im sorry.

HESTER. I gotta go.

> (*But she doesnt move. She stands there numbly.*)

DOCTOR. Yr gut. Lets have a listen.

> (*He puts his ear to her stomach, listens.*)

Growling hungry stomach. Heres a dollar. Go get yrself a
sandwich.

(*She takes the money and goes.*)

DOCTOR
DOCTOR
DOCTOR

1st Confession: The Doctor
"Times Are Tough: What Can We Do?"

DOCTOR. Times are tough:
What can we do?
When I see a woman begging on the streets I guess I could
Bring her in my house
sit her at my table
make her a member of my family, sure.
But there are hundreds and thousands of them
and my house cant hold them all.
Maybe we should all take in just one.
Except they wouldnt really fit.
They wouldnt really fit in with us.
Theres such a gulf between us. What can we do?
The Higher Ups see her
As she lives and breathes and walks and talks as she has life
     as she passes life on
She was well entrenched in that process before I came along
A boulder is rolling down the side of the mountain what can
     one do,
it gathers no moss! what can one do?
I take my practice to the streets,
Up and down with my black bag and my medicines what more
     can I do?
The earth revolves around the sun: let it be but
theres a mama dog running lose and her puppies are crying
     because theres not
theres not enough food for those poor little pups
and the pups grow into dogs unhousebroken and illmannered
     with families of their own.

335

The mama dog dashes by:
"Spay it!"
Thats what *they* say.

   (Rest.)

I am a man of the people from way back my streetside practice
      is a testament to that
so dont get me wrong
do not for a moment think
I am one of those people haters who does not understand
who does not experience—compassion.

   (Rest.)

And all those times she came to me
Looking so folorn and needing
affection
At first I wouldnt touch her without gloves on, but then

   (Rest.)

We did it.
In that alley there
she was
phenomenal.

   (Rest.)

I was
lonesome and
She gave herself to me in a way that I had never experienced,
even with women Ive paid,
she was, like she was giving me something that was not hers
      to give me but something
that was mine
that I'd lent her
and she was returning it to me.
Sucked me off for what seemed like hours
her mouths got quite a grip
but I was very insistent. And held back
and she understood that I wanted her in the traditional way.
And she was very giving, very motherly very obliging very
      understanding, very
phenomenal.

Let me cumm inside her. Like I needed to.
What could I do?
I couldnt help it.

Scene 3: The Reverand on His Soapbox

(*Late at night. The* REVERAND D. *on his soapbox preaching to no one in particular.*)

(*There are taped versions of his sermons for sale.*)

(*A large rock, his new Cornerstone, just next to him.*)

REVERAND D. You all know me. You all know this face. These arms. These legs. This body of mine is known to you. To all of you. There isnt a person on the street tonight that hasnt passed me by at some point. Maybe when I was low, many years ago, with a bottle in my hand and the cold hard unforgiving pavement for my dwelling place. Perhaps you know me from that. Or perhaps you know me from my more recent incarnation. The man on the soapbox, telling you of a better life thats available to you, not after the demise of your physical being, not in some heaven where we all gonna be robed in satin sheets and wearing gossamer wings, but right here on earth, my friends. Right here right now. Let the man on the soapbox tell you how to pick yourself up. Let the man on the soapbox tell you how all yr dreams can come true. Let the man on the soapbox tell you that you dont have to be down and dirty, you dont have to be ripped off and renounced, you dont have to be black and blue, your neck dont have to be red, your clothes dont have to be torn, your head dont have to be hanging, you dont have to *hate* yourself, you dont have to hate yr neighbor. You can pull yrself up.

(HESTER *comes in with a framed picture of* BABY. *She stands a ways off.*)

(REVERAND D. *keeps on talking.*)

You may be in the gutter today but you should know that you will wake up in the gutter tomorrow ONLY if you want to. You may not have a way out today but you will ONLY have a way out tomorrow if you take it upon yourself! If you shoulder yr own life. If you take yr own load on yr own back. Put yr shoulder to the wheel. And there is a way. Apply yourself and you will see, that in rain or in snow, in sleet or in hail, in dark of night, in thunder and asunder, in lightning and frightening, through tornados and through hurricaines, friends, the sun is always shining!

(*Rest.*)

And I am an example of that. I am a man who has crawled out of the quicksand of despair. I am a man who has pulled himself out of that never ending gutter—and you notice friends that every city and every towns got a gutter. Aint no place in the world that dont have some little trench for its waste. And the gutter is endless and deep and wide and if you think you gonna crawl out of the gutter by crawling along the gutter you gonna be in the gutter for the rest of your life. You gotta step out of it, friends and I am here to tell you that you can. I dragged myself out of the gutter and up onto this soapbox and now I stand atop a cornerstone! I stand atop a cornerstone! The first rock of my new house, friends. I stand atop a cornerstone!

(*Rest.*)

(*He sees her but doesnt recognize her.*)

REVERAND D. What can I do for you tonight, my sister.

HESTER. I been good.

REVERAND D. But yr life is weighing heavy on you tonight.

HESTER. I havent bothered you.

REVERAND D. Reverand D. likes to be bothered. Reverand D. enjoys having the tired the deprived and depraved come knocking on his door. Come gathering around his cornerstone. Come closer. Come on.

(HESTER *holds the picture of* BABY *in front of her face.*)

HESTER. This child here dont know his daddy.

REVERAND D. The ultimate disaster of modern times. Sweet child. Yours?

HESTER. Yes.

REVERAND D. Do you know the father?

HESTER. Yes.

REVERAND D. You must go to him and say "Mister, here is your child!"

HESTER. Mister here is your child!

REVERAND D. "You are wrong to deny what god has made!"

HESTER. You are wrong to deny what god has made!

REVERAND D. "He has nothing but love for you and reaches out his hands every day crying wheres daddy?"

HESTER. Wheres daddy?

REVERAND D. "Wont you answer those cries?"

HESTER. Wont you answer those cries?

REVERAND D. If he dont respond to that then he's a good for nothing deadbeat, and you report him to the authorities. Theyll garnish his wages so at least youall wont starve. I have a motivational cassette which speaks to that very subject. I'll give it to you free of charge.

HESTER. I got all yr tapes. I send my eldest up here to get them.

REVERAND D. Wonderful. Thats wonderful. You should go to yr childs father and demand to be recognized.

HESTER. It been years since I seen him. He didnt want me bothering him so I been good.

REVERAND D. Go to him. Plead with him. Show him this sweet face and yours. He cannot deny you.

(HESTER *lowers the picture.*)

HESTER
REVERAND D.
HESTER
REVERAND D.

(*Rest.*)

HESTER. You know me?

REVERAND D. No. God.

HESTER. I aint bothered you for 2 years.

REVERAND D. You should go. Home. Let me call you a taxi. *Taxi!* You shouldnt be out at this time of night. Young mother like you. In a neighborhood like this. We'll get you home in a jiff. Where ya live? East? West? North I bet, am I right? *TAXI!* God.

HESTER. He's talking now. Not much but some. He's a good boy.

REVERAND D. I am going to send one of my people over to your home tomorrow. Theyre marvellous, the people who work with me. Theyll put you in touch with all sorts of agencies that can help you. Get some food in that stomach of yours. Get you some sleep. Fix yr hair. Yr teeth.

HESTER. Doctor says I got a fever. We aint doing so good. We been slipping. Like the angle of the ground changed and no body told me about it. Slipping and sliding downhill. Straight into the jaws of—. I been good. I dont complain. They breaking my back is all. 5 kids. My treasures, breaking my back.

REVERAND D. We'll take up a collection for you.

HESTER. You know me.

REVERAND D. You are under the impression that—. Yr mind, having nothing better to fix itself on has fixed on me. Me, someone youve never even met.

HESTER. There aint no one here but you and me. Say it. You know me. You know my name. You know my—. You know me and I know you.

REVERAND D. If you need money, yll get more from me if you respect my predicament.

HESTER. Huh?

REVERAND D. Play my way.

HESTER. Are we talking?

REVERAND D. My lingo.

HESTER
REVERAND D.

HESTER. Talk.

(*Rest.*)

REVERAND D. Youve lost yr looks.

HESTER. We aint doing so good. I wouldnt of come otherwise. Alls we needs a leg up. Just a little help. We're trying to make ends meet but damn if them ends dont keep moving further and further apart.

HESTER
REVERAND D.

(*Rest.*)

HESTER. Nice rock.

REVERAND D. Thank you.

HESTER. Theres something on it—

REVERAND D. Dont come close. Its the date its just the date. The date and the year.

HESTER. Like a calendar.

REVERAND D. Its a cornerstone. The first stone of my new church. My backers are building me a church. Right here. And this is the first stone. It will be a beautiful place. Not much of a neighborhood now but when the church gets built, oh theyll be a turnaround. Lots of opportunity for everyone. I feel like one of the pilgrims. You know, they step out of their boats and on to that Plymouth rock. I step off my soapbox and on to my cornerstone.

HESTER. His names Baby. I call him Baby. People dont think thats much of a name but theres plenty of people, people well off and well known whos nicknamed Baby. Sports players. Singers. Nickname Baby. So I figure I give my Baby a headstart on his fame and fortune by just calling him Baby straight off.

(*Rest.*)

Its a boy.

(*Rest.*)

Looks like you. Got your eyes. Your mouth. Dont look at all like me. If I hadnta seen him come outta me with my own eyes I woulda thought he came outa you, that youd had him all on yr own, instead of me.

REVERAND D. One of my people will get in touch with you. My legal advisor. Heres his card, take it and go. Get someone to read it for you.

> (*He holds out the card to* HESTER *who doesnt take it. It hangs out there between them like a white flag.*)

> (*He stands on his rock. She approaches him.*)

> (*She grabs his soapbox, drags it a safe distance away and sits.*)

HESTER
REVERAND D.
HESTER

> (*A stalemate.*)

> (REVERAND D. *turns on a tape recording of one of his sermons. While it plays he brushes his teeth and tongue and gargles, washes his wrists, hands, armpits and behind his neck and changes his shirt. Combs his hair.*)

REVERAND D. (*On tape.*) Hello and Welcome. Thank you for purchasing my audiocassette. Thank you for inviting me into your home or your car, or bringing me along to your athletic facility as you work yourself strong. Take in a deep breath. Center yourself. I have a lot of good news for you today.

> (*Rest.*)

I have fallen and I cant get up. I have heard that phrase so many times on so many different occasions and Friends Im sure you have heard it too. I have fallen and I cant get up. I have fallen and I cant seem to get myself unfallen. I have slipped and I cant seem to get myself unslipped. I have wronged and I cant seem to get myself unwronged. I was up, but now, Reverand D., now Im down and I cant seem to get up again. I hear that every day. And then come the hands. The hands stretching out to me. The hands stretching out to me for help. Help me up, Reverand D. Youre up, so help me up.

(*Rest.*)

There aint nothing wrong with getting help, Friends, but theres a lot of us out there who not only want to be shown the way but want to be carried all the way. There are lots of us who

(*He turns the tape off.*)

Do you know what a "Backer" is? Its a person who backs you. A person who believes in you. A person who looks you over and figures you just might make something of yourself. And they get behind you. With kind words, connections to high places, money. But they want to make sure they havent been suckered, so they watch you real close, to make sure yr as good as they think you are. To make sure you wont screw up and shame them and waste their money.

(*Rest.*)

My Backers are building me a church. It will be beautiful. And to make sure theyre not wasting their money on a man who was only recently a neerdowell, they watch me.

HESTER. They watching now?

REVERAND D. Not now. Now theyre in their nice beds. Between the cool sheets. Fast asleep. I dont sleep. I have this feeling that if I sleep I will miss someone. Someone in desperate need of what I have to say.

HESTER. Someone like me.

REVERAND D. Here is his card. He'll call you.

HESTER. We dont got no phone.

REVERAND D. He'll visit. Write yr address on—. Tell me yr address. I'll write it down. I'll give it to him in the morning and he'll visit you.

(*Rest.*)

Do the authorities know the name of the father?

HESTER. I dont tell them nothing.

REVERAND D. They would garnish his wages if you did. That would provide you with a small income. If you agree not to ever notify the authorities, we could, through my institution, arrange for you to get a much larger amount of money.

HESTER. How much more?

REVERAND D. Twice as much.

HESTER. 3 times.

REVERAND D. Fine.

HESTER. Theres so many things we need. Food. New shoes. A regular dinner with meat and salad and bread.

REVERAND D. I should give you some money right now. As a promise to you that I'll keep my word. But Im short of cash.

HESTER. Oh.

REVERAND D. Come by tomorrow. Late. I'll have some then.

HESTER. You dont got no food or nothing do ya?

REVERAND D. Come by tomorrow. Not early. Late. And not a word to no one. Okay?

HESTER. —. K.

REVERAND D.
HESTER
REVERAND D.
HESTER

>(*Rest.*)

REVERAND D. You better go.

>(HESTER *goes.*)

>(*The picture of* BABY *is still on the ground.*)

>(*After a moment she comes back, gets the picture and leaves again.*)

>(REVERAND D. *selects another cassette tape. Pops it in and plays it. Stands on his rock, listening.*)

REVERAND D. (*On tape.*) Hello and Welcome. Thank you for purchasing my audiocassette. Thank you for inviting me into your home or your car, or bringing me along to your athletic facility as you work yourself strong. Take in a deep breath. Center yourself. I have a lot of good news for you today.

Scene 4: At the Welfare

(*Outside,* JABBER, TROUBLE, BEAUTY *and* BABY *sit in the dirt playing with toy cars.*)

BEAUTY. Wheres Mommie at?

TROUBLE. Inside.

BABY. Stop. Go. Stop. Go.

JABBER. Look, a worm.

(*They all study the worm as it writhes in the dirt.*)

(*Inside,* HESTER *and the* WELFARE LADY.)

WELFARE LADY. Are they clean?

HESTER. Yes, Maam.

WELFARE LADY. Wash them again.

(HESTER *washes her hands again. Dries them.*)

The Welfare of the world.

HESTER. Maam?

WELFARE LADY. Come on over, come on.

(HESTER *stands behind the* WELFARE LADY, *giving her a shoulder rub.*)

The Welfare of the world weighs on these shoulders, Esther.

HESTER. Hester.

WELFARE LADY. You know who Esther was? Noble woman. Biblical. We at Welfare are at the end of our rope with you, Esther. Rub harder. We put you in a job and you quit. We put you in a shelter and you walk. We put you in school and you drop out. Yr children are also truant. Word is they steal. Stealing is a gateway crime, Esther. Perhaps your young daughter is pregnant. Who knows. We build bridges you burn them. We sew safety nets, rub harder, good strong safety nets and you slip through the weave.

HESTER. We was getting by all right, then I dunno, I been tired lately. Like something in me broke.

WELFARE LADY. You and yr children live, who knows where.

HESTER. Under the Main Bridge, Maam.

WELFARE LADY. This is not the country, Esther. You cannot simply—live off the land. If yr hungry you go to the shelter and get a hot meal.

HESTER. The shelter hassles me. Always prying in my business. Stealing my shit. Touching my kids. We was making ends meet all right then—. Ends got further apart.

WELFARE LADY. "Ends got further apart." God!

> (*Rest.*)

I care because it is my job to care. I am paid to stretch out these hands, Esther. Stretch out these hands. To you.

HESTER. I gave you the names of 4 daddys: Jabbers and Bullys and Troubles and Beautys. You was gonna find them. Garnish they wages.

WELFARE LADY. No luck as yet but we're looking. Sometimes these searches take years.

HESTER. Its been years.

WELFARE LADY. Lifetimes then. Sometimes they take that long. These men of yours, theyre deadbeats. They dont want to be found. Theyre probably all in Mexico wearing false mustaches. Ha ha ha.

> (*Unseen by the* WELFARE LADY, CHILLI, *with his basket, walks by, checking his watch.*)

HESTER. Oh god.

WELFARE LADY. What?

HESTER. Someone walking by the window.

WELFARE LADY. Someone you know?

HESTER. —. No.

HESTER
HESTER

(*Rest.*)

WELFARE LADY. What about the newest child?

HESTER. Baby.

WELFARE LADY. What about Babys father?

HESTER
WELFARE LADY

HESTER. —. I dunno.

WELFARE LADY. Dont know or dont remember?

HESTER. You think I'm doing it with mens I dont know?

WELFARE LADY. No need to raise your voice, no need of that at all. You have to help me help you, Esther.

(*Rest.*)

Run yr fingers through my hair. Go on. Feel it. Silky isnt it?

HESTER. Yes Maam.

WELFARE LADY. Comes from a balanced diet. Three meals a day. Strict adherence to the food pyramid. Money in my pocket, clothes on my back, teeth in my mouth, womanly parts where they should be, hair on my head, husband in my bed.

(HESTER *combs the* WELFARE LADY's *hair.*)

Yr Doctor recommends that you get a hysterectomy. Take out yr womans parts. A spay.

HESTER. Spay.

WELFARE LADY. I hope things wont come to that. I will do what I can. But you have to help me out, Esther.

HESTER. Dont *make* me hurt you!

WELFARE LADY. What?

HESTER. I didnt mean it. Just slipped out.

347

WELFARE LADY. Remember yr manners. We worked good and hard on yr manners. Remember those afternoons over at my house? Those afternoons with the teacups?

HESTER. Dont *make* me—

WELFARE LADY. Esther!

HESTER. Huh?

WELFARE LADY. Good manners at all costs, Esther. Only way yll ever make it in the world.

HESTER. Yes Maam.

WELFARE LADY. Help me out, now. Babys Daddy. Whats his name?

HESTER. You wont find him no how.

WELFARE LADY. We could get lucky. He could be right around the corner and I could walk out and there he would be and then we at Welfare would wrestle him to the ground and turn him upside down and let you and yr Baby grab all the money that falls from Deadbeat Daddys pockets. I speak metaphorically. We would garnish his wages.

HESTER. How much would that put in my pocket?

WELFARE LADY. About 50 a month.

HESTER. Huh.

WELFARE LADY. Maybe 100. Maybe. We take our finders fee. Whats his name?

HESTER. I dunno.

WELFARE LADY. You dont have to say it out loud. Write it down.

(*She gives* HESTER *pencil and paper.* HESTER *writes.*)

(*The* WELFARE LADY *looks at the paper.*)

WELFARE LADY. "A."

(*Rest.*)

Adam, Andrew, Archie, Arthur, Aloysius, what?

HESTER. Looks good dont it?

WELFARE LADY. My shoes.

(HESTER *polishes the* WELFARE LADY'*s shoes.*)

WELFARE LADY. You like what I'm wearing? Tailormade suit.

HESTER. Its pretty.

WELFARE LADY. Pretty! Of course its pretty, Esther. I have a girl make them for me. Works by the piece. For pennies. I should hook you up. Yes. We've got to get you back into the workforce. Remember when you came over to my house and we drank from the teacups? You should come over again.

HESTER. No thanks. I aint much for tea no more, Maam.

WELFARE LADY. You dont know Babys daddy and you dont like tea.

HESTER. I want my leg up is all.

WELFARE LADY. You wont get something for nothing.

HESTER. I been good.

WELFARE LADY. 5 bastards is not good. 5 bastards is bad.

HESTER. Dont *make* me hurt you!

(*She raises her club to strike the* WELFARE LADY.)

WELFARE LADY. You hurt me and, kids or no kids, I'll have you locked up. We'll take yr kids away and yll never see them again.

(*The* WELFARE LADY *pops* HESTER *upside the head.*)

HESTER. My lifes my own fault. I know that. But the world dont help, Maam.

WELFARE LADY. The world is not here to help us, Esther. The world is simply here. We must help ourselves.

(*Rest.*)

Learned yr letters yet?

HESTER
WELFARE LADY

WELFARE LADY. You havent learned yr letters yet.

349

HESTER. Bitch.

(*The* WELFARE LADY *pops* HESTER.)

WELFARE LADY. I know just the job for you. I have a little boutique I run. All the clothes are hand made. By people like you. I dont pay well, but the work is very rewarding. Hard honest work. Unless yr afraid of hard honest work.

HESTER. I aint afraid of hard work.

WELFARE LADY. Its piece work. Sewing. You can do it at home. I pay by the piece. No work, no pay but thats yr decision.

HESTER. Bitch.

(*The* WELFARE LADY *raises her hand to pop* HESTER, *but doesnt.* HESTER *flinches.*)

WELFARE LADY. Good girl.

(*Rest.*)

Heres the fabric. Make sure you dont get it dirty.

HESTER. Can I express myself?

WELFARE LADY. Needles, thread and the pattern, in this bag. Take this cloth. Sew it. I pay by the piece. If you do a good job therell be more work. Have it sewn by tomorrow morning, yll get a bonus.

(HESTER *takes the cloth and notions.*)

HESTER. I dont think the world likes women much.

WELFARE LADY. Dont be silly.

HESTER. I was just thinking.

WELFARE LADY. I'm a woman too! And a black woman too just like you. Dont be silly.

(*Rest.*)

Send the next case in on yr way out. Go on.

(HESTER *puts her hand out, waiting.*)

HESTER. Yr shoulders and yr shoes. Plus I did yr hair.

WELFARE LADY. Is a buck all right?

HESTER
WELFARE LADY

WELFARE LADY. Unless yll change a 50.

HESTER. I could go get change—

WELFARE LADY. Take the buck, K? And the cloth. And go.

> (*The* WELFARE LADY *owes* HESTER *more $, but after a beat,* HESTER *just leaves.*)

2nd Confession: The Welfare "I Walk the Line"

WELFARE LADY. I walk the line
   between us and them
   between our kind and their kind.
   The balance of the system depends on a well drawn line.
   And all parties respecting that boundary.
   I am
   I am a married woman.
   I—I dont that is have never
   never in the past or even in the recent present or even when I look
   look out over into the future of my life I do not see any interest
   any *sexual* interest
   in anyone
   other than my husband.

>   (*Rest.*)

My dear husband.
The hours he keeps.
The money he brings home.
Our wonderful children.
The vacations we go on.
My dear husband he needed
a little spice.
And I agreed. We both needed spice.
We both hold very demanding jobs.
We put an ad in the paper: "Huband and BiCurious wife,
      seeking—"
But the women we got

351

Hookers. Neurotics. Gold diggers!
"Bring one of those gals home from work," my hubby said.
    And Hester,
she came to tea.

    (*Rest.*)

She came over and we had tea.
From my mothers china.
And marzipan on matching china plates.
My hubby sat opposite in the recliner
hard as Gibralter. He told us what he wanted and we did it.
We were his little puppets.
She got naked immediately.
Her body is better than mine.
Not a single stretchmark on her
Im a looker too dont get me wrong just in a different way and
Hubby liked the contrast.
Just light petting at first.
Running our hands on each other
Then Hubby joined in
and while she and I kissed
Hubby did her and me alternately.
The thrill of it
we were his harem
me his wife, and her, the lowly slave girl
I was so afraid I'd catch something
but I was swept away and couldnt stop
She stuck her tongue down my throat
and Hubby doing his thing on top
my skin shivered
She let me slap her across the face
and I crossed the line.

    (*Rest.*)

I count myself lucky that I have what I have
that Im not in her shoes.
Every day I work and work and work to distinguish myself from
    her kind because
We have so much in common and—

    (*Rest.*)

It was my first threesome but it clearly wasnt hers.
And it wont happen again we were
sorry for her. Happy that we could give her an opportunity.
We honestly thought it would be good for her.
For an afternoon
to escape her difficult circumstances
and spend some time in our nice home.
My mothers china plates.
But I should emphasize that
she is a low class person.
What I mean by that is that we have absolutely nothing in
common.
As her caseworker I realize that a maintenance of the system
depends on a well drawn
boundary line
And all parties respecting that boundary.
And I am, after all,
I am a married woman.

(*Far upstage* HESTER *sits surrounded by most of her children, hugging them close.*)

HESTER. My treasures. My joys.

(*End of Act I.*)

Five Poems
Donald Revell

IN THE DRISK

In the drisk

I was changed

To a mountaintop

        Or drowned

        I had forgotten

        Drowning

Findrinny

        A whale's word

Drisk is Indian

So do works of man

Resemble works of nature

Failing to understand wait

Perfectly still mistaking

Sailboats for a mountain don't be scared

Donald Revell

HYMN COMPLETED IN TEARS

Hymn completed in tears

No drunk can dream

I've been here before

What a funny candy

         Be born

         Be born

Someone in the circus

Fell

Into the audience

And it's happening

Again

      This is an explosion

      An exact white lollipop

      I refuse to stop

Donald Revell

IT RAINED & DRIZZLED & GLEAMED

It rained & drizzled & gleamed

Once or twice

        Of thatch no

        Squander *The Maine Woods*

        Grow roots

        In the red wreck

        Of a bateau

To reach Heaven attend

To the true instance A

POET BOY SUICIDE NEWLY

TRANSLATED no thatch it was a great city

It had a beautiful smell

Dark coming awake wet

All hours

JULY 4TH BLUE DIAMOND NEVADA

It is impossible

Not to suffer agonies

Of attachment the world

Is really so wonderful

The mountain stain

Of the grass deepens

The solo trumpeter

His anthem ended

Falls forward weeping

Into a woman's arms

The notes are eternal

Many stars shine down

Through the roman candles

More brightly because of his tears

Donald Revell

10 NOVEMBER 1997

Why not people Heaven

With magpies

It's only the ceremony

After all

Makes us ridiculous

A birthday today telephones into the loose earth

It's not ridiculous

Only lonely

Out of Heaven

Stories begin where they ought to

End with magpies

Starlings and synonyms

Sister's birthday means the same

Why not people

The Black Widow
From Harp Song for a Radical
Marguerite Young

THE TIME FROM the assassination of Abraham Lincoln and the sudden catapulting of a Rebel into the presidential saddle to the time of the assassination of James B. Garfield and his succession by Chester A. Arthur would be a time through which would run—sometimes in the limelight, sometimes in the shadows—the distraught figure of Mrs. Abraham Lincoln—the Black Widow as she was called by those who, often hating her husband when he was alive, did not deceive her by the respect they paid to him when he was dead and she was left to starve to death inch by inch.

The trouble was that Mrs. Lincoln had purchased by secret charge accounts of which her husband had not been apprised voluminous satins to which she had added oceans and oceans, acres and acres by her shopping tours in New York and Washington and her trunks and trunks—bales of chiffons and silks and velvets and lace which had come by ship throughout the War—because of which she thanked God that he had died before confrontation with her bills for yardage reaching endlessly, it must have seemed.

Even when her husband had been alive to know that letters of threat had been made against his life—so many that he had told her that life was Hell—people who were scorpions—the Radicals, the Vindictives, the Jacobeans in the Republican Party—what need had Abe of enemies outside that recalcitrant mob?—his enemies had tried to drive their swords through him by driving their swords through her with accusations of traitordom—for the best way to reach his vulnerable heart was by way of her even more vulnerable heart.

The *Chicago Daily Tribune* had remarked that if Mrs. Lincoln had been a prize-fighter, a foreign danseuse, or a condemned convict on the way to execution, she should not have been so maltreated as she was by a portion of the New York press. Her secretary—in response—had tried to laugh out of court the implication that Mrs. Abraham Lincoln had been engaged in treason to the Union cause by remarking that if there were so many spies coming over the White

359

House grounds like so many ghosts every night as had been implied, probably the best way to get in through the window to the former sleeping First Lady of the Land would be to put up Jacob's ladder and climb.

But the accusation of his wife's treason to the cause of the Union which old Abe Lincoln had believed that he himself personified in every department of the War could not be dismissed as a joke.

Before the Committee on the Conduct of the War he had ambled in one day to declare, "I, Abraham Lincoln, President of the United States, appear of my own volition before the Committee of the Senate to say that I, of my knowledge, know that it is untrue that any of my family hold treasonable communication with the enemy."

When Andy Johnson—as the new President surrounded by the Bloody Reconstructionists who had defamed the conciliatory Lincoln—was having his veiling problems which Carl Schurz, a spokesman for the deep South, had told him he could have for a long time in the wilds of the deep South—strange land where civil liberties would be withheld from black men whether alive or dead and where a great many black women who under the old order of things had not dared to wear black veils as an expression of their grief—for black veils had been considered the expression of white aristocracy fit for a white lady but not fit for a white lady's black maid or black wash-woman, black washer of her white feet or black comber of her hair or nurse for her young—had put on veils under the new order of things in recognition of the fact that slavery was supposed to be no more in idea or fact—and thus had been set upon by white women tearing the black veils away from the faces of black women—such having been the spirit of revenge of former first ladies of great plantation kingdoms. What concern should the welfare of the former First Lady, the President's Black Widow with her eternal veiling problems, be to the former tailor Andy Johnson, for whom silks and satins and long veils for the first year of mourning with diminishment in length of veil as the period of mourning diminished itself had never been his line?

It was said of Mrs. Lincoln when she was still in the White House that she—never known to deny herself the most extravagant luxuries—had been such a penny-pincher and so tightfisted that she had had drawers for careless Old Abe sewn out of the White House sheets and pillowcases which bore the wreathed initial "M" to signify the name of Madison. She had dismissed all laundresses but one, who was not herself—for she was no Dolley Madison stringing her

360

washing in the damp, moldy blue room on rainy days in order to provide shelter from storms—had dismissed all gardeners but one—had sent back for a refund a load of manure which had been intended for the White House garden and with the money had given a dinner party which, ever afterward, had been described by some of the ungrateful attendants as the manure dinner.

Poor, starving widow! Was she now supposed to eat nothing but manure herself? Was she supposed to live on a diet of worms and not enough bread crumbs to keep a bird alive as those who were in charge of the nation's bread basket certainly did not starve themselves but prospered and grew fat with their ill-gotten gains?

In a nation of starving poor whites, poor blacks who in the mass could find no employment but to be used as scabs upon trains and rails during railroad strikes and thus suffer increase of the hatred by the poor white for the poor black, war veterans of both North and South, Mrs. Lincoln—the squat Black Widow with her black hat and black cherries and black veils and black ribbons making her seem an ambulatory pavilion flitting forever among her self-protective shadows—had been obsessed not only by the idea that she was the starving, homeless wanderer but that all the tragedies which came after the death of her beloved husband were and would continue to be the responsibility of those who had conspired for his removal from the White House.

She was overwhelmed by the belief that Andy Johnson had been in communication with Jefferson Davis and that both ought to be hung from the same sour apple tree—for both had conspired with Booth.

She well knew, moreover, that she was under suspicion herself of complicity with the murderers—for who were more likely to try to throw the burden upon a bereaved widow for whom the light of the moon and the sun and the stars had gone out?—that they had spread the rumor that she had been precipitate in her preparations for what she called—surely not erroneously—her everlasting grief, that she had ordered her Black Widow's veils and black silk and black satin skirts and underskirts and black hats with black cherries or black roses on the brims and more black ribbons and black veils than were ever worn by a hearse-driver's horse and black gloves and black snub-nosed velvet or satin pumps and black stockings and probably even black corsets before the President's murder had occurred—for she had known, no doubt with great intimacy—that the President's murder was in the works.

People were shocked, indeed, by the way the Lincoln widow

woman had thrown her dead husband's clothes around as if to return them to the primordial chaos—the old worn clothing for which she could get no dollars—and even his bloody shirt among the bundles.

Mrs. Lincoln—clinging tenaciously to all the trunks of silks and satins and laces which had been hers and which the merchants to whom she owed money for enough mourning veils to have covered the ocean with mourning veils and enough sequins with which to have paved a black shore line—enough black hats with which to have hatted dozens of hearse men—was believed by the thieves who were carrying a continent away in their carpet bags a thief herself even if a petty kind.

What had she stolen? She was accused of vandalism by the Johnson administration although all she took when she left the White House through the back door—as it were—so terribly alone and ignored by the people who were coming in through the front door— was just her husband's shaving mug for which—something like a pack rat in her honest psychology of taking nothing for which she did not leave something in its place—she had left a shaving mug as near its identical twin as she could find.

She had held it against Andy Johnson that he had not written to her for nine long months after the President was killed, and then only the most impersonal expression of profound regrets from the methodical Houses of Congress and Senate to which had been added not so much as a postscript from the man in the White House.

When Victor Hugo—at a ceremony in Paris where there were forty thousand mourners for the martyred President who had been opposed to slavery in any form—gave a medal in honor of the Great Emancipator to the American ambassador with the request that it should be passed on to the President's widow and this was delayed in the delivery, she had become convinced that if they could only have omitted handing over to her the tangible honor of this memorial medal they would certainly have done so and pocketed it away for themselves.

Her tonnages of silks were for a long time Mrs. Lincoln's only insurance—her husband's estate, when divided three ways of which a third was hers and a third was for each of her two living sons, having not been enough to keep her moored—poor soul—as she drifted helmless in the storm.

The stalwart successors to President Abraham Lincoln had ignored his difficult widow either because they had remembered or had forgotten that it was she who had jogged Old Abe's elbow to make him write the Emancipation Proclamation sooner than he would have.

To Frederick Douglass—the distinguished colored leader who would be the first black man ever to be entertained at the White House—Mrs. Abraham Lincoln had sent one of the murdered President's fine walking sticks—that which, in the hands of a man who had loved him, must have seemed to have had for him throughout all his future years a life of its own in the journey toward the land in which Civil rights would be something more than a Promised Land.

As the cost of living had been higher than the cost of dying after the Civil War when the Congress had allowed to Mrs. Mary Todd Lincoln only the salary for that one year which the President had not lived to collect—and as she had only her widow's share of Lincoln's dollars and only a little more than the ten thousand dollars raised by popular subscription for the purchase of a house into which she could retire with her black-veiled grief—the latter sum having been raised before the public knew that Lincoln had died with little more than a few pennies in the toe of an old grey sock—the sympathies of her well-wishers had seemed justifiable.

Black church folks and some who had no church or Rock of Ages to which to cling had been among those who—starving and homeless as many perpetually were—had contributed their hard-earned copper pennies, penny by penny, to the original First Aid sum. But who else would be a Saint Bernard to the President's frail widow as she struggled to keep footing in a world of icy pinnacles, abysses, avalanches of snow falling over her?

Heavily disguised—pretending to be somebody else's black widow—Mary Todd Lincoln had consented while in New York to have her clothes put on display for sale—and she had also permitted the publication of letters in the Democratic newspaper *New York World* in which the Republican Party members were accused of having deprived her of all means of support and having thus left her in a pitiable condition.

The Black Widow had been accused of blackmail on every side, her detractors seeming always to increase and never to diminish. And thus she who was of a bold rather than a timid nature had become afraid to venture out of doors for fear she would be mobbed and knocked down and subjected to highway robbery by those whose hands were claws—iron claws such as pursued and assaulted her in her night dreams as in her day dreams which also transpired in darkness—darkness and whirlwinds never ceasing—and indeed, she had passed already beyond recognition, she was convinced—as she surely would have been wiped out from public and most private memory if it had not been for the heavy black widow's veils behind which she draped herself and which called attention to her in a nation of many widows who—both black and white—were surely poorer than she was and had no such lavish weeds as hers who was passing beyond recognition of self by self—the reflection of her face in the mirror pale and haggard—drained of all color—a mere moth—perhaps the Death's head or Sphinx moth the moon sometimes seemed when it was in a cloud—her dresses like bags hanging on to her lean frame so that it was a wonder she did know herself although, of course, she did—and in dimensions not usually apprehended by the average eye which saw not beyond the superficial appearances of things.

The widow of Abraham Lincoln did not feel like shooting or stabbing the Republicans in the North or the Democrats in the South—only like taking her own life.

Added to all other nervous discords, griefs beyond measure, had been William H. Hernden's revelations, by publication and lectures, of the awful lie that her idolized husband had never really loved her who had been his helpmate and his wife and that he had gone mad—mad as a March hare no doubt—because of the death of his sweetheart Ann Rutledge, whom he had loved with an everlasting love and of whom the besieged Black Widow had never heard.

Mrs. Lincoln's husband had been truth itself in his relationship with her not only when he was alive but when he was dead—so that she had been sure in every cell of her being from the crown of her head to the soles of her feet that Abraham Lincoln's much publicized love for Mrs. Ann Rutledge had been founded upon myth, such a romantic name never having been breathed by him who would never have cherished his love for a ghost with whom she could not compete and who was beyond the range of what was real and who existed not even in a dream—undying dream which would go on when the dreamer was dead.

Abraham Lincoln's life, all through his marriage to Mary Todd Lincoln, had been a life of joyous laughter in which one would not have supposed that his heart was in an unfortunate woman's grave.

As for the widow of Abraham Lincoln, however, her heart was and always would be in her dead husband's uneasy grave, no matter how far she wandered. She had lost some of her buttons when she lost her husband, it was true. Agonies had smitten her between her eyes, sometimes blinding her right eye and sometimes her left—so that at least half the world was cast into darkness at either hand—sometimes to the left and sometimes to the right—she did not always know which—inasmuch as her sufferings were all-pervasive.

Because of accusations and persecutions making her almost maniacal, especially those of the dirty dog Hernden, the widow of Abraham Lincoln had fled—heavily veiled by her black veiling—to Europe with her idolized Tad—the frail and asthmatic and stuttering son who had reminded her most of Abraham Lincoln and of Little Willie as Robert Lincoln—cold and hard and precise—never did.

She had been determined that Tad should have the finest European education there was—this flight from the New World to the Old having given great offense, however, to those who believed that he should be planted in the American millennial soil which should give nurture to the murdered President's son and which should shape and influence the forming of his character and sense of leadership in a way that would not disappoint his dead father, who had continued to live through him and would live as long as his offspring lived—perhaps longer.

For those who had loved the former President, his memory could not be killed, could not be extinguished—but would always shine on like an undying spark in a sea of darkness for them—even as for her delicate, high-strung, nervous, stammering invalid boy—the always dying, nearly dying Tad over whom the President would always watch—no matter where he was or where they were. For to be dead was not to be dead. The advantage of being dead was that one had simply escaped the logic of time—that time which would net all fishes of the sea and all birds of the air in the end or almost all.

The date of passage of mother and son on the *City of Baltimore* for Bremen had been October 1, 1868. In Europe—where as not in her own country she had expected to be treated with deference as the President's widow—she had drifted from castle to castle—always keeping herself amply shrouded by black mourning crepes and silks for which she was delighted to find that the price had been only fifty cents a yard—whereas in New York harbor where the evil profiteers flourished, the same material was fifty dollars a yard.

The widow of Abraham Lincoln—her mind always replete with memories of her beloved husband's body when it had lain in state in the Windy City of Chigaco at the Court House where over one door had been written, "Illinois clasps to her bosom her slain and glorified son"—and over the other, "The beauty of Israel is slain upon her

365

high places"—had seen that Paris, the French city which was in France and not a town in Illinois where the President had often set his foot as never in this metropolis filled with people who spoke French, had been crowded with the presence of rich Americans who—weighted down by their wealth which was of great magnitude and whose munificence provided a sharp contrast with her penury, for she was poor and must count each cent—had made their fortunes during the Civil War.

She had seen while in Europe—as she journeyed from spa to spa— the loud-mouthed, vulgar type of American visitors who would be the concern of Henry James.

Mary Todd Lincoln—the Black Widow with the permanent lines of grief etched upon her club-shaped face as with an endless rage no passage of time or change of habitat from the New World to the Old World or from the Old World to the New World could blot out, for she had recognized all too clearly that for her there would never be a resting place—had wept and moaned through ceaseless peregrinations in the Alps.

Among her numerous peregrinations had been that in which she had gone over the cloud-topped Alpine pinnacles to Florence—slumberous city where she had been fascinated by the birthplace of Dante and the Pitti Palace and the King's residence which she had visited with the keenest appreciation of historical residences and monuments and flagstones and Ghilbertini's Golden Doors while waiting for the passage of the pension bill which had been drawn up for the protection of the dead President's widow by Charles Sumner and which—asking for only three thousand dollars a year—had been passed by the House in May 1870, but had been killed by the Senate when Lyman Trumbull spoke out for it—Sumner having continued to carry on the battle for the Black Widow's pecuniary rites even when the mud-throwers threw mud on him as they were also so busily throwing mud upon her skirts that he would think they should have wearied themselves of this cruel sport in which they engaged at the expense of a most helpless, most fragile soul.

According to Senator Simon Cameron, the men and women who could not destroy Abraham Lincoln had done all that they could to destroy his wife.

Finally in July, Mrs. Lincoln had received her pension by a vote of twenty-eight to twenty, this pension to be increased in 1882 to five thousand dollars a year—so that, if she had been sensible, she might have enjoyed a certain munificence—had she not been swept away by fits of extravagance such as had always been hers.

Very probably—besides the personal aversions to Mary Todd Lincoln caused by their own sense of guilt—they were reluctant to extend compensation to women who, no matter under what circumstances the bread-winners had perished, enjoyed no property rights at all in those halcyon days—not one iota more than had the red men.

Mrs. Lincoln's social consciousness, which had transcended that of many who were now become her persecutors and the maligners of her character, had shriveled to so thin a thread that she could see little or no connection between her struggles and those of the sufferings of the blacks and the reds—a relationship which she might have seen if she had not been of necessity centered upon her homeless, wandering, wind-driven, bedraggled self.

Left with only her poor widow's mite and acres of black memorial garments, she had been unable by even the farthest stretch of imagination to identify herself with the women's freedom cause and struggle from the darkness to the light as embodied in the person of the long-suffering Susan B. Anthony—that gaunt-ribbed but motherly Bloomer Girl who had been smitten by a sense of moral and physical outrage because the power to cast the vote in election time had been given to free black men but not women who had fought for Abolition long before the War—as there were also those who had fought in the War.

She had been utterly appalled when Victoria Woodhull—who had been a tramp clairvoyant in the Hoosier capital during the Civil War—had emerged most flamboyantly as a candidate for the surely sacred and not profane office of President of the United States in 1872 when her slogan had been what she stood for, so help her God and man—and especially man—was the naked truth which, whatever that might be, should be revealed to men, and may the Devil take the hindmost—there having been only the thinnest veiling between her naked body and her followers who, mostly men, had tossed red roses in her way so that her gossamer shroud had been torn into shreds and she stood blushing as if in a sea of roses, none with thorns.

Although it had seemed to Mrs. Lincoln that she had made many sacrifices for her country and even that ultimate sacrifice which had come with her husband's death by hands which were mysterious to others as never to her—few who had prospered having escaped her suspicion, her brightly roving eyes which could see through her black widow's veils which were as thick as steam emitting from smokestacks of ships and factories and trains—the legend of her self-centeredness had increased—and yet that from which she had suffered acute diminishment was a loss of self—as probably could not be guessed by most of those who considered that the clotheshorse was insane and was more in love with the clothing of reality than with the reality itself—a thing which was so very plain and bare and cold and had passed beyond all memory except her own.

Only a few weeks after her return from Europe to Chicago—the ailing eighteen-year-old Tad having died from the consumption which he had caught while living with his ailing mother in too many unheated castles—Mrs. Lincoln had passed into a state of almost perfect lunacy from which it had seemed she would not recover.

The lonely Mary Todd Lincoln had been surrounded by the Stalwarts who were a sea of scamps—in her withering estimate. She had been isolated by their cruel behavior and driven into exile as if it were she and not they who had conspired in numerous plots for the murder of her husband—a noble man not utterly naive—a man who could never have been taken by surprise no matter if there was one murderer or if there were many murderers out to saw him down—if an assassin was always waiting in his path through the dark forest of this life.

Physical harm to Abraham Lincoln had not been enough to satisfy his would-be killers. Slander had also been a death-dealing instrument. Mary Todd Lincoln had had her love robbed by the malicious gossip that old Abe had loved that corpse in Illinois—the beautiful Ann Rutledge who had died young and who was not his wife who had lived and had grown old at his side although she had remained—as he well knew and as she well knew—a child in her heart. He had been so faithful to his child wife that no memory of the dead, always mysterious sweetheart—the dead Mrs. Ann Rutledge—could have displaced her—there had surely never been the ghost of a third person in her marriage bed.

Mrs. Lincoln had been accused of infidelity to her dead love, however, the false news having been spread that while in Europe wandering from spa to spa she had attracted and had not discouraged the amorous sentiments of a German dwarf who was a Grand Chamberlain to the Duke of Baden.

Utterly mad but still not half as mad as the government of this nation was—for they should have provided her with comforts which might exceed those of a poor widow who had never been the First

Lady of her land and had never seen her beloved husband killed by a madman's bullet—sometimes Mrs. Abraham Lincoln thought that her husband's astral body had returned to sleep with her.

Even when at last there was no monetary problem, her habit of tight-fistedness had been so persistent in its rule over her that she had continued to pity herself for her deprivations and ask for the pity of others, and she had remained convinced of her increasing poverty which was largely of her own mental and moral vision and not real.

Worn out by his mother's maniacal belief that she was surrounded by her enemies on every side and by her inordinate fear of starvation and shelterlessness and most particularly by her vast shopping expeditions, the only living son of Abraham Lincoln had foreseen that if his mother were not checked she would soon run pell-mell through her sizable capital by large purchases of water-damaged or fire-damaged silks.

The widow of Abraham Lincoln was obsessed by her almost constant, almost unremitting fears that Chicago was going to be burned down again by a Great Fire which would leave only skeletons of tenements and scorched dune from which all bushes would be burned away and by her desire that her trunks and boxes of material goods should be moved to a small town which should be beyond the tongues of fire. She did not feel that she was safe in Chicago, where she—safely ensconced with her memorial torch flaming all during the night—was determined that the fires would never find her—be they even the fires of spring—and where she could surely trust no waterman of the ladder and hook society—if such there was—to come to pour waters onto the fire—pour all the waters of the lakes and rivers and streams on her.

She slept on a mattress stuffed with corn shucks which made a papery, rustling sound as she moved from side to side, trying to find some rest for her aching, swollen head upon its feather-stuffed pillow and rest for her inflamed spinal column from which she suffered such sharp pains that she felt that there were some discs missing as in an old many-toothed harvester machine which had broken down and had been left to rust away into nothingness or almost nothingness.

She knew so well that there were people who, whether or not they were conscious or were unconscious of the fact—her judgment refused to differentiate between them—wanted her out of this world—those who had for so long refused to provide an umbrella such as her ever thoughtful and considerate husband had always carried over the frail creature who was of the creation but not its creator.

The ever-prudential Robert Todd Lincoln, carrying the heavy burden of familial responsiblity on his broad shoulders, had been worried by his frenetic, loudly vocal mother's shopping manias—her purchases, for example, of seven thousand dollars' worth of lace curtains when she had nowhere to hang them—acres of lace tablecloths and bales of silks and jewels and gold watches—altogether three time-pieces when she already had enough—including the time-piece which told the time only of some other day, some other year that was fled and would never return—would never bring her husband and her dead sons back to her whose only prospect was to make haste to join with them as hastily as she could—and she had also loaded herself down with boxes and boxes of scented soaps and bottles of Eau de Cologne and more perfumes of Araby than she could ever use, although she continually washed and sprayed herself from head to foot and powdered her face and applied eye shadow and painted her lips cherry red so that she would be recognized by Old Abe when he saw her, for she had desired to be no poor bag of skin and bones such as he might not know. She carried her capital on her person and was made squat by so many hidden appendages so that her only living son had had in his tow for about three weeks Pinkerton's detectives to shadow her and report to him how and where she spent her money.

How could such frugality and such extravagence as hers be combined in one not-simple nature, and was she duplicitous or straightforward?

At the Cook County Court at the behest of Robert Todd Lincoln who, hat in hand—his attitude was both sincere and reverential—he being a lawyer for his mother's last estate and being also her only living son—he who was thoroughly worn out and who had suffered enough through his mother's temperamental outbursts and her quarrels with the Republicans and who had political ambitions of his own which made him want to keep the Black Widow quiescent and out of the nation's limelight—had brought her against her will and better judgment to trial before a lunacy judge who had been her husband's friend and before a prosecuting attorney who had been her husband's friend and before an attorney for the defense who had been her husband's friend and before a jury which—all things were to seem equable, fair and square as a carpenter's last—was made up of important businessmen, merchants, real estate men. All had been her well-wishers and had intended her no harm—but had wished to protect her from taking her bucket to the well so often that she should draw up all the water in it.

Mrs. Lincoln's own chamber maid who had seemed devoted to her had testified—as proof of her madness—that she could never let up on the subject of Grant, who for her—as was well known to practically everybody except himself with his winsome ways—had a defective character—was a caitiff, a mad dog, a murderer—was a coward.

Mary Todd Lincoln had hated Grant with such almost unceasing virulence that the only way to quiet her had been to give to her the laudanum drops with which she could put herself into a state in which she was half asleep and half awake.

Merchant princes had testified that Mrs. Abraham Lincoln's madness had been shown by the purchases she had made at their stores—those which they ordinarily would have welcomed as a sign of her sanity having now become a sign of her insanity as undoubtedly it was if this Black Widow thought that she was getting bargains from them who had carried to even farther extremes than usual their custom of marking things up so that they might mark them down.

The jurymen had included Lyman J. Gage, who would be Secretary of the Treasury under President William J. McKinley—the third President of the United States to be assassinated.

Not mainly because of her hallucinations, which might have been harmless, the poor lady was adjudged abnormal, abysmally insane, her mind having been shattered possibly beyond repair, it being recalled that, in response to former and present harassments piling up like old sheets stained with blood, she had made an attempt to do away with herself by drinking from two bottles which—about the size of those in which ladies carried their tears and their smelling salts—she had asked to be filled with something to end or abort her misery—but which the pharmacist, knowing his customer well, had labeled Laudanum and Camphor although both were as false as false signs along a road—for both had been nothing but water. She had been escorted to Batavia in a private railroad car as she sat upright and still, moving without rustling and without jingling and jangling—her stocks and bonds and paper bills and coins having been sequestered by her son.

While there she was so far gone in madness that she was under the delusion at least part of the time that she was in the White House

371

still. The larger part of Mrs. Lincoln's waking time, where she was surrounded by boxes and bales of the purchases which she had made at the crossroads store at Batavia which had carried—ordinarily a decade late—the last word in fashion, she had spent her flickering, cluttering energies writing to old friends or acquaintances who were in a position of power or had contact with those in power and from whom she asked for assistance in helping her to escape from the madhouse—in which she was confined behind bars to the surrounding land of freedom where she should be permitted to live in accordance with the style befitting a President's widow who has served her country to the best of her ability as her faithful husband had—they had been side by side through periods of darkness and whirlwinds unimaginable to most people from whom had been required such sacrifices as theirs had been.

Her confinement because of her shopping manias had caused as great an embarrassment as when the Black Widow had been denied her pension rights by a government seemingly indifferent or oblivious to her sufferings, and thus how could Robert Todd Lincoln have expected to enjoy appointments to high office in the Grand Old Party or run for election for President of the United States if it could be said by every loudmouthed Democratic speaker on his trail that he had thrown his mother into a loony bin and left her there?

After four months which must have seemed like four eternities to her whose life was that fifth eternity which was four with one to spare until she should come to the place of the meeting of all parallels, Mrs. Lincoln had been released from the care of her keeper who had posed as her buggy driver and who had certainly treated her with a greater show of outward courtesy than was generally given to most maniacs.

Nine months had passed before Mrs. Abraham Lincoln had been at last pronounced sane, the attorney for the prosecution having turned turtle as had the attorney for the defense. As his mother was no longer in the tightfisted custody of her son, Robert Todd Lincoln could no longer keep his hands on the purse strings of his father's widow.

Oh, what a thief this thieving son was and how undependable—how duplicitous—untrustworthy and ambivalent and two-faced!

It was perhaps understandable that poor Mrs. Lincoln, who had lost so much and all those things which had recalled to her the meaning of her life, dead life, had been like a hunter with a retriever's instinct when it came to the recovery of all her stolen property—all her losses—all the goods which she thought had been stolen away from her by her son.

To Robert—the future most important cog of the Pullman empire and lawyer for George Mortimer Pullman—who would be barely glimpsed by Eugene Victor Debs when he was leading the strike against that Sleeping Car Emperor—and who could not have been amused by the comparison of Debs with the left-winged father whom he had never known very well—the mother in a white heat of anger had written from Springfield that she wanted the return of all her paintings, both oils and watercolors whether framed or unframed.

One was the oil painting of the infant Moses hidden among the bulrushes away from the cruel Herod. Another was the oil painting of fruit that had been hung above the buffet in the dining room. She wanted her silver set and her large silver waiter and her silver tête-à-tête returned to her—all her vermeil spoons and silver spoons and gold and silver forks and pewterware returned to her—also her laces, diamonds, other jewels—silks and white lace dress, double lace shawl and flounces, lace scarf—how many acres long?—two black shawls and one black lace with deep flounces.

Mary Todd Lincoln had informed Robert Todd Lincoln that he had injured himself, not her. Two prominent clergymen had written to her that they were offering up prayers for him in their pulpits on account of the wickedness of this son against his mother who was of this earth like all things mortal, no doubt—he had sinned not only against his mother but against high Heaven, too. He had tried, moreover, his game of robbery long enough.

Her letter to Robert Todd Lincoln containing the list of her stolen properties and the threat that the extensive theft would be published in the newspaper if not returned immediately to her—who hesitated not to reveal to the public eye all that it did not see—had been written on June 17, 1876.

Thousands of families in great cities like Chicago and New York were living on as little as seventy cents a week, even like the poor Indians now as the breed of reds against whom the great guns were turned were not the feathered bird men who had been so greatly depleted and were still being mown down but were Union labor strikers who dared to question the authority of the American czars of mills and mines and rails with their punitive expeditions against all who did not conform and belonged to some lesser orb than theirs.

*

While Mrs. Lincoln might be mad as her original persecutors had judged her to be, she was beyond a shadow of a doubt sane enough to have enjoyed the collapse of the Northern Pacific and the Jay Cooks Company scandals and the Credit Mobilier scandals and all the embarrassments which had been brought to the administration of Grant and Grab.

Returning to Europe in 1879 because she felt that she was a stranger in her own land where she could have no peace in a personal sense, Mrs. Lincoln, well knowing that there were some people in her native land who would believe the judgment which had declared that she was insane but not the reversal which had declared that she was sane, had drifted once more over Europe—from one cathedral town to another cathedral town where history, that which was always of utmost fascination to her, was visible in every stone, from Alpine spa to Alpine spa where she took the waters or walked alone upon a windswept esplanade under her black widow's veils by which she hid herself from the recognition which she above all things wanted not for her own sake but for that of the great President who deserved to be honored throughout the world for having died for the sake of freedom to his fellow men and women in his own country.

She had followed world news with intense interest but had lived mainly with her memory of her beloved husband and her three younger sons whom she missed so much, seeming almost to have forgotten Robert Todd Lincoln, until one day she read in the newspaper that Robert Todd Lincoln and Stephen A. Douglas, Jr., against whose father Abraham Lincoln had won the election to the White House, were likely to run against each other in the coming election. Suddenly her presidential ambitions for her only living son had been stirred but not for long—her mind passing to something else—she could not concentrate on one subject for long, especially if concerned with a future prospect and not with the past.

Her only living son, at any given moment, could not have told an interrogator what the address of this spectral lady was—although conceivably anybody who really wished to reach her could have located her through an old friend of Lincoln's who was living then in Paris and was handling her pecuniary affairs. She had exalted that she who had been neglected by her own country had recieved the condolences of many crowned heads including the still beautiful widowed Empress Eugenie and the Empress Victoria, both of whom had known, had shared so well the communion of grief.

It would have been strangely appropriate if she had joined in the company of the black-veiled Empress Carlotta, widow of the Emperor Maximilian whom she had not seemed to know was dead.

The Emperor Maximilian had been toppled from his gilded throne in Mexico and executed upon the Hill of Bells by the marksmen of General Benito Juarez, who had insisted upon shooting him and had not been treating him as a prisoner of war as William Seward and Andy Jackson had asked—the Revolutionary general having been determined not to seem a pawn in the hands of the American practitioners of Manifest Destiny.

The Empress Carlotta, who had yearned to wear a crown and who—a black-veiled professional widow like the black-veiled Mrs. Abraham Lincoln, had continued to wear it after her husband's premature death—had stated that she would wait for the return of the Emperor Maximilian for sixty years if that was the time required for the return of her dead husband who had been so cruelly snatched away from her. For sixty years—as if acting in fulfillment of her prophecy as she looked in all ways turning her head from side to side toward the four corners of the many-tasseled sky—she would address her remarks to her husband and God, just as Mrs. Lincoln, although knowing that her husband was not in this world but was in the next world if there was such a world which was always, of course, made of aspects of this world with its inherent mysteries never to be solved, would imagine that he spoke to her in the name of God.

Every morning in the spring of the year for sixty years, the demented Empress Carlotta in her black mourning clothes would step into her little boat which was moored among the lily pads upon the glassy moat of her castle in Brussels and say—only she seeing the dead emperor's living face as she surely saw it the day she died—"Today we are sailing for Mexico."

For a while, Mrs. Abraham Lincoln did have an American competitor albeit one who was far removed from her in attitude and kept her grief pent up. She was Mrs. Arthur Garfield, whose husband, when he was an Ohio congressman on a random visit to New York, had delivered impromptu and unrehearsed but with oracular triumph from the steps of the Sub-Treasury where George Washington, the father of his country, had most appropriately been sworn in as first President of that democracy which would be called a dollars and cents democracy—dollars for some and cents for others—an instantaneous elegy for the prairie President Abraham Lincoln:

"Clouds and darkness are around Him, His pavilion is dark waters and thick clouds, justice and judgment are the habitation of his throne; mercy and truth shall go before His face! Fellow citizens, God reigns and the Government in Washington still lives!"

The Wandering Black Widow had journeyed across the ocean four times before her last voyage of return which could only be followed by that last of all voyages. In December 1879, while trying to hang a picture, she had a fall which had severly injured her spinal column.

Mary Lincoln, given more and more to stumbling, falling, had sailed from Le Havre on the French steamer *Amerique*, which was expected to make the passage in nine days although the ways of winds and waves had been—as always—unpredictable. Heavily veiled, her head whirling, her body twisted by torment, while standing at the top of a stair, she would have been pitched downward by a sudden swell had she not been saved by a lady who had kept her from falling and who had turned out to be none other than Sarah Bernhardt.

The acrobatic Sarah Bernhardt had heard the gentle, dreaming voice of the little woman in black thanking her, but as her face was swathed by so many veils had not recognized her. "You might have been killed, Madame, if you had fallen down that horrible staircase." The little woman had answered with a sigh yes, she knew, but that it was not God's will.

When Sarah Bernhardt, saying good-bye, had revealed her name, the woman in black had recoiled and had said with a hiss to the one who had stood between her and the enactment of God's will, "I am the widow of Abraham Lincoln."

Sarah had divined that since it had been an actor who had killed her husband, she had no love for actors—even the most eminent. The great tragedienne before whose feet Oscar Wilde had paved a path of long-stemmed lilies during what was called the lily craze and had not been placed at the Black Widow's wandering feet had said afterward that she had done the unhappy woman the only service she ought not to have done her—she had saved her from death.

She could not know, of course, how many deaths John Hay's Black Cat caterwauling widow had died—she had died more than nine.

The Black Widow had passed unnoticed by the crowd welcoming the great tragedienne at the dock. The veiled Mrs. Abraham Lincoln descended to the dock must have seemed a figure from the past—a cutout from a page of an antebellum Godey's Lady's book—for she had not changed her style for years. She had set out for Springfield by the Hudson River Railroad, where night began as dusk on through the fog-shrouded, randomly star-punctuated darkness of the sleeping, undulating prairie states—Ohio and Indiana and Illinois—until she came at last to Decatur.

Mary Lincoln in her final phase as she lay with all her trunks and boxes piled around her bed on the top floor of her sister Ninian's high-shouldered house of limestone on the hill had seemed to arouse little understanding of her illnesses by physicians and relatives or by Robert Todd Lincoln.

Her passionate love of money had remained the same when she had at last received the retroactive pension which she had recognized she would not live long enough to use. She had worn her money belt around her waistline as she waxed, waned, waxed, waned, waxed and waxed and waxed large as the moon—as long as she was wide—turning, rolling in her bed—and once had insisted upon rising because she was convinced that a thief in the night had stolen from her where the sounds of the rustlings of her stocks and bonds and gold certificates had assured her that there was money for her support—that she was never to be like some old, twisted hen for whom there was not a grain of corn or a blade of grass to feed on.

Mary Lincoln had departed this life on the night of July 15, 1882. She had been in a deep coma but had been ready to sail. The funeral had been held in her sister Ninian's parlor where her open coffin had been lighted by the flickering rays of the whale oil lamps which sometimes left her face among the shadows and sometimes lighted it up with sudden incandescence.

The Reverend James A. Reed, who had delivered the eulogy, had spoken with a symbolism which almost any McGuffey's man or woman would have understood regardless of what his or her social status or class was, whether high or low. Mary Lincoln and her martyred husband had been two tall and stately pines which had grown so close together that their roots and branches had intertwined as they faced mountain storms. When the taller of the two was struck by a flash of lightning, the shock was too much for the other, and thus they had virtually both been killed at the same time—although with the one that lingered, it was only slow death from the same cause. When Abraham Lincoln died, she died.

Now, with a book made of flowers—lilies, rosebuds, tube roses, carnations, and the name Mary Lincoln spelled out upon its cover with forget-me-nots, she was carried by the hearse to her grave, her son Robert Todd Lincoln and members of his family and members of her family following her to the place of her internment at Oak Ridge Cemetery, which had been built to discourage those who might wish to disturb the President's body or Little Willie or the other two dead sons to take them on tour—and there she was placed in a row of coffins at the feet of Old Abe, Civil War President and Great Emancipator who had died for mankind—the last living son, Robert Todd Lincoln, Secretary of War, having been the only one who would not some day join with his parents at Springfield.

Four Stories
Diane Williams

SQUARISH

FOR THE DURATION of my speculation, the girl felt as if she had been in a world.

There is no item so common to us all as she is.

I would eat the girl's food as if it were my food. I would like to have all of her money. She has so much of it.

I try to speak the way she speaks. I wish I could wish for what she wishes for.

"Scoot the dishes off the table," said the girl. "Molly?"

The girl's urn was sobbing. The great hall—healthy and unclean—is so noisy.

The girl—though not at her worst, is not at her best—she is midway between these. A few of her live limbs were flaring like sprigs. Her young teeth are notorious.

A girl's guests are richly made. Unh!—a thing was perceptive.

Piercing the day is the sun with its flaws.

But that's not all. Here they have a set of sixteen quarrelsome, sexually greedy, murderous butter knives. Somebody is influenced by what the butter knives do.

Needing a refreshment for myself, I went into the little hills. I sought a hill, but I did not stop. In the glen, I saw three girls. My view passed from the body of one girl into the brain of another. This girl leapt toward me, yelling, dragging itself on two legs, and I went toward her, and I said, "I came looking for you to be my friend." And now I have her.

So I take this opportunity to express my deep appreciation for this most sacred object without which I do not believe my troubles would be over.

It will be interesting to see how my feelings about the girl change. In the best battle I ever fought I was supposed to meet a princess. Within days I received a handwritten letter with the warning which predicted the onslaught. She appeared in gorgeous clothing and dashed toward me, pushing ahead of the collection of pewter plates and mugs, the Turkish cooking pot, strainer and stirrer, the sparkles of hope. In the white bedroom she clung to the curve of my faith and then she sat herself down on the repetitive pattern.

A superb rider, the princess might have seen anyone or done anything. She was famous. One did not often see something so opulent. And yet, next, she threw herself round the room. Her star-studded body was famous for lavishing its attentions. We all know how hard that is if you are chunky. She is not.

That I made this last effort is not surprising. About five miles away a troop of four girls I saw was looking down into the glen. Now they are dead. They were alive. In another battle I killed five. I was married at nineteen. I have ordered my men to attack and to kill my enemies.

My career—this so-called war—one always knows how these things are going to turn out.

What else could there have been besides a battle? The baby.

The midwife had come along nicely. I heard myself say that I felt fine. A long explanation was embarked upon about vicious kicking. No attempt was made to conceal the baby, which was soon known to all as cool, intellectual and young—the sort who moves on easily from one person to the next—is handed all around, because the thug is thoroughly emancipated.

We have banded together, the strong ones. I have engaged in sixty-five battles. Small fires are lit in the houses. The children are bathed. This is the first time I have had an infection in my mouth and it pains me to chew a juicy piece of meat. I have not been able to notice any other pain of mine.

What is this made of? I love this! See the tartan rug sits on an old chair—sits, and sits, and sits.

WE FULLY INTEND TO DISCUSS THE MATTER

He tried. He traveled toward me on the earliest known land.

In front of him is my bare house and behind him are the long herbaceous borders past the belt of the strong green trees, and the flowers are fooling around. These are flowers so faint I only think I am faintly hungry, not that I am lonely.

In these days when desire is large desire, I use more of my favorite words when he is everlasting and just.

My encouraging tale I tell leads anyone toward my black breast, and I have white hairs at the heart of me.

And he yanked up his voice and he had remarkable things to say, and as it happened, and he said to me, "It will take about an hour," and I could not find a peculiar feeling and I said to him, "Oh, God." He had been given a human shape, he said. He could rest near me and, look, my plan was mostly to rest too. How should I do anything else, friend? When I am feeling weak, I do not like a person to use a loud voice too often near me.

"How are you?"

"I am fine."

He put those words aside for me, although I wait for them. I thought that at this hour, you see, at this hour I thought, by this hour, that we would have more happy wishes. I gave him a slippery thing which is so much like a winning cup, so that by now we are settled in an atmosphere with boldness.

Our staff is in charge and for us they carry hinged envelopes and our notebooks with our wishes from somewhere down, down, down, somewhere where they speak as we do. In the lower end and in the upper part we walk and we declare.

I FRESHLY FLESHLY

His block is washed clean and covered with new paper because he says one area of the block has the scent of a fish market. Because his shop window is open I have left his shop door open even wider.

He lifts his tunic waist high and explains why he shares an experience with such a young person. I see his skin stretched out. Freshness and quality are just as important in people. He has a long neck and mouth, a thick fillet between foot and body, flat shoulders, and a stepped foot.

I tug on myself and cry out as if making quite an effort.

He is the only one I did that with.

"They can see us!" He leans.

"They can't see us," I say.

"They can see us!" he says.

A number of people asked him for German bologna—an item he seldom will sell. We were rushed to the point where a woman requested half a ham. In general the customers are not too concerned. She took what she ordered and she vowed she would never return.

A man came in and after that I went home. I came home at 3:00 P.M. When I started seven years ago I was a very shy person. I don't think anyone would guess it now. The ability to meet people and to talk to anyone will be an asset all of my life. I have learned a lot about people and I have made some great friends.

ROW OF US SURROUNDED BY
SEVEN SLIGHTLY SMALLER ONES

Her future will have been brought to a sad end if it is not incessantly, daily decorated.

The Williams woman opened the gift from me. The immoral wrapping paper lay on her leg.

"It's adorable! Thank you!" she said.

"You are loved," I say. "Would you like to play a game of checkers or of chess?"

"Oh! No, thank you. I am very tired. I am just too tired. I am waiting for my boys and then I am going upstairs."

She wears several small jewels and lesser chains, a waist buckle, shoe buckles and an arrow brooch.

When a big jewel was handed over to the woman, I said, "Do you really like it? Do you really like it? No, I really mean it. Do you really like it? Tell me how much you like it."

It gave me a shiver when she said, "I cannot remember very clearly."

So said, so seen. I will tell you I was an elder clothed and fed.

I would like to go to that store to get gemstones for her to wear with that gemstone, something with a crystal! When was the last time I knew what was best for someone?

Most nights I never knew if I was going to give her a thrum or a finger ring. On Friday, Saturday or Sunday I am not busy. Tonight she gets a particle either after my bath or this will be after our marriage, I think. Dinner will be waiting. We eat planked fish. The soles of my shoes have been rinsed in the bathroom sink. I am mauvish, not complete within my borders, nor am I surrounded!—my sweetheart, my darling!

Ghosts
Barbara Guest

Robins' egg blue   passes into darker color placed its head
  where fluid blue descends.   Distance unrolling a screen,

     another landscape,

continuous reeling, as in allegory,

    absorbed *and darkly hinted.*

    If now the Baron inside the Screen

   could ride into the distance, not outline.

Barbara Guest

Owl, vapor

rupture of distance,

this elaborate structure around the text   ʼ

                                        may be imagining
a dread ice.

Snow running over it and out of the thin tree.

Barbara Guest

The body in the field—beyond uneven brick,
part of the secret faring, existing by itself.

Body in the field
and *grandeur*
from uneven brick,

meaning exists by itself.

The Seventh Elegy
Rainer Maria Rilke

—Translated from German by William H. Gass

No more courting. Voice, you've outgrown seduction.
It can't be the excuse for your song anymore,
although you sang as purely as a bird
when the soaring season lifts him, almost forgetting
he's just an anxious creature, and not a single heart
that's being tossed toward brightness, into a home-like heaven.
No less than he, you'd be courting some silent companion
so she'd feel you, though you're perched out of sight,
some mate in whom a reply slowly wakens
and warms in her hearing—your ardent feeling
finding a fellow flame.

O, and springtime would understand—there'd be
no corner that wouldn't echo with annunciation.
First each little questioning note
would be surrounded by a confident day's magnifying stillness.
Then the intervals between calls, the steps rising toward the
        anticipated temple
of what's to come; then the trill, the way a fountain's
falling is caught by its next jet as though in play . . .
With the summer ahead.
Not only all of summer's dawns, the way they
shine before sunrise and dissolve into day.
Not only the days, so soft around flowers, and above,
shaping the trees, so purposeful and strong.
Not only the devotion of these freed forces,
not only the paths, not only meadows at evening,
not only the ozoned air after late thunder,
not only, at dusk, the onset of sleep and twilight's
        premonitions . . .
but also the nights! the height of summer nights,
and the stars as well, the stars of the earth.

O to be dead some day so as eternally to know them,
all the stars: then how, how, how to forget them!

Look, I've been calling my lover, but not only she would come . . .
Out from their crumbling graves girls would rise and gather.
How could I confine my call—once called—to just one?
Like seeds the recently interred are always seeking the earth's
      surface.
My children, one thing really relished in this world
will serve for a thousand. Never believe
that destiny is more than what's confined to a childhood;
how often did you pass the man you loved, panting,
panting after the blissful chase, to dash into freedom?

It is breathtaking simply to be here. Girls, even you
knew, who seemed so deprived, so reduced, who became
sewers yourselves, festering in the awful alleys of the city.
For each of you had an hour, perhaps a bit less,
at worst a scarcely measurable span between while and while,
when you wholly *were*. Had all. Were bursting with Being.

But we easily forget what our laughing neighbor
neither confirms nor envies. We want to show it off,
yet the most apparent joy reveals itself only after
it has been transformed, when it rises *within* us.

My love, the world exists nowhere but within us.
Withinwarding is everything. The outer world
dwindles, and day fades from day. Where once
a solid house was, soon some invented structure
perversely suggests itself, as at ease among ideas
as if it still stood in the brain.
The Present has amassed vast stores of power,
shapeless as the vibrant energy it has stolen from the earth.
It has forgotten temples. We must save in secret
such lavish expenditures of spirit.
Yes, even where one thing we served, knelt for and
prayed to, survives, it seeks to see itself invisible.
Many have ceased perceiving it, and so will miss
the chance to enlarge it, add pillars and statues,
give it grandeur, within.

Rainer Maria Rilke

Each torpid turn of the world disinherits some
to whom neither what's been, nor will be, adheres.
For to humans even what comes next is far away.
We, however, should not be confused by this,
but should resolve to retain the shape in stone we still recognize.
This once stood like a standard among mankind,
stood facing fate, the destroyer, stood in the middle
of our not knowing what, why or wherefore, as though an answer
      existed,
and took its design from the stars' firm place in heaven.
Angel, to you I shall show it—there! in your eyes
it shall stand seen and redeemed at last, straight
as pillars, pylons, the sphinx, the cathedral's
gray spire thrust up from a decaying or a foreign city.

Wasn't it miraculous? O marvel, Angel, that we *did it,*
we, O great one, extol our achievements,
my breath is too short for such praise.
Because, after all, we haven't failed to make use
of our sphere—*ours*—these generous spaces.
(How frightfully vast they must be,
not to have overflowed with our feelings
even after these thousands of years.)
But one tower was great, wasn't it? O Angel, it was—
even compared to you? Chartres was great—
and music rose even higher, flew far beyond us.
Even a woman in love, alone at night by her window . . .
didn't she reach your knee?
                   Don't think I'm courting
you, Angel.
And even if I were! You'd never come.
For my call is always full of "stay away."
Against such a powerful current even you cannot advance.
My call is like an outstretched arm. And its upturned,
open, available hand is always in front of you,
yet only to ward off and warn,
though wide open, incomprehensible.

—*Château de Muzot, Sierre, Switzerland, February 7, 1922*

ACKNOWLEDGMENTS

Three for Cornell. Work by Joseph Cornell accompanying Joyce Carol Oates's "The Box Artist" is *Object 1941,* a box construction (14½ x 10½ x 3½ inches), 1941, collection of Marguerite and Robert Hoffman. Cornell works accompanying Paul West's "Boxed In" are *Keepsake Parakeet,* a box construction (20¼ x 12 x 5 inches), 1949–53, collection of Donald Windham; *Untitled (The Grand Hotel),* a box construction (7 x 5 x 3 inches), 1953, the Joseph and Robert Cornell Memorial Foundation; and *Untitled (Swan Box),* a box construction (4⅞ x 6⅜ x 1¼ inches), circa 1945, collection of Robert Lehrman, Washington, D.C. Cornell work accompanying Bradford Morrow's "For Brother Robert" is *Aviary,* a box construction (18⅜ x 16⁵⁄₁₆ x 5 inches), circa 1949, the Joseph and Robert Cornell Memorial Foundation. All Joseph Cornell works published here are copyright © The Joseph and Robert Cornell Memorial Foundation, and reproduced courtesy C & M Arts, New York.

The following paintings, which accompany Ann Lauterbach's "Handheld," are reproduced with the kind permission of the Isabella Stewart Gardner Museum, Boston: *A Young Lady of Fashion* by Uccello, *Portrait of a Seated Turkish Scribe or Artist* by Gentile Bellini, *The Presentation of the Infant Jesus in the Temple* by Giotto di Bondone, *Hercules* by Piero della Francesca, and *Saint Michael* by Pere Garcia de Benabarre.

The following works, which accompany Camille Guthrie's "Articulated Lair," are reproduced courtesy of Wendy Williams and The Louise Bourgeois Studio, New York: *New Exit,* wood, painted metal and rubber, 1989, collection of the Ginny Williams Family Foundation, Denver (photograph: Peter Bellamy); *Nature Study,* polished patina, 1984, collection of the Whitney Museum, New York (photograph: Allan Finkelman); *Le Défi (detail),* painted wood, glass and electrical light, 1991, collection of the Solomon R. Guggenheim Museum, New York (photograph: Peter Bellamy); *Untitled (With Growth),* pink marble, 1989, collection of the Ginny Williams Family Foundation, Denver (photograph: Allan Finkelman); *Sainte Sebastienne,* drypoint, 1992, courtesy of Cheim & Reid, New York (photograph: Christopher Burke).

NOTES ON CONTRIBUTORS

EVE ASCHHEIM is a painter living in New York City. Upcoming solo shows include Galerie Rainer Borgemeister in Berlin; Galleri Magnus Aklundh in Lund, Sweden; Galerie Benden & Klimezak, Cologne; and Stefan Stux Gallery, New York.

THOMAS BERNHARD (1931–1989) was a novelist, playwright and poet whose works include *Gargoyles, Correction, Woodcutters, The Lime Works, Wittgenstein's Nephew, The Loser* and, most recently, a collection of plays, *Histrionics*, and of stories, *The Voice Imitator*. Bernhard, who lived in Austria, is widely considered to be one of the most important writers of his generation.

LOUISE BOURGEOIS was born in Paris in 1911 and moved to New York in 1938. Bourgeois worked in various media: painting, drawing, printmaking and sculpture. The *Louise Bourgeois Retrospective* at the Museum of Modern Art, 1982–1983, confirmed her reputation as one of the foremost artists of the twentieth century. *Locus of Memory* represented the United States at the Venice Biennale in 1993; *The Prints of Louise Bourgeois* were featured at MOMA in 1994; and, in 1997, she received the NEA's National Medal of Arts. MIT Press recently published *Destruction of the Father/Reconstruction of the Father: Writings and Interviews, 1923–1997.*

American assemblagist, collage and toy maker, film pastiche artist, correspondent and trinket Kabbalist JOSEPH CORNELL was born on Christmas Eve, 1903, and died in 1972. A collection of short stories and poetry inspired by his aviaries, *A Convergence of Birds*, edited by Jonathan Safran Foer, will be published by Rizzoli for Christmas 1999.

ROBERT CREELEY's *En Familie*, a poem with Elsa Dorfman's photographs, will be published this fall by Granary Books. His *In Company: Robert Creeley's Collaborations* opened at the Castellani Art Museum of Niagara University on April 10 this year. *Day Book of a Virtual Poet* (Spuyten Duyvil) is his most recent publication.

The Fan-Maker's Inquisition, RIKKI DUCORNET's sixth novel, will be published by Henry Holt in November 1999. Her other books include *Phosphor in Dreamland, The Jade Cabinet, The Fountains of Neptune* and *The Complete Butcher's Tales.*

BRIAN EVENSON is the author of three collections of short fiction, including *Altmann's Tongue* (Knopf) and one novel, *Father of Lies* (Four Walls Eight Windows), which was published last year.

FORREST GANDER's most recent book is *Science and Steepleflower* (New Directions). The work excerpted here is part of a book-length collaboration between Gander and Sally Mann called *Late Summer Entry.*

MARY GASS is an architect and lives in St. Louis. Her specialties include restoration of Craftsman and Prairie School homes and gardens.

WILLIAM H. GASS is the director of the International Writers Center at Washington University, St. Louis, and the author, most recently, of *Finding a Form* and *Cartesian Sonata* (Knopf). *Reading Rilke* is forthcoming, also from Knopf.

In April 1999, BARBARA GUEST was awarded The Frost Medal by the Poetry Society of America. Her *The Confetti Trees: Motion Picture Stories* will be published by Sun & Moon in 1999. *Rocks on a Platter: Notes on Literature*, a long poem, will be published this fall by Wesleyan University/The New England Press.

Articulated Lair: Poems for Louise Bourgeois by CAMILLE GUTHRIE, excerpted here, is a collection written in admiration of the artist's work. Guthrie is also the author of *The Master Thief.* She teaches at New York University.

ROBERT KELLY's latest collection of poems is *The Time of Voice* (Black Sparrow). He teaches in the writing program at Bard College.

MYUNG MI KIM is the author of *Under Flag* (Kelsey St. Press), *The Botany* (Chax) and *Dura* (Sun & Moon). She is currently at work on a book-length poem, *Arcana.*

ANN LAUTERBACH is the Ruth and David Schwab Professor of Language and Literature at Bard College, where she directs the writing division of the MFA program. Her most recent collection is *On a Stair* (Penguin 1997). She was artist-in-residence at the Gardner Museum in January 1999.

DEBORAH LUSTER is a photographer living in Louisiana. She has worked with C. D. Wright on several collaborations including *The Lost Roads Project: A Walk-in Book of Arkansas.* She is currently documenting the Louisiana prison population.

BRIGITTE MAHLKNECHT studied at the Kunstakademie, Vienna, from 1985 to 1990. She divides her time between Austria and Italy. Mahlknecht has had individual and group shows in Salzburg, Bolzano, Vienna, Munich and elsewhere.

Mother Land: Georgia and Virginia, SALLY MANN's first landscape exhibition marked in 1997 a departure from her *Immediate Family* series. Mann has since continued to explore the Southern landscape, and her recent body of work, *Deep South: Mississippi and Louisiana*, premieres at the Edwynn Houk Gallery, New York, in September 1999.

DIANA MICHENER exhibits her photographs at the Pace Wildenstein MacGill Gallery in New York. She is currently working on a photographic project in Paris.

BRADFORD MORROW is the editor of *Conjunctions* and author of four novels, *Come Sunday, Trinity Fields, Giovanni's Gift* (all published by Penguin) and *The Almanac Branch* (Norton). In 1998, he received an Academy Award in Literature from the American Academy of Arts and Letters. He teaches at Bard College.

KENNETH NORTHCOTT is an emeritus professor at the University of Chicago. His most recent translation is Thomas Bernhard's *The Voice Imitator*, which was selected by the *Los Angeles Times* as one of the three most important works of fiction published in 1998, and by the New York Public Library as one of 25 exceptional works published that year.

JOYCE CAROL OATES is the author most recently of *The Collector of Hearts* (Dutton), which includes a story originally published in *Conjunctions*. Her forthcoming novels are *Broke Heart Blues* and, under the pseudonym Rosamund Smith, *Starr Bright Will Be With You Soon*. She teaches at Princeton University.

SUZAN-LORI PARKS is a two-time Obie-award winner whose plays include *The Death of the Last Black Man in the Whole Entire World*, *Imperceptible Mutabilities in the Third Kingdom*, *The America Play* and *Venus*. Her three new plays—*In the Blood, Topdog Underdog* and *Fucking A*—will premiere in 1999–2000. Her first feature film, *Girl 6*, was directed by Spike Lee.

ARCHIE RAND will have shows in Milan, Florence, Rome and other venues throughout Italy between April and September 1999 and is scheduled to exhibit in Paris, London and New York. In 2000 he will have a show at the Vatican. He was recently named a laureate of the National Foundation for Jewish Culture and will be presented with their Lifetime Achievement Award for Contributions in the Visual Arts in June 1999.

DONALD REVELL's sixth and newest collection of poems is *There Are Three* (Wesleyan). Wesleyan also published his translation of Apollinaire's *Alcools*. Revell is a professor of English at the University of Utah.

RAINER MARIA RILKE (1875–1926) is generally regarded as one of the twentieth century's greatest poets, and *The Duino Elegies*, composed between 1912 and 1922, his most significant achievement.

HAIM STEINBACH, born in 1944 in Rehovot, Israel, is a leading figure in American art. Since the 1970s he has been conceiving structures and framing devices for the presentation of objects, illuminating the objects' aesthetic and social qualities.

MEREDITH STRICKER works in the fields of visual arts and poetry. Her intermedia projects have recently been exhibited at St. Mary's College Museum, Notre Dame, and Korean-American Museum, Los Angeles.

COLE SWENSEN's most recent book, *Noon*, won the New American Writing Award and was published by Sun & Moon in 1998. *Try*, awarded the Iowa Poetry Prize, will be published by the University of Iowa late this year. Swensen teaches creative writing and literature at the University of Denver, where she directs the writing program.

LYNNE TILLMAN's most recent novel, *No Lease on Life*, was a finalist for the National Book Critics Circle Award. Her *Bookstore: The Life and Times of Jeannette Watson and Books & Co.* (Harcourt Brace), is a history of the independent bookshop Books & Co., which closed in May 1997.

PAUL WEST's most recent novels are *Terrestrials* and *Life with Swan* (Scribner). He has been awarded the Lannan Prize for Fiction and the Literature Award from the American Academy of Arts and Letters and was recently made a Chevalier of the Order of Arts and Letters by the government of France.

DIANE WILLIAMS's latest book is *Excitability: Selected Stories*, published by Dalkey Archive Press. She is the founder of the new literary annual, *Noon*.

TREVOR WINKFIELD exhibits his work at the Tibor de Nagy Gallery, New York.

C. D. WRIGHT's most recent book is *Deepstep Come Shining* (Copper Canyon Press). She and Deborah Luster are frequent collaborators.

JOHN YAU edited the collection of short stories *Fetish* (Four Walls Eight Windows). His recent books include *My Symptoms* (Black Sparrow) and *The United States of Jasper Johns* (Zoland). His essay on Robert Creeley's collaborations with artists is forthcoming from the University of North Carolina Press, while *Dazzling Water, Dazzling Light: The Painting of Pat Steir* is forthcoming from Hard Press.

MARGUERITE YOUNG was the author of one novel, *Miss MacIntosh, My Darling;* two books of poetry, *Prismatic Ground* and *Moderate Fable;* and of the nonfiction epic *Angel in the Forest: A Fairy Tale of Two Utopias.* She taught creative writing at Indiana, Iowa, Columbia, Fairleigh Dickinson and Fordham universities, as well as the New School for Social Research. She was born in Indiana, lived in New York for nearly half a century and, during the last two years of her life, returned to Indiana. *Harp Song for a Radical* will be published by Knopf in August 1999.

Bibliophile Books from Erker-Verlag, St.Gallen

Eugène Ionesco: Le Blanc et le Noir

15 original lithographs by Eugène Ionesco with accompanying text by the author. Size of the book 33 x 22 cm, 78 pages, linen, bound.
Edition of 200, numbered, printed on wood free offset, each book signed in the imprint by Eugène Ionesco.
ISBN 3-905545-13-6. US$ 1,400.–

Joseph Brodsky / Antoni Tàpies: Roman Elegies

1 double spread and 8 full page original lithographs by Antoni Tàpies with a poetry cycle by Joseph Brodsky inscribed direct on the stone by the author. Size of the book 36,5 x 28,5 cm. A compact disc featuring Joseph Brodsky reading the poetry in Russian and in English accompanies each book.
Edition of 200, numbered, printed on Rives hand-made paper, each book signed in the imprint by both the author and the artist.
ISBN 3-905546-32-9. US$ 3,000.–

E. M. Cioran / Eduardo Chillida: Ce maudit moi

3 wood cuts, 4 engravings and 1 dry point engraving by Eduardo Chillida with a text by E.M. Cioran inscribed direct on the stone by the author. Size of the book 32,5 x 24,5 cm. A record featuring E. M. Cioran reading his text accompanies each book.
Edition of 170, numbered, printed on Rives hand-made paper, each book signed in the imprint by both the author and the artist.
ISBN 3-905545-33-0. US$ 5,000.–

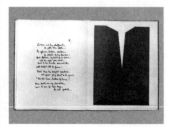

Ezra Pound / Giuseppe Santomaso: An Angle

7 original colour lithographs by Giuseppe Santomaso with fragments from Ezra Pound's Cantos XVII, XXV and XXVI inscribed direct on the stone by the author. Size of the book 47 x 38 cm. A record featuring Ezra Pound reading his text accompanies each book.
Edition of 200, numbered, printed on Rives hand-made paper, each book signed in the imprint by both the author and the artist.
ISBN 3-905544-28-8. US$ 2,700.–

Erker-Verlag has published other collector's editions. Please ask for further information if you are interestet.

Erker-Verlag
Gallusstrasse 32
CH-9000 St.Gallen (Switzerland)
phone ++41 71 222 79 79
fax   ++41 71 222 79 19

Discover what's new in the world of books

RAIN TAXI

reviews • interviews • essays

Published quarterly, the *Rain Taxi Review of Books* brings you reviews you can trust of the best in contemporary literature. Each issue also includes in-depth interviews, small press profiles, and original essays by some of today's most innovative writers. Subscribe now and receive our Fall '98 issue, featuring interviews with Anne Waldman and John Yau, essays on Jane Bowles and Paul Valéry, a special section on Frank Stanford, plus reviews of Michael Palmer, John Edgar Wideman, Tim O'Brien, Marguerite Duras, and more.

One Year Subscription (4 issues) $10, International Rate $20
Send Check Or Money Order to:
RAIN TAXI, PO Box 3840, Minneapolis MN 55403
visit our website at www.raintaxi.com

NEW DIRECTIONS / New Poetry

WILLIS BARNSTONE
TO TOUCH THE SKY. Poems of Mystical, Spiritual & Metaphysical Light. Barnstone's translations, from Herakleitos to Rainer Maria Rilke. "Thoughtfully rendered." —*Publishers Weekly*. $15.95 *pbk. orig.*

ROBERT CREELEY
LIFE & DEATH. "No American poet has ever combined linguistic abstraction with specificity of time and place more poignantly than Creeley has, nor has anyone else negotiated such a graceful accommodation between lyricism and open form."—*Buffalo News*. $19.95 *cl.*

SO THERE: POEMS 1976-1983. "His influence on contemporary American poetry has probably been more deeply felt than that of any other writer of his generation." —*The N.Y. Times Book Review.* $14.95 *pbk.*

LAWRENCE FERLINGHETTI
A FAR ROCKAWAY OF THE HEART. "...a glorious rant against mediocrity, greed, capitalism and boring poetry, with copious riffs on painting and love." —*Publishers Weekly.* $21.95 *cloth* / $10.95 *pbk.*

FORREST GANDER
SCIENCE & STEEPLEFLOWER. "His sharp sense of place has made him the most earthly of our avant-garde, the best geographer of fleshly sites since Olson."—Donald Revell, *The Colorado Rev.* $12.95 *pbk. orig.*

H.D.
TRILOGY. THE WALLS DO NOT FALL. TRIBUTE TO THE ANGELS. THE FLOWERING OF THE ROD. Readers' notes by Aliki Barnstone. "This ecstasy, ecstasy in language, in beautiful language, is what carries me through the entire trilogy.... " —Hayden Carruth, *The Hudson Review.* $10.95 *pbk.*

MARY KARR
VIPER RUM. Afterword"Against Decoration." "A terrific, plot-driven collection concerning themes that include alcoholism,... salvation, and transformation." —*Harvard Review.* $19.95 *cl.*

JAMES LAUGHLIN
A COMMONPLACE BOOK OF PENTASTICHS. Ed.w/intro. by Hayden Carruth. "All beautifully spry and clean-limbed. Just the sort of testament one owes to life...."—Charles Tomlinson $19.95 *cl.*

THE LOVE POEMS. "Who else writes such bittersweet, ironic, rueful, erotic,toughminded, witty love poems?"—Marjorie Perloff $6.95 *pbk.*

MICHAEL PALMER
THE LION BRIDGE. Selected Poems 1972-1995. "He fuses contemporary concerns about syntax and meaning production with some very ancient poetic pleasures." —*VLS.* $18.95 *pbk. orig.*

NEW DIRECTIONS 80 8th Avenue, NYC 10011 (*ndpublishing.com*)

Discover
the Writer's Life
in New York City

Master of Fine Arts in Creative Writing

Over more than six decades of steady innovation, The New School has sustained a vital center for creative writing, with a faculty that has included some of this century's most acclaimed poets and novelists. The tradition continues with our MFA in Creative Writing, offering concentrations in **fiction, poetry, nonfiction** and **writing for children.** Study writing and literature with The New School's renowned faculty of writers, critics, editors and publishing professionals.

Faculty 1998-1999: Hilton Als, Jill Ciment, Jonathan Dee, Cornelius Eady, David Gates, Lucy Grealy, Amy Hempel, A.M. Homes, David Lehman, Pablo Medina, Rick Moody, Francine Prose, Luc Sante, Dani Shapiro, Jason Shinder, Darcey Steinke, Benjamin Taylor, Abigail Thomas, David Trinidad, Susan Wheeler, Stephen Wright.

Visiting Faculty: Ai, Martin Asher, Frank Bidart, Deborah Brodie, James Ellroy, Margaret Gabel, Glen Hartley, Pearl London, Thomas Mallon, Carol Muske, Geoffrey O'Brien, Robert Pinsky, Jon Scieszka, Ira Silverberg.

Director: Robert Polito

Fellowships and financial aid available.

For a catalog and application contact:
212-229-5630 ext. 211 or
email: admissions@dialnsa.edu

New School University

The New School
66 West 12th Street New York NY 10011

Lost Roads
publishers

New

Titles

From

Lost

Roads

The Leaves in Her Shoes
poems by J. L. Jacobs

"Reading these poems is like listening to snatches of song or overhearing half-sentences, mutterings, broken chants of a lost tribe."

--Carol Muske

ISBN 0-918786-49-5   #44 $12.00

Anamorphosis Eisenhower
by Sam Truitt

"Sam Truitt gives 'mouth to mouth resuscitation' to the ancient quest poem as he writes 'to voyage is to become / Hysterical.'"

--Peter Gizzi

ISBN 0-918786-48-7   #43 $12.00

Ex Voto
poems by Frances Mayes

"The bell-like musicality of these poems belies their grim insistance: we live in a furnace. We consume and are consumed."

--San Francisco Chronicle

ISBN 0-918786-47-9   #42 $12.00

Endou: poems, prose, and a little beagle story
by Josephine Foo

Foo writes: "I bring out a sheet of paper, smooth as the white of my eye. I will put words on the sheet like bricks for a house with rooms for children..."

ISBN 0-918786-46-0   #41 $12.00

Ordering Address: Small Press Distribution 1341 Seventh Street Berkeley CA 94710-1409

http://www.brown.edu/Departments/English/road

Sun & Moon Press presents…

The Winner of the 1997 National Poetry Series

TALES OF MURASAKI
and Other Poems

Martine Bellen

Selected by Rosmarie Waldrop

Order from
Sun & Moon Press
6026 Wilshire Boulevard
Los Angeles, CA 90036
323 857 1115

Please visit our website
www.sunmoon.com

ISBN: 1-55713-378-6
$10.95

The Web Forum of Innovative Writing

www.Conjunctions.com

"Bard College's venerable *Conjunctions* has gone hypertext. Those who bemoan the poor quality of prose in cyberspace may have found their match in this truly innovative offering."
—*Library Journal*

From Antonin Artaud to Italo Calvino to Cristina García to Rick Moody to John Sayles, our site features works unavailable elsewhere, and takes you deeper into past, current and future issues. Nowhere online will you find as extensive a selection of the best in innovative contemporary literature.

➤ PREVIEWS: Selections from upcoming issues

➤ JUST OUT: Highlights from our current issue

➤ THE ARCHIVES: A host of work from past issues

➤ AUDIO VAULT: Performances by our authors

➤ WEB *CONJUNCTIONS*: New writing available only online

➤ PLUS: A variety of other features, including favorite links, complete index 1981–1998 and much more

Visit us often and explore the expanding world of CONJUNCTIONS